The River with No Bridge

Sué Sumii (1902–97), social reformer and writer, was born in Nara prefecture. An outspoken advocate for victims of discrimination, notably the *burakumin*, Japan's former so-called "untouchable" class who are in Buddhist eyes unclean, she devoted her entire life to breaking down barriers of inequality among people. She came to challenge the widely accepted belief that those who are disadvantaged are destined to remain so. Her most prominent protest against *burakumin* lies in her seven-volume *The River with No Bridge* (1961–92). Her other works include novels, essays, short stories, stories for children, and a personal narrative consisting of a series of transcribed dialogs with various people, including her daughter, Reiko Masuda.

Susan Wilkinson graduated with First Class Honors in Japanese studies in 1979 from the University of London's School of Oriental and African Studies. A freelance translator and editor, she resides in Tokyo.

Sué Sumii
The River with No Bridge

Translated by
Susan Wilkinson

TUTTLE PUBLISHING
Tokyo • Rutland, Vermont • Singapore

Published by Tuttle Publishing, an imprint of Periplus Editions (HK) Ltd,
with editorial offices at 364 Innovation Drive, North Clarendon,
Vermont 05759 and 130 Joo Seng Road #06-01, Singapore 368357

ISBN 0-8048-3327-3
ISBN 4-8053-0650-5 (for sale in Japan only)

Printed in Singapore

Distributed by:

Japan
Tuttle Publishing
Yaekari Building, 3F, 5-4-12 Osaki,
Shinagawa-ku, Tokyo 141-0032.
Tel: (813) 5437 0171;
Fax: (813) 5437 0755;
E-mail: tuttle-sales@gol.com

North America
Tuttle Publishing
364 Innovation Drive
North Clarendon, VT 05759-9436
Tel: (802) 773 8930; Fax: (802) 773 6993
Email: info@tuttlepublishing.com
www.tuttlepublishing.com

Asia Pacific
Berkeley Books Pte Ltd
130 Joo Seng Road #06-01,
Singapore 368357.
Tel: (65) 6280 1330;
Fax: (65) 6280 6290;
E-mail: inquiries@periplus.com.sg
www.periplus.com

05 07 09 10 08 06
1 3 5 6 4 2

Contents

Translator's Introduction

JAPANESE women have, at least in the eyes of the West, an image of submissive acquiescence in a male-dominated society, but such an image could hardly be less applicable to writer Sué Sumii. Born in Nara prefecture in 1902, she left home at the age of seventeen and came to Tokyo to make her living as a writer. Her first job was with the publishing house Kodansha, but her rebellious spirit soon asserted itself, and she left in protest over the discriminatory conditions of employment for women members of the staff. A year later, her first novel was published, and she married the writer Shigeru Inuta, who was involved in a left-wing-oriented farmers' literary movement, the Nomin Bungei Kai, that opposed the privileges of the landowners. By the early 1930s, with the rise of ultranationalism in Japan, the repression of liberals and leftists intensified and the magazine edited by Inuta was suppressed, as was everything he wrote. This contributed to his growing ill-health, and it was Sué Sumii's writing, mainly of children's fiction, that supported them and their four children, and was to continue to do so for the rest of their married life.

Inuta died in July 1957, worn out from the long struggle with illness. Sué Sumii has described how, as she gazed at the face of her dead husband, she was suddenly overwhelmed by the realization that "everything I'd given Inuta over the years was being repaid a thousand-fold." Not only was he showing her how precious life was, but also that everybody was bound by the same inexorable law of Time. He seemed to her to be saying that if there were such a thing as fate, it was the limits set by Time alone and had nothing to do with a law that determined one's lot in life. Sumii suddenly saw surrounding her dead husband the faces of those disadvantaged because of the commonly held belief that it was their fate to be so; in particular, she saw the faces of those forced to leave their village on Unebi Hill, at the beginning of the Taisho era (1912–26). It was to lead her to write her thought-provoking and moving six-volume novel, *The River with No Bridge,* about Japan's little-known outcasts, the *burakumin.**

The people forced to leave their village on Unebi Hill were *burakumin,* or "new commoners," as they were still known for some time following their legal emancipation in 1871. Their village was called Hora (Michi, in the novel), and in the *History of the Imperial Tombs* (by Shuho Goto), published in 1913, it was pointed out that "both the government and the people seem quite unconcerned about the fact that there is a cemetery of the 'new commoners' on Unebi Hill, overlooking the tomb of Emperor Jinmu." It went on to protest that "the unclean corpses of the 'new commoners' are being buried on this most sacred hill; they are rotting in this hallowed soil, their bones remaining there from generation unto generation. It is outrageous to permit a group of 'new commoners' to live between the Imperial Tomb and the sacred hill. . . . " Apparently, it was so outrageous that 208 households, or 1,054 people, were forced to leave in 1917.[1] How had these people become outcasts and why was their presence considered so defiling?

Until their legal emancipation, the outcasts were known as *eta,* or "much filth." Over the centuries, they had come to be viewed as in some way different and physically inferior to the rest of the population, even animal-like, as is shown by other derogatory names for the *eta,* such as *yotsu* meaning four (inferring four-legged, or animal-like), and *ningai,* or "other than human." Racially no different from other Japanese, their long association with occupations considered defiling had gradually made the outcasts themselves seem hereditarily defiled in the eyes of the majority population. This defilement was felt to be somehow communicable, or contagious, like a germ, so that the rest of society wanted to have as little direct contact as possible with the *eta.* As a result they were forbidden to live outside their own villages, or to marry those who were not *eta* like themselves.

The early beliefs of Japan's indigenous Shinto religion concerning purification and defilement were influential in the development of an outcast group. Uncleanness was the greatest *tsumi,* or thing displeasing to the gods. Death, disease, and wounds, as well as menstruation and childbirth, were all sources of uncleanness, to the extent that there were special parturition huts to separate pregnant women from the rest of the household. One of the later names for outcasts was *sanjo-no-mono*, believed originally either to refer to the homeless who sought refuge in abandoned parturition huts, or to the midwives. With the introduction of Buddhism from the Asian continent, the killing of animals and eating of meat also came to be considered unclean; thus, by the eighth century, butchers, tanners, and makers of leather goods had joined midwives and undertakers as a defiled group.

The first known written reference to the *eta* is in a thirteenth-century document that states the word *eta* is a corruption of *etori*, or food-gatherers, the title of those in the Department of Falconry in charge of butchering cattle to feed the falcons and dogs. This work was considered of low status, and when the Department of Falconry was abolished in 860, due to the influence of Buddhism, the *etori* lost their hereditary occupation and it is likely that some survived by working as butchers, or in other similar occupations considered "defiling."

The *eta* were relatively prosperous during the Ashikaga shogunate (1338–1573) and Momoyama period (1568–1603). The fact that their occupational specializations were taboo for non-outcasts gave them monopolies in their trades, and, in an age of constant civil war, their skills in working leather, bone, and gut were in much demand for the manufacture of saddles, armor, and bowstrings. Military lords induced them to settle on their estates, offering incentives such as the tax-free use of land, and in this way *eta* communities spread from western Japan, where they had been concentrated, into other parts of the country, such as eastern Honshu. The outcasts were able to expand their trades into new areas, such as basket weaving and straw-sandal making, and the caretakers of tombs were also absorbed into the *eta* segment during this period. (These were descendants of the tomb guards, a slave group that had existed in the Nara period [646–794].) Many of the ancient burial mounds in the Nara, Kyoto, and Osaka areas had an *eta* community in their vicinity, including the village of Hora described above.

In the relative peace of the Tokugawa period (1603–1868), trades such as leather-work and tanning lost the importance they had held during the time of civil war, while, on the other hand, the perception of the defiled nature of the *eta* strengthened. A rigid social hierarchy was established, with the military at the top, farmers, artisans, and merchants below, and the outcasts right at the bottom. The *eta* were bound by many legal restrictions, which were enforced with increasing frequency from the middle to the end of the period. The *eta* were easily recognizable, as they were not allowed to dress their hair in the same way as commoners, had to use a rope instead of a sash to bind their kimonos, and were sometimes obliged to wear a patch of leather on their clothes as a badge of their defiled status. They were only permitted to marry other *eta* and could not live outside *eta* villages, nor enter the service of commoners as servants. They were forbidden the privilege of sitting, eating, and smoking with commoners and of crossing the threshold of a commoner home. In 1859, a time when discrimination against the *eta* was at its height, a notorious judgment was handed down in the case of an *eta* youth who had been killed by non-*eta*. The magistrate decided that an *eta* life was worth only one-seventh of that of a commoner and therefore six more *eta* would have to be slain before the guilty parties could be sentenced to death.

The Meiji Restoration of 1868 brought an end to the feudal Tokugawa regime and to the two hundred years of Japan's seclusion from the rest of the world. One of the social reforms that followed the Restoration was the legal emancipation of all outcasts in 1871. However, equality before the law did not mean an end to prejudice and discrimination. In many ways, the position of the *eta* worsened as they lost their monopolies in trades such as butchering and leatherwork, and, moreover, they were now required to pay taxes and do military service for the first time. Furthermore, the settled communities and specialized trades of the *eta* meant that they continued to be easily identifiable as "new commoners," or former outcasts. This made them scapegoats and sometimes victims of violence for the feelings of frustration of ordinary citizens, for whom all the changes that took place following the Meiji Restoration meant financial difficulties and insecurity.

By the beginning of the twentieth century, Western political ideas of liberalism and democratic rights began to influence some of the *burakumin* and led them to form associations to try and overcome the continuing discrimination by raising their own education and living standards, in the hope that this would influence the majority population to treat them as equals. However, the self-improvement movement had little effect and a more radical emancipation movement, favoring "direct action," began to emerge. *Burakumin* leaders were particularly active in the Rice Riots that broke out in 1918 following the sharp increase in the price of rice, the main staple. After the riots, these same leaders began to demand that the government give direct help to improve the economic and social conditions of the *burakumin*. In 1920, for the first time, the government gave them financial support and began to sponsor organizations to deal with their problems, largely from a desire to prevent the spread of revolutionary ideas among the *burakumin*. This did not deter young *burakumin* leaders from forming a new, militant movement, the Suiheisha, or Levelers' Society—named after one of the radical movements during the English Civil War—with the aim of removing all inequalities. On March 3, 1922, the Suiheisha held its first national convention in Kyoto; it was attended by two thousand representatives from *buraku* all over the country. The Suiheisha flag was unfurled: a blood-red crown of thorns on a black ground. The declaration that was read out at that convention was an interesting mixture of Marxist and religious language. Written by Mankichi Saiko, the son of a Buddhist priest, it began, "*Burakumin* throughout the country, unite!" and ended, "The time has come for the martyrs' crown of thorns to be blessed. The time has come for us to be proud of being *eta*."[2]

Set between the years 1908 and 1924, the six volumes of the *River with No Bridge* mirror the development of the awareness of *burakumin* of their rights and dignity as human beings, which lead to the formation of the Suiheisha. In the background are the actual events that took place during this period: the execution of the radical writer and thinker Shusui Kotoku, for allegedly plotting to assassinate the Emperor; the death of Emperor Meiji; the Rice Riots; the Korean Independence Movement; and the massacre of Koreans in Tokyo after the Great Kanto Earthquake.

In particular, the first volume (this translation) traces the questioning of the system by an individual child, Koji. Koji's growing sense of injustice derives not only from the prejudice he meets from other children and the teachers at school, but also from the content of what he is taught. The purpose of education in prewar Japan was to train children to become docile and loyal citizens. The more liberal education policies of the early Meiji era were soon replaced by a doctrinaire system centering round the idea of *sonno aikoku*—reverence for the Emperor and patriotism. School textbooks came under the direct control of the government, and children were taught the overriding importance of the Confucian virtues of filial piety and loyalty. They were constantly told that the Japanese state was one family and that the Emperor was the father of the nation; and just as children had to behave with filial piety toward their parents, so their main duty to the father-Emperor was loyalty. These principles were set out in the Imperial Rescript on Education, which, together with a copy of the Imperial Portrait, was issued to every school from 1891 onward. Shinto beliefs were increasingly used to reinforce the idea of the sacredness of both the national family and the father-Emperor. In the textbooks, Shinto mythology was presented as historical fact, and children were taught that the Imperial family had been commanded to occupy the throne by Amaterasu Omikami, the Sun Goddess and the divine founder of the Imperial line. The Imperial Portrait and Rescript on Education were sacred objects, and, in the case of an outbreak of fire at a school, they had to be saved before anything or anybody else, even at risk to life. The Imperial Rescript was often recited at school ceremonial assemblies, the scroll held in white-gloved hands, and there were cases of teachers having to resign, sometimes even committing suicide, over an impropriety such as a mistake in the reading, or for dropping the scroll.

It is not difficult to see how useful such an education system, with its deliberate indoctrination of children in the sacred nature of the State, was to the militarists when they came to power in the 1930s, nor, on the other hand, to see that since the State and its symbols were held to be so sacrosanct, it was all too easy to despise those traditionally viewed as being at the very bottom of the social scale, outside so-called "normal" society. In the Japan of the Meiji era, the change in attitude toward the *burakumin* on the part of the majority population had not kept pace with the change in the legal status of the former outcasts. Compulsory education and military service applied to the *burakumin* like everybody else but it was often in the schools and the army that they suffered from the worst treatment.

One of the leaders of the Suiheisha movement, Kyotaro Kimura, in some respects the model for Koji in the *River with No Bridge,* has written of the severe discrimination he suffered at higher elementary school. The *burakumin* children all had to sit together in the classroom; and in the playground, the other children avoided them. They could not use the same pails or cups without their being snatched

away with cries of "dirty," and the other children were continually abusing them with insults, such as "You stink!" or "Filthy
eta!" openly in front of the teachers. Eight children from his *buraku*
started school at the same time as Kimura. By the second term, their
number had halved and, by the third term, only two of them were
left. As in the novel, his *buraku* also suffered a fire that destroyed
many homes, largely because the fire brigade of a nearby village
turned back when they saw it was only an "*eta* fire."

While the discrimination that occurs in the *River with No Bridge*
is based on the actual experiences of people like Kyotaro Kimura,
Koji's view of the world, particularly of what he is taught at school,
is that of Sué Sumii herself. Although not a *burakumin,* she was brought
up in the same area of Nara prefecture in which the novel is set,
and, like Koji, was six years old in 1908. She remembers the army
maneuvers that year attended by the Emperor and how people
searched the site of the Emperor's temporary headquarters afterward
and brought back any souvenirs they could find, such as the remains
of the Emperor's cigarettes marked with the Imperial seal. She also
remembers how she laughed over the story of another souvenir. A
lavatory for the Emperor's sole use had been set up at the headquarters
and apparently somebody had found a specimen of Imperial feces
there. While laughing at the stupidity of grown-ups, six-year-old
Sumii had been struck by the thought that a sacred being like the
Emperor should defecate. In fact, as an infant, she had suffered
from feelings of revulsion over the feces her own body produced and
would try and hold back from defecating as long as possible, with
the result that she was always being scolded for dirtying herself. This
had led eventually to a severe sense of inferiority and bashfulness
when she started school. Sumii later wrote that when she heard the
story of the Emperor's feces, she thought to herself, "If the Emperor
craps, it must mean he eats food too. In that case, he's no different
at all from me." She claims that all sense of inferiority left her there-
after and that far from suffering from shyness at school, whenever the
Headmaster lectured them at morning assembly on the sacredness
of the Emperor and their indebtedness to the father of the nation,
she would retort to herself, "The Emperor's not a sacred *kami*. He's
just an ordinary person who smokes cigarettes, eats food, and craps
like everybody else."

The insight afforded Sué Sumii through her own childhood experiences enabled her to see that the veneration of the sacred and the rejection of the despised are really two sides of the same coin. Her conviction is:

No one is born more than a human being.
And no one is born less than a human being.

I would like to take this opportunity to express my deep appreciation to the author, Sué Sumii, for her constant encouragement and endless patience in answering all of my queries concerning this translation.

Sources:

1) The account of the forced removal of the village of Hora appears in *Naraken suihei undo shi* [History of the Suihei Movement in Nara Prefecture] (Kyoto: Buraku Mondai Kenkyujo, 1972).

2) I am indebted for the account of the history of the outcasts to George de Vos and Hiroshi Wagatsuma, *Japan's Invisible Race: Caste in Culture and Personality* (Berkeley and Los Angeles: The University of California Press, 1966) and to Shigeaki Ninomiya, "An Inquiry concerning the Origin, Development and Present Situation of the *Eta* in Relation to the History of Social Classes in Japan" (Paper delivered to the Asiatic Society of Japan, December 1933).

The River with No Bridge

1

Stars and Frosts

I

Hoh-ee, hoh-ee . . .

"*Somebody's calling. Somebody's calling to me.*"

The girl started running, blown along by the wind.

Hoh-ee, hoh-ee . . .

"*Somebody's calling. They're calling to me.*"

The boy too was running before the wind.

The girl shouted back; so did the boy. Then they caught sight of each other. Between them lay a small ditch in which water trickled away from a paddy field, golden with its ripe crop of rice.

"*Fudé!*" *cried the boy, and Fudé realized with a start that she was no longer a young girl and that the boy was her husband, Shinkichi.*

She had not seen Shinkichi for a long time, not for many years, but now there he stood on the opposite bank. Bracing herself, she was about to jump across when, all at once, the ditch became a swift-flowing river and she was cut off from her husband.

On the other side of the river, Shinkichi started to run upstream. Fudé ran upstream as well: there was bound to be a bridge somewhere.

"*Oh, there's one!*" *and she hastened breathlessly toward it. But the bridge was only the arch of a rainbow; a rainbow that grew wider and wider as it swept smoothly up into the heavens.*

There was no choice but to go farther upriver. Fudé and Shinkichi raced on until they found their way blocked by a great iceberg, looming out of the mist. They both turned round and began to run back downstream: there had to be a bridge somewhere . . .

The river broadened out and flowed with increasing force. Fudé caught the sound of Shinkichi's breathing: he was panting hard, almost gasping for air. Why was he so out of breath? The snow. Yes, of course, it was because

3

of the snow that had been falling on the opposite bank and now lay several feet deep. Shinkichi was sinking in it and would soon be completely buried.

Fudé began to cry unashamedly, overcome with longing; she yearned for Shinkichi with her whole being.

"Fudé, Fudé."

Fudé awoke. Her mother-in-law, Nui, was tapping her on the shoulder.

"It was only a dream," she thought; yet she still ached with longing.

Hands resting on her breast, she asked, "Did I talk in my sleep?"

"No, not a word. But you were gaspin' like you couldn't breathe. I thought you must be havin' a bad dream so I woke you."

Fudé sighed in reply and Nui rearranged her pillow.

"It just struck four, we can go back to sleep for a bit. Do us good. With all this night work, we're never in bed before twelve."

All the same, Nui knew that she would not fall asleep again: maybe it had to do with her age, but recently she had taken to waking up at three and would lie there thinking her "useless thoughts" until it was light enough to make out the lattice frame of the screen door.

Fudé did not feel as if she would drop off again either, although she usually slept deeply until about five. She groped in the darkness for her kimono, which she had spread over the quilt, and pulled it up over Koji, who was lying beside her.

"I bet it's frosty this mornin'," said Nui, feeling for her kimono to cover Seitaro. He and Koji were her grandsons, the children of Shinkichi and Fudé. Seitaro was ten, and Koji, six.

Ever since Koji's birth, Seitaro had liked to snuggle up to his grandmother and had never spent a night away from her side. But he was no crybaby; on the contrary, away from home he behaved like a young ruffian, always the leader when he and his friends played soldiers: after all, he bore the weight of glorious history on his shoulders, being the son of one of the Fallen Heroes of the Russo-Japanese War.

"Mother, I dreamed of Shinkichi," Fudé blurted out suddenly, after pondering her dream for a few moments.

"Did you?" Nui turned towards her. "What happened?"

"It was a funny sort of dream. Shin and I were children again, least that's what I thought, but then suddenly it seemed as if we'd grown

up. There was this great river between us and no matter how hard
I tried I couldn't get across to him."

"Why not?"

"There wasn't any bridge. We ran upstream, no bridge; downstream, no bridge. And meanwhile, this blizzard had come on. Shin
was gasping for breath and slowly sinking down in the snow, there
before my very eyes. I just didn't know what to do."

Fudé did not mention her yearning but Nui understood only too
well: what else would she feel for the husband she would never see
again?

Nui lay back, folding her hands over her breast, and pictured her
son gradually being buried in the snow. She could not dismiss it as
a silly dream. No, there was no doubt about it, Shinkichi must have
died that way.

Koji was two at the time and Seitaro, six; Shinkichi himself, at
twenty-nine, had been in his prime. Just after war with Russia had
been declared, he was called up on February 10, 1904. He left Japan
from Hiroshima on April 20 with the Second Army. On May 5, they
disembarked on the Liaotung Peninsula.

After landing on the continent, they found themselves literally in
a battlefield: starting with the engagement at Chinchou Ch'eng,
there was fierce fighting near Telissu, Tashichiao, Liaoyang, and,
finally, the Shaho River. The weather grew bitterly cold, with deep
snow, and at the Shaho River the tide turned against them for a
while and many lives were lost. They rallied, however, and, during
the decisive battle that followed, Shinkichi's short life of twenty-nine
years came to an end.

Of course, the official dispatch informing them of Shinkichi's
death made no mention of how he met his end, but the date of death,
December 3, made Nui and Fudé imagine snow and ice. They were
both afraid of speaking of this: the thought of the bitter cold, rather
than of the actual fighting, was what conjured up his death most
vividly.

Her eyes brimming with tears, Nui spoke as if to herself, "You
never had so much as a warm woolen shirt even when you was little,
did you Shinkichi?"

"Mother," said Fudé in a low voice, after a pause.

"Yes?" whispered back Nui.

"I can't help feeling Shin must have frozen to death in the snow,

after coming to me in a dream like that. What do you think?" Fudé
asked in an even lower voice.

"Matter of fact, I'd decided the same thing myself."

"I'm not surprised. I mean he couldn't have walked in all that
thick snow, even with only a slight wound, could he? He must have
frozen to death."

"Fudé, where's the sense in us going over it all now?"

"But I can't bear it. He just stood there staring at me as if he was
longing to come back."

"You know why that is, don't you? It's because you never stop
thinking about him."

"I know. All the same, a man's still got a soul, hasn't he, even when
he's dead?"

"I suppose he does. But if a man don't get his way when he's alive
it's not likely to make any difference when he's dead, even if his
soul does go leaping and flying about all over the place."

Nui gave a wry smile and stretched out her limbs. She was born
in 1852 and had lived now for fifty-six years. Nobody could deny
that her life had been one of continual hardship and suffering but
her will to go on living was as firm as ever; after all, she still had the
use of her arms and her legs. "With large hands like those, she'll
never have any trouble earning a living," an old man reputed to be
a palm reader had said of her in the autumn of 1871. She was almost
twenty then and about to go as a bride to the home of the Hatanaka
family. Her husband, too, who had died the previous year, used to
compliment her: "You're born skillful, with those long fingers of
yours." And they had both been proven right, because it was Nui's
dexterity, whether with a hoe, or needle, or the materials for sandal-
making, that brought in a living. Despite the handicap of illiteracy,
her confidence in being able to survive was unshakeable. Tensing the
muscles in her outstretched limbs, she knew that she could—indeed,
she must—live for another twenty years; by which time Seitaro
would be thirty, and Koji, twenty-six, and both of them would certainly be able to read and write with ease.

Nui raised her head. "Seitaro's a promising lad, I know, but I've
got a feeling Koji's going to do even better."

"Mm," murmured Fudé absent-mindedly, still turning the dream
over and over in her mind.

She was well aware, of course, without her mother-in-law telling her, that it made no difference even if Shinkichi's soul did find its way back every night. Shinkichi belonged to the other world now; he was beyond reach, he made no response. Nevertheless, he was still alive in her dreams; he breathed and spoke in them, and Fudé was in love with him. She was in love with the husband who stared silently at her with a look of anguished longing such as she had never seen during their married life together.

Koji suddenly stretched out his hand to his mother's breast. Fudé caught hold of the small hand, wide awake at last.

"I mean, take last night; Koji was writing such difficult characters on his slate again, all by himself," continued Nui.

"Yes, he can already write *hiragana* easily and some of the other children in the first year haven't even learned *katakana** yet."

"I'd like him to have a real good education."

Fudé made no response.

"From now on, you'll need to be educated."

Fudé was silent.

"If you're educated, you can do anything."

"Do you really think so?"

It was Nui's turn to fall silent.

"If you ask me, I don't think it'll make a scrap of difference whether the children have a good education or not. We're *eta,** aren't we? Though when it comes to war, we end up the wives and mothers of dead soldiers like everybody else."

Nui said nothing.

Fudé closed her eyes. She saw the wide river; the swift-flowing water; the countless footsteps along the banks. Although the snow had melted, the footsteps were clearly imprinted there . . .

Was she still dreaming? She opened her eyes again. The papered screen of the adjacent workroom was a pale gray. Dawn was breaking.

Fudé gently released Koji's hand and Nui guessed that she was about to get up.

"I'd sleep a bit longer if I was you, Fudé. I'm sure you had that bad dream because you're tired."

Fudé's period had begun the previous day.

II

How fair is the land of Yamato,
A land enriching our history,
Bathed in moonlight at Mikasa,
Perfumed with cherry at Yoshino.

In Nara, the ancient capital,
Which has prospered from age unto age,
Many thousands of sturdy young men
Are flocking to join our regiment.

May the Yamato soul fill our rifles,
And our swords burnish the glory
Of this our flawless, sovereign land,
Unequaled throughout the world.

We are as children before our Lord,
And our Lord is like our father.
Loyalty and devotion rest on
Wisdom, benevolence, and courage.

This was the song of the Fifty-third Nara Regiment. Led by Seitaro, about thirty strapping lads from the village of Komori climbed down the west bank of the Katsuragi River singing it at the top of their voices. Then battle began, and they fought long and hard until the pampas grass growing by the river was veiled in the gray light of dusk. On the way home, their singing gradually died down as the sight of the approaching village with its lights and curling smoke brought them back to reality. They began to imagine the sour faces and scolding voices of their parents: "You little good-for-nothing, playing about all day long. Draw some water, or light the fire, and be quick about it or else!"

Seitaro was certainly no exception and his grandmother roared at him as he came in, "Silly boy, wasting your time every day playing soldiers when you could be giving us a hand. And to think you'd of left school by now if things hadn't changed."

"That's right," Seitaro nodded with obvious approval. "I might be an apprentice."

Nui could not help smiling, and Fudé's mouth also twitched as she lit the stove fire. That year, the elementary-school course had been extended from four to six years and Seitaro had unexpectedly enrolled for the fifth grade. As he was not fond of school, this was too much of a good thing as far as he was concerned; especially as some of his friends had already left at the end of their fourth year and either gone to serve an apprenticeship in Osaka, or stayed at home to help look after younger brothers and sisters. However, for the son of a Fallen Hero of the Russo-Japanese War, it was a point of honor to at least finish primary school.

Relieved by the smiles of his mother and grandmother, Seitaro went over to the stove. "Mm, sweet potatoes! Come on, let's eat."

The lid was half off the pan and the sight of the round slices of sweet potato dancing about with the grains of rice in the gruel made him feel even hungrier.

"I just put the potatoes in, so they won't be done yet. Watch the fire for a minute, will you."

Leaving Seitaro in charge, Fudé went to wipe the wooden floor of the two-mat* room that had served many generations of the family as living room, playroom, and sometimes guest room for entertaining the neighbors.

Koji had been playing there with his shell top, but when his mother began cleaning the floor, he went over to the stove.

"You should've come, Koji. We've been fighting hand-to-hand in the middle of the river today. It was really exciting," whispered Seitaro, feeding the stove fire with straw.

"I don't like playing soldiers."

"You're a softie," and Seitaro pretended to punch him.

This did not escape Nui. "If you go on playing soldiers all the time, Seitaro, you'll turn into one. I can't see why you think it's such fun to behave in that frightening way. Koji likes his books, so he doesn't want to be bothered with them silly games."

"But all the most important men are soldiers. Lieutenant-generals and generals are ever so important. And d'you know, Gran, there's a Field Marshal who's even higher up than they are. And above the Field Marshal, there's the Emperor, the Supreme Commander."

Nui's eyebrows suddenly shot up and Fudé bent her head even lower as she wiped the floor; it was as if the sky had become a heavy weight pressing down on her and she bit her lip hard.

"Are you going to be a soldier when you grow up, Seitaro?" Koji asked, with a glint in his eye.

"Course I am. I'm already a general, aren't I?"

"Ah, ha, ha! Seitaro's the general of all the mischief-makers round here all right."

Koji burst out laughing at his grandmother's words.

"Mother, supper's ready," Fudé called presently, putting the pan down on the clean floor and stirring the gruel with a wooden spoon.

Nui went out and shook her apron under the eaves, giving a dry cough as clouds of dust rose into the air. Whenever there was a lull in the farm work, she and Fudé wove the upper side of hemp-soled straw sandals, in the workroom adjoining the living room. In fact, they spent more hours doing this than anything else, and, with only half-an-acre of arable land, their main occupation was really sandal-making rather than farming.

The four of them now sat down on the floor around the pan.

"Eat as much as you can. They say sweet potatoes make you clever," said Fudé, ladling an extra big slice into Seitaro's bowl.

"No, they don't, they just make you fart. But I like them a lot, though."

Seitaro took a large bite. The potatoes seemed to have absorbed the flavor of the rice gruel and were particularly delicious. They also made the rice go further, and, during the lean period before the harvest, when they had to be very frugal with what little rice was left, sweet potatoes became their staple food.

As she served herself, it suddenly occurred to Fudé that she still had not wiped her face, and she reached for a cloth. Nobody would have called her a great beauty, but, with her round face and fair complexion, she was not bad looking and was popular with the people in the neighborhood. Although only thirty-three, her dark, slightly reddish hair had already lost its gleam; not really surprising considering the hard life she led, where it was a luxury even to use hair oil once a year.

"Eat some greens, too; they're good for you."

Fudé pushed the bowl of greens toward Seitaro, who had been eating only the gruel. The greens, known as "stalks," were radish leaves preserved in salt and had rather a piquant flavor; but they were not the sort of food that appealed to children.

"Those stalks are chicken food," and Seitaro held out his bowl for his fifth helping of gruel. The next minute, he was ready for a sixth, and Fudé looked rather taken aback.

"You're not still hungry! You'll eat so much you won't be able to move. Try standing up."

"You're in for a shock," chuckled Nui, crunching the stalks.

"I'm not called Frogfish for nothing, and I can still eat another two helpings."

Seitaro could not help sniggering at his own retort. He had acquired the nickname of Frogfish because his mouth was so large. Fudé thought he resembled his dead father in this respect; and Shinkichi had undoubtedly taken after his mother. Nui's mouth was exceptionally big for a woman's, but this was her attraction and it mirrored her manly outspokenness.

The pan was empty, and Frogfish, full at last, gave a satisfied burp. Now there was nothing else to do but go to bed: due to a shortage of firewood, households only lit a fire for a bath once every seven to ten days in that area, the heart of the Yamato basin, and children usually went to bed shortly after their supper of gruel. Koji, however, settled down, as he often did, under the lamp that his mother and grandmother used for their night work and started to untie his bundle of schoolbooks. It was not yet seven.

"Seitaro, why don't you do some homework, too, for a while." Fudé tried to sound as serious as possible, as she was already starting to yawn.

"But tomorrow's a festival. I don't need to do any homework tonight."

Fudé remembered that the next day was November 3, the Emperor's Birthday.*

"That's lucky," said Nui, her hands moving busily as she worked. "We're going to start the reaping tomorrow, Seitaro, so please come straight home instead of playing soldiers. We'll need your help. The ceremony will finish in the morning, won't it?"

"What, are you starting the reaping already?"

"We are. It's a bit soon really, but the army's beginning Grand Maneuvers in a few days, and when they start, horses and troops will be trampling all over the place. They all say it's better to reap any rice that's ripe enough before they begin."

Seitaro nodded in agreement. He knew about the Grand Maneuvers, of course, and, infected by all the commotion over them, he and his friends had been playing soldiers with even greater fervor for the last few days. The children in his class talked of nothing else. Some boasted, "We've got an officer coming to stay with us," while others, proud of the number of troops who would be quartered with them, retorted, "Well, seven soldiers are coming to stay at our place." In fact, about forty thousand soldiers from four divisions—the Osaka Fourth, the Kyoto Sixteenth, the Himeji Tenth, and the Nagoya Third—would be surging into the small Yamato basin. It was unprecedented for the Grand Maneuvers to be held there and, not unnaturally, people were in a state of unusual excitement.

"All right, I'll help."

"Me, too," said Koji, following his brother's example; after all, this was nothing less than a family emergency.

The next morning, instead of the usual dark blue apron over his kimono, Seitaro wore a black muslin sash, while Koji was dressed in a lined kimono of brown cotton, replacing the unlined one he had worn continuously since the end of the summer. Fudé had given much thought to her children's appearance on the Emperor's Birthday.

III

On the east side of Ohashi Bridge, over the Katsuragi River, there was a path that sloped gently down to the entrance gates of a school, Sakata Primary School, which Seitaro and the other children from Komori attended. The elementary-school course having only just been extended to six years, there were at present only five grades and Seitaro was in the top one. There were two hundred and seventy-three pupils, and of these eighty-one came from Komori, a larger number than from any of the other villages. But the Komori pupils also had the lowest rate of attendance, as was clearly shown by the flag that Seitaro always shouldered to and from school. The flag was certainly splendid, with its design of a white cherry blossom on a purple ground, but Seitaro felt no pride or pleasure in being its bearer because of the five white stripes in the bottom corner.

Sakata Primary School served the five villages of Hongawa, Komori, Sakata, Shimana, and Azuchi, and, that April, it had provided them with flags that displayed from one to five white stripes. The attendance rate of each village was officially announced at the end of every month, and the pupils who had made the best showing were presented with the flag with only one stripe; the second best, the flag with two; and, of course, the worst, that with five.

The aim of the scheme was obviously to improve attendance through making the villages compete with each other, and no doubt it achieved a certain measure of success. For the children from Komori, however, it was nothing but a source of humiliation: with many of them absent for anything from six months to one, two, or even three years, they had no hope of ever gaining any flag other than the five-striped one.

As leader of the Komori group, Seitaro had to receive it at the end of every month, and every day without fail he had to carry it to school and back. The black-painted flagstaff was uncomfortably heavy and he always ended up carrying it in a slovenly fashion over his shoulders.

But on this particular morning he held it high as he passed through the school gates, over which two national flags, with their emblem of the sun, were crossed imposingly. Since there was to be a ceremony today, he had come without his bundle of books and could grip the flagstaff firmly with both hands.

Although school usually began at eight forty, nine o'clock came and went without the bell being rung for assembly because the ceremonial hall was still being made ready. The children in the playground were certainly not bored. Both girls and boys were running around in delight at being dressed up in their "best" clothes: those who normally came wearing aprons had on sashes, while those who wore sashes were now arrayed in the formal *hakama* divided skirts; and most of them had on clogs that were higher than usual, too, the highest being those called *pokkuri,* which had an insole of woven straw.

One group, however, had been sitting in a corner of the playground at the north end for quite some time. It was a spot with a fine carpet of grass that had spread from the nearby bank of the Katsuragi. Toyota Matsuzaki, a boy who sat next to Seitaro in class, was at the center of the group and had been reading aloud from a thick book with a red cover, which lay open on his knees. He turned the page: "Next, 'The Broken Bow,'" and raising his voice, began reading again.

The bow was called Full Moon and it was very powerful. One arrow from it was enough to shoot down any animal, however large, or any bird, however swift. People from all over the world longed to own Full Moon, and its price soared up and up, until it was worth a mountain of gold.

Now, there was a very rich man called Kanamaru of Hodaka, from the land of Tadara. Nobody knew how he had become so wealthy, but it was common knowledge that old Kanamaru was terribly strong: some people thought he had probably conquered another country and taken all its treasure, while others thought he must possess magic powers and could make gold and silver whenever he wanted. Nevertheless, it was a fact that no matter how hard they all worked they just grew poorer until they could only afford to sip the thinnest gruel, while Kanamaru lived off the fat of the land, with hundreds of servants and an estate of thousands of acres.

But at last Kanamaru grew tired of his life of luxury, and he ordered his servants to go and find him something more diverting. One day, Fukumaru, his favorite servant, heard about the rare and precious Full Moon and told his master.

Kanamaru leapt up. "I would willingly part with half my wealth to have such a bow," he said; and in due course the powerful bow did indeed come into Kanamaru's possession for half his wealth.

When he at last set eyes on Full Moon, Kanamaru grew angry because the bow did not look at all splendid or powerful. In fact, it looked so ordinary that he thought he must have been cheated. Fukumaru smiled: "It is difficult to tell whether the bow is strong or not without shooting at some target. As a test, might I suggest that you try hitting that great rock in the garden. If this bow really is Full Moon, you should be able to split the rock easily."

"Yes, you are right," nodded Kanamaru, and he fitted an arrow to the bowstring. Taking aim, he drew it and let fly the arrow. There was an exploding sound, the ground shook, and the great rock lay there, neatly split in two.

Fukumaru ran up to Kanamaru and, bowing his head respectfully, said: "Master, this day you have become the King of Tadara; you are no longer just a man of wealth. As long as you are in possession of Full Moon, nobody will be able to defy your command."

"Then let us set off without delay and see what this bow can win for us."

The next day, as an interesting game to dispel his boredom, Kanamaru set off to conquer the people of Tadara. At first, the people resisted, but before long they realized that they would certainly be killed by the arrows from Full Moon if they did not surrender, and before the end of the year Kanamaru had become the King of Tadara.

Kanamaru now set about attacking all the neighboring kingdoms without exception, to the north, south, east, and west. At first, the people of these countries fought back fiercely, but gradually they also came to realize the might of Full Moon, and within seven years every one of them had surrendered. Kanamaru, the conqueror of so many lands, became known as the Great King.

"All of these victories are due to Full Moon. It is truly my most precious possession."

The Great King expressed his gratitude over and over again, but he was disappointed that Full Moon looked neither splendid nor mighty. When he mentioned this, one of his vassals replied: "Your Majesty, the sculptor, Takamura, who is celebrated throughout the world, has just landed in our realm. Might I venture to suggest that Your Majesty order him to decorate the bow with his carving. Like gold lacquer, carving will not fade with age, and the work of the renowned Takamura is said to be so skillful that if he carves a rose the most exquisite fragrance fills the air; while if he carves a lion, a fierce and terrible roar resounds far and wide."

Naturally, the King summoned Takamura immediately, and the sculptor was delighted at the King's command. Three years and three months later, Takamura presented the King with the bow decorated with his carving.

"I hope that it will meet with Your Majesty's approval. For my part, I cannot but feel that this is my greatest work."

The King was thrilled as soon as he saw it. Full Moon was decorated with a design of King Kanamaru shooting down a lion.

"Full Moon does indeed now look like a royal bow. The celebrated sculptor has excelled himself. Splendid, splendid," cried the vassals in praise. The sculptor, Takamura, was duly rewarded to his satisfaction, and he departed for another country.

The following day, the King set off with many of his vassals to go hunting. It was in the middle of autumn and scores of rabbits were frisking hither and thither. The King fitted an arrow to Full Moon and aimed at a young rabbit that went running by. The arrow flew through the air, faster than light, and pierced the rabbit's back—or

so the King thought—when suddenly the bow snapped in two and
the arrow fell, piercing his right foot.

"Aaah, agony!"

The King desperately tried to pull the arrow out but it would
not give an inch; it had passed straight through his foot and was
wedged firmly in the ground.

"Help!" thundered the King. "Quick, help me! There's a big reward for anybody who'll help."

At last, his vassals came running up and tried to pull out the arrow,
but without success.

"Cut it off! Cut off my foot!" screamed the King, and his vassals,
in panic, did as he commanded. The Great King fell to the ground
instantly and breathed his last.

Now, why had Full Moon, the most powerful bow in the world,
suddenly snapped in two? One of the vassals picked up the broken
bow and examined it. Then he nodded. Full Moon had broken
just at the point where the King's neck was carved: the sculptor must
have cut too deeply there in trying to capture the King's protruding
chin.

Time passed. Many wars broke out among countries far away across
the sea and their people suffered continuously. But Tadara remained
at peace and its people were content. They had all heard about King
Kanamaru's tragic death and nobody wanted to become rich, much
less a king. It is said that even now in Tadara, King Kanamaru's footprint can still be clearly seen at the spot where he was pinned to the
ground.

"The end," said Toyota, and, as he raised his head, his eyes met
Seitaro's. "Want to borrow it?"

Seitaro hesitated, but Koji tugged at his sash from behind; there
was no doubt that he wanted to borrow it.

"Who'd want to read a book like that! It's a pack of lies," sneered
Senkichi Sayama, who had slipped in among the group during the
story. He was also in the fifth grade.

Toyota tucked the red-covered book inside his coat. "They're
fairy stories, not lies. You'd learn a lot if you read them."

Senkichi burst out laughing. "Idiot. What can you learn from a
book like that! It's the schoolbooks you read to learn things."

Everybody suddenly fell silent. Senkichi's home was in Sakata, and it was well known that his family was the wealthiest in the village.

"What's up? Is there a fight?" Senkichi's chums crowded round.

Seitaro was sitting on the roots of a cherry tree and without moving he replied, "It's not a fight. Sen's just being rude about Toyo's book."

"What book?"

"This one," said Toyota, letting them catch a glimpse of the red book under his coat. On this festive day, he was wearing a lined, dark blue *kasuri** kimono and a matching *haori* coat. Over the kimono, he wore a pleated *hakama* skirt in strong duck cloth.

"What's it about?"

"It's nothing but lies. He said you could learn a lot from it so I said it's the schoolbooks you read to learn things."

"That's right," Senkichi's friends agreed.

Seitaro grew more and more irritated until he could no longer remain seated. He jumped up and in a fierce voice, which surprised even himself, cried, "It's them schoolbooks that are full of lies!"

"Oh, are they! Where then? What sort of lies? Go on, tell us," retorted Senkichi just as forcefully.

"All right, I will . . . " But Seitaro could not collect his thoughts quickly enough.

"What, can't you tell us?" A scornful smile spread across Senkichi's face.

Although Seitaro knew he should take no notice, Senkichi's sneer was like a dagger through his heart. He sprang back: "That story about the god who flew down from heaven to Mount Takachiho in Hyuga.* That's a whopper for a start."

Senkichi and his friends looked at each other; they had not been expecting such an answer.

"So the teachers' lessons are lies, are they?" Senkichi challenged, a few moments later.

"Yes, nothing but lies."

"Well, is his Majesty the Emperor a lie then? His Majesty's descended from the goddess Amaterasu, and if what the teachers tell us about Amaterasu is a lie that means His Majesty the Emperor's a lie too, doesn't it?"

Seitaro was taken aback.

"You can't answer that one, can you? I don't know why a creep like you even tries to sound clever. You're just a scruffy poor kid who doesn't even wear *hakama* on the Emperor's Birthday. Toyo said he'd lend you that book 'cause he's only come here recently and doesn't know anything yet. But if he did lend it to a creep like you, it'd end up stinking so much it'd be ruined."

Only four boys guffawed at this, but Seitaro felt as if a typhoon had struck him. In fact, not one of the children from Komori was wearing the formal *hakama* skirt; some of them were even in their usual stained kimonos, with grubby aprons. They were all obviously "scruffy poor kids." Poor kids probably did smell, but this was not the reason for Senkichi's remark: it was because they were *eta*. Seitaro felt a lump in his throat and he fought to hide his tears. Just then the bell rang for assembly.

"Sei, I'll lend you the book after school."

Toyota tapped the book through his coat. He was from Osaka and had started coming to Sakata Primary School in September, at the beginning of the fall term. He lived with his mother in Shimana. Seitaro did not know anything else about him.

IV

Ra-ta-tat, ra-ta-tat—the hard sound, like the rattling of a winnower, was from a light machine-gun.

Pop, pop, pop—the rifle sounded like a balloon bursting.

Indifferent to the sounds of fierce fighting, Fudé and Nui were weaving straw sandals. The rice they had reaped on the third was still drying over racks out in the fields, but they were sure that the soldiers would not go so far as to trample it down. None of the soldiers were quartered in Komori, and it was completely removed from the atmosphere of excitement and festivity that had seized the villages of Sakata, Hongawa, and Shimana.

The previous day, Seitaro had been running around until dusk following the tracks of the soldiers, and this morning too he could hardly gulp his breakfast down fast enough.

"What's the point of watching the Maneuvers over and over again. You just get starving hungry racing around like that."

"But it's really exciting! And today the Emperor's coming to watch them from Miminashi Hill. That'll make the troops fight hard."

Stuffing a sweet potato into the breast of his kimono, he dashed out. Several hours later, the fighting did indeed seem to be moving toward Miminashi Hill and, from the continuous light-machine-gun fire, it was apparent that both sides were intent on wiping each other out.

Koji had sat silently in the corner of the workroom since morning. It was an ideal place for him to read because it was the sunniest spot in the house and, in the evening, a lamp hung there.

Right from the start of the maneuvers, Koji had been completely lost in his book. Wondering what he could be reading, Fudé bent over to have a look. The tiny characters were packed closely together on the page; the print was even finer than in the fifth-year textbooks belonging to Seitaro.

"Can you read such a difficult book, Koji?"

"Mm."

"And you understand it?"

"Mm."

"What's it about?"

"It's a story."

"Is it good?"

"Mm."

"Try reading me a little."

Koji raised his head for the first time and smiled shyly.

"Who lent it to you? Whoever it was, it was very kind of them to part with an expensive book like that."

Nui also had a look. The bright red cover dazzled her.

"Toyota who lives in Shimana lent it to Seitaro. Toyota's from Osaka."

"And you're reading it, Koji? That's very clever of you."

"No, it isn't. There's *kana* next to all the hard characters so it's easy to read.

" 'The bow was called Full Moon and it was very powerful,' " Koji began, but then he stopped. "I think I'll read you the story about the bow another time."

Fudé and Nui's eyes were shining; it had been a moment of pure delight, a wave of sunshine suddenly flooding into their lives. What a promising grandson! What a clever son! A few flies had landed on the son's little back and were crawling about there.

In the evening, Seitaro came running back, starving as usual, but before starting his supper he announced with an air of importance:

"The troops are camping out tonight. They're not going to stay in the villages because they're losing the battle. So Sakata and Shimana have come off worst and I'm the lucky one."

"Why's that?"

"I can go and see their camp. The troops who should've stayed in Sakata and Shimana are going to guard the bridges over the Katsuragi."

Seitaro's enthusiasm was infectious and Fudé found herself growing excited.

"I think I'd like to go along too."

"Let's all go. I'd certainly like to see the soldiers," said Nui quite seriously.

"Why don't we steam some sweet potatoes and take them along. One or two of the soldiers might enjoy them."

"Oh yes, that's a good idea! And our potatoes are really tasty."

For a few moments, Seitaro hovered there on the earth floor in a state of ecstasy.

After supper, they all set about steaming the potatoes. The only land that the Hatanaka family owned was a small allotment, about an eighth of an acre, next to the house. Over half the land was used for growing sweet potatoes, and as these were such a precious food, especially when rice was scarce, the family was all the more anxious to share them with the troops.

It was just ten. Afraid that the potatoes might grow cold, Fudé left them in the pan, which she placed in a basket, strapping it to her back.

"Seitaro, you go ahead and see if any of the soldiers want one."

"Goodie!" cried Seitaro delightedly and sped down the moonlit path toward the river.

Here and there along the riverbank groups of soldiers were squatting down, still with knapsacks on their backs. Seitaro approached one group by the bridge.

"Do you want a sweet potato, sir?"

"What's this? You brought us some potatoes? Well, thanks, I wouldn't say no to one."

A tall soldier held out a large hand.

"My mom's just bringing them."

The soldier thanked him again, imitating the local dialect, at which the other soldiers burst out laughing.

A moment later, Fudé appeared, followed by Koji and Nui. Fudé put the basket down on the ground and Nui's lantern shed a faint light on it.

"It's really very good of you. We're much obliged."

The soldiers gathered round at once, lured by the appetizing smell.

"They're nice and hot!"

"What a treat!"

"You couldn't have thought of anything better."

One after another, they reached into the pan.

"Are you here until the morning, sir?" asked Nui.

"It depends on how the fighting goes."

"What a pity you couldn't put up for the night and take it easy."

"Happily, though, many will be discharged after these maneuvers. I mean, if this were a real war there'd only be a few who'd be going back alive."

"Yes, my son died in the war at a place called Shaho."

"That explains it. Most people wouldn't dream of coming out at this time of night to bring us hot potatoes. But even your children . . . I can't thank you enough."

"Yes, thanks a lot."

"They were delicious."

"Take care, sonny."

"Work hard at school."

The large hands of the soldiers patted Seitaro and Koji on the head. The two boys were thrilled but there was also a lump in their throats.

The next morning, Seitaro leapt out of bed.

"Come on, Koji. Let's go and have a look."

"Yeah," and Koji sprang out of bed too; he knew where they were going without Seitaro explaining.

At that early dawn hour, the frost looked like snow as they ran along the path through the fields, and their bare feet were soon bright red. They rushed on to the bridge panting hard, their breath white in the chill morning air, but as they looked round, there was no sign of life at all; only the frost-bent pampas grass on the riverbank.

"The soldiers have left already," sighed Seitaro, breaking the silence.

In fact, the detachment at the bridge had been forced to abandon its position in the middle of the night and had been pushed back farther and farther to the north.

Koji breathed hard on his numb hands.

V

"School again tomorrow," sighed Seitaro, finishing his supper of gruel.

After enlivening the Yamato basin for the last four days like a brilliant festival, the army Grand Maneuvers had finally been brought to a close with a parade in Nara. Seitaro was as forlorn as when he had to put on the dirty, striped kimono he wore every day, after wearing his best dark blue one. Naturally, he realized he could not always wear his best kimono, but he never failed to feel miserable when the time came to change. Similarly, he felt lost now that the machine guns, regimental flags, horses, and troops were leaving, even though he knew they could not stay forever.

Fudé understood this mood of Seitaro's: he loved wearing his one best kimono so much because of the coarseness of his ordinary clothes; and it was the very drabness of the life he led that made the splendor of festive occasions so intoxicating. Fudé had felt exactly the same herself but this only made her speak to him all the more severely.

"I'd have thought you'd be glad to be going back to school tomorrow. You can't run around looking at guns and cannons forever, can you? And it's a busy time for us farmers. We'll be glad to see the backs of those soldiers."

"You'll both have to work all the harder at school after four days break," Nui added. She put her hand on Koji's head, "Won't you, Koji?"

Koji grinned.

"You, too, Seitaro. Mind you keep your nose to the grindstone now. If you don't watch out, Koji'll be outstripping you."

Nui started to stroke Seitaro's head; it was much warmer than Koji's.

"I like soldiers better than old books," he retorted, tossing his head to try and shake off his grandmother's hand.

"But you have to study to be a soldier." Fudé neatly turned the tables on him.

"That's right. A boy won't make a good soldier if he don't work hard at school," followed up Nui.

Seitaro was silent for a moment. Then he said, "It's no use, Gran. You can't be a good soldier if you only go to primary school. All them officers are from good schools. If only I could go to a good school, too, I'd become a general." He stared back at his grandmother.

"Ah, ha, ha! I don't mind a bit if you don't become a general."

Nui stood up and changed the position of the lamp, in readiness for another evening of sandal-making, while Fudé set about her humble chores: clearing away the pan, wiping up the soot marks it had left, and washing the dishes. She then settled down by Nui and began work. They could weave about twenty pairs of sandals a day, but it brought in only a pittance when the cost of raw materials had been deducted; which meant they had to work all the more diligently.

Koji sat down beside them, and, with his slate before him, he opened a book. For a while, Seitaro hung around twiddling his thumbs. Then he reached into Koji's bundle of school things and pulled out the book of fairy stories with the red cover.

Fudé was watching him. "Seitaro, if you want to be a soldier you'd be better off doing some arithmetic."

"I'm no good at arithmetic."

"All the more reason to work hard at it."

"Won't make any difference."

Koji stopped writing on his slate. "I bet Master Hidé the priest's son is good at arithmetic."

This remark was rather unexpected, but they all nodded. Hidéaki was the only middle-school* student in the whole of Komori, and his father, Shuken Murakami, was the resident priest at An'yoji, the village temple of the Shin sect.* Hidéaki cycled to school and wore a jacket with a stand-up collar and gold buttons; and Koji had long regarded him with a mixture of envy and respect: Master Hidé could do all the things that were impossible for the rest of them; in fact, there was nothing he could not do. It was not so surprising therefore that he should have mentioned him.

"Do you want to go to middle school when you're older, Koji, like Master Hidé?" asked Fudé, bending down to peep at his face. A feeling of both hope and fear seized her at the thought of the unknown future.

"Mm. But I don't want to be a soldier, though."

"You needn't if you don't want to. I don't really like them much myself. And look at Master Hidé. Even though he goes to middle school, he's not going to be a soldier. He'll be following in his father's footsteps at the temple."

"D'you mean that's decided already?" cried Seitaro, sounding both shocked and angry. He felt as if he had been sharply rebuked—told that just as Master Hidé was going to succeed his father at the temple, so this house would be coming to him and he had no choice but to be a farmer and to make sandals. In that case, what a waste of time it was going to school. How idiotic to go on sweating over arithmetic!

But had not his hero, Hideyoshi Toyotomi,* risen from being a mere servant who carried his lord's sandals to a mighty general who conquered the whole country? After all, even if you were only a farmer or a sandal-maker, "where there's a will there's a way," as the teacher had taught them only the other day.

On the other hand, it was obvious that you had to go to a first-class school if you wanted to become a great soldier. And you needed money for this. And his family was poor.

"No, it's no use," he cried out silently and rushed into the darkness of the next room. Two mattresses were spread on the floor there. He crawled under the quilt of one and pulled it up over his head. The only way of fending off the enemy that came to attack him again and again with all these contradictions was to hide in the fortress of his bed. Here at least he was safe and could laugh or cry a little without the fear of anybody knowing.

"What can you do with him! I wonder why he hates schoolwork so much," said his grandmother, with the flicker of a smile.

"But, Mother, we can't help him, can we, if there's something he doesn't understand. Don't you think that must make the schoolwork seem even worse to him?"

"I suppose you're right. After all, it was thanks to Seitaro that Koji learned *hiragana*. Like anything else, you can't get on without the right person to help you."

"No, you can't," agreed Koji. His brother had been the first to write out *hiragana* for him, arranging each symbol next to the corresponding one in *katakana*. Since then, every night he had practiced copying his *katakana* textbook onto his slate in *hiragana*. This evening, too, he had copied out one of the stories in his reader. It was his

favorite and, wanting to stick up for the brother who had slunk off
to bed, he began to read it out loud: "A dog carrying a fish in its
mouth came onto the bridge. It looked down into the river and saw
another dog with a fish in its mouth. The dog wanted that fish, too,
and gave a bark. Then the fish fell out of its mouth into the water."

"Well, I never!" There was a perplexed expression on Nui's face
as if she wanted to laugh but could not.

"There's some funny stories even in a school reader," giggled Fudé,
looking pleased at her son's display of talent.

"It doesn't do to be too greedy. Going and dropping his precious
fish in the river like that," and Nui guffawed like a man. Then a look
of relief crossed her face. She had sensed something in the short story
that overwhelmed her: it was not only a story with a moral; it was
far deeper than that. It moved her more than all the stories about
people who became rich and famous, or who sacrificed their lives
out of loyalty or devotion. But she could not find the words to express
what she felt to Fudé. She could only hide her feelings for the time
being by laughing at the greedy dog.

"I feel sorry for the dog," said Koji, who had been staring at the
book, and he turned it toward his mother and grandmother to show
them the picture of the dog with the fish in its mouth looking down
into the river. The next moment, it would have lost the fish and
both Nui and Fudé could picture it running away forlornly, its tail
between its legs in disappointment and regret. Like Koji, they could
not help feeling sorry for it. In the twinkling of an eye, it would be
punished for its greed. A dog was not even allowed to desire one
more fish; whereas among men, greed and avarice flourished. There
were people who took pride in their wealth and social standing,
indifferent to places like Komori where the villagers could scarcely
afford gruel three times a day. But was it not through greed that
they had acquired this wealth and position?

Neither Nui nor Fudé, however, could voice such thoughts, which
remained locked inside them.

"Koji, that story's enough for one night. Go to bed now. School
starts tomorrow," said Fudé quietly.

Seitaro quickly pulled his brother's pillow next to his own. Until
his mother and grandmother had finished their work, he would sleep
by Koji's side.

VI

The next morning, there was a clear, blue autumn sky, and the mountains surrounding the basin seemed to slumber so peacefully that it was hard to imagine the whirlwind of the Maneuvers had ever disturbed their repose.

It was now apparent that, in spite of all the excitement and emotion engendered by the Emperor's supervision, the Grand Maneuvers had been nothing more than a heavy burden on the people living in the basin; and taking place just at harvest time, the farmers had been hit harder than most. The one consolation was that it looked as if the fine autumn weather would continue for a while, and before it broke they would have to hurry and finish the reaping and threshing of the rice.

After sending Seitaro and Koji off to school, each with a packed lunch, Fudé and Nui dragged out the cart as if they had not a moment to lose. They piled in a straw mat, an iron-comblike threshing device, and some baskets, as well as a lunch box and water flask: even though the field was only about six hundred yards away, they could not afford to waste time going home for the midday meal.

The rice that they had reaped before the Maneuvers was almost too dry by now, and the pointed leaves were as sharp as thorns. To protect themselves, they wrapped old aprons round their heads and tied on cloth shields, like mittens, for the back of their hands.

In the next field, separated from their own by a low ridge, there were three people reaping: Tosaku Nagai, his wife, Sayo, and daughter, Natsu, all from Komori. They were so intent on trying to work faster than each other that they did not pause even for a moment to chat, and not a word passed between Fudé and Nui either. The two families continued to work silently all morning.

At last, as she unpacked their lunch on the ridge between the fields at midday, Fudé called out, "A good crop this year, Sayo. About fifteen bushels, I'd say."

"Fifteen bushels! You must be joking," retorted Tosaku, shaking his head.

"Twelve-and-a-half at the most," added Sayo.

"But at least you own your land so the whole lot's yours." Nui unwound the apron from her head. "Not like us tenant farmers. We'll only get about three out of the twelve-and-a-half, plus the straw. There's nothing harder than being poor."

"All the same, Mrs. Hatanaka," said Sayo, setting out her family's lunch next to Fudé, "Twelve-and-a-half bushels don't go very far in a family of nine. Like this morning, I must have cooked about two pints of gruel, and the pan was pretty heavy I can tell you, and it's quite a job for a woman to lift it off the stove. Anyway, in the twinkling of an eye, every single drop had disappeared into their great bellies."

She burst out laughing, and Fudé and Nui joined in; they could vividly picture the large pan, with the bubbling gruel lapping at the brim and the grains of rice sinking to the bottom. Very few families in Komori cooked a fresh panful every morning; most of them merely added some water to the leftovers from supper and had "warmed up gruel" for breakfast. It was enough simply to have something to eat, whatever it might be, and they relished even the roughest mixture of boiled rice and barley; as did the two families sitting on the ridge who were about to have this for their lunch. For a while, the five of them munched contentedly and then there was a loud gulp as Tosaku drank some water.

"There's an old saying," Tosaku said and then paused for breath; "You may dread your guest leaving but you're relieved when he's gone. Now, I like the army as much as the next man and I thought I could watch the Maneuvers for another two or three days at least, but I can't say as I'm sorry now they're over."

He turned and smiled at Fudé, who was just swallowing her last mouthful and could only nod.

Sayo leant toward Nui. "He's just like a little boy. You'd never think he was turning fifty. We can do without those old Maneuvers can't we, Mrs. Hatanaka?"

"I suppose so," Nui smiled awkwardly, hiding her feelings.

"But everybody's been saying you Hatanakas enjoyed them more than anybody else in Komori," butted in Tosaku impatiently. "I mean, going to all the trouble of steaming sweet potatoes to take to them soldiers, and on such a bitter night, too. Not the sort of thing most people'd do. We've all been downright impressed, you being so thoughtful on account of Shinkichi dying in the war."

"Very grateful, I'm sure." Nui laughed exaggeratedly, as if to say, "Do you really think we took the soldiers potatoes because we enjoyed the Maneuvers?" Only Fudé understood, however.

Tilting up the flask, Sayo poured some water into her bowl and drank noisily. Then she pulled the towel round her head tighter.

"Well, we don't like them Maneuvers. It beats me what the rich get out of them, what with all the rice being trampled down when it's ready to harvest. If you ask me, Maneuvers are no different from the pranks the young rascals around here get up to. The Emperor and them generals are the only ones that enjoy them, and they'd enjoy anything because they don't have anything better to do. They don't have to worry where their next meal's coming from, like us."

"You shouldn't say things like that so loudly. If a cop heard, he'd cart you off to the station like a shot."

Tosaku looked all around dramatically and his daughter Natsu giggled.

"The old woman is born envious," he continued, filling his pipe and striking a match. "Each of us comes into this world carrying Fortune's Box on our back. If you're lucky, you've got a king's crown in your box, but if not, and it's the life of a beggar, there's nothing you can do about it. Envying the king and grumbling won't change things. Look over there. His Majesty the Emperor's only got to visit that hill once and they build a road so wide there you wouldn't recognize the place. That shows you how almighty the Emperor is." Tobacco smoke drifted up Tosaku's forehead, through his long hair, and slowly faded away into the air.

Nui shifted her gaze from Tosaku to Miminashi Hill. As he said, a whitish road, especially built for the Imperial visit, wound round the flank of the hill like a broad sash. Even the vegetation had to submit to the might of the Imperial Throne!

Fudé noticed a white, shiny grain of rice in the cloth in which she was wrapping her empty lunch box. Putting it in her mouth, she silently chewed on it with her front teeth. Had Shinkichi died in the war because he was unlucky? If so, who decided whether a man would be lucky or not? The *kami?** The Buddha? But were not the *kami* and the Buddha fair to everybody? Fudé's face grew flushed; she felt tense and confused.

Natsu stood up. "That road must be very wide."

"Yes, about twelve feet, I'd say. Must have been quite a job felling all those trees and spreading the gravel. It may be small but a hill's still a hill, and it's a fair distance to the top, winding round and round like that. It was soon finished though. The power of the Emperor is quite something."

"But, Dad, it wasn't the Emperor who built the road. It was done by all the farmers over there."

"You stupid girl! You don't have to tell me that. The Emperor, a *kami*—or so they say—stooping so low as to do a common job like road building! I've never heard of such a thing!"

"Is the Emperor really a *kami?*" asked Natsu, after a pause.

"Well," Tosaku seemed to hesitate, as if no longer certain.

Seeing this, Natsu grew bolder. "The *kami* can go up to the sky or down to the sea in a flash, so if that's what the Emperor is, he could get to the top of the hill easily without a road. But look at all the trouble they've gone to building such a wide one. That means the Emperor finds it as hard as everybody else to climb hills, doesn't it?"

"You'll be punished saying things like that!" roared Tosaku as he looked around him again.

Natsu slipped back swiftly among the rice and began reaping. It was rumored that when the harvest was over, sixteen-year-old Natsu was going into service in Osaka.

The children at Sakata Primary School had also finished lunch and were now gathering round Senkichi Sayama in the playground. He was the center of attention because of the "magic glasses" hanging round his neck. A few children had already been allowed to peep through them and, in high spirits, were loudly boasting:

"I could see all the trees and paths on Miminashi Hill as if they were right next to the school. They're a soldier's binoculars. But only the top soldiers have binoculars like that. And I had a look through them!"

"I saw some people threshing. And the thresher, too; they were so clear."

"I saw a factory chimney. I almost jumped seeing it so near."

"Well, I saw an oxcart. The ox lifted up its tail and dropped ox dung. Ha, ha, ha!"

"Fibber!"

"I am not. It did drop ox dung."

"Idiot. Of course an ox drops ox dung!"

Everybody roared with laughter and in the midst of the merriment,

Senkichi shouted out, "All those who want to look through my binoculars must line up and wait their turn."

The children formed a long line behind Senkichi and, rather hesitantly, Koji joined the end. He noticed Seitaro standing some distance away from them. "Maybe Seitaro doesn't want to look through the magic glasses," he thought, feeling sorry that his brother would miss such a treat.

The binoculars passed from child to child down the line under the supervision of Senkichi's best friend, Shigeo Iwase. The children were still in a state of excitement over the Maneuvers and, led by Senkichi, they started to chatter about rifles and machine guns, scouts and buglers, and eventually the soldiers who should have been quartered with them, at which point the talk grew even more animated.

"Four soldiers were meant to stay with us and we'd got all new mattresses and pillows made. Then we felt like idiots when it suddenly turned out they weren't coming."

"They said five soldiers were coming to stay at our place, and then they said they couldn't 'cause they were losing the battle, and they all went away."

"Some officers were quartered with us and so we'd bought heaps of fish and beef, and a great barrel of saké. But there's no time to eat when you're losing a battle, and now we've got to finish it all by ourselves. We'll be stuffing ourselves forever!"

"Ha, ha! It's no good being on the losing side."

"It's bad enough in the Maneuvers, but it's even worse in a real war."

"Only the Russians and Chinese lose in a real war."

They all laughed again.

But Seitaro, who was still standing apart from the rest, neither spoke nor laughed. He was not alone in being silent; none of the children from Komori had anything to say because none of the soldiers had been quartered with their families.

Senkichi Sayama caught sight of Seitaro. "It's all right for Sei and the others from Komori, isn't it? They've got nothing to worry about. They couldn't care less if the soldiers lost and went away because there was never any chance of them staying with them."

"That's right."

It was not Seitaro who answered back but Shigemi Nagai, one of

Tosaku Nagai's daughters and Natsu's younger sister. At school, she was known as "Hachimero"; which could mean a tomboy, or, more harshly, a hussy.

Shigemi paused and looked around quickly at her Komori friends before continuing, "We couldn't put them up in Komori because we're all poor. We don't have any spare mattresses and we can't afford to buy nice things to eat. But Sei's family steamed some sweet potatoes for the soldiers camping on the river bank. You lot didn't give them anything to eat, did you, even though they were meant to stay with you. We did a lot more for them in Komori."

"What! Sweet potatoes!" shrieked Senkichi, and all the others collapsed with laughter.

Seitaro felt as if he had been knocked over. "They're all laughing at me," he thought. "They're laughing at me because I'm poor. 'We bought heaps of saké and fish but you only had sweet potatoes—' that's what they're saying. The soldiers were pleased with them though. They even patted Koji and me on the head."

Wanting to explain this to the other children, he mustered up courage and spoke quickly:

"The soldiers camping out enjoyed having some nice hot potatoes on such a cold night."

"Those soldiers are from the Nagoya division," said Senkichi, speaking with deliberate slowness. "They don't know these parts. D'you think they'd have eaten the potatoes if they'd known you're from Komori? On top of losing the battle, the poor things ended up eating *eta* potatoes! Stinking *eta* potatoes!" and he held his nose, pretending to vomit.

It was Toyota Matsuzaki's turn to have the binoculars. "I don't want a look," he said, pushing the binoculars away and stepping out of the line.

"Well, why bother to wait your turn then?" Shigeo's tone of voice and stance clearly showed his annoyance at Toyota's rebuff.

"We don't have to lend them to anybody who doesn't want a look," snapped Senkichi, glaring at Toyota.

"I don't know what he's got to be so stuck up about. What's so special about a pair of old field glasses?" Toyota gripped Seitaro's shoulder. "Come on, Sei, let's go."

"Ha, ha! Look, one's an *eta* and the other's a bastard. Just right for each other, they both stink!"

Senkichi was suddenly punched in the chest, and the next moment a full-scale fight had broken out.

"Teacher, they're fighting! Teacher, they're fighting!"

"Teacher, teacher, the *eta* are making trouble!"

Word of the fight soon reached the staff room, upsetting the midday calm.

VII

The wooden storm doors at the front of the house facing the road were all closed and inside there was semi-darkness. Koji slid open the screen doors of the workroom and sat down there. Across the narrow backyard where the washing was hung out to dry, the door of a makeshift shed was wide open, revealing a straw mat, a winnower, an old sack, some bundles of straw, and, in the corner, a mortar for polishing rice. A stillness lay over these objects as if they were aware of their owners' absence.

Tick-tock, tick-tock, tick-tock—Koji glanced at the clock; it was nearly three. "Seitaro'll be back at three," he said in a small voice, not really believing it. "Seitaro'll be back at three," he repeated a little louder. But it became increasingly obvious that his brother would not be back by then.

"They dragged him off to the staff room all covered in dirt from the playground and the teacher hit him when he kept on struggling. No, he won't come back at three." Koji's face suddenly contorted and the tears streamed down his cheeks.

Presently, he reached inside his toy box and brought out some shell spinning-tops. His fingers were still damp from wiping away his tears, which helped him to wind them up more neatly than usual. When satisfied, he let one go. It was a good throw and the top spun smoothly with a whirring noise. Koji quickly wound up the next and set the two tops spinning together.

"Keep going, Sei, keep going. Keep going, Toyo."

The third was bright red. Koji spun it full of confidence but, as if it were angry, the top flew through the air and hit the door. Koji wound the lifeline again.

"Come on, keep going!" The top whirled round smartly this time. "Shige, don't give up. Please don't give up."

Koji was playing in deadly earnest: the red top really was "Ha-chimero."

Ding, ding, ding. The clock chimed three. Koji strained his ears; he could hear people talking in the distance. Maybe Seitaro was among them.

He ran out to the front of the house. Seven or eight children, with a purple flag in their midst, were following the path as it curved toward Komori; and Seitaro was not among them. Koji swallowed hard, fighting the feeling of panic which gripped him. He started to walk toward the flag.

"Sei's been made to stand holding the buckets, Ko."

"He won't be back for ages yet."

"Not before dark."

Did they care at all, Koji wondered as the children surrounded him. He glared at his brother's friends and then pushed his way out of the group and sped like the wind toward school.

Sei's been made to stand holding those buckets, he thought. Those heavy buckets full of water!

The weight of them distorted Koji's face.

Seitaro almost fell to his knees again and again, giving way under the weight of the buckets, but each time he caught sight of the Head-master he braced himself once more. The Headmaster, who was in charge of the fifth grade, had handed down the punishment him-self.

"You may not put the buckets down until you understand that you should not have hit Senkichi Sayama and until you show that you are truly sorry for what you have done," he repeated several times.

Even if it meant standing there all night, even if his arms were pulled out of their sockets, Seitaro was determined to go on holding the buckets, and he felt sure that Toyota was equally resolved. But the color was draining from Toyota's face, second by second, and he had almost reached the limits of his endurance.

As if he could not bear to stand back and watch, Mr. Egawa, the senior teacher, called out to them, "Don't be so obstinate both of you. Hurry up and apologize. After all, you shouldn't have hit Sayama."

"No, leave them. They obviously still think they are in the right. We must knock some sense into them."

However, no sooner had the Headmaster uttered these words than Mr. Egawa went over to the two boys. "Hatanaka." He put his hand on Seitaro's shoulder.

Seitaro felt tears welling up in his eyes. The touch of that hand brought happy memories of his first year at school flooding back: Mr. Egawa had been his teacher then and had often quietly placed his hand on Seitaro's head or shoulder.

"Put the buckets down."

The order was gently given and the two boys lowered their buckets. At once, a cold sensation shot through their shoulders, followed immediately by a tingling in their fingers; they had been delivered from humiliation and the blood was coursing through the veins of their arms once more.

"Apologize to the Headmaster." Mr. Egawa put his hand on Toyota's shoulder. "He has business to attend to and must be leaving now. Hurry up and apologize and then you can go home at once. Your mother's bound to be worried about you."

"But I haven't done anything wrong, sir." Toyota addressed his remark to the Headmaster rather than Mr. Egawa.

"What do you mean you've done nothing wrong! Do you think it is all right to hurt Sayama?"

The Headmaster had just put on his hat but now he snatched it off and flung it down on the table. The three other teachers who were working in the staff room pretended not to be aware of what was going on.

"Sir, it was me who hit Sen," cried Seitaro so loudly he even startled himself. At the same time, Toyota unexpectedly picked up both the buckets again.

The Headmaster took this as a personal affront.

"Well, if that's the way you feel, you can stand there until the morning," he roared, sweeping out of the room.

"Put down those buckets and stop being so stubborn," said Mr. Egawa. "Now, it seems that when Sayama refused to show you his binoculars, you both got angry and hit him. If that's really what happened then you are both in the wrong, aren't you?"

"That's not how it was, sir, that's a lie. The Headmaster only believes Sen, but Sen said rude things about us."

"I see. Well, you'd better tell me all about it right from the beginning. The other teachers will listen as well. What started the fight?"

"Sweet potatoes."

The lady teacher sniggered discreetly but the other two, who were young men, laughed outright.

"Well, what happened?"

"He said they stank. They stank 'cause they were *eta* potatoes."

The teachers stopped working and looked at each other.

"Then you hit Sayama?" continued Mr. Egawa, after a moment's pause. His low voice sounded tense.

"Yes, that's right. Sen's always calling me an *eta*. Some of the others do, too. Sir, I hate being called that more than anything. And it's not something I can change, however hard I try. Please tell me what I can do about it, sir, please."

"Yes, I see. I understand only too well, now. And Matsuzaki, you got angry because your friend, Hatanaka, had been insulted."

"Yes," Toyota began, but then he closed his mouth: naturally he had hit Senkichi because of Seitaro but, even more, on his own account. He had been called a bastard; and that was not something he could help, any more than Seitaro could help being an *eta*. Nevertheless, he had been abused as if he were ugly; tormented as if he were evil; and when that happened all he could do was hit back. His grip on the buckets tightened.

"For goodness sake put them down. I understand everything and tomorrow I'll explain it all to the Headmaster."

Mr. Egawa wrenched the buckets from Toyota's hands and took them outside.

"Now hurry along home; it will soon be dark."

"Yes, sir."

Toyota and Seitaro both bowed and the three teachers all gave a slight nod back. Then they rushed to the school gates where they drew together for a moment. "Toyo," said Seitaro, "Sei," said Toyota; and they ran off in opposite directions.

"Seitaro!"

It could not be, so late . . . Yet there was no doubt that it was Koji who came scampering like a puppy toward him from the shadow of the riverbank.

"Koji, you mustn't tell Mom or Gran about this."

"No."

And not another word was spoken. The evening breeze played with the hems of their kimonos as they crossed over to the west side of Ohashi Bridge.

VIII

"You're very late, aren't you?" Fudé stared at Seitaro suspiciously. She and Nui had just arrived back from the field with the baskets of rice.

"I was busy after school."

Seitaro handed his bundle of books to Koji and helped his mother and grandmother unload the baskets.

"That's all right then. I was afraid you'd got into trouble and been kept in."

"Well, I didn't."

Nui smiled. "There's nothing so terrible about misbehaving and getting into a fight, so long as you don't come home blubbering about it. Boys will be boys, and you can't be playing with dolls, can you, Seitaro?"

Nevertheless, Nui felt secretly worried about him. "Something's the matter. I know something's happened," she thought, impatient to find out what it might be.

That evening, Fudé lit the fire to heat up a bath. It was the first time for many days and she was longing for one, especially after work like threshing, which left her covered in white dust from head to foot, even her eyelashes. But when Seitaro and Koji had had theirs, she invited the neighbors round for one, too, as was usual in the village, and waited her turn until the very last.

Seitaro and Koji completely forgot their tiredness and stayed up, sitting by the lamp. Their nearest neighbors, a couple who lived on the north side, also lingered by the brazier as if they had been asked round for the evening—which was understandable, since the only chance they had to enjoy themselves and indulge in some lively gossip was once or twice a month when they got together with the other villagers for a bath. Fortunately, the husband, Hirokichi Shimura, not only had the gift of the gab but a constant supply of stories as well. He worked as a carrier and traveled far and wide, sometimes pulling a cart laden with goods right into the heart of the Yoshino mountains, or to Osaka and back.

Tonight, Hirokichi waited for Fudé to finish her bath before opening his mouth and revealing a set of yellow, tobacco-stained teeth.

"I heard a good one today," he began.

"Tell it to us over a cup of tea," said Fudé, feeling sociable.

"Oh, don't bother," Hirokichi's wife, Kané, waved her hand. "It's not worth making him a cup of tea; you never know what he's talking about half the time. If he gets tired of talking, a glass of water will do."

"Now I ask you, what's a fine man like myself doing married to such a cold-hearted woman," cried Hirokichi in high spirits.

"Talk about a happy couple: What's happened to this story we're all dying to hear?" Nui, too, seemed to have quite forgotten her weariness.

"Well, now," Hirokichi slapped his knees, "it is with great trepidation that I announce the following story is about His Majesty, the Emperor. I'm sure you and Koji know that the Emperor came to the Maneuvers, Seitaro. Well, some fella picked up His Imperial Majesty's stub ends. What a find!"

"Where did he find them?" asked Seitaro, his eyes shining.

"That I couldn't tell you, but it must be somewhere around Miminashi Hill."

"But stub ends aren't any use."

"Now that's where you're wrong; you obviously don't realize their real worth. These are stub ends marked with the Imperial seal and graciously left by His Majesty. They're cigarettes that have been in the Emperor's mouth and you won't find anything like them no matter how hard you look. The fella that picked them up has really hit the jackpot. He'll treasure them like a family heirloom. Anyway, this other man, that lives nearby, heard about it and he decided he wanted a keepsake of His Majesty, too. So off he went to the hill to have a look round but there wasn't any more stub ends. So he used his brains and . . . hee, hee, . . . what d'you think he found, Sei?"

"Footprints."

Fudé, Nui, and Kané burst out laughing at the thought of the man trying to take home a footprint.

Hirokichi paused and then said, "Well, it seems he did take back a keepsake."

"He scraped up the soil the footprints was in," scoffed his wife.

Hirokichi shook his head. "With *your* brains you'll never guess; I'll have to tell you. He found the Emperor's crap. He's a smart fella all right."

They were all taken aback.

Hirokichi continued in an increasingly exultant tone of voice. "The Emperor spent a day and a night at Miminashi Hill and this fella was sharp enough to realize that even His Majesty has to crap."

"Even a *kami?*" asked Koji in a small voice, staring up at the family *kamidana,* the altar to the guardian spirits of the household, above the doorway leading into the bedroom. Hirokichi's story was incomprehensible to him: he could not even imagine the teachers at school crapping like everybody else, much less the Emperor, who was meant to be a *kami.*

Nui and Fudé were overcome with mirth.

"I've heard of the Water-Fetching ceremony at Nara's Nigatsudo, but this is the first time I've ever heard of the Crap-Fetching ceremony on Miminashi Hill," said Kané, wiping away tears of laughter.

Seitaro silently shook himself; there was so much he wanted to say he did not know where to begin.

With his pipe in his mouth, Hirokichi added, "Funny what a difference there is between people when we're all the same human beings. There they are, treating the Emperor's crap like treasure, but in our case, they think even the rice we grow is dirty and stinks." He raised his eyes to the ceiling.

Seitaro gave a start and then froze: maybe Hirokichi had heard about the trouble at school; maybe he was hinting at the sweet potatoes when he talked about their rice stinking.

"Koji, let's turn in now. It's half past nine already," he urged.

Koji shook his head, showing a stubbornness unusual for him. "I'm not a bit sleepy. I want to listen to some more stories."

Seitaro grew increasingly nervous. He was afraid Koji might blab about what had happened that day and he wanted to shield his mother and grandmother from the hopeless pain of the jibe about "stinking potatoes."

Koji leaned toward Hirokichi. "Uncle, what's a bastard?"

"A bastard? What are you talking about?"

"It's about a person."

"A person?"

"Yes, I heard one boy call another boy a bastard."

"Ah, I've got you now. I bet the one who was called that went red."

Koji made no reply.

"Or did he get angry? They usually do. A bastard's a child who hasn't got a father."

"Are me and Seitaro bastards then?"

There was another explosion of laughter. Fudé tapped Koji on the shoulder.

"You've got a father, Koji."

"No, I haven't. He's dead."

"Yes, but he was alive when you were little. The boy who's a bastard never had a father right from the start."

"Yes, he has. Toyo said his father in Osaka sent him that book with the red cover," retorted Seitaro, unable to remain silent.

"Ha, ha. He's too much for me. I'm blessed if I can answer that one. We'd better be off." Hirokichi stretched himself, twisting his hips from side to side, and stepped down to the *doma.**

"But if a bastard's out of the top drawer, it doesn't matter, of course," he suddenly remarked as he looked for his straw sandals. "That Yanagihara, for instance—the lady-in-waiting of the second rank or whatever they call her—she's no more than the Emperor's concubine really. But her son's the Crown Prince, isn't he? In the old days, all the lords had twenty or thirty concubines, the shogun more like fifty, and all them concubines' sons was important samurai. Not like us. Our kids are always looked down on, legitimate or not. We stink, same as our rice."

"Don't talk such rubbish! We've just had a good bath, haven't we?" Kané laughed and went out just ahead of her husband.

"All right, all right." Hirokichi trotted after her.

Fudé and her family felt dazed for a moment as if a whirlwind had swept out. Nui broke the silence:

"Seitaro, did you play with this Toyo today?"

"Yes. I went over to Toyo's."

"What's his mother like?"

"Very pretty."

Seitaro escaped to the bedroom.

"I wonder if he did play there." Nui looked at Fudé with a suspicious expression on her face.

Fudé was staring vacantly at the lamp, not yet recovered from the whirlwind. "Our rice stinks. Our children stink," she thought, the words sinking down inside her like sediment.

"Come over and play at my place during the winter holidays, and I'll come over to yours, too," Toyota suggested to Seitaro the next day at school.

"Is your mother pretty?" asked Seitaro, who felt greatly relieved when Toyota smiled proudly; he had not lied to his grandmother last night after all.

When he saw Senkichi, Seitaro squared his shoulders to show he was quite ready to hold the buckets again any time. Senkichi looked away, raising his hand to his right cheek which was still slightly swollen.

IX

"You're back just in time, Seitaro. We're going to start treading the mortar."

Fudé's nasal voice brought Seitaro to a halt. His mother was kneeling on the ground cleaning the bottom of the mortar. Seitaro wanted to cry out "that's done it"; he hated treading the mortar more than any other job, especially if it contained barley. However, he could not complain or run away because Koji was already standing there, very upright and with a strangely solemn expression on his face, obviously waiting to help.

"All right, I'll tread as long as you like," he replied, there being no alternative. "Is it going to be barley or rice?"

"Rice; rice for dumplings," said his grandmother, who was sitting on a mat under the eaves of the shed making a thick length of rope. She looked up, opening her large mouth to laugh. She was using only the best fresh straw, long in the stalk, and each time she twisted it, she stretched the upper part of her body and threw back her head.

"Rice for dumplings?" repeated Seitaro disbelievingly, going over to his grandmother. "You're not joking?"

"No, of course I'm not. Look inside that measure."

It was quite true. The pale mass of unpolished rice at the bottom of the thirty-pint measure, beside the mortar, was certainly the sticky kind used to make dumplings.

"Are we going to make dumplings then?"

"We are. Your mother's very considerate and she thought you and Koji must be dying to have some again."

"But it seems a bit odd." Seitaro wrinkled up his nose, unconvinced.

Koji was still looking as solemn as ever; undoubtedly he knew all about it.

Fudé adjusted the pestle and poured the rice from the measure into the mortar. She then sprayed it with water, as the rice tended to crack if it were too dry.

"There's not much, so it won't take long before the bran starts rising. Then you can go and play, Seitaro."

"No, I'll stay and tread till it's finished. Mom, why are we having dumplings?"

"Because you'd both like some, that's why." As she said this, Fudé's nose twitched as if it tickled.

"I'd better eat as many as I can then. You'll see, Frogfish'll gobble up ten at one go."

Seitaro climbed onto the step on one side of the treading beam and Fudé and Koji climbed up on the other. Then they all pressed down on the beam with their feet, forcing up the pestle attached to it. The next moment, they released the pressure and the pestle fell with a heavy thud into the mortar, which was secured in the ground.

Worked by foot in this way, the mortar "polished," or removed the bran layers of husked rice and barley, and if a different kind of pestle were attached to the beam, it could also be used to produce flour from beans and grains. It was known as a Chinese mortar, indicating its country of origin, and was an indispensable piece of equipment for the farmers thereabouts. But treading the mortar was monotonous and exhausting work; and even when the rice had been pounded two or three hundred times, there might still be no sign of the outer coat coming off.

Seitaro lifted his foot off the treading beam to change legs and, at once, Fudé felt the full weight of the pestle. She laughed, "Frogfish may eat a lot but it makes him strong all right. And he'll be even stronger by New Year's after tomorrow's dumplings."

"We're having them tomorrow, then?" Seitaro's spirits rose at once. The next moment, however, Fudé's words made him grow serious.

"Yes, we're going to make an offering to your father."

Of course, tomorrow was December 3, the day his father had died in battle in snowy Manchuria. Seitaro no longer wanted to boast of the number of dumplings he could eat. He trod the mortar as hard as he could, his forehead bathed in sweat.

Koji felt the same. Having known from the start that the dumplings were to be an offering, he had been working steadily without saying a word. As was his wont, he was thinking intently about his father's death. He could not understand why his father had died in the war, and the more he thought about it the more puzzling it became.

"Other fathers are alive and well. They're alive and getting on with their work. So why did my dad have to go to the war? It'd be much better if he hadn't gone to such a dangerous place."

Koji only remembered one thing about his father: his large, square-shaped head. It had looked like the square, earthenware foot warmer, known as a *banko,* and had felt faintly warm, too. Shortly before he was drafted he gave Koji a ride on his shoulders, and Koji vaguely remembered being afraid of falling off and clinging tightly to his father's head.

He had never mentioned this to anyone: this father with the slightly warm *banko* head belonged to him alone; and he was afraid that if he tried talking about him, they might say that his father's head had not looked like that at all.

He could see the square *banko* head now, moving along in front of him, in time with the pestle. Koji pressed his lips together even tighter and went on treading.

"I'd say the bran's risen now," Nui remarked after a while; she could tell this from the sound of the pestle, without looking inside the mortar.

"Yes," agreed Fudé, fixing the treading beam in place with a wooden bar.

Seitaro and Koji sank down onto their grandmother's mat and stretched out their tired legs.

"I bet your legs ache. Never mind, there's bound to be a treat in store after helping with the treading. Even the dumplings'll taste nicer, you'll see," Nui comforted them.

Seitaro silently rubbed his knees but Koji put his hand on his grandmother's shoulder and said, "I don't understand, Gran."

"And you so good at school! What is it?"

"It's not to do with school, it's to do with Dad."

"Your dad? I'm not surprised you don't understand. I know you're bright but there's not much chance of you remembering him when you was only two at the time."

"No, it's not that, Gran. I don't understand why Dad went to the war."

"He went 'cause there was a war," retorted Seitaro.

Koji stared at his brother.

"I don't know why that war broke out, either," said Fudé, sifting the bran from the rice. "War's a funny thing when you think about it."

"War's a quarrel," chipped in Seitaro again.

Fudé nodded, "Yes, I know, but why did the Emperor, who's meant to be a *kami*, have to get us mixed up in something bad like a quarrel?"

"Well, Russia started it. If the Emperor hadn't done anything, Russia would have conquered us. That's why we went to conquer them instead."

"Then war's nothing but a land-grabbing demon," laughed Nui lightheartedly, wanting to dismiss all the talk of war with a joke.

Undeterred, Koji asked again, "I still don't understand, Gran. Why did Dad die when Japan won the war?"

"What a thickhead," and, half in fun, Seitaro gave Koji's head a push. "It doesn't make any difference who wins if you've been hit by a bullet. You'll die anyway."

"But if you die, that's losing."

"Well, we didn't lose. We won."

"Even though Dad died?"

"Of course, we won. That's why Dad died. And the other soldiers, too. They all died so we'd win."

Koji was bewildered. He looked at the length of rope Nui had twined. It lay behind her; one foot, two feet. Each time she stretched, the rope grew, and he felt that at any moment it might come and wind itself around him.

"He died so we'd win. We won even though he died. Did we though?"

He felt stifled; also rather angry. Treading on the rope, he shouted, "But he shouldn't have died!" At once, he saw his father's *banko* head again, growing larger and larger.

Nui sighed. "No, he shouldn't've died. Shin was very fond of dumplings, but he'll never enjoy one again now, no matter how many we offer up."

"But Gran, Dad won," insisted Seitaro, growing red in the face. He could not bear to think of his father unless it were in terms of victory.

Fudé put the sifted rice back in the mortar; it would have to be pounded again until the bran had been completely polished away. She rearranged the towel covering her head and climbed back onto the treading step, intending to continue work by herself. Seitaro quickly ran over to join her and so did Koji.

"Didn't he, Mom? Even though he died . . . " Seitaro began, but his mother stared across at him almost crossly.

"I'll tell you the way it was. The Emperor won the war and thousands of soldiers including your father died in it."

"There, as usual your mother couldn't have put it better. That's the way it was. Now d'you understand, Seitaro?" Nui jumped to her feet and started pulling in the length of thick rope, which soon grew into a coil more than an arm's span in width.

Thirty minutes later, the glutinous rice was fully polished and the white grains gleamed in the twilight. Fudé rushed over to the well with it.

Seitaro and Koji heard her sniff many times as she washed the rice; they knew it was not only because of the cold. And neither of them had enjoyed pounding the rice for an offering of dumplings their father could no longer eat.

X

"Koji, look at this," said Seitaro, opening his clenched hand on a level with Koji's eyes.

Koji stood on tiptoe and stared at the object on his brother's palm. "It looks like a top," he thought, his head on one side.

Seitaro laughed at him. "It's a metal top, and it's very strong." He placed it in Koji's hand.

Koji examined it from every angle. It was slightly smaller than his own wax-filled shell ones and heavier, too, being made of iron.

"Where d'you get it?"

"Toyo gave it to me. He said in Osaka the metal ones are much more popular. I bet it'd beat a shell top straight off."

"How d'you know?"

"Bet it would. If you don't believe me, let's try."

Koji searched the dark room until he found his three shell tops while Seitaro quickly wound up the metal one.

Fudé looked round from the corner in the *doma* where she was busy clearing up after supper. "What about your homework tonight?"

"We'll do it later," replied Seitaro excitedly, and let the top go with a sharp tug of the string. Not to be outdone, Koji pulled the string of his as well. The two tops seemed to size each other up, sometimes spinning near, sometimes farther apart, in the middle of the wooden floor of the two-mat room; and then, the metal top moved obliquely toward its opponent and rammed into it.

The shell top feebly rolled over twice and came to a halt. It lay motionless, as if dead, while the metal one continued to spin round it triumphantly.

"Hee, hee. See how strong it is." Seitaro picked up his victorious top delightedly. "Let's try again."

"All right, I'll play with this one." Koji wound up his red top.

But it lost even faster than the blue one before it. The first collision was too much for it and it went flying into the *doma*.

"Seitaro, that's enough. There's nothing to be proud of in beating Koji at a game like that," scolded Fudé, picking up the red top. Seeing it pitifully dented in the middle, where it bulged, she said sharply, "I'd like you to stop now."

Koji took the top from his mother a little shamefacedly and immediately noticed that it was injured.

"Oh, it's hurt."

"Ah, ha, ha! It's lost. The metal top's beaten it all right, just like I said."

Koji was silent.

"Those old shell tops don't stand a chance against a metal one."
No response.

"This top's as strong as a bullet 'cause it's made of iron that's been beaten in the middle of a fire. D'you want it?"

"No." Koji shook his head. Besides being vexed, he felt grieved as well: his top had been alive. Although now filled with wax instead of flesh, its shiny skin was still flecked with its original purple spots and it had always revived when he wound up the lifeline, humming a song in a loud or a soft voice, or telling him stories of the sea he had never seen.

These seashell tops were to him precious playmates. He put all three in a box and tied it up.

"I'm never going to spin my tops again."

"I'm pleased to hear it," said Nui, who had already begun her evening sandal-making. "Can't stand them games of chance. And don't go playing it at school, either. It's no better than gambling. And you too, Seitaro, you'd do better to be getting on with your schoolwork instead of messing about with games like that. Promise your father you will when you pray before the shrine tomorrow. Promise him you'll work hard at school and do well in life."

Seitaro quickly crawled into bed before his grandmother had finished. The victorious metal top lay beside his pillow, its pointed end sticking up in the air.

The next morning, he awoke to the sound of the pestle pounding the polished glutinous rice into a dough for the dumplings. His brother raised his head with a start.

"Shall we get up?"

But Koji pointed to the metal top. "Are you going to play with that again?"

"You bet. I'll win every time. I'll beat all those weedy shell tops everybody's got."

"Poor things."

"Who? The boys that lose?"

"No, the shell tops."

"Why are they poor things?"

"'Cause people make them fight."

Seitaro was nonplused.

"They make the shell tops fight each other and they get hurt."

"Ha, ha, ha . . . "

"It's true, Seitaro. The shell tops are saying they don't want to fight anymore. When I'm older and I can go to the sea, I'm going to put them all back there 'cause that's where they live."

"Where does the metal top live then?"

"I don't know. Why don't you ask it?"

Seitaro was at a loss for words; what Koji was saying sounded like nonsense to him but he could think of no suitable retort. To hide the awkwardness of the situation, he leapt up with a meaningless shout.

Koji lay there by himself staring at the metal top. He began to feel as if it were alive as well and, leaning over, he whispered to it, "I bet you don't like being made to fight either, Metal Top. And it'd hurt if you got wounded, so why don't you say you don't want to next time, and run away. You don't want to die in a fight, do you?''

Koji suddenly saw his father's big *banko* head spinning round and round in front of him like a top.

"Dad."

"Yes, your father's here," said Fudé, opening the doors of the family shrine.

Nui came in with the offering of dumplings piled on a small stand. She placed it in the shrine before the tablets inscribed with the names of the deceased members of the family.

"Wash your face, Koji, and then come and say a prayer."

Koji sat on the quilt of his bed watching while his mother lit a candle and his grandmother struck the small bell—ting, ting. They both knelt there together praying quietly—"Praise to Amida Buddha."

Fudé turned round, aware of Seitaro standing at the foot of Koji's bed.

"What are you doing standing there, Seitaro? Quick, come and pray before the shrine."

"Seitaro and me are going to pray together. I'll just go and wash my face," said Koji, defending his brother.

"Yes, that's a good idea," his grandmother agreed at once. She remained before the shrine murmuring to herself until Koji returned.

"Now, both of you, have a good talk with your father. You can tell him anything you like," said Fudé, standing up.

"Tell him something nice and make him happy," added Nui, in a serious tone of voice.

"Mm," nodded Seitaro, striking the bell; but he looked as if he might burst out laughing at any moment. Koji bent his head and giggled, thinking his brother looked very funny.

Nui too was seized with a strong desire to laugh. "It's all right being a child, isn't it? No cares in the world. But I suppose that's why they grow up. If they had lots of worries they'd be shrinking instead. Ha, ha, ha."

Seitaro waited for his grandmother and mother to leave.

"You know those shell tops of yours, Koji? Well, what about putting them back in the sea as soon as we can?"

"In the sea? But I can't go to the sea."

"Yes, but I've got a good idea. The Katsuragi flows straight into the sea at Osaka."

"Oh!" Koji's mouth hung open as he saw a golden light streak away like an arrow, carrying the shells right out to sea.

"Then if we let them go in the river . . . "

"They're bound to find their way to the sea."

"Whoopee!" He had never heard anything so wonderful!

"When'll we let them go?" he asked a moment later.

"The sooner the better."

"What about on the way to school?"

"All right. But we can't drop them in the river from Ohashi Bridge."

"No, they'd faint if we dropped them from such a high place."

"We'll have to climb down to the river and put them back in the water properly."

Koji pressed his hands between his knees to stop himself from dashing off there and then. Lowering his voice, he whispered, "You won't tell anybody, will you?"

"No, it's a secret. Dad's heard it all though."

"He's different."

"Let's have breakfast quick and get to the river before the others. We'll put them in as far downstream as we can, so they'll be nearer the sea."

Koji and Seitaro saw the blue morning sky reflected in the quiet-flowing river of winter and the three shells traveling down the current to their home in the sea.

The offering on the stand glimmered like a white flower in the fading candlelight.

XI

The winter crop of wheat had sprouted three leaves; the barley, four; and the broad beans, five. In three days, December would be over; the holidays were fast approaching for Koji and Seitaro.

Koji did not mind school. When he first started, he had been terribly shy and had not dared say a word; but now he had many friends and could even talk to his teacher, Miss Kashiwagi. Nevertheless, as he hurried through the school gates after Seitaro, he felt excited at the thought of the coming holidays.

"We've all got to help clean the school," cried four or five girls, who came running out clutching bamboo brooms.

"Why are we doing the cleaning in the morning?" asked Shigemi Nagai.

"The District Governor's coming."

"You're kidding!"

"Yes, he is! You never know, you might even get a prize this year, Shigemi."

"Don't be silly. D'you think they'd give a prize to any of us from Komori?"

Seitaro went into the school by himself and put Komori's flag in the stand by the staff room. One flag was already there; the flag with a single stripe, which Sakata had received for the best attendance rate in November. Seitaro noticed Senkichi Sayama and Shigeo Iwase wiping the staff-room floor, undoubtedly in preparation for the District Governor's visit.

"Can I help, Sen?" he called through the glass door.

Senkichi looked up and, seeing Seitaro, gave a broad grin and deliberately turned his back on him, while Shigeo went on with his cleaning as if unaware that anyone had spoken. For a moment, Seitaro was rooted to the spot: he could not very well leave all of a sudden, and yet he couldn't decide whether he should go into the staff room or not.

Helping him out of this quandary, Mr. Egawa said, "Give us a hand, Hatanaka, as you're early, and go and tell everybody to get the hall ready."

"Yes, sir."

Seitaro returned to the playground and called his friends. In order to prepare the ceremonial hall, they had to remove the wooden partitions separating the classrooms of the third, fourth, and fifth grades, after which they set up a platform at one end, arranged some chairs, and carried in the organ. Usually, they got the hall ready to celebrate New Year's in the afternoon, after the autumn-term reports had been distributed, but this year, there had been a change in plans owing to the District Governor's visit. As they worked, they were all wondering who would be awarded a prize.

At about ten, two rickshaws bearing the District Governor and another gentleman arrived at the main entrance of the school. Four teachers, including the Headmaster, rushed out to welcome them and the visitors swaggered inside, to the reception room. Seitaro knew that the other gentleman was the District School Inspector, the most important man after the Governor. The Inspector reminded Koji of the priest at An'yoji, having the same red face and bushy eyebrows like a hairy caterpillar. As for the District Governor, who sported a finely trimmed mustache that curled up at the ends, he looked exactly like the man in the picture hanging in the chemist's. (Koji did not know that this was an advertisement for a ginseng elixir.)

The prize-giving ceremony had hardly begun when Koji was amazed to hear the man with the caterpillar eyebrows call, "First grade, Koji Hatanaka." Instinctively, he looked at Miss Kashiwagi, who nodded back to him from behind Mr. Caterpillar Eyebrows. Like a top that had been set spinning, he quickly went up to the District Governor.

"The same grade, Machié Sugimoto."

As Koji returned to his seat, he bumped into Machié and somebody giggled.

Prizes were given to pupils in the second and third grades, and it would soon be the turn of the fifth.

"Maybe Seitaro or Toyo'll get one." Koji's heart began to thump but this faint hope soon faded as Mr. Caterpillar Eyebrows announced the names of Senkichi Sayama and Kinu Miyajima, a girl whom he did not know at all. What would happen next? Koji placed the thick notebook, the District Governor's prize, on his knees and waited in a state of nervous expectation.

Mr. Caterpillar Eyebrows moved over to the platform on which the District Governor was standing.

"I am now going to ask each of you in turn a question. There is no need to be frightened or shy, just answer as best you may." He gazed round at all the children. "Machié Sugimoto, what good deed have you done recently?"

Machié hesitated for a moment but she caught sight of Miss Kashiwagi, who was looking at her encouragingly, and managed to stutter, "I, I rubbed my mother's shoulders for her."

"Ah, so you showed devotion to your mother, did you? Well done. Now, Koji Hatanaka, what good deed have you done?"

"I put my shell tops back in the river."

There were sniggers here and there around the hall; what was so praiseworthy about throwing shell tops away, they seemed to mock. But Mr. Caterpillar Eyebrows nodded approvingly.

"That's very good indeed. Top-spinning is a form of gambling and a most unsuitable game. All those of you who have shell tops must throw them away in the river or break them today, without fail."

Nobody sniggered this time: most of the boys had shell tops and to have to throw them away or break them was no laughing matter.

Koji was troubled. Every day for the last twenty days, on his way to and from school, he had looked down at the Katsuragi River with a feeling of the utmost joy and satisfaction. It was true that sometimes, during a fine spell when the river shrank to a narrow trickle, he would feel uneasy about the well-being of the shells; but in his heart, he never really doubted that they were safely continuing their journey back to their home. He felt sure that putting them in the river was the best thing he could have done and had no hesitation in announcing it to the school. Yet, Mr. Caterpillar Eyebrows had now ordered that all those with shell tops must throw them away or break them.

He wanted to shout back "that's not what I meant," but he knew that this would not be tolerated. Had he not been told constantly, ever since he first started school, that it was his duty to humbly obey those in authority? And although Mr. Caterpillar Eyebrows might not be as important as the District Governor, he was certainly more so than the Headmaster.

Koji's ears turned scarlet as he stood there motionless, looking down. The children round about glanced at him curiously out of the corner of their eyes: they knew that he was naturally bashful, but even so, the School Inspector's lavish praise was certainly making him blush very red.

"Next, Senkichi Sayama. Do you know the name of the edict which His Imperial Majesty was pleased to hand down in October?"

Senkichi was silent.

"You don't know? Very well, anybody who does know, please raise their hand."

Koji stole a look behind him. In the back row to the right, Toyota Matsuzaki had raised his hand.

"Yes, what is the answer?" Mr. Caterpillar Eyebrows pointed to Toyota.

"The Boshin Edict."

"Very good. Now, the District Governor is very kindly going to tell us why His Majesty, the Emperor, handed down this edict."

Mr. Caterpillar Eyebrows moved back to his former place.

Compared with the teaching staff, who were all wearing the uniform jacket with a stand-up collar, the District Governor looked the height of dignity in his frock coat. He began in a suitably formal tone:

"Boys and girls, recently His Majesty, the Emperor, has been pleased to issue the Boshin Edict. His Imperial Majesty fears that we, His subjects, intoxicated by our great victory in the Russo-Japanese War, are losing our spirit of thrift and diligence and turning toward a life of increasing luxury.

"Japan has indeed been victorious. However, we have been left with a great debt, as the war cost two thousand million yen. This means we have had to borrow two thousand million yen from other countries. Divided among our population, it is equivalent to forty yen per person. Each and every one of us, from the newly born babe to the old lady of ninety, has borrowed forty yen. Nevertheless, day by day we are growing more extravagant and prices are continually rising. This has been a source of great concern to His Majesty, the Emperor, and His Majesty has graciously urged His subjects to be more frugal.

"Boys and girls, it is very important that all of you explain this carefully to your families when you return home today."

The District Governor continued speaking in this vein a little while longer and the children all stared straight up at his mustache, completely unable to make sense of what he was saying. They felt that it must be good for them to listen to something as incomprehensible and mystifying as this; and besides, they had been taught that they must pay particular attention to such speeches. On the whole they behaved well, therefore, apart from occasionally sniffing when their noses started to run.

Presently, the District Governor gave a slight bow and stepped down from the platform. Miss Kashiwagi struck up the national anthem on the organ.

The children came to life at once and began singing at the top of their voices. Koji joined in and his crimson ears gradually returned to their normal color.

When he came out into the corridor, Toyota gave him a big grin; and this time, Koji really did flush with embarrassment. Senkichi rushed past, obviously suffering from the shame of not being able to answer the District Governor's question.

XII

Komori had the lowest attendance rate in December, too, and, in accordance with the rules, Seitaro received the fifth-rank flag. Although this was not very pleasant for him, there was nothing he could do about it, since the children had stayed away in order to work for their families.

Going out of the school gates, Seitaro noticed the wheel tracks of the rickshaws and immediately recalled the District Governor's curling mustache and the School Inspector's red face.

"His Imperial Majesty has called on each and every one of his subjects to work hard and to be thrifty": if these words of the District Governor were true, then the Emperor could have no idea how poor Komori was and how hard they all worked, even to the extent of the children staying away from school. The Emperor was said to be the father of his people, but he obviously knew nothing whatsoever about them. Seitaro felt like hitting out at something and he suddenly began running faster and faster. The purple flag fluttered in the biting westerly wind, which stung his face.

Koji and the other boys ran to keep up with the flag, and the girls, including Shigemi, hurried after them, panting hard. When they came onto the bridge, they could see Komori spread out before them, its thatched roofs huddled up together as if trying to share the burden of knowing that one day they would crumble away. Here and there, columns of smoke rose up into the air, the smoke a beautiful deep mauve, which, as Seitaro knew, was due to the straw and chaff they burnt as fuel. The mauve smoke would be a symbol of their poverty for as long as it rose from Komori stoves.

On the outskirts of the village, Seitaro handed the flag to a friend, Yozo Samita, who was also in the fifth grade. The flag was kept in the entrance of the priest's living quarters at An'yoji and, as Yozo lived nearest, Seitaro always entrusted him to take it there.

"I bet they'll be pleased over at your place today, Sei. Koji's the first one that's ever got the Governor's prize," said Yozo, looking delighted himself as he took the flag.

Seitaro laughed, or at least appeared to; inside, he did not feel like laughing at all. While delighted that Koji had won the prize, he felt inexplicably as if he had been betrayed and also as if he himself had betrayed something. All the same, when he actually crossed the threshold of his home, he started to grow excited.

"Mom, Gran, Koji's got the Governor's prize," he yelled.

"Well done!"

Seitaro and Koji were thrilled at the sound of this voice, which did not belong to either their mother or grandmother. They could hardly kick their sandals off fast enough before rushing into the room with the family shrine.

Their uncle Yuji had just finished praying there. He was Fudé's elder brother and lived in the village of Ino in Shimokawa *mura,** about four miles from Komori. They usually visited their uncle's home about once or twice a year, while he came over two or three times, not for pleasure but to give them a hand with the farm work.

Fudé and Nui opened out the diploma. Although illiterate, even Nui could decipher the characters "Koji Hatanaka."

"If only Shin were alive . . . " and the tears streamed down her smiling face.

"Let's see your report then," said Fudé, pulling it from the breast of Koji's kimono. He had been given an "A" in all his subjects.

"Gosh, he's even got an 'A' for deportment," cried Seitaro in amazement, as he peeped at the report.

"Of course he has. Otherwise he wouldn't have got the District Governor's prize, even if he'd an 'A' for all his other subjects," said Fudé.

"But up till now nobody from Komori's ever got a good mark for deportment, even if they did behave all right."

"You may have thought they were behaving all right, but the teacher looked at it different."

"I s'pose so. But what is deportment anyway? It doesn't have anything to do with the kimono you've got on, does it?"

"No, it doesn't," replied his uncle.

"And it isn't bad deportment if your hair's too long?"

"No."

"But the teacher once said we kids from Komori had bad deportment 'cause our kimonos are dirty. Koji's never is though 'cause he doesn't play soldiers and he doesn't have to carry a baby brother or sister round on his back, either. That's why he got an 'A.' "

"While your kimono's always getting torn and dirty playing soldiers, I suppose."

"Mm, but don't Ken and Kei play soldiers, Uncle?"

"You bet. That's all they ever do. I don't know how many times they've mucked up their kimonos since the autumn. Now why don't you come over during the holidays and play with them?"

"Don't encourage him. He'll go marching over to your place ready to be His Majesty, the Supreme Commander," joked Fudé.

Her brother frowned, trying not to laugh.

"Ken'ichi and Keizo have this girl *kami* who's even mightier than the Supreme Commander. It seems they heard about her from a student at middle school. A long time ago, there was this war between France and England that lasted more than a hundred years. And there was a young girl then, living in a country district of France, called Jeanne d'Arc, who went to the King of France saying as how the *kami* had spoken to her. Well, in the end, they put her on a white horse and she rode at the head of the French army—and, funnily enough, from then on the French had victory after victory. They regained all the castles the English had taken and the war came to an end. So, if you're thinking of playing soldiers, Ken'ichi and the others are bound to take along Nanaé, to be this Jeanne d'Arc, you see."

"Gosh," sighed Seitaro, in wonder and envy; while Koji, who had been drinking in every word, his hand on his uncle's knee, wished he could hear more about the girl on the white horse.

"I bet Nanaé doesn't know what's going on when they cart her off to play soldiers like that," said Fudé, giving a sad smile at the thought of her little niece, who was two years younger than Koji, being dragged round like a plaything.

"But if you had a Jeanne d'Arc you'd win," sighed Seitaro, wishing that he too had a younger sister like Nanaé.

As a special treat, Fudé did not mix any barley with the rice for lunch, much to the delight of Seitaro and Koji. Their uncle, however, kept protesting apologetically, "I'd be fine with boiled rice and barley, or gruel. Rice is such a terrible price these days."

"I'm not giving you gruel when you've come all this way to help cord the bales," answered Fudé, as she served him; and Seitaro and Koji now realized the reason for their uncle's visit.

As soon as he put down his chopsticks, Yuji tied a towel round his head and went out to the shed. There were a number of baskets there filled with rice that had already been husked in a hand mill. Nui and Fudé measured the rice into straw bags, and Yuji secured either end with a round lid, and weighed and corded them. Seitaro and Koji were kept busy, too, holding bags steady and helping to tie them up.

"The Emperor and Governor haven't a clue how we sweat, telling us to work harder like that," thought Seitaro, kicking the dirt floor of the shed; the soles of his bare feet tingled with irritation.

"Times are bad for poor farmers like us, and that's for sure. The landlord reckons on the price of rice going up and so he doesn't want money, the rent's all got to be paid in rice. It leaves us with hardly enough to live on ourselves. How are you managing over at Ino?" asked Fudé, as her brother finished cording one of the bales.

"We eat Nanking rice. Seeing as we can get a good price for our own rice, it seems a pity not to sell it and buy that cheap foreign stuff. Don't you eat it at all?"

"We would but Seitaro says he doesn't like it."

"You're too fussy." Yuji looked at Seitaro and laughed.

Seitaro stamped round the sack he was holding. He did not dislike Nanking rice because of the red and blue grains in it, or the strong smell; it was simply that he hated the way children from other villages jeered, "Komori kids stink even worse eating stinking Nanking rice." He usually came home for lunch and had some gruel.

But he would not have dreamed of telling his mother and grandmother about this: the deeper the wound from the ridicule and ill treatment he suffered at school, the more he felt bound to keep it secret from his family.

"What I can't figure out, Yuji," said Nui presently, "is why times is so hard when we won the war?"

"I'm none too sure of that one either," replied Yuji, tightly cording a second bale. "But, you know it's only the poor that's hit, the rich are getting richer hand over fist. The landlords've been lining their pockets all right, what with the price of rice going up. Just think, before the war five bushels was only about thirteen yen. Since last year it's gone up to over sixteen. They say that on their low wages, the people working in the factories in Kyoto and Osaka can only afford bran with a tiny bit of rice mixed in."

"You know I've always thought it funny, Yuji," remarked Fudé. "When Shin died, I got three-hundred-yen's worth of government bonds, but, at four percent interest, they only bring in twelve yen a year, not enough to buy even five bushels of rice. But the officers that are still alive have all gone up in the world, haven't they, and made a bundle in the bargain—some of them are even barons and viscounts now. Well, why do the powers that be have to treat them so different from the rest of us? In the schools, they teach that the Emperor's our father and we're his subjects, and we're all brothers and sisters."

"That's the way of the world for you."

"But don't you think it's wrong?"

"Even if it is, what can we do about it? We're just . . . " Fudé's brother kicked the corded bale and it rolled over and over toward Seitaro.

"I'll come over in the winter holidays, Uncle, I promise," said Seitaro, sitting astride the bale.

"I hope you will. Then you can play soldiers. And if you don't like Nanking rice, we'll cook something special for you."

"I'll come, too," said Koji.

"Of course, you're coming. And make sure you bring that District Governor's prize to show Keizo and Ken'ichi."

Koji felt his ears turning red again. In fact, he wanted to see Jeanne d'Arc: the pretty, doll-like face of Nanaé had impressed itself on his memory like the picture from a transfer.

The next day, Fudé and Nui crossed Ohashi Bridge many times, pulling the cart laden with bales of rice. The rent in kind for their half acre of land was about twenty-three bushels of rice, enough to fill about eleven-and-a-half sacks, which meant that they had to make four journeys to the landlord. Each time, Seitaro and Koji helped to push the cart uphill to the bridge; they would have pushed it all the way but Nui and Fudé refused, not wanting their children to see the contempt with which the landlord, Keizo Sayama, treated them.

Seitaro and Koji stood on the bridge gazing downstream into the distance as they waited for the cart to return. Without saying a word, each of them knew that the other was wondering if the shells had reached the sea yet.

The mountains surrounding the basin quietly watched the wisps of cloud floating across the sky.

2

Manju Buns

I

Flowers of snow
Falling petals
Blossoming
On the windowpane
Fan tucked in belt
They dance
Round and round

Koji was singing and dancing gleefully as the snowflakes fluttered down onto his bald head, which Fudé had just shaved.

Nui slid back the screen doors of the workroom with a bang.

"How well you sing, Koji," and she laughed.

"That's a girl's song," mocked Seitaro disparagingly, his head held fast between his mother's knees.

"Now, don't move, Seitaro," said Fudé, gripping his head even more firmly.

Seitaro gave a start and shut his eyes as the cold razor neared them. He could see the snow whirling down even with them closed. The brave snow troops: with a silent roar, they had come from the gray country to take the fields and allotments, the gardens and roofs.

He tried to keep still for as long as possible, but eventually he could no longer bear it and his eyelids started to twitch.

"Right, that'll do." Fudé put down the razor and took off the towel wrapped round his neck. He dashed out into the garden like a top set in motion.

Although it had only been falling for ten minutes or so, the snow

58

was already settling on the dry, hard ground and the garden looked white. With any luck, there would be several inches by tomorrow morning. A thrill of joy surged through Seitaro at this prospect, and he began singing at the top of his voice.

> The snow advances over the ice
> And both rivers and paths are hidden.
> Leave not behind your fallen horses,
> This land belongs to the enemy.

Nui not only slammed the doors shut this time, without a word of praise, but after a few moments she called out crossly, "Koji, Seitaro, you'd better come in. You've only just had your heads shaved and if you get wet from the snow, you'll catch your death."

Neither Seitaro nor Koji wanted to go in, even though the snow was melting as soon as it fell on their bald heads, and trickling down onto their collars. They went inside the shed instead and opened the back door. From there, they could see the tall chimney of the town cotton mill to the right and, to the left, the banks of the Katsuragi stretching away to the upper reaches of the river; and even further off, they could see the mountains of the Katsuragi Kongo range towering up into the sky.

Koji gazed around him. "There's snow everywhere," he said, looking overwhelmed.

"What d'you expect?" replied Seitaro, feigning indifference to hide the wonder he felt at the snow's magnificence: it had almost captured the whole of the basin.

"Seitaro, why does it snow?"

"Don't you even know that? It's instead of rain."

"Oh." Koji stood on tiptoe staring across the fields. The winter crop of barley and vegetables was being hidden by a snow cap . . . Maybe it felt cold to the vegetables? No, it didn't . . . But maybe the barley was chilly? No, it wasn't. Both the barley and the vegetables definitely liked the snow.

Snow: Koji thought it very mysterious; Seitaro had said it fell instead of rain but somehow that did not sound right. Maybe snow was the clear blue sky breaking into little pieces and falling to the ground.

He lifted up his face and called out from the doorway:

> Flowers of snow
> Falling petals
> Blossoming
> On the windowpane

A snowflake fluttered down on to his forehead in reply.

"Koji," whispered Seitaro, "I'm going over to Toyo's tomorrow, after the New Year's Day ceremony. You can come too if you want to."

Koji did want to: he was curious to see Shimana, as he had never been there before, and he was sure that Toyota would have all sorts of storybooks to show him. The one drawback was that to get to Shimana they would have to go through Sakata and he was frightened of going there.

"I don't want to."

He drew back from the door and rubbed his wet feet on a bundle of straw.

"Why not? Toyo's expecting you."

"Shimana's such a long way away."

"No, it's not, it's right near Sakata."

"There's lots of frightening kids in Sakata."

"What d'you mean? Sen and Shige? Ha, ha, they'll run a mile when they see me."

Koji did not reply.

"We're not going to do anything wrong, we're just going to go through Sakata on the way to Toyo's. There's nothing to be afraid of about that."

In spite of what he said, Seitaro felt uneasy at the thought of going alone; he could imagine somebody hiding in the shadows ready to shout out *eta*, or throw stones at him as he went past. Yet he wanted to visit Toyota and he had accepted the invitation over two months ago.

"Koji, can you come and help," called out his mother. Koji guessed the reason at once: he was needed to clean the globe of the lamp.

As Seitaro shut the back door, placing the bar across it, he was seized with a desire to stand by his brother.

"I'll come tomorrow," he announced.

In the gloom of the shed, Seitaro nodded as if pleased.

Cleaning the oil lamp was always left to Koji's small hand, which now passed round and round the inside of the globe polishing it until the glass was unrecognizably clear. Nui was watching him and, looking rather troubled, she said, "I'm looking forward to you getting bigger soon, Koji, but who'll clean the globe when you can't get your hand inside it any more?"

"Well, we'll have electricity instead," he replied, as if this were self-evident.

Nui could not help laughing. "Yes, with electricity we won't need to clean the globe. It'll be convenient for our night work, too, and it's safer than an oil lamp."

"A poor village like Komori isn't likely to get electricity and that's for sure," said Seitaro in an adult tone of voice.

Fudé laughed this time. "Very true. So you'd better grow up as fast as you can and get a job."

"I'm not going to grow big and strong on that gruel we have every night, Mom. All it does is fill you up."

"You young rascal." Fudé lit the lamp and lifted the pan of gruel off the stove. "You may only get gruel but look how thick it is. In other families it's just like water."

"Yes, thank you very much." Seitaro jokingly bowed his head in contrition.

After supper, Fudé hung the lamp in the workroom and brought out a bundle.

"What's that?" asked Seitaro in surprise.

"Something you'll like. Have a guess."

Koji sensed that it was something for his brother and himself. Seitaro lifted up a corner. "Kimono!" he shouted.

"No, *haori*," answered Fudé, undoing the bundle. Inside were two *haori* coats, both with a bright, white splashed pattern, one with a large print and the other smaller.

"Is this one mine?" Seitaro held the coat with the smaller pattern against his knees and then put it on his head. "I've been wanting a *haori* for ages," he sighed. Unexpectedly, he felt slightly flat now that his wish had been fulfilled.

"I like them too," said Koji, holding the larger-patterned one.

"So you like the *haori* do you?" Fudé smiled, stroking his head.

"Well, you're both pleased then. Why don't you try them on to show me." Nui blinked as if she were dazzled. It was she who wanted to see Koji and Seitaro dressed in *haori* for the New Year's Day ceremony, and she had made them herself, taking time off from her sandal-weaving. Yet the feeling that now stole over her was more one of sadness than of joy.

Seitaro put on his *haori* very carefully, as if afraid of getting it dirty, and Fudé tied the front cord fastenings. They were made from four black-and-white strands and, when tied, their tassels pointed straight up. They looked very manly and he could not help smiling at them.

Nui helped Koji on with his. The cord fastenings were shorter than Seitaro's and the tassels did not stick straight up; but they suited a little boy like him and he was very pleased with them. He twirled round in front of his grandmother.

"Do I look nice, Gran?"

"You both look very nice in them," replied Nui, trying to look serious. "Anybody'd think you was from a really good home."

"I'm going to Shimana tomorrow with Seitaro. Can I wear my *haori*, Mum?" asked Koji, whirling round once more in front of his mother.

"All right, but where are you going in Shimana?"

"We're going to Toyo's," said Seitaro. "The boy who lent us the book with the red cover. He's been asking us over for ages."

Nui and Fudé remembered hearing about Toyota; surely he was the "bastard," the boy with the pretty mother. Nui imagined a beautiful woman with her hair done up in the *marumage* style.

"Well, you'd better go and see him then, but mind you behave well."

"You don't need to worry about that. Koji's got an 'A' for deportment and the Governor's prize as well. And didn't you just say anybody'd think I was from a good home in this *haori*, Gran?"

"Ah, ha, ha! Dear, oh dear." Nui wiped her eyes, both amused and pleased; at the same time, she was aware of a dark spot that could not be erased with laughter and which made her uneasy.

As if she had caught this uneasiness, Fudé said, "I hope you will go over to your friend's, but does his mother know you're from Komori?"

Seitaro was startled. "I don't care if she does or not," he retorted at once. "Toyo's my friend, not her."

"That's true." Nui felt slightly relieved and settled down to her evening work. "I suppose you're giving back that book tomorrow," she said, changing the subject. "Why don't you read me one good story before you do?"

"You'd better ask Koji; he's read more of it than I have."

Seitaro took off his *haori* and sat down by the chaff fire of the brazier, ready to listen to a story himself.

Koji looked down shyly. 'I like the story about the bow. I've read it hundreds of times. Is that all right, Gran?"

"It certainly is."

"Yes, I'd like to hear that one too," said Fudé. "Didn't you promise to read it to us before?"

"Yes, I did."

"I'll enjoy it all the more then."

The circle of light around them suddenly grew brighter as Fudé turned up the wick of the lamp. That moment, the wind rose and snowflakes fluttered against the shutters.

Koji knelt very upright, his knees together, and started reading. Tick-tock, tick-tock—the hands of the clock on the wall moved round; it seemed to be following the story.

Several times, Fudé and Nui gave a sigh as they listened; although it was only a story, parts of it sounded strangely familiar: "No matter how hard they all worked they just grew poorer until they could only afford to sip the thinnest gruel, while Kanamaru lived off the fat of the land, with hundreds of servants and an estate of thousands of acres." And Kanamaru's wealth had bought him the powerful bow, Full Moon, which he used to conquer many lands, until eventually he was known as the Great King.

The story sounded only too plausible: were they not poor themselves in spite of working so hard; and, this very evening, had they not sipped gruel again for supper?

However, Kanamaru shot an arrow into his own foot and died, after which there were no more wars because nobody in Tadara hankered after wealth, much less the power of a king.

"If there hadn't been a war, Shinkichi'd still be alive to this day. All them guns and warships, they're nothing but machines to kill people with," thought Nui, biting her lip.

Although Nui and Fudé had only heard about such things in conversation and neither of them had ever seen a gun or a warship, it was not difficult to imagine their terrifying destructive power;

they were simply another form of the mighty bow, Full Moon, of the
story. But this bow had finally snapped and the King had been
wounded and died. Would the guns and warships ever shatter and
disappear; would the generals, field marshals, and the Supreme
Commander ever die and war cease?

"Thank you for reading us that story, Koji. I'll remember it till
the day I die," said Nui, her hands moving busily over her work.

Fudé was silent for a while and then got up and went outside, as
if she were going to relieve herself.

It was no longer snowing and the moon could be seen sailing
through stormy clouds. Fudé sank to her knees and thrust her right
hand into the deep snow; the first big fall since Shinkichi's death.

II

Thump, thump—the sound of somebody stamping the snow off their
wooden clogs could be heard.

"Good day to you!"

It was the distinctively mellow voice of Mr. Otaké.

"Come in," Fudé called back, and quickly cleared away the
remains from lunch as Mr. Otaké brought out his pipe and stepped
up into the living room.

"We've certainly been having some snow," said Nui, fetching a
small brazier from the workroom.

"Yes, it's not often we get so much. Should mean a bumper crop
of wheat and barley this year."

"It'd better," said Fudé smiling, and she settled down to work,
leaving Nui to chat with the visitor.

"Where are the boys off to? I just met them the other side of
Sakata."

"They're going to see a friend in Shimana that asked them over,"
replied Nui as casually as possible, trying to give the impression that
there was nothing unusual about this: she knew only too well how
Mr. Otaké would react and, sure enough, as he pulled at his pipe, a
look of amazement spread across his face. A few moments later, he
put down his pipe, unable to remain silent any longer.

"My word, times have changed. When I was a lad, you didn't dare
go to other villages. You knew they'd start shouting *eta, eta,* and
throw stones at you if you did."

"Yes, same when I was a girl. What's the difference in our ages again?"

"I'll be turning fifty-two soon. I'd say I'm about five years younger than you."

"Then you must've been born in the fifties."

"That's right, 1857."

"So you'll remember the Edict* in 1871?"

"I'll say I do. How old were you at the time?"

"Nineteen."

"I was fourteen. My goodness, we was overjoyed when we heard His Imperial Majesty had granted an edict like that. We thought from the next day on that nobody'd ever call us *eta* or Four-Fingers* again. Ha, ha, ha."

"It was like a sad joke in our village. I'm sure you've heard as how the head of the *mura* called our local headman over to see him. 'I know them officials have brought out this *eta* edict,' he said, 'But you needn't think you can start rejoicing yet; it won't make a scrap of difference for at least a hundred years.' Well, my heart sank when I heard that, I can tell you. Up till then, we girls couldn't even wear a sash because of what we was, and just when I thought I'd be able to dress like everybody else at long last, the *mura* headman had to go and say a thing like that."

"Yes, yes, I remember something of the sort. And people didn't know whether to be angry or happy when they found out he only said it out of spite . . . That was thirty-seven years ago now and we'd still be *eta* for a long time yet if the headman had been right."

"But we're still treated different, Mr. Otaké, like he said," remarked Fudé from the workroom.

Mr. Otaké refilled his pipe. "That's only to be expected. Old habits die hard. But as your mother-in-law was saying, when she was young, girls couldn't even wear a sash. I only had a piece of rope round my waist too when I was a lad, and the girls wore an apron. And none of us went to school, either. But now, if you've got the means, you can wear anything you like, even a *haori* or a Western-style suit; and the children can go to school as well. Look at your son, he went and got the District Governor's prize, didn't he? At this rate, I'm sure things will soon get better for us."

"They'd better, that's all I can say. There's nothing different about us, is there? It snows on our village the same as on all the others, and it melts the same, too." Nui rubbed her large, work-roughened hands together over the brazier.

"You're right there, people are all the same. The only difference is that some are rich and some poor, but if you work hard enough you can bridge that gap. And your family's doing all right, Mrs. Hatanaka; with that money from the army, you're better off than most in Komori."

"What are you talking about, Mr. Otaké! Us two women have to support this family by ourselves and it's hard making ends meet, I can tell you."

"It's a lot easier for women on their own, men just go and spend all the money on drink and cigarettes. By the way, there's some good quality straw over in Shimana. D'you want me to get you some? It's always longer in the stalk than straw from other places and it's in great demand for sandal-making."

"We'd been thinking of asking you, seeing as you got us some last year. What sort of price is it selling at?"

"With rice so high, it's a bit more than last year. But don't worry, leave it to me."

"I thought rice'd been getting cheaper again recently."

"Well, the market price is always on the move."

"They say some people have made a fortune on the rice market, not that we know much about it."

"I'll say they have. The authorities frown on gambling as a rule, and keep a tight check on it, but the rice market's a different kettle of fish altogether and there's nothing illegal about gambling on that. If ever I make some money, I'd like to have a go myself, just once. Not that I'm likely to get the chance, mind you. Ha, ha! Now, I'll bring the straw over when the roads are clear again. How much do you want, about one *tan?*"*

As a middleman dealing in sandal-making materials, such as straw, bamboo-sheath, and hemp, Mr. Otaké felt very pleased at having settled a transaction. He stayed for a while longer chatting, but when the clock struck one he hastily tucked up the skirt of his kimono and left.

"I wonder if Seitaro and Koji are still at their friend's," said Nui, looking a little worried.

Fudé glanced up at the clock. "All the other children came back from the ceremony before eleven, so they've been gone about two hours.''

"Maybe they're having such a good time, they've been invited to stay for a meal.''

"Yes, maybe they have.''

"It'd be nice if that boy's mother gave them a meal, knowing they're from Komori. I wonder though.''

"Yes, I feel a bit uneasy about it.''

"All the same, she's a bit different herself and I'm sure she's had her fair share of suffering. You never know, she might be kind to them.''

"I'd like to have her son round at the old-style New Year.* I can't help wondering what the boy's like.''

Fudé was confessing her true feelings but, as she spoke, she suddenly felt ashamed: she suffered continually from discrimination herself and yet here she was showing unusual curiosity in this illegitimate child and his mother. She slid back the screen doors, feeling as if she were stifling. A lump of snow fell from the roof with a thud.

"I'm sure most of it will have melted by tomorrow," said Nui cheerfully; the agreement to buy more straw had put her in a good mood.

III

The earth wall which faced the veranda was white as if it had been polished. A number of old azaleas, a nandin shrub with bright red berries, and a camellia with crimson flowers grew in the garden, as well as a fat pine tree, with branches soaring high up into the sky. There were many other trees and shrubs besides, the names of which Seitaro did not know, and a stone lantern covered in moss. This was the garden of an annex belonging to a large house, and the annex was the home of Toyota and his mother.

At first, Seitaro felt too shy to look around him openly. But, as they played games of cards, backgammon, and hide-and-seek, his spirits gradually rose until he felt completely at home and his stomach started to rumble hungrily at the smell of red bean soup with dumplings.

"It's nothing special, but I hope you'll eat as much as you want," said Toyota's mother with a smile, and she placed the pan of soup on the brazier to keep it warm.

"She's lovely, isn't she," said Seitaro, full of admiration.

Koji was amazed by Toyota's mother; with her fair complexion and red lips, she looked so very different from his own. Her black hair was done up neatly in the *marumage* style, as if she were about to go out visiting, and her hands were pink and smooth, quite unlike Fudé's rough, chapped ones. Could she really be a mother? She seemed more like a being from a faraway land to him, imagining, as he did, a mother to be somebody who toiled from morning to night.

When they had eaten their fill of the soup, Toyota's beautiful mother returned.

"Did you enjoy the soup?"

"Yes, I did," replied Koji, smiling bashfully.

"You must come over again and I'll make you some more. I hope Toyota will visit you, too."

"But we haven't anything so nice to give him."

"Ah, ha, ha . . . What a polite little boy you are. Toyota's going to do much better when he visits you. There isn't a family as well-to-do as yours in Sakata, now is there?"

"But we're poor."

Toyota's mother laughed even more at this. "You're the biggest landowners in Sakata, as I'm sure your older brother knows. Why I heard about your family as soon as we moved here."

She went out of the living room carrying the remains of the soup. Toyota closed the sliding doors tightly together.

"Sei, please don't tell. Please don't tell her the truth," he said, with an imploring gesture and turning a little red.

Seitaro felt as if he too were flushed, but in fact his face was rapidly growing pale; only his ears burned like fire, and so did Koji's.

The clock struck one.

"We'd better be going." Seitaro stood up, anxious not to lose control and say anything hurtful.

"You aren't cross, are you?" asked Toyota, also standing up.

"No, I'm not." Seitaro's face grew distorted as he tried to smile.

"If you're going then, I'll see you home."

"Don't bother, the road's bad."

"I'll wear shoes." As if it had suddenly occurred to him, Toyota added, "You can have any book you want, Koji, the book of fairy stories you borrowed and any others as well. Go ahead, choose what you want.''

''Just this one,'' replied Koji, the book he had meant to return tucked under his arm.

''You're not going already, are you? Why don't you stay and play a bit longer?'' said Toyota's mother, seeing them as far as the path through the garden. Neither Seitaro nor Koji could bring themselves to reply.

Toyota lived in the middle of Shimana, which consisted of about sixty houses, and it took them seven or eight minutes before they reached the outskirts.

''You needn't come any further, Toyo.'' Seitaro scraped the slushy snow from his wooden clogs on the signpost at the end of the village.

''My mother's stupid, isn't she?'' said Toyota, walking on, ''She's pleased if I say my friend's Senkichi Sayama from Sakata but she'd be angry if I said my friend's Seitaro Hatanaka from Komori. That's why I told her a lie.'' He stamped down a patch of snow.

''You shouldn't lie to your mother, Toyo.''

''Why not?''

''It's not respectful to her.''

''Ha ha, not respectful! That's a good one, Sei.'' Toyota picked up a handful of snow from the roadside, pressed it into a hard ball and threw it. He burst out laughing again. ''If it's wrong to lie to your parents, what about that story, the 'Yoro Waterfall,' about the son who gave his father river water to drink, pretending it was saké. That's worse than what I did.''

''It really did taste of saké, though, and it made his father happy so it didn't matter.''

''Well, it's the same with my mother. It made her happy to think you were Sen. I haven't been disrespectful at all, I've been a good son.''

Seitaro could think of no answer to this. What Toyota had said sounded reasonable enough, yet there was something not quite right about it.

He noticed they had almost reached Sakata and came to a halt. ''Don't bother to come any further with us.''

''It's not far now. I'll come with you to your home.''

''Your mother'll be angry if she finds out.''

"It's all right, she won't find out."

"Will you say you went to Sen's house then?"

"I'll see."

Seitaro felt uneasy, aware that Toyota would not get away with this lie forever. "No, you'd better go back now. Me and Koji will be fine."

Even Toyota could not go on refusing, and, picking up another handful of snow, he threw it in the direction of Senkichi Sayama's house.

Koji glanced back towards Shimana. "Look, Master Hidé, the priest's son is coming," he cried excitedly.

The middle-school student in a black cloak, riding toward them on a bicycle, was undoubtedly Hidéaki. If they ran along beside him, they would be able to cross the "barrier" of Sakata safely; and even if there were any troublemakers there, they would be no match for a middle-school student like Master Hidé.

Seitaro quickly took off his white cotton *tabi* socks and got ready to start running. "Take off yours, too; you don't want to get them dirty," he said to Koji, who began untying them; the socks Fudé made them had long laces.

They had expected the bicycle to pass by without stopping but it suddenly came to a halt in front of Seitaro.

"Are you going home, Sei? Do you want a ride, Ko?"

Did he mean on the bicycle? Koji stared at Hidéaki, the laces of his *tabi* dangling down.

"You're not afraid, are you, Ko?" laughed Hidéaki. "There's no need to be. Ride it a little way. I'll push."

"Go on, Ko, have a ride," said Toyota, giving him a shove toward the bike.

Hidéaki caught him up and placed him on the saddle. "Hold onto the handlebars," he said, and Seitaro quickly took Koji's *tabi* and book.

"Bye." Feeling relieved, Toyota waved as hard as he could.

"Goodbye," called back Koji nervously, afraid of falling off in spite of clinging tightly to the handlebars.

Before turning the corner into Sakata, Seitaro looked back and waved to Toyota again. He was standing where they had left him, staring after them.

"Sei, did you know the Sayamas live here?" asked Hidéaki, as they passed a thick earth wall with a granite foundation.

"Only too well. Sen's in my class."

"His older brother's in mine, too."

"Sen got the District Governor's prize."

"So did Ko, didn't he? And his is the real thing. That's why I'm giving him a ride—to celebrate."

A dog barked from the direction of a row of storehouses; they felt as if it were barking at them. A wooden door in a nook in the wall opened and a face peered out: it was Senkichi. He shut the door at once, without a word.

Hidéaki continued to push the bicycle along at the same speed. "Is that a book in your parcel, Sei?"

"Yes, it's a book of fairy stories."

"Do you like fairy stories?"

"Mm, but Koji likes them even more. The friend you just met gave it to him."

"I envy you having a friend like that."

"Does he mean he doesn't have any friends?" wondered Seitaro. "But, if Toyo's mother finds out we're from Komori, she'll never let us see each other again either." He bent his head; something seemed to be pressing down heavily on the back of his neck.

There was another curve in the road; they were almost out of Sakata. Once they had left it, they would be near their school; and once past the school, they would be in sight of the bridge. Even though they were with Hidéaki, Seitaro still felt apprehensive and he wanted to reach the bridge as soon as possible.

As they rounded the bend, they saw for the first time that there were seven or eight children ahead, playing merrily with shell tops in front of a shop that sold cheap millet cakes.

"Now what's going to happen? Will they let us go by without saying anything or not?" wondered Seitaro, his mouth suddenly dry.

Was it his imagination or did Hidéaki also look tense? "Yes, there's going to be trouble . . . " Seitaro clutched the socks and book tightly as he started to give way to a feeling of panic.

They passed by without incident, however. The children were absorbed in their top-spinning and seemed uninterested in the little group from Komori.

Seitaro was as relieved as if he had just crossed a steep pass, or emerged from a dark tunnel. He looked up at the sky.

That very moment, a burst of laughter assailed them from behind.

> The middle-school *eta*
> Sits down on his chair;
> He scratches some words,
> But first he scratches his ass
> And then he scratches his head.

The abusive chanting continued.

> The *eta* kids wear *eta haori;*
> They're *haori,* but *eta haori.*

"I'll get you for that!" Seitaro kicked off his clogs and ran back barefoot.

The children could not scuttle into the shop fast enough.

"You shouldn't have anything to do with those *eta* children. The *eta* are frightening and they soon get angry and want a fight. If the parents find out, they'll come over here beating a drum, ready to attack us all," said the shop lady, sitting on the edge of the raised floor, one leg tucked under her, the other dangling down. The children had kicked away one of her clogs in the *doma* and she could not reach it with her foot. As she bent down to pick it up, she suddenly noticed Seitaro.

"I'll scold them myself, so please don't be cross. The little scamps really are a nuisance," she said; but the smile on her face stung Seitaro more than any insult. He scooped up a handful of slushy snow and threw it into the shop entrance.

"Here's your clogs, Seitaro." Koji got off the bicycle and arranged the clogs in front of his brother, when he returned.

Seitaro picked them up. "I'll go back barefoot, it's not far now."

"You'll catch a cold. Here wipe your feet on this."

Hidéaki handed Seitaro the small towel tucked in his sash and insisted that he put his clogs on.

When they had crossed the bridge, they found that the side of the riverbank that faced southwest was quite dry, without a trace of snow; the dry grass bathed in warm sunlight. There was a view of Komori from there, and of course it was safe territory. The three of them sat down, Koji in the middle.

"You mustn't get angry, Sei, no matter what other people say about you. You're no better than they are if you do, and it only makes them say worse things."

Hidéaki took off his hat and rubbed his brow; his hairline was wet with sweat. He had a thin face with a straight nose and his build was slight, suggesting that he must have found it hard work pushing Koji along on his bicycle through the mud and slush.

"But they even called out nasty things at you. It made me so angry I wanted to hit them all, one by one."

Hidéaki said nothing.

"I don't mind if they shout *eta* at Koji and me, but they dared to call you that, too, and you're not even an *eta*."

Seitaro took off his clogs and let the sun warm the soles of his feet. He could not help feeling embarrassed when he saw how blackened and chapped his heels were.

Hidéaki remained silent for a while, tearing at the withered grass. At last, he said, "Sei, I *am* an *eta*, you know."

"You're not, I know you're not. That's not true," Seitaro cried, shaking his head violently.

"Yes, it is."

"No, it's a lie!" Seitaro took a deep breath. "You're the priest's son, and a middle-school student; there aren't any *eta* at middle school."

"If you're born in Komori, you're an *eta*, Sei, whoever you are—priest, scholar, rich man, it makes no difference. And all the relatives of people from Komori are *eta* too."

"But why?"

"I don't know, it's always been like that."

"Do they call you an *eta* at school, then?"

"Yes, they do."

"You should punch them."

"It would only start a fight. I'm thinking of changing schools instead, and going to one further off."

Hidéaki blew away the grass he had pulled up and a piece landed on the front of Seitaro's kimono. He stared at it.

"There's a novel called *The Broken Commandment*.* The story's made up, of course"; Hidéaki began tearing up the grass again and rubbing it between his palms. "But it's about a man called Ushimatsu Segawa, who graduated from a teacher-training college and became a higher elementary-school teacher. He suffered a lot because they found out he was an *eta*. You can read it when you're a bit older, Sei."

"Where did it happen?"

"In Nagano prefecture. Have you heard of it?"

"Yes, we learnt about it in geography. It's a long way off, though. Are there people like us even there?"

"It seems so."

Seitaro rubbed his bare feet backwards and forwards on the grassy bank: not out of irritation, or uneasiness exactly; he simply felt that unless he moved everything would grow hazy, as if a spider's web were being woven around him.

"What happened to that teacher?" asked Koji, who had been listening quietly.

Hidéaki smiled at his unexpected question. "He went to America in the end. He apologized to his pupils and said he was an *eta* and shouldn't have tried to hide it."

"The teacher apologized?" Koji looked very disbelieving.

"Yes, he said he'd done wrong and he bowed low over his desk and apologized."

Seitaro picked up his clogs and beat them together like wooden clappers. The cheap clogs made a dull, heavy sound and a lump of damp earth fell off them onto his knees. He flicked it away roughly.

"He was a bad lot. Fancy apologizing like that. He should've punched all the ones that called him an *eta*. That's what I'd have done."

"What about you, Koji?" asked Hidéaki, resting his hand on Koji's shoulder. "Would you punch them too?"

"No, I wouldn't. I'd show them by studying hard."

"Showoff!" and Seitaro thumped Koji on the head.

"You shouldn't hit Koji like that, Sei."

Seitaro hung his head and, to cover up his feeling of shame, he said, "Will you lend me that book some time? I don't mind reading myself. I've had a go at this one lots of times." He undid the parcel and showed Hidéaki the book; the title, *Tales of Kings of Many Lands*, was printed on the red cover in gold characters, so fine they were barely legible.

"What a splendid book. I like fairy stories very much. I bet you've got some good stories in your school readers as well. Like that one about the dog with the fish in its mouth that it went and dropped in the river. A slave—that's somebody the king and the well-to-do looked down on, like people do us—a slave in a country called Greece made it up a long, long time ago."

Seitaro and Koji blinked and said not a word: they were too surprised.

Fancy Master Hidé even knowing things like that! It just showed how stupid those brats were to be rude to him, thought Seitaro, putting on his clogs in high spirits.

They arrived home about three o'clock and each brought out two tangerines from under the tuck at the waist of their kimono; these had been distributed at school in celebration of New Year's.

"Here you are, Gran," said Seitaro, putting a tangerine in Nui's lap, while Koji placed one in Fudé's.

"How kind of you both to save them for us," said Fudé, bowing her head in thanks.

Koji began peeling his. "The teacher said 'if you eat them on the way home, you're no better than a beggar.' There's nothing worse than being a beggar, is there, Mom?"

"That's right."

"How does a beggar get to be a beggar?"

"Because he spends all his time enjoying himself and never does any work."

"Yes, anybody'll end up a beggar if they're always having nice things to eat and enjoying themselves," added Nui.

Munching on a piece of tangerine, Koji wondered to himself, "Then how did we get to be *eta*?" But he was afraid to ask this question aloud; he had recently begun to realize how uncomfortable and upset his mother and grandmother would become if he asked them such a question.

"That was delicious." Having finished the tangerine, Fudé rubbed the peel on the back of her hand to smooth her chapped, cracked skin. Seitaro watched with a heavy heart, remembering the pink hands of Toyota's mother.

"Did you have a good time? Was Toyota's mother nice?" Fudé asked rather pressingly.

"Yes. She gave us some delicious red bean soup," he replied, trying hard to push away the memory of those pink hands.

"She does sound a kind-hearted lady. It's because of all she's been through . . ."

Fudé wiped her hands on her apron and began work again. Her fingers moved like lightning; a sign that she was feeling pleased.

Seitaro grew increasingly gloomy. He was deceiving his mother, like Toyota. And his deceived mother was happy; in fact, he had to deceive her to make her happy.

"What about going over to see your uncle at Shimokawa tomorrow?" she suggested, as if seeking to add to her happiness. "He asked you to come over during the winter holidays, and you both promised to go. He and Ken will be expecting you."

"Will you come with us, Mom?"

"Yes, I'd like to."

"It'll make a nice change for you," said Nui, encouragingly.

"But we can't walk to Shimokawa with the roads in such a state. They're terribly muddy with all the snow melting," Seitaro said, trying to sound practical.

"Yes, you're right. We'd better wait until the spring holidays," Fudé replied, believing him.

As he took off his *haori,* Seitaro thought, "There, I've gone and lied to her again." He knew full well that however heavily it snowed, it would pose no hardship to visit his mother's family and see Ken'ichi, Keizo, Nanaé, and the rest of his cousins. Only there were the barriers presented by Sakata and the other villages on the way, and these he was afraid of crossing together with his mother. What would he do if insults were hurled at them, like the one today about *eta* kids in *eta haori?* Folding up his coat awkwardly, he ground his teeth.

The following morning, a card from his cousin Ken'ichi arrived unexpectedly. Seitaro was thrilled; it was the first time he had ever received a card addressed to himself. Holding it up on a level with his eyes, he read aloud:

"Nanaé's got measles. Dad says he doesn't want Koji to catch them so don't come over now, come in the spring holidays. We aren't going to have any more battles until Jeanne d'Arc is up again. That's because we'll lose if she isn't with us. Jeanne d'Arc is Nanaé."

"Ken writes well, doesn't he? Ha, ha, ha," Nui laughed loudly, pleased of course with Ken'ichi's card but even more delighted by the ease with which Seitaro could now read.

Koji was sitting beside them, staring outside at the traces of snow; all he saw though was Nanaé's face resting on her pillow. "Master Hidé told us yesterday that the relatives of Komori people are *eta* too," he thought. "I wonder if Nanaé's one. Maybe they'll treat her different when she starts school and make fun of her like they do us."

The glare of the snow was harsh and Koji shut his eyes; at once, Nanaé's face grew even clearer.

IV

It was February 1, New Year's Day by the old calendar, and, with the traditional decorative straw rope hanging in the doorway and the dumplings prepared, it felt like New Year, in contrast to the official festival a month earlier. Unfortunately, it was also a Monday.

"What a nuisance having to go to school today," Seitaro said with a grimace, wrapping some toasted dumplings in bamboo.

"You can't get your own way all the time . . . But maybe the Headmaster will give the school a half-day holiday, seeing as everybody's celebrating New Year," said Fudé, packing up Koji's lunch.

"No, he won't," replied Seitaro, shaking his head. "The old spoilsport'd think he was losing out. And anyway, he's always going on about how we ought to give up the old-style February New Year and keep the new one 'cause it's one of the Three Great Festivals* and 'cause the Emperor does this important ceremony at half past five in the morning. He says it's disloyal to the Emperor if you work then and don't hang the national flag out. So why on earth would he give us a half-day holiday today?"

"Well, I never; so that's what the new one's all about, is it? And I thought it was just a festival for them officials and townsfolk," said Nui, stirring the *zoni*, a soup with vegetables and dumplings for New Year's Day. "All they ever seem to think about at school these days is ceremonies to do with the Emperor. Not like when I was a girl, we didn't have them Three Great Festivals then. We had five holidays, the seventh day of the first month, the third of the third month, the fifth of the fifth month, the seventh of the seventh month, and the ninth of the ninth month. I know we've still got the Dolls' Festival on

March 3 and the Boys' Festival on May 5 but, on the whole, it was
a lot more fun in the old days.''

For a moment, Nui's expression became youthful, and she sighed
once or twice as she recalled the last fifty years. Suddenly, the past
slipped from her grasp. She looked down at her hands holding the
pan of *zoni* and could not help smiling—they looked like decrepit old
rakes; but then, they had been working hard all these years, scraping
together a living.

Fudé sat down in the living room and served the *zoni*. This made
it seem even more like a special occasion to Seitaro and Koji, who
were used to seeing their mother eat breakfast hurriedly, either
sitting on the edge of the raised wooden floor or standing up. Nui too
made herself comfortable and dug into the dumplings with great
relish—there could be no doubt that Shinkichi's weakness for them
came from her. The bean curd, radish, and taro in the soup were
much to her liking as well, and, as she ate her third helping, she said,
''I'm giving you both some pocket money when you get back from
school today, seeing as you've helped such a lot with the *yokiri* of
late. You can buy a kite, or a pack of cards, or anything else you
want.''

''It's for New Year's,'' thought Seitaro and Koji, growing increasingly excited.

Yokiri was the work of cutting out the *yo,* the top segment of the
stalk, which was the only part of the straw that was used for weaving
the upper sides of sandals; the ear was used for making brooms. The
straw from Shimana that the middleman Shohei Otaké had brought
round in January had not been cheap at four yen a *tan,* but it was
of a high quality and good material to work with. Seitaro and Koji
had spent most of the previous day doing *yokiri* in the shed, skillfully
wielding an old sickle, the handle of which was missing. They had both
felt that New Year's Day would come faster if they worked instead
of playing with their friends, which was natural enough considering
that the life of their family revolved around work and there was never
a day when they could forget it. For Seitaro and Koji, there was no
other way of making time pass more quickly.

However, Nui was touched by her grandsons' helpfulness and
wanted to give each of them some money, thinking they were growing
up to be sensible and considerate. Fudé was moved too. Although
she sometimes asked them to help with the *yokiri,* at heart she wanted

at all costs to spare them such work. "I hope my generation will be the last to do sandal-making. I can't bear to think of Seitaro and Koji having to do it," she would say to herself, whenever she worked with the straw they had prepared so well; and this was why she went into the shed presently, when they had left for school, and settled down to do some *yokiri* herself.

"Fudé, why don't you take a break from work, just for today?" suggested Nui, tapping her on the shoulder.

Fudé laughed. "*Yokiri's* not work, Mother." So Nui settled down beside her and they both worked in the shed until midday.

Koji arrived home at two o'clock, an hour later than usual, and hastily undid the cloth in which his schoolbooks were wrapped.

"What, are you going back to your books already?" asked Fudé suspiciously.

Koji shook his head. "No, I want to dry my wrapper."

"Did you get it dirty?"

"Mm."

"How did you do that? You haven't been fooling around on the way back, have you?"

"No, I haven't. But they made us go and collect sand after school."

"Collect sand? Sand from the Katsuragi?"

"Yes, and then we had to carry it back to the playground. They said it's to make the playground look better."

"That's not a bad idea I suppose, but they didn't have to have you do it on New Year's Day. I think that's a bit unfair of the teachers," said Fudé, and she gave a bitter smile as she recalled Seitaro's words. He had certainly been right about the Headmaster; why, even the children in the first year like Koji had been kept later than usual. Perhaps Mr. Otori, the Headmaster, had ordered them to collect sand as a punishment for showing disloyalty to the Emperor by celebrating New Year's in February. Mr. Otori was a small landowner in Azuchi whose fervent patriotism was well known, since he was forever declaring in public how much he revered the Emperor and esteemed General Nogi; even Fudé had heard talk of it.

She hung Koji's wrapper, made from two pieces of brown striped cotton, on the washing pole to dry. She could picture him running along the dry riverbed busily scraping up the sand; the seams of the soaking wet wrapper were full of it.

"I'm going to have my dumplings, Mom."

Koji sat down on the wooden floor and, pushing his schoolbooks to one side, he opened his lunch box.

"What, you've left your lunch!" exclaimed Nui and pushed the small brazier toward him. "Toast them over this, they'll be hard by now. I'm surprised at you though, taking them nice dumplings with you and then leaving them."

"The others all came to have a look though, 'cause I had such a nice lunch, and so I couldn't eat more than one."

"You silly boy, letting them put you off like that," scolded Nui, feeling nevertheless that this was in keeping with his character. The children from Komori hardly ever ate "nice" white dumplings made entirely of glutinous rice, and neither did the children of the poor tenant farmers in Sakata, Shimana, and Azuchi; they had probably brought dark-colored ones for lunch, made of unpolished crushed rice, mixed with only a few grains of the glutinous variety. And of course they would tease a timid boy like Koji, partly out of envy, making him too embarrassed to eat.

Not like Seitaro. A slight twinkle of amusement appeared in her eyes as she pictured him munching white dumplings with an air of defiance, even smugness. But was he still collecting that sand? She glanced up at the clock. "I don't suppose Seitaro will be coming back yet."

"No, his grade'll have to collect sand after their fifth class."

"I've no doubt he'll be starving when he does get back, like a true Frogfish." Nui turned over the dumplings on the wire grill; they were much softer now and a smell of burnt soy sauce pervaded the room, whetting her appetite. She thought again of Seitaro's hunger.

But Seitaro was not feeling particularly hungry at that moment; he was enjoying collecting the sand and ran as fast as he could back and forth between the river and the playground; by the time his friends were bringing back their second load, he was already carrying his third. On his fourth trip, he scraped together a large pile, intending it to be his last. Suddenly, he let out a cry.

"What's the matter, Sei? Have you hurt yourself?" asked Toyota. Seitaro grunted vaguely, squatting on the riverbed.

"You've hurt yourself, haven't you?"

Another grunt.

"Where've you hurt yourself?"

Toyota took a step toward him and at once, Seitaro sprang up and began running along the riverbed, as if to escape his friend. There was obviously something wrong and Toyota sped after him, his feet crunching into the sand. "Wait, Sei, wait for me!" he cried at the top of his voice.

There were many loops and curves in that part of the river. Toyota grew uneasy, as if he was rushing into an unknown world, but Seitaro showed no signs of nervousness or fear; a more violent emotion seemed to be pressing him forward.

At last, he came to a halt and fell down onto the sand. When Toyota ran up, he whispered, "It's no good," and smiled sadly.

"What's no good?"

Seitaro made no reply.

"Where are you hurt?"

"It's hurt, not me." He opened his right hand and Toyota was amazed to see a shell top there.

"It's only a top, isn't it? What about it?"

"I found it in the sand."

"Somebody must've thrown it away. But why run all the way here with an ordinary old top like that?"

"Well, you see, it's a shell top that me and Koji put back in the river ages ago. We put it back 'cause . . . ''

A wagtail flew slowly zigzag downstream, every so often alighting on a post on the riverbank and wagging its tail; and even when it had finally disappeared from view, Seitaro was still busy explaining all about the shell top.

"I understand why you did it now. You're both poets." Toyota stared again at the shell in Seitaro's hand.

"What's a poet?"

"Somebody that thinks beautiful things."

"H'm." Seitaro looked down embarrassedly.

"You are, you're both poets. Imagine knowing this one had been left behind and couldn't get to the sea 'cause it was hurt. I'd never have realized a thing like that."

"But the other two aren't here anymore. This hurt one just couldn't swim well enough. I wanted to find some water downstream so I could put it back but it's no good, the river's dried up everywhere."

"Why not leave it here? Maybe it'll rain tonight."

"All right. But Toyo, promise not to tell anybody, they'd only think it was stupid and laugh at us. Not that I care if they do, but if Koji hears about it, he's bound to start worrying. He's sure all three of them have got back to the sea."

"You can trust me, I won't tell. Here," and Toyota hooked his little finger round Seitaro's and then they pressed their palms together to seal their secret pact.

After gently burying the injured red shell in the sandy riverbed, it occurred to them that their classmates would be starting to go home by now. They ran back upstream. As expected, the others had disappeared and all they found were two cloth wrappers awaiting their owners amidst a confusion of footprints. They quickly scraped up some sand and Seitaro took off his apron and filled that as well.

There were still seven or eight children in the playground but their wrappers now held schoolbooks, not sand. They began teasing Seitaro and Toyota.

"What have you two been up to?"

"I bet you've been hiding somewhere and playing."

"Idiots, d'you think we'd bother to hide! If we wanted to play, we'd play here in our playground," Seitaro answered back loudly, emptying his sand onto the heap, which already looked like a small mountain. Fragments of mica-schist sparkled there in the late afternoon sun.

The Headmaster came out of the school and the children beat a hasty retreat.

"Come on, Toyo," urged Seitaro, but the Headmaster's voice stopped them in their tracks.

"Hatanaka, Matsuzaki, you're not going home yet. I'm well aware you have both been hiding somewhere and playing. You must go and collect some more sand. Didn't I say right at the start that all grades had to go and collect sand at least three times."

"But sir, I've been four times, five counting the sand I brought in my apron," said Seitaro quietly, the utter truth of this giving him courage.

To Mr. Otori, his boldness merely sounded like the sort of impudence he would expect from Komori children. "If that's the sort of stubborn attitude you are going to take, you can remain standing where you are!" he snapped and stalked off.

"Today, without buckets," whispered Toyota with a giggle and Seitaro sniggered.

"Sei, I must've started to think like you, I feel as if that shell's alive now," said Toyota presently, scooping up sand from the heap with both hands. "I like what Ko said about feeling sorry for the shells 'cause people make them fight and they get hurt. I feel sorry for people, too. They're made to fight when they don't want to, same as the shells. What d'you think about that war, Sei? I mean, war's when people are made to fight, isn't it?"

"Mm, that's what I've been thinking. My dad was made to fight in the war with Russia and he was killed, just like one of them shell tops."

"Why d'you like playing soldiers so much then?"

Seitaro fell silent.

"If you join the army, you'll be one of the first that's made to fight."

"But," Seitaro thrust both hands deep into the sand heap, "Nobody'll call me *eta* or Four-Fingers anymore if I'm a soldier."

Toyota also silently plunged his hands into the sand.

"I don't care how hard it is, I'd rather be a soldier than be called names like *eta* and Four-Fingers, even if they make me crawl forward under heavy fire in a battle."

"I know how you feel, Sei," said Toyota, after a moment's pause. He drew out two large handfuls of sand from the heap, his fingers tightly clenched around them, and then threw the balls of hard-packed sand with all his might, as if they were hand grenades. Grabbing his cloth wrapper, he ran off. At the staff room window, he called out loudly, "Sir, please can we go home now?"

"Yes, off you go." The Headmaster stuck his head out of the window, smiling uncomfortably. "What about your books?"

"I'm leaving them in my desk. I can't wrap them up in this cloth, it's too wet."

"And Hatanaka's?"

"Sei's is much wetter than mine because he carried a lot more sand."

The Headmaster withdrew his head at once.

"Silly old fool," muttered Toyota, beating the wet cloth against the school gatepost. Seitaro stopped for a moment to wring out his apron and suddenly recalled his grandmother's words, "I'll give you both some pocket money when you get back from school today." A smile spread across his face as he thought of what he would like to buy.

"Goodbye, Sei," called Toyota, relieved to see his friend looking happier.

The days were noticeably longer now and the winter wheat and barley were shooting up as if they sensed the arrival of spring.

V

That evening, Seitaro and Koji were in a state of bliss, feeling warm and cozy after their bath, full after their supper and with a five-sen nickel coin shining in their palm.

"What a nice New Year's! Koji, what are you going to spend your money on?" asked Fudé, affected by the happiness of her children.

"Nothing, I'm going to keep it."

"But you can buy whatever you want."

"I'd rather have the money."

"Yes, it's better to have the money I suppose." Fudé laughed sadly; as if for the first time, she realized that a coin had its own special attraction, however little it might be worth.

Now that he actually felt the five sen in his hand, Seitaro too was strangely loathe to part with it, in spite of the many things he had wanted to buy. It gave him a thrill of pleasure to throw the coin up in the air and catch it again as it came tumbling down.

"There's an ear of rice on this five sen, isn't there, Seitaro?" said Koji, after tossing his own coin up in the air for a while in imitation of his brother.

"Yes, that's right."

"Why did they put an ear of rice on it?"

"'Cause an ear of rice is something good."

"Why's it good?"

"Well, rice is food, isn't it? The staff of life. And so it's good, isn't it?"

"Mm, and the people that grow it must be good, too."

"Yes, they are."

"We grow rice."

"That's why we're good as well."

"Good people are different from well-to-do people, aren't they?"

"Yes, good people are the ones that do all the work and well-to-do people are the ones with a lot of money."

"Are important people rich too?"

"I'll say. If you get to be important you make a bundle, but if you don't have any money to start with you'll never be important. So whatever way you look at it, they've all got loads of money."

"How much have they got? One measureful or two?"

This was greeted by an explosion of mirth from Nui and Fudé. Nevertheless, there was something sad about the innocence of such a question, springing as it did from the experience of a child who had known only poverty. Fudé felt a lump in her throat.

"We'll soon have enough saved up to fill a measure or two ourselves, Koji," she said. "We grow rice and we use the straw to make sandals, too. If there are any *kami* about, they're bound to see how hard we work and reward us."

"I wonder what Dad's up to. He ought to come and help us quick if he became a *kami* when he died," said Seitaro. His funny criticism made Fudé and Nui want to laugh again.

"Well, we're all fit and enjoying New Year's Day. That shows Shin's helping us from the other world. I've felt as strong as a horse ever since he died." Nui clenched and unclenched her hands over the brazier—yes, she knew she could work for many years yet. Just then, they heard the sound of footsteps at the front entrance.

"Sei, can I come and play?"

It was Kiyokazu's voice. He was the eldest son of their neighbor, the carrier Hirokichi Shimura, and was in the same grade as Seitaro, although he missed school most of the time, unlike his sister Harué, in the third grade, who was hardly ever absent. When Harué was at home she usually played with Koji, and now she called out, "D'you want to play cards, Ko?"

"Come in," said Fudé, stepping down to open the screen door.

"Good evening," said Kiyokazu, who bowed to Nui with a quick bob of his head. He felt shyer of Nui, with her large, firm, masculine mouth, than anybody else in the neighborhood; and yet he could not help liking her at the same time, perhaps because his own grand-mothers were no longer alive.

Kiyokazu and Harué stepped up into the living room and at once began laying out a set of picture cards. These matched up with another set of cards with sayings on them and when a saying was read out, the object of the game was to try and be the first to spot the corresponding picture.

"You read the cards, Auntie," urged Harué.

"It's no fun at home 'cause Mom can't read. It's lucky yours can, Sei," said Kiyokazu, jerking his knees restlessly.

"That's right, Kiyo," Nui looked sharply at him across the brazier. "So enjoy yourself playing cards tonight, but be sure you go to school tomorrow and no playing truant. Your mother couldn't go to school even if she'd wanted to. It's not her fault she can't read, like me."

"Yes, you don't know how lucky you are, Kiyo, being able to go to school," added Fudé. "Make the most of it and go without fail from tomorrow. I know it'll please your father."

"All right, all right, I'll go from tomorrow then," said Kiyokazu, as he finished shuffling. "Now Auntie, start reading the cards. The winner gets a nice dumpling."

"So that's his game, is it," laughed Nui and fetched several white dumplings from a store in the cupboard. Wanting to have enough for at least the first three days of the New Year holidays, she had pounded three 3-pint measures of glutinous rice, an unusually large quantity for Komori, where people had so little land to cultivate.

Kiyokazu and Harué, already familiar with the pictures, each won a game, but the third time they lost to Seitaro.

"Well, you can't expect to beat the top of the grade," said Kiyokazu gravely.

"What are you talking about, I've never been top," replied Seitaro in an equally serious tone.

"Yes, but everybody knows you're really the best."

"No, I'm not. Senkichi Sayama is."

"Him! He's just the teacher's pet."

"Now, now, you can settle that later. Have a dumpling; they're done now. Like they say, you can't fight on an empty stomach." Nui gave each of them one of the dumplings she had been toasting. They were round, as was the custom in that region, and the children dug into them eagerly.

"Mom, what does this mean?" asked Koji, unexpectedly breaking the silence he had kept until now. On the card he showed his mother were written the words "three years even on a stone."

Fudé inclined her head slightly. "I'm not sure, but maybe it means that just as even a cold stone'll grow warm if you sit on it three years, things are bound to get better, no matter how hard they are, if you stick it out long enough."

"Yes, that must be it," cried Seitaro, slapping his knees; his mother's interpretation sounded most convincing to him.

"D'you think so?" Kiyokazu looked doubtful. "I've been sticking it out at school for four years now, but it never gets any better."

"Well, that's because you're always playing hookie," said Nui.

"But I don't see any point in going. The teachers think we're all troublemakers from Komori and as soon as anything's wrong, the other kids always say it's our fault. I don't care what they say about having to study, I don't like school."

Nui nodded and made sure that Kiyokazu had the last New Year's dumpling.

He was stuffing it into his mouth when his mother, Kané, opened the door and called out good evening. She noticed her son at once. "I can see that Kiyo's having a lovely New Year's."

"And me," announced Harue.

"Ha, ha, I know what you're both up to, using cards as a trick to get dumplings." Kané stepped up into the room.

"Now don't go and spoil things, Mom," warned Kiyokazu.

"I won't spoil anything; I'm only going to watch. I'm sure you don't mind your mother just watching a game of cards at New Year's, do you? It only comes once a year."

"I don't mind. But d'you know what the cards mean, Mom?"

"Of course I do; I'm the teacher, aren't I?" protested Kané vigorously and then subsided into laughter.

"Well, what does this one mean, 'three years even on a stone'? Sei's mother's just given a real good answer."

"Then I'd better give a good one too, seeing as I'm four or five years older. Now, let me see, 'three years on a stone.'" Kané's expression grew serious as she stared up at the ceiling. Presently, smoothing her apron over her knees, she said, "Not that you could sit on a stone without moving for three years, mind you, you'd end up dead. You can't expect to eat if you don't work every day."

"Too true," agreed Nui.

Kiyokazu grinned embarrassedly. "No, you've got it wrong, Mom. It's not 'three years on a stone' but 'even on a stone'; there's an 'even' and that makes a big difference, doesn't it?"

"Mm, I suppose it does. So it's not 'three years on a stone' but 'three years even on a stone'. That word 'even' makes it a bit tough. Now, if you sit still for three years, even on a stone—of course you couldn't really, but just suppose you did—even a cold stone will slowly get warm.''

"That's it. That's right," cried Harué, clapping her hands in delight because her mother's explanation was like Fudé's.

Kané continued more confidently, "And as the stone gets warmer, you get used to sitting there, so you don't mind it anymore, however hard it is. And in the same way, if you live in a place long enough, no matter how poor it is, even if it's like Komori, you get quite fond of it in the end. There's no place like home, as they say.'' Pleased with her explanation, Kané gave a contented chuckle.

The grin on Kiyokazu's face had gradually given way to an expression of bewilderment: he was neither impressed with his mother's explanation nor did he agree with it—in fact, he found it rather lame—yet there was some truth in it that he could not deny.

Fudé and Nui had a similar reaction; they could not help feeling that Kané's interpretation was nearer the truth. "Three years even on a stone," "adversity polishes the gem"—there was undoubtedly wisdom as well as common sense in the old proverbs and maxims, but, as Nui thought to herself, much of it was inapplicable to Komori. "It's a sharp thorn we've been sitting on these hundreds of years, not a stone. We've tasted all the suffering that life has to offer, and more besides, and what's come of it? Has anything got better? It's like Kané says, we've just got used to sitting on the stone and somehow we manage to keep going.''

"But why do us Komori folk have to sit on a stone, anyway?" thought Fudé.

And Seitaro declared to himself, "Let's get up from that stone. Rise up and kick it away!''

He stuck out his elbows, "Right, let's play," and another game began. As quick as a flash, he spotted the picture that matched up with the card Fudé was reading.

"Isn't he good!" exclaimed Kiyokazu. "It's 'cause he eats such a lot. You can't beat Frogfish.''

"Don't talk such rubbish. Sei's a bright lad because he works so hard at everything. And so must you, Kiyo, you mustn't be lazy and miss school anymore. You won't find work in any of the shops or factories in Osaka if you don't finish the sixth grade, you know,'' said Kané, her voice suddenly quiet. A gust of wind swept over the roof, rattled the back door, and shook the well-sweep.

The next day, Kiyokazu made an appearance at school after a
long absence. He stood for a while surveying the mound of sand in the
middle of the playground; it seemed indifferent to his presence, and
the swings and the crossbeam that should have been so familiar
looked coldly away.

In the lunch hour, Seitaro and Toyota carried him over to the sand
heap and pushed him right to the top; and then, at last, Kiyokazu
felt that he belonged in the school. He guffawed noisily, the sand
tickling his bare feet.

After that, Kiyokazu never missed a day until the ceremony on
March 27, marking the end of the school year. And he successfully
moved up into the sixth grade; he did not know that he had ranked
second from the bottom in his class that year.

VI

If only the gruel were not so hot, fretted Seitaro, wishing to be off
as soon as possible. Today, the dream he had cherished since last
year was coming true and he was going with Koji to visit his mother's
family in Ino, in Shimokawa *mura*.

Koji too sipped his breakfast with obvious impatience. "I'm going
to get dressed now," he said, when he had finished a bowlful.

"Ino's a long way from here. You'll get hungry if you don't eat
more than that," said Fudé, an anxious expression on her face, and
began serving another helping.

"I don't want anymore. I can't eat it." With mixed feelings of
excitement and nervousness jostling around inside him, Koji was
not just full—he was bursting.

"Are you so excited to be going over to Ino? Not that it's so surprising; even at my age I still dream of going to Mother's." And,
with a chuckle, Nui helped Koji to get dressed.

Fudé took a ten-sen silver coin out of her hand-sewn purse and
wrapped it first in paper and then in a cloth.

"Buy them a present with this, Seitaro. Do you know the cake
shop in Hayasé, just before you get to Ino?"

"Yes, it's on the corner of the road turning off to Ino."

"That's right. They've always sold nice *manju* buns there, and
your grandfather's very fond of them. You can get twenty for ten
sen; that'll make a good present."

"All right." Seitaro tucked the ten sen into his sash.

"I'd better give you some pocket money, too." Nui pressed a copper two-sen coin into the hands of each of her grandsons.

"I've still got the five sen from New Year's, Gran, so now I've got seven sen altogether."

"Me, too," said Koji, his face lighting up. Nui quietly stroked his head.

"Now, you both look after yourselves. And if they ask you to stay the night, that's fine by us."

"No, we'd better not." Seitaro shook his head, a little shamefacedly. Nui caressed him in turn; she was reluctant to part with this precious grandson who did not like spending even one night away from her.

Fudé went a few steps of the way with them. "And don't forget to say that I'm very busy at the moment but I'll come over when things slacken off." This was certainly not a polite excuse: when the frosts were over and the cherry trees began to blossom, ceremonies and festivals took place every day at the temples and shrines and there was a sudden increase in the demand for bamboo-sheath and hemp-soled straw sandals. Fudé and Nui received more orders then from wholesalers than they could handle, and, partly from a sense of obligation to them, they felt that they could not take off even one day.

The dirt roads had dried to a whitish shade after several days of fine weather, and as they walked along Seitaro and Koji found their brand-new hemp-soled sandals light and comfortable. Once, they turned to look back at Komori. It was wreathed in a long ribbon of smoke from the fires lit for breakfast.

On the outskirts of Sakata, Koji whispered, "It looks as if they're all still asleep, doesn't it?"

"Yes," whispered back Seitaro.

The houses in Sakata appeared unwilling to let in the morning: many of them lay behind large gates that were shut, while the front doors of those right by the road were only half open. It was the first day of the school holidays and the children were no doubt stretched out contentedly in bed.

"What a good thing we left so early. An hour later and I bet those kids'd come running up and start calling us names," thought Seitaro, his relief tinged with a sense of triumph. He made an effort to walk as slowly as possible past the houses where the children in his class lived, including the large home of Senkichi Sayama. The minute they were finally out of Sakata, however, he took to his heels as if suddenly buffeted by a strong wind; he was trying to get away not from some terrifying enemy but from the fear of an unknown monster.

Startled and half in tears, Koji sped after his brother, eventually catching up with him by a field of Chinese milk vetch.

"Don't cry, Koji. I only ran 'cause I thought I saw a lark over here."

Koji turned a deaf ear to this apology. With a sulky expression, he tore up some vetch and tossed it at his brother. Seitaro caught one and held it up to his lips; it tasted faintly sweet, either because of the dew or the nectar.

"I bet it's sweet."

"Mm, it is. Have you ever sucked the nectar?"

"Lots of times." Koji also held a flower to his lips and then the two of them set off again, heading for the Soga River.

Miminashi Hill had been hidden by the riverbank and the woods, but once they were across the Soga it appeared straight in front of them, with Unebi Hill slightly to the right. They were now out of the Sakata district and Seitaro breathed a sigh of relief; he was free of the bonds that had shackled him.

"Ino's still a long, long way off, isn't it, Seitaro?"

"Course it is, we've only just set out. You're not tired already are you?"

"No, I'm not."

Koji walked along briskly to show that he was not weary in the slightest. "It's still a long, long way off," he kept repeating to himself. One of Ino's attractions for him was its distance; such a faraway place made him imagine something wide and remote; and wide, remote things were beautiful. He lifted up his voice in a song he had learnt only the previous day:

> The snow on the window
> Gleams like a firefly

The sun slowly rose higher in the sky and from every village, people began to emerge carrying picks and spades. Presently, the track ran by the side of a brim-full reservoir, the brown grass on its bank dotted with green horsetails, purple violets, and yellow dandelions. Seitaro paused for a moment.

"A long, long time ago, there were lots of great battles here."

"Who fought them?"

"First of all the *kami* and then famous men."

"Why did the *kami* and famous men fight battles?"

"To destroy the villains. All they ever did long ago was fight battles with villains. You'll see when you do history at school."

"Didn't they have to work in the fields?"

"The fields? Yes, I wonder what they did about that." Seitaro looked around him. The yellow rape, now in full bloom, shone in the morning sunlight, and ears of barley fat with life itself looked up at the sky contentedly. Both now and in the past, men surely had to grow food wherever they were. But how had they existed in the so-called Age of Gods, far back in the mists of time?

"Even long ago, I'm sure they grew rice and barley, Koji. If they hadn't, there wouldn't be any people about now," he said with conviction.

"But they couldn't have if they didn't do anything except fight battles, could they?"

"The ones that worked in the fields didn't fight battles. The battles were against the villains."

"Who were the villains?"

"There were lots of them. Round here, there were the Shiki brothers; they were terribly strong."

"What had they done wrong?"

"I don't know; they didn't tell us at school."

"What happened to them?"

"They must've been killed, 'cause they lost the battle."

Koji was mystified: it seemed very strange to think that the sacred *kami* would kill people in a battle; and yet the teachers at school would hardly lie or teach them things that were incorrect.

A few more bends in the track and the Asuka River came into sight; and after crossing the river, they were near Ino. As they entered Hayase, Seitaro took out the cloth from his sash and unwrapped the ten-sen coin.

In the cake shop, the buns filled with sweet bean paste, known as *manju*, were displayed in glass-topped boxes. They appeared to be freshly cooked, as the glass tops were milky with steam.

"Ten-sen worth of *manju* please," said Seitaro.

"Ten-sen worth?" repeated the lady, who looked about his mother's age.

Seitaro put the coin on the glass top.

"Where have you come from?"

"Sakata."

"Goodness, that's a long way. You're brave boys, aren't you? And where are you off to now?"

Seitaro was silent.

The lady carefully arranged the twenty buns five to a row, in two layers, on a broad piece of bamboo-sheath. Tearing off a strip of sheath, she quickly tied the parcel up and covered it with a piece of pinkish newspaper.

"Right now, hand me that cloth of yours and I'll wrap it up safe for you. Where did you say you was off to, sonny?"

Seitaro remained silent. He was trying with all his might not to turn red, but the harder he tried the more he blushed. The lady looked from one to the other of them suspiciously; and her eyes followed them as they left, the bundle of *manju* tucked under Seitaro's arm. When they quickly took the turning to Ino, she said to herself, "*Eta*, that's what they are. Though at first sight, you'd think they were boys from a good home."

Gingerly, she picked up the coin from the glass top.

VII

There were about one hundred and fifty houses in Ino, lying along the banks of a tributary of the Asuka River. They were mostly thatched, but one building was conspicuous in having a high, tiled roof; this was the main hall of Manseiji temple.

Fudé's family lived opposite the temple, and theirs was the only house with a gateway; it was not, of course, comparable with the imposing entrance of Manseiji, but nevertheless, it was a source of pride to Seitaro.

Shortly after midday, about thirty boys, the "crack unit" of Ino, assembled in front of this gateway, and together with Special Volunteer Seitaro marched off westward without a moment's delay. Soshichi chuckled with pleasure as he watched them go, his eyes resting on his grandson Seitaro in particular.

This merry band of men was armed to the teeth with branches and bamboo sticks of various shapes and sizes, weapons of amazing versatility, serving one minute as rifles and the next, in the heat of battle, as cannons and machine guns. Such an army was surely invincible.

> Mightiest in the world
> Are the sons of Japan;
> Our fleet numbers thousands,
> Our troops in the millions,
> What, then, have we to fear?
> Let us load our guns
> With the soul of Yamato
> And strike at one fell swoop . . .

Soshichi chuckled again as he listened to the singing, which gradually grew fainter. He pictured the advance of the brave troops: dandelions being trampled down by straw-sandaled feet and goggle-eyed frogs leaping into the ditches in fright.

"These days, all children seem to like playing soldiers," he said, as if to himself, slowly going back into the house.

"Well, I don't, Grandad," declared Koji, seated before a small table and an oblong-shaped brazier.

"You like books better, don't you, Koji? Maybe clever children are a bit different," remarked Nanaé's mother, Chié, her hands moving nimbly over her work; like most of the women in Ino, she made thongs for clogs and sandals on the side.

Soshichi sat down opposite Koji and leaned toward him. "Playing soldiers is all right, but it's even better if a boy likes reading. What's that you're looking at, Koji?"

"It's a good book."

"It's a prize Kei got yesterday. What did you get, Ko?" asked Nanaé from nearby.

"All the books for the second grade."

"Well done," said Chié, looking as pleased as if he were her own son. But Koji would have much preferred Keizo's prize; it was like the red-covered book belonging to Toyota Matsuzaki.

"Can you understand it?" asked Soshichi.

Koji nodded. "Yes, it's full of nice stories. Shall I read you one, Grandad?"

"Yes, you do that." Soshichi started making twists of paper, which he then wove into tobacco pouches; a pastime he had taken up only recently.

Expecting a well-known story, he was surprised when Koji began to read one he had never heard before, but he listened quietly, mindful of his grandson's feelings.

The house belonged to a very wealthy family and was often full of guests—well-dressed gentlemen, elegant ladies, and little girls with pretty ribbons in their hair. They always enjoyed themselves immensely, singing, dancing, and feasting to their hearts' content. Of course, they had every reason to be lighthearted, being rich, of good family, and without a care in the world. How had they achieved this? It was said that their ancestors had distinguished themselves in battle long ago; and indeed, whenever the ladies and gentlemen grew tired of merrymaking, they always talked of their ancestry, of connections with royalty, and of men famed for their skill with horse or bow.

The little girls also talked a great deal about their families, but about their own fathers rather than remote ancestors.

"My father's a minister. He's the most important person after the King," said one little girl.

"That's during peace time. When there's a war, *my* father's more important because he's a general," said another.

"But you've got to have lots of money when there's a war or else you can't buy any weapons, or even uniforms for the army. My father's the richest man in the country, and so he must be the most important, too," said a third.

At that, a little girl with blue ribbons, who had been hesitating to speak, plucked up courage. "My father's the owner of a newspaper," she declared more loudly than any of the others. "You all know what a newspaper is, don't you? Well, you're finished if they print something bad about you, even if you're a millionaire, or a general, or a minister, because people won't trust you anymore. My father says he may not have a crown but he's like a king. So I think he must be the most important man in the land."

The little girls were silent for a while and then the minister's daughter spoke:

"I think we're all very fortunate to have such fine fathers. The unlucky children who come from poor homes can work and study as hard as they like, but they'll never get on in the world and be able to live in comfort like we do. We were born under a lucky star and we must join hands and make sure we keep the happiness we've been blessed with. We must always be good friends so that other children can't rob us of our good fortune."

"Yes, we must, we must!"

The little girls all joined hands and danced round and round in a circle.

A boy had been crouching beneath their window, weeding a flowerbed. He was the son of the gatekeeper and had heard the whole of their lively conversation. He sighed many times, for his own father was poor and almost as wretched as a slave. The little girls had said that children from poor homes had no hope of ever doing well and the more he thought about this, the sadder he grew. But he fought back his tears and worked all the harder, knowing that it would help to lighten his father's load.

Time passed—over a hundred years—and the house where the rich and famous had so often gathered was rebuilt on an even more lavish scale than before; but not by the descendants of the former owners. No, it was rebuilt by all the people who lived in that land, and on one of the pillars of the entrance the words "The Children's House" were inscribed in large letters. It really was a house for children, full of all their favorite things, a place where they could study, rest, or play, and eat anything they liked. All the children visited it and had a wonderful time, but before leaving they never forgot to pause in front of the photograph hanging in the entrance hall, and say "Thank you, Father. We'll come again soon." This was a photograph of a man with a beaming smile; the very same one who, as a boy, had overheard the little girls' conversation. Most of the children knew about this but sometimes children from abroad, who had come to play there, would ask in surprise, "Why do you all call the man in the photograph 'Father'? Is he really your father?"

Then the children would stand up very straight and answer proudly, "Yes, he is. He's the father of us all. He did all sorts of difficult things for us because he said that not a single person in our country ought to suffer from being poor. That's why we don't have a king here anymore, living in luxury, or high-and-mighty ministers, or generals who take pride in killing people, or rich men who think it's clever to cheat. And that's why we all work together now and call this man 'Father.' Don't you think he's the finest father in the whole world? We children love him very much.''

Although he made some mistakes and faltered occasionally, Koji managed to finish the story with the help of the readings in *kana* beside the difficult characters.

His grandfather paused in his handiwork. "Well done, Koji. What a long story you've read me. I'm not surprised you were top of your class."

"Yes, you read very nicely," complimented Chié, putting down her needle. "Keizo hasn't even glanced at the book yet, even though it's his prize. He's too busy playing soldiers."

Such praise did not please Koji at all: neither his grandfather nor his aunt had made the least mention of the story itself. "I wonder what Grandad and Auntie think about it. Fancy there being such a marvelous country somewhere and such a wonderful man . . . ''

Unable to openly show his dissatisfaction, he began reading the story, which was called "Our Father," once more from the beginning. His grandfather resumed his paper-twisting but, after a few moments, suggested tentatively, "What about a different one this time, Koji?"

"But I like this one, Grandad."

"Do you? I wonder why."

"It's such a good story."

His grandfather was plainly surprised; it had not occurred to him that his little grandson would try to understand what he was reading.

"I'm proud of you, Koji. Imagine you understanding it."

Koji felt even less pleased; as if he were being patted on the head in mistake for somebody else. But he cheered up presently and asked, "Don't you like the story, too, Grandad?"

"I do. Ha, ha, ha."

"Honest?" asked Koji again, to make sure; he did not altogether believe his laughing grandfather.

"Yes, I really do." Soshichi gave the paper a firm twist, pressing hard with his fingertips.

Nanaé had sat down quietly by Koji, and, apart from occasionally

peeping up at him and her grandfather, she had been playing with
the Ichimatsu doll in her lap. It was about a foot high, with thick black
hair, and sparkling eyes, delicately tapering at the corners. And it
had a long-sleeved kimono with a pattern of pine, bamboo, and
plum, and a gold brocade sash. Soshichi had bought it in the town
for his granddaughter when she had had the measles, hoping that
she would lie quietly in bed with it until she was better; and since
then, Nanaé and her doll had been inseparable. By now it was looking
rather worn, but the grubby cheeks made it seem endearingly alive
and Nanaé had only grown even more attached to it. She and the
doll, which had acquired the name of Yaé, were like sisters.

Nanaé pressed her cheek to it. "Did you listen to the story, Yaé?
It was good, wasn't it?"

"Ah, ha, ha . . . Even Nanaé thinks it's good," laughed Soshichi
delightedly, but the next moment his expression grew serious. "All
the same, it's only a story, isn't it? Like a picture of some dumplings—
it won't fill you up when you're hungry."

"Yes, things don't happen that way in real life," echoed Chié, a
stern look appearing in her eyes.

Koji wriggled uncomfortably, feeling as if he had been scolded.
That moment, Keizo came bursting in through the back door, panting
so hard it was obviously something important.

"Nanaé, aren't you coming? We're all waiting."

"I don't want to," cried Nanaé, fleeing to the safety of her grandfather's lap.

"You silly, we'll lose if you don't come."

"If that made you stop playing soldiers, it'd be a good thing.
Somebody's going to get hurt one of these days, you wait and see,"
scolded Chié.

"But it's the Hundred Years War. Nanaé's got to come."

"What's the Hundred Years War?"

"It's a war that happened a long time ago between England and
France."

"What's the point of imitating other countries' wars? Downright
silly, that's what it is."

"We've fought all the Japanese ones. And besides, Sei's keen on
doing the Hundred Years War, too, and he's waiting for Nanaé.
With a girl on our side, we'll win in no time."

"With a girl on your side you'll win in no time! Sounds a funny sort of war to me," Chié could not help giggling.

Keizo wiped away the black beads of sweat on his temples with the flat of his hand. "We've fought the Hundred Years War loads of times and we always win 'cause Nanaé joins in. You must know that, Mom. But if she doesn't want to play today, I'll take that Ichimatsu doll instead. It'll be the same 'cause it's a girl."

"Will you lend it to him, Nanaé?" asked Soshichi, peering down into his granddaughter's face.

"Just for a little while," suggested Chié, wanting to settle the matter.

"All right," agreed Nanaé at last.

Keizo tied the doll to his back with the same plaited cord he used to secure Nanaé when he carried her. His mother and grandfather laughed as they watched him run back to join the others. Not that he cared: his country was in great peril and the only person who could save it was Jeanne d'Arc.

VIII

The house at Ino was not particularly large, with no more than four rooms—an eight-mat, a six-mat, and two four-and-a-half-mat—but its high white gables looked down on the roofs of the neighboring houses, and the front of the rice storehouse, next to the shed, was decorated with a black-and-white pattern, giving it an air of prosperity. At the back of the house, too, there was a roofed well, with a pulley and a thick hemp rope, where it was possible to draw water without getting wet on rainy days. This well caught Koji's fancy more than anything else at his grandfather's.

As he pulled the rope, he suddenly remembered the times children from other villages had jeered at him—"Look at that poor good-for-nothing *eta*." "I wonder if they're all *eta* at Grandad's," he thought. "Master Hidé, the priest's son, said all the relatives of Komori people are *eta* too, but they look well-off here. There's a gateway, a tiled roof, a storehouse, and a well with a pulley."

Soshichi noticed his grandson pulling the well rope and came hurrying out anxiously onto the verandah. "Take care you don't slip, Koji," he called.

"I will," replied his grandson meekly.

Soshichi did not have any favorites among his grandchildren, but he felt a particular concern for Seitaro and Koji because their father had been killed in the war; and of the two, he felt closest to Koji, whose face was the image of Fudé's.

Koji gulped some water and then, wiping his mouth, returned to his place by the brazier. Chié stepped down into the *doma* and busied herself preparing the afternoon meal—in this region, it was the custom to have four meals a day, including one in the middle of the afternoon. Nanaé followed her mother, hovering about the sink and stove, and Koji and his grandfather were left alone in the room.

Soshichi stared at his grandson, still gripped by the feeling of unease and apprehension that had overtaken him a few moments before. "I wonder if the other children at school make him cry, too, with names like *eta* and Four-Fingers. And even if he doesn't suffer much from that sort of thing now, while he's still only a child, I expect he'll have a hard time of it when he's a bit older," he thought; but he pretended to smile and said cheerfully, "You've got a bright future ahead of you, Koji, with your love of books."

Koji stared silently at one of the pages of Keizo's storybook.

"Don't you think so?" pressed his grandfather.

"What, Grandad?"

"I said you've got a bright future, with your love of books. Would you like to study to be a teacher?"

Koji did not reply.

"Don't you want to be a teacher?"

"Yes, I do."

"Well then, that's what you'd better do."

"I can't Grandad."

"Why not?"

"We're poor good-for-nothings." A bitter little smile crossed Koji's young face, at the sight of which his grandfather felt a sharp pang: it showed that Koji was already aware of himself as an *eta*. Soshichi wanted to weep unrestrainedly; he wanted to face the invisible enemy that was trying to crush them as *eta* and strike out at such hatred with all his might. At the same time, he needed no one to tell him how utterly futile that would be.

"Ha, ha, ha . . . So you're poor good-for-nothings, are you?" he laughed, with tears in his eyes—his way of avoiding a collision with the *eta* wall confronting him. Now sixty-five, he still did not really understand why they were what they were. Not that he was illiterate: on the contrary, he was one of the most educated men in Ino, with the result that his thinking was permeated with Confucian ideas, such as "Heaven cannot support two suns, nor earth two masters." He believed that as long as one sun shone in the heavens, it was quite natural for there to be one sovereign ruler in the land, supported by a glittering array of officials and dignitaries. The only aspect of this scheme that he could not figure out was why there were people like themselves despised as *eta*. Why did there have to be *eta* at all? He had resigned himself to being one by thinking that it must be his karma; but this was merely a form of self-deception to make life bearable. Moreover, he himself realized this; at heart, he did not really believe in such ideas as predestination. Stroking the edge of the brazier, he said, "But there are families much poorer than yours, Koji. And poverty's nothing to be afraid of. If you work hard enough, you're bound to do well in the end."

"Were you poor to start with, Grandad?"

"We certainly were. Not that we're all that well-off now."

"Yes, you are. You've a storehouse and a gateway, like well-to-do people have."

"You'll soon be building a gateway and a storehouse at your home, too."

"No, we won't."

"Why not?"

"We live in Komori."

Soshichi was taken aback.

"Grandad, Komori's an *eta* village."

"Who said a thing like that?"

"Other people do. They all do."

There was silence.

"Grandad, what is an *eta?*"

"I don't know myself," replied Soshichi, shaking his head vigorously. Koji looked down: he felt that his grandfather had shaken his head to admonish him never to mention the word *eta* again.

"It's true what Master Hidé said," he thought. "All the relatives of Komori people are *eta*. Grandad's family, too, even though they look so well off. That's why he's angry and doesn't want me to talk about it again."

He turned over the pages of the book, pretending to read. Presently, Nanaé came to tell them that the meal was ready.

"It doesn't look as if the troops are coming yet. I think I'll join Koji and start without them," Soshichi said, settling down beside his grandson. As a special treat, there was a bowl heaped with white rice on the small tray before each of them.

They were still eating when the sound of the troops' triumphant return reached their ears. Each was singing a different song:

"Defending or attacking, the iron battleship . . . "
"With a thousand miles before us . . . "
"Our country is so far away . . . "

When they caught sight of the trays set for the afternoon meal, however, they revealed their true colors and with one voice, cried, "Oh, I'm starving!"

Seitaro was carrying the Ichimatsu doll with the long-sleeved red kimono. He had been playing the part of the white horse on which Jeanne d'Arc rode, but now that the battle was over he suddenly felt embarrassed and quickly undid the cord that tied the doll to his back. Chié went behind him and deftly caught it.

"Yaé's tired, Nanaé, you'd better put her to bed soon."

Nanaé immediately spread a small mattress in a corner of the room and lay down beside her doll.

> Sleep, little one, sleep,
> Be good and don't cry;
> Sleep, little one, sleep.
> Mommy will hug you
> And kiss you good night.

An atmosphere of quiet and peace stole over the room, and Soshichi looked the soul of contentment.

All at once, the calm was shattered as Nanaé started screaming. Koji was so startled he could not say a word.

"Whatever is it? Has a wasp stung you?" asked Soshichi and tried to pick her up.

Nanaé pushed him away. "My doll! My doll!"

"What's the matter with your doll?"

"She's lost her thumb!"

They all put down their chopsticks in surprise. Chié rushed over to Nanaé and picked up the doll.

"Oh dear, so it has," she sighed. Sadly, the doll's right thumb had been knocked off.

"Put it back! Quick, put it back! Put her thumb back!" cried Nanaé again and again between sobs.

"There, there, I'll put it back for you. There's no need to cry so," said her grandfather, and walking over to the family shrine at the back of the room, he took down the present of *manju* buns which had been placed there as an offering.

"Here you are, Nanaé, here's a red *manju*. You can have as many as you want." Chié desperately tried to soothe her daughter.

But Nanaé continued to crouch on the floor sobbing, "I don't want one. I don't want a *manju*. Put my doll's thumb back!"

Seitaro did not know what to say in apology: although of course he had damaged the doll quite unwittingly, there was no denying that he was to blame; nor that the dainty little hand now had only four fingers.

Soshichi stood there sorrowfully, his arms folded. "Throw it away. I'll buy you a much better one," he said after a while.

Nanaé sprang up immediately. Her grandfather was staring at her sternly, as if he might take the doll from her at any moment.

"You mustn't. You mustn't throw her away." Clutching the doll, Nanaé rushed over to Koji, who now seemed the best person to help since her grandfather was always singing his praises.

Soshichi's expression softened. "Stop crying then and play with Koji. I'll give you some *manju* to share with your doll."

He gave each of the five children two buns, one white and one red. Keizo started munching them at once, but Ken'ichi slipped his into the breast of his kimono and dashed out of the back door. Seitaro ran after him.

"I'm not going to play soldiers anymore, Sei."

"I'm too tired even if I wanted to."

"You did fight well today."

"That's 'cause the commanding officer's so good."

"Are you really going to be a soldier, Sei?"

"Yeah. Anyway, you have to join up, like it or not, if you pass the test," replied Seitaro, assuming an air of authority.

"It's tough being a soldier, though."

"I don't care."

"The commanding officer's orders are *our* orders. Know what that means?"

"Course I do," said Seitaro, dispatching a red *manju* in two bites.

Beyond the shed there was some wasteland, in a corner of which stood two persimmon trees, leaning over slightly. On the other side was a path, which ran between cultivated fields.

Ken'ichi shinnied up one of the persimmon trees, sat down on a branch, and brought out his *manju*. "You bought them at that cake shop in Iwase, didn't you? This pine spray is their mark."

"You don't miss much, do you?"

Seitaro also climbed up the tree and brought out his remaining white bun; as Ken'ichi had said, there was a pine-spray trademark on it.

"I'll come with you as far as there when you leave."

"You don't have to," said Seitaro earnestly; he intended to pass the shop as quickly as possible and did not want to have to say goodbye there.

"Sounds as if Nanaé's stopped crying," remarked Ken'ichi presently. "A couple of *manju* and the crybaby's laughing again. It's awful when she starts howling, though."

"It's my fault. It's no use crying over spilt milk, but I wish I'd been more careful. I was charging about like mad, like a good horse, and the doll's thumb must've caught on a branch and broken off."

"It doesn't matter. It's a wound of honor. Anyway, the real Jeanne d'Arc had a much worse time of it."

"But . . . "

Seitaro glanced quickly at Ken'ichi and a feeling of doubt crept over him. "Doesn't he mind at all? Doesn't it bother him it's only got four fingers now? I bet he'd be upset if he'd been called Four-Fingers, like I have," he thought; but he could not bring himself to talk about it. He hastily clambered down the tree, brushing against the new buds.

On returning to the house, they found Nanaé in the best of spirits, carrying her doll on her back. Now that Koji had tied a bandage around the damaged hand, she was fonder than ever of Yaé, much to the relief of Seitaro and Ken'ichi.

Soshichi was in the back room, quietly wrapping up some money to give to his two grandsons who would shortly be returning to Komori.

IX

The four boys had left Iwase behind them and were approaching the Asuka River. At the bridge, Seitaro stopped. "Don't come across with us or else I'll want you to come even further."

"All right, you both run across and we'll watch from here," said Ken'ichi.

Koji set off at a trot, with Seitaro close behind. When they reached the other side, they turned round to find that Ken'ichi and Keizo had followed as far as the middle of the bridge. They called goodbye to each other and then parted, Seitaro and Koji hastening home into the late afternoon sun, and Ken'ichi and Keizo walking slowly away from it. Presently, they all turned round once more, but by then they could only see the banks of the Asuka River.

"Will it be dark before we get home, Seitaro?" asked Koji anxiously, quickening his pace.

"No, don't worry. It's still light for a while, even after the sun's gone down." Nevertheless, Seitaro too was uneasy.

He suddenly recalled the small package his grandfather had pressed into his hand when they were about to leave, and at once his uneasiness vanished. He quickly pulled out his purse and, sure enough, there was the package stuffed inside.

"Gosh, fifty sen!" He came to an abrupt halt.

Koji turned hot all over.

"Would you believe it, Grandad's given us fifty sen, so they must be well-to-do." Seitaro wrapped the money up again and stuffed it back into the purse.

"We're poor, aren't we, Seitaro?"

"Yes. Can't be helped though, because Dad was killed in the war. Ken's Dad was out on business today. No wonder they can save a lot, doing business as well as farming all those fields."

"What kind of business?"

"The thongs they make in the village. Ken's Dad takes them to Osaka."

"And I bet he brings them back a nice present."

"Yes, he's a good father."

At these words, Koji recalled the father of the story, who, as a boy, had been shunned by those lucky enough to be well-born, rich, and honored. In the end, though, he had succeeded in building a country where children from any home could be happy; a country without an extravagant king, or high-and-mighty ministers, or generals who killed people, or the cunning rich who made money by cheating others. Koji liked the sound of this father; he would certainly have got rid of all those who hurt them with names like *eta* and Four-Fingers . . . He walked along briskly, staring down at his toes.

They were halfway home when a dog started barking furiously somewhere in the village they were nearing. Although they liked dogs, it was frightening when they barked. They took to their heels and started to run through the village. All at once, three women came out of a side street ahead. They had bundles on their backs and two or three pairs of bamboo-sheath sandals in their hands.

"They're from our village." A look of relief crossed Koji's face at having found some trustworthy fellow travelers.

Seitaro had also noticed the women. One was Shigemi Nagai's mother, Sayo, and the other two were Yozo Samita's grandmother and the wife of Shohei Otake, the straw and hemp middleman, generally considered to have the readiest tongue in Komori. But Seitaro felt more like hiding than trying to catch up with them: even in a village where they were unknown, they would soon be recognized as *eta* in the company of women peddling sandals. He hunched his shoulders and looked down, afraid that the women would notice them.

In vain, however. Shigemi's mother turned round and cried out, "Look, if it isn't Seitaro. On your way back from Ino with Koji, aren't you? Let's go together. Nice to have a bit of company."

Yozo's grandmother, too, evidently felt it unfriendly to say nothing. "Yes, come on. Ah, ha, ha," she laughed.

There was no escape. Maybe he should try and overtake them. And that very moment, a good opportunity presented itself as the three women stopped in front of a house by the road in the hope of selling their remaining sandals. Seitaro grabbed Koji's hand and ran as fast as he could. Before Shigemi's mother and the others knew anything about it, they were past the house.

"Sandals, sandals, who'll buy some sandals?" some children cried mischievously. "One *shin* five *shin* a pair. Down to one *shin*. Only a few left. A bargain at one *shin*."

Seitaro was as shaken as if he had been knocked flying. "One *shin* five *shin*"—the Komori pronunciation of one sen five rin—he could have wept to hear it being mimicked in this way. It was no better at school either; and whenever the Komori children were called on to read, they would feel embarrassed about their accent even before they had begun. Inevitably, this made them stammer and falter all the more, until the teacher would scold them: "You Komori children really are hopeless."

What a relief it would have been if he could have given way to his feelings now and sobbed. Instead, he began singing loudly.

> The enemy forces are in disarray,
> Although many thousand strong . . .

He and Koji gradually lost sight of the Komori women and presently the banks of the Soga River appeared, stretching away to the north and south. They no longer dreaded the thought of dusk, as once across the river they would be in Sakata *mura*. Suddenly the light faded in the west and a breeze swept across the fields, rustling the ears of barley.

"Seitaro," called Koji, for no particular reason, drawing closer to his brother, who took hold of his hand.

Do-ng, do-ng. In the distance, a temple bell started ringing.

"Seitaro." A note of disquiet had crept into Koji's voice. Seitaro put his arm round his brother's shoulders.

Do-ng, do-ng. Dong, dong, dong.

"It's the fire bell." Seitaro's heart began pounding.

Startled, people dashed out of their houses along the Soga and ran up the river bank.

Do-ng, do-ng. Sakata's temple bell was also ringing. A fire must have broken out. Seitaro's mouth went dry. "There's a fire, there's a fire," he kept repeating to himself breathlessly, dragging Koji along.

"It's not Sakata. It's further off," roared a man crossing the Soga.

"Perhaps it's Komori, then."

"Yes, it must be."

"No, it's the other side of Komori."

Women stood on the bank all shouting at once, while men raced toward the Katsuragi.

"Is Komori on fire, Seitaro?"

"I don't know yet," snapped Seitaro, but inside he felt certain that it was, and maybe . . . He saw the panic-stricken faces of his grandmother and mother.

They reached the outskirts of Sakata.

"Where's the fire?" asked a man.

"Komori," replied a woman.

"Might have guessed."

"Yes, it's an *eta* fire."

Leaving the voices behind them, Seitaro and Koji eventually found themselves in front of the school. They could see fingers of flame across the river and there was a rumbling sound, as in an earthquake. In a daze, they started running across the bridge.

"Come back! It's not safe for children." A pair of large hands grabbed hold of Seitaro's collar and picked up Koji. They were hauled back unwillingly to Sakata.

Seitaro peered at his brother when they had retreated behind the school. His face was wet with tears.

"Don't cry, Koji. Our house isn't on fire."

"Isn't it? Honest, Seitaro?"

"No, it isn't. I can see it."

It was almost dark. Seitaro stared across at Komori, shaking violently. Every now and then, he caught a glimpse of the shed roof in the midst of dancing flames.

"Look, it's burning down! It's burning down!"

A clamor of voices resounded along the top of the riverbank.

"An *eta* fire certainly burns well."

"Wouldn't be such a bad thing if a place like Komori did burn to the ground."

"And all those *eta* with it."

Senkichi, Shigeo—they were all voices he recognized. Seitaro suddenly realized he was pressed flat against the bank.

"I want to go home," sobbed Koji.

"Just wait a bit. We can't cross over yet."

"But I'm worried about Mommy and Gran."

"They'll be helping to put the fire out."

Pop-pop, pop-pop. It was the unearthly sound of bamboo splitting.

Maybe a thatched roof was on fire; or maybe the flame fingers were reaching out after some new prey.

Heave. Heave. A hand pump was being pulled across the bridge.

"Ugh, there's a horrible smell," said a woman's voice.

"Disgusting," agreed an old man.

"That's the *eta* for you. Even their fire stinks."

"It really does stink."

Smoke billowed toward the bridge as the wind began blowing from the west, and a strange smell filled the air.

"They say a child started it."

"Dreadful little brat!"

"Well, it's what you'd expect from an *eta* brat."

"They haven't the slightest idea about right and wrong, have they?"

"All the parents' fault, of course."

The black night sky was alive with twirling sparks. Seitaro and Koji slithered down the bank like a pair of young puppies; they were going to try crossing by the riverbed.

3

The Rainbow

I

The flames devouring the ridgepole lit up the blossoming winter crop of rape with the harsh brilliance of lightning. Seitaro and Koji stopped dead in their tracks. A terrible sight met their eyes: their home was burning down. As they stood there trembling, what seemed like a gust of wind swept over their heads with a roar.

"Seitaro."

Koji tried to shout but he could only whisper. His mouth was dry and his tongue as stiff as a sun-bleached cloth. Seitaro was the same. Much as he wanted to comfort Koji, he was completely numb.

Water spurted from a hose; that of a solitary hand pump. Nevertheless, it rallied the people at the scene of the fire. They began dashing about, shouting, cursing, and getting angry; a sure sign that they had come back to life.

"Koji!" Seitaro's voice returned.

"Seitaro!" Koji's tongue could move again.

"The danger's over."

"Are you sure?"

"Yes, look over there."

He was speaking the truth: the fire that had brought down their ridgepole had suddenly shifted away from the shed and flames were now licking at the charred remains of houses in the opposite direction. It looked as if the shed would be saved and the two boys rushed toward it, the stifling air scorching their throats.

"Gran!"

They spotted their grandmother standing beside the broad bean plants behind the shed.

"Seitaro! Koji!"

As Nui flung her arms round the two boys, they saw her large mouth contort, drawn down at the corners. Their lips too quivered and the tears started to flow.

"There, there, don't cry. You mustn't cry. I don't mind about the house one little bit. Just so long as you're both safe, that's all that matters."

The broad bean flowers were a pale blur.

"Mother! Mother!" cried Fudé, running toward them. Seitaro and Koji could see her easily by the light of the flaming timbers.

"Oh, I've been so worried about you both . . . It doesn't matter about the house. Doesn't matter a bit." And her mouth contorted like Nui's.

By the time the fire was finally put out, after having gutted fifteen houses, nobody had any idea how late it was. As the pump stopped, a new blaze flared up.

"Where's the one who started it?"

"It was him."

"It was not. It was you."

"We'll drag the culprit off to the police."

"Whoever started the fire's going to jail."

This exchange made Seitaro and Koji tremble anew as they helped to carry back to the shed all the tools that had been taken out to the vegetable patch. If what the people on the river bank had said were true and a child had started the fire, could that child be thrown into prison? And who could it possibly be?

"It's not me."

All the same, they both felt apprehensive, as if somebody were glaring at them from behind.

As Seitaro crawled into the straw bed Nui and Fudé had improvised, he remembered the money his grandfather had given him. Afraid that he might have dropped it when he was running about in panic, he thrust his hand into the breast of his kimono. Nothing. He quickly felt his sash and found a hard lump; it was his purse. Although he had no recollection of doing so, he must have tucked it in there to keep safe.

"Gran, look what Grandad in Ino gave me. Fifty sen." Seitaro pressed the purse into his grandmother's hand.

"Well, I never, fifty sen!"

"I don't need it. You keep it, Gran."

Nui sank into silence, her mouth beginning to tremble again. Seitaro wriggled down into the bed, the straw rustling under the thin mattress.

"Seitaro, I'm scared." Koji snuggled up to his brother.

"There's nothing to be scared about. The fire's over now, isn't it?"

It was not the fire that Koji was afraid of, it was something else; but he could not talk about it because he knew Seitaro would be afraid, too. It was that man with the saber, whose shoes squeaked when he walked. Even in ordinary clothes, he was so frightening he made your blood run cold; and tonight, he was wandering around looking at the remains of the fire.

"Let's go to sleep." That was the way to shut out all their fears and Seitaro drew Koji close to him.

"Sleep well, both of you. Me and your grandmother have still got a lot to do." Fudé inspected the straw bed and tucked it in here and there before leaving the shed.

"Seitaro, what d'you think's happened to Master Hidé?"

"I don't know. I bet he's all right though. He lives a long way from here."

Seitaro wondered why Koji had suddenly remembered him, although he too had been thinking of Hidéaki, confronting him with the question that was preying on his mind: "They said an *eta* fire stinks. 'That's the *eta* for you. Even their fire stinks.' But why do we *eta* stink, Master Hidé?"

That moment, somebody's shoes creaked near the eaves of the shed. Seitaro held his breath. He could feel Koji stiffening.

"Are you in bed already?"

What a surprise; it was Hidéaki's voice. Seitaro cheered up immediately, as he did when he heard the beating of the drum at a festival.

"No, I'm still up." Seitaro leapt up even before he spoke.

"It doesn't matter if you are or not. I heard you'd both gone over to Ino today and came round to see if you got back safely. I just bumped into your grandmother. It's a relief to know that all of you are all right."

"Yes, we got back a while ago and the house was on fire. How did it start, Master Hidé?"

"Three policemen are trying to find that out now."

The glowing embers still shed some light and Hidéaki managed to thread his way through the assortment of old tools to their straw bed.

"When Koji and me got to the riverbank by the school, we heard somebody say a brat from Komori started it. D'you think it's true?"

"They don't know how it started yet, but as Mr. Nagai's was the first house to catch fire . . . "

"Mr Nagai's, you mean where Shigé lives?"

"Yes. It's awful because one of Shigemi's younger brothers is missing."

"It's Takeshi, isn't it?" whispered Koji, who had been listening behind Seitaro.

Hidéaki peered over at him. "Yes, it is. All the others are in the main hall of the temple."

"I wonder what's happened to him." Seitaro also spoke in a whisper; it was impossible to talk about something so dreadful in an ordinary voice. And what about Shigemi and Takeshi's mother, Sayo, who had been trying to sell her last pairs of sandals amid the callous jeers of "one *shin* five *shin*"? He suddenly saw her again, looking such a fright with her dishevelled hair.

Hidéaki must have been reading his thoughts. "Shigemi's mother's running all over the place like a madwoman."

Seitaro put his hands to his head trying to stop the chill sensation that was creeping up his spine. But he could not ward off the feeling of dread so easily—Takeshi's burnt, blackened face already haunted him.

Takeshi, the fourth of six children, was due to start school on April 1, and at the beginning of March Koji had promised to lend him all his first-grade books. They were bound to be as good as new since they were Koji's, Sayo had remarked when asking to borrow them, and perhaps that would help Takeshi to do well at school, too.

Koji had wanted to lend him the books even without such compliments. He liked Takeshi as much as "Shigemi Red Top" and had secretly made up his mind to look after him at school, since he would be in the grade above. Now, his chin began to quiver at the thought that Také might have been burnt to death.

"It's raining," said Hidéaki, breaking the short silence.

"Yes. Sounds funny, doesn't it, sploshing like that."

"It probably sounds different after a fire."

"And it smells horrible." Seitaro started at what he had blurted out. It was true nevertheless; a most pungent smell filled the air and he felt better for saying so outright. He continued, half-joking, "It stinks. A Komori fire really stinks!"

Hidéaki laughed. "Of course, it does. The fumes drift over here in this sort of weather and besides, all sorts of dirty things have been burnt, too, you know. It's enough to make anybody from another village run away holding their nose, crying, 'It stinks, it stinks.' "

The fumes that Hidéaki had mentioned were sulphurous acid and had an overpowering smell. However, as a bleaching agent, sulphur was vital to Komori's important sandal-making industry, as Seitaro was well aware. There were several manufacturing wholesalers in Komori, each of whom had an oven in the corner of his shed, where sandals were bleached overnight by fumigating them with sulphur. The ovens were known as "fumigators," and everybody took it for granted that sulphurous fumes leaked from them to a certain extent.

However, this evening, the "*eta* fire" certainly did smell dreadful, perhaps because one of these ovens had been damaged and fumes were pouring out of it, or, as Hidéaki had suggested, the damp weather was causing the smell to concentrate and drift over the village.

It began to rain more heavily. Hidéaki pricked up his ears. "It's only a shower. It'll have cleared up by tomorrow. Talking of which, Seitaro."

Now what was coming? Seitaro clasped his hands around his knees and wiggled his toes, impatient to know, yet strangely anxious as well.

Hidéaki bent his head as if to peer out at the rain. "I'm going to Kyoto first thing in the morning."

Seitaro rubbed his shins and gulped twice, his chin resting on his knees. "You're starting another school then?" Although he did not mean to show sadness or reproach, he sensed both as he asked that short question, and Hidéaki's sigh suggested that he did, too.

"I don't want to, but it can't be helped. It's not so bad if they call you names at primary school, because you've got lots of friends. But there are only two or three *eta* at middle school."

Seitaro bit his lip: it was far more painful to hear the word *eta* from Hidéaki than from children from other villages.

"You'll be back for the summer holidays, won't you?" he asked, deliberately changing his tone.

"Yes, I'll come back on July 25, I think."

"July 25? All right, I'll look forward to that."

Seitaro was pleased to know the exact date; there was an air of certainty about it. At the same time, the thought crossed his mind, "What will Master Hidé do if they call him *eta* at the Kyoto school, too"; but he did not dare ask this. He swallowed and simply called out "Master Hidé," which was his way of saying goodbye.

"Look after yourself, Koji, and work hard at school," called back Hidéaki, who went out into the rain to return home.

Seitaro crawled into bed. He lay still, clutching the quilt tightly, but the lump in his throat grew bigger. The harder he fought to hide his tears from Koji, the more difficult it became.

Koji pressed his face against his brother. "I wish I was old enough to go and study in Kyoto."

II

He felt something hard. A copper one-sen piece. He found another; a copper two-sen piece this time. Then a nickel five sen. And a silver ten sen. Gosh, a twenty sen and a fifty sen! There was no need to go on searching, the riverbed all around him was buried in coins.

Seitaro's heart was pounding; his body felt as light as a feather— was this what they meant by "walking on air"? Quick, before anybody else came; before the others found out. Breathlessly, he began scraping up the coins on the sand.

"We've got a measureful already, Seitaro. I can go and study in Kyoto," exclaimed Koji, with a broad grin. He was dressed in the uniform of a middle-school student.

"We've got two measurefuls now, Seitaro. Shall we go home?" he said again.

Seitaro stood up. Although the sky immediately above him was blue, everywhere else was gray. There was a rustling sound. The pampas grass on the river bank quivered and some soldiers appeared.

"Oh, when did you soldiers get here?" he asked.

He was about to approach them when he became aware first of his feet and then the rest of his body, as he drifted back into consciousness.

It had only been a dream. Immediately, everything grew clear again and he sprang up, his body having regained its normal weight. His sense of time and space returned.

A bell tinkled.

"What, is that the shrine?" Seitaro barely managed to suppress a hoot of laughter. He had only just realized what the square box standing by his straw bed was. Not that there was any reason why he should have recognized it as that most solemn and awe-inspiring of objects, the family shrine. He had worshiped, or been made to worship, before it all his life, in the shadow of the doors that Fudé and Nui opened with such reverence; but now, viewed from behind, he saw that it was no more than a large soot-stained box.

A look of piety on her face, his grandmother was praying with joined hands, thanking the Lord Buddha for keeping her family safe.

"Thanks to Your merciful protection, we're all alive and well . . . Praise be to Amida Buddha."

Seitaro remembered Takeshi. "Gran."

Nui peered over at him. "Ah, you're awake, Seitaro. What a time we had last night searching for Také."

"Is he all right?"

"He came out from under the floor of the temple."

"The temple floor! He must have been hiding there."

"Yes, I suppose so. He must've been terrified of the fire."

"I'll lend him my books," said Koji, already starting to undo his bundle.

"You can see about them later, after you've washed that dirty face."

Nui's face was also dirty, and so was the towel covering her head, but without a word Seitaro and Koji ran over to the well.

It was a fine morning, the sudden rainfall in the middle of the night having cleared up by dawn, as it often did in the spring. They gazed up at the sky; it seemed to stretch on without end, perhaps because of the disappearance of the fifteen houses, which until last night had huddled there together.

"You two up already? You should have slept a bit longer." Fudé, who was preparing breakfast near the well, turned toward her children, her eyebrows smoke-blackened.

"Yes, we should, with such a nice bed made specially for us."

Fudé laughed in spite of herself. "We're lucky the shed escaped. We couldn't have made you a straw bed if that had gone too."

"How awful."

Fudé chuckled again.

Koji was standing stock-still, staring at the debris from the fire. The remains of the stove looked rather unpleasant, like a corpse. Maybe stoves were different from other things and really alive.

Even though they only had a dirty towel to rub their faces with, Seitaro and Koji felt better after washing, more like they usually did in the morning. They looked up at the sky once more.

"Let's have breakfast." Fudé spread a straw mat under the eaves of the shed. The chipped *kanteki,* or small portable stove, the black kettle, the gray bowls, and the dirty bamboo chopsticks had all had a very narrow escape.

"Seitaro, Koji, help yourselves to one of these if you want," said Nui, opening a picnic box. Inside, there were five rice-balls, left over from the emergency rations distributed last night. Judging by the sesame seeds floating about in the gruel, some of them had been used to make breakfast.

"Now, dig in, both of you. No use in fretting over what we've lost. We'll just have to work all the harder and build another home," said Fudé, as she filled Seitaro's bowl, trying to resign herself to their misfortune.

"It doesn't bother me. Také's come crawling out from under the floor like a baby turtle and everybody'll be happy at having a new home. What could be better?" Seitaro joked on purpose.

"Ha, ha, ha . . . We was all in a fair old state over Také, though, I can tell you," laughed Nui. "We thought he'd got caught in the fire, seeing as he started it, and burnt to death."

"I'd have gone crazy if I'd been his mother. I was worried enough as it was imagining Seitaro and Koji trapped in them flames, even though I knew they still hadn't got back from Ino."

Color returned to Fudé's face as she sipped her gruel, the liquid soothing her scorched throat.

"Good morning. Having breakfast, are you?" called Kané from the burnt remains of her house. It was now all too apparent how densely packed the houses had been; Kané's, separated from their own by an alley, seemed no more than a stone's throw away.

"We're just finishing. Isn't it terrible what's happened!" Nui repeated for the hundredth time; although surprisingly enough, each time she said it, it was with a fresh surge of emotion.

Kané walked over to them. "Well, it was that brat who started the fire. And that's why he hid under the temple floor. My goodness, even if they beat the living daylights out of him it won't make up for what he's done. D'you realize, we've lost everything?"

"But you can't help wondering why he did such . . . " Fudé faltered.

"He's Tosaku's brat, that's why. Like father, like son. Out to make trouble, the pair of them. They put us up at the temple last night, so I know all about it. They're going to drag Tosaku and his brat off to the police station today."

Kiyokazu came running up. He looked all around him curiously, a broad grin on his face.

"You ninny!" roared Kané, boxing his ears. "Are you pleased everything's burnt to the ground?"

"Who'd be pleased about that? But it's happened and there's nothing we can do about it," said Kiyokazu in a sagelike tone.

"Well, if you think you'll be going to school now that we're ruined, you've got another think coming."

"But I never did want to go to school."

"So that's why you've got that silly grin on your face."

"That's right."

Kiyokazu sat down on the edge of the mat beside Seitaro, his kimono open at the front, revealing a pair of black legs that seemed to have been smeared with ash; souvenirs of last night's desperate fight. Making no mention of the fire, however, he whispered in Seitaro's ear, "Master Hidé left for Kyoto early this morning. I saw him go with my own eyes."

Seitaro made no response.

"Did you know?"

Seitaro looked down, still saying nothing.

"I think he must've got fed up with that middle school, so he's going somewhere else." After another silence, Kiyokazu added, "I'm going to Osaka."

"Who on earth would take on a ninny like you there!" bellowed Kané.

In reply, Kiyokazu sang the words of a popular song he had picked up: "You may not love me but somebody does, or where would I be now?" Everybody roared; everybody, that is, except Koji, who had undone his bundle and was absorbed in looking through the first-grade

readers he had promised to lend Takeshi. The pages slowly grew
blurred.

"Did you start the fire, Také? It's a lie, isn't it?" he thought.
"Then you've got to tell them what really happened."

But how could Také possibly say anything at all in front of that
frightening man with the long saber and the creaking shoes. If it
were him, he would not be able to say a word.

Koji's tears overflowed, and, as he brushed them away, in his
mind's eye he saw a train. It was like the train he had seen once at
Takada station; and Master Hidé was on it, going away to Kyoto,
which was even further off than Osaka.

Koji wiped his eyes again.

III

Word of the fire at Komori flew around Sakata, Hongawa, Shimana,
and Azuchi on a capricious wind, and from early in the morning the
villages were buzzing with it. In particular, the parents of children attending Sakata Primary School used it as a good opportunity to
deliver a warning to their offspring.

"They say it was only a child that started the fire over at Komori,
so you see how frightening they are. Now you watch out at school.
You're not to play with any of that Komori bunch or you'll be
picking up their bad habits in no time."

Toyota Matsuzaki also received a lecture from his mother, Nami,
over breakfast. "I don't care how much you want to see the remains
of the fire, Toyota, you must not go to Komori. They'd set upon you
straight away if you did. They're not like the rest of us; you can
never tell what they're going to do. Apparently, last night's fire was
started by a little child only in the first or second grade. And at that
age, a child from a good home would still be frightened of matches.
Talking of which, do you remember that lantern race you took part
in on Sports Day, when you were in the third grade? You and another
boy couldn't light your candles and you ran with them out. Well,
that's what little boys from a good home are like. Just think of it,
though, a Komori child only in the first grade went and started a
fire. Don't you think it's frightening? You really must take care—not
that you've got any friends in Komori, of course."

Toyota listened quietly, with a resigned expression, obviously prepared to hear the lecture out, however long it was to last. Of course, he disagreed with everything his mother said. Since last night, he had been worrying about Seitaro and Koji and intended to run over to Komori this morning to make sure they were all right. First of all, though, he had to set his mother's mind at rest and gain her trust.

Smiling docilely like a boy from a "good home," he whispered to himself, "She really believes I am from a good home, with all that talk about how I still couldn't light a match even as a third grader. Doesn't she realize how awful it is? She must be blind. Blind and stupid!"

He suddenly felt that all adults were blind, especially Mr. Otori, the Headmaster, who seemed completely insensitive to the feelings of his pupils.

"I'd like to go and play in Sakata today, Mommy." He put down his chopsticks.

"Yes, all right, as long as it's Sakata or Azuchi." Nami smiled, "I suppose you're going over to the Sayamas'?"

"Where else?"

"I think you'd better take them a present. There are quite a few of those millet cakes left, the ones your father brought."

His father, the owner of a cotton wholesale business in the Motomachi district of Osaka, was in his fifties but still a handsome man with a pale complexion. At the end of every month, he came rushing over to see them and then left again just as hurriedly. Until he was in the third or fourth grade, Toyota had accepted his love unreservedly, thinking that all fathers behaved in this way; recently, however, he had begun to realize that there was something different about him, and therefore something different about himself and his mother, too. Only, he did not know what to do about it; he simply had to accept the fact that there were parents like his own.

After quickly clearing away the breakfast things, Nami picked out the choicest cakes and wrapped them up in a purple crepe cloth, feeling obliged to make the gift as attractive as possible.

"That's a fine present. I bet Sen'll be pleased." Toyota stared up at the ceiling, too guilty to look his mother in the face.

On reaching school, he found Senkichi Sayama and his friends stationed outside the gates. They were unusually excited, the fire in

Komori having given them another opportunity to indulge in a sense of their own superiority.

Senkichi's mood was all too obvious: instead of the ordinary "Toyo," he addressed him formally by his surname. "Ah, Matsuzaki. Where are you off to?"

"Guess," parried Toyota, playfully trying to get rid of him.

Senkichi grinned, "Oh, I see. You've got relatives in Komori, haven't you?"

Following his lead, all Senkichi's chums guffawed, whether they understood what he meant or not.

"Of course, I have. I'm Japanese, aren't I? So all men are my brothers and the Imperial House is our head family."

"Smartie." Senkichi changed his tone, "You'd better watch out though, Toyo, if you go there. Their blood's up today, all right. Any outsider's likely to get beaten up. And ever since last night, it's been stinking something awful 'cause three of those *eta* were burnt to death."

"They weren't?"

"Yes, they were. That's why Komori's fire had blue flames."

"Idiot!"

Everyone laughed again; this time paying court to the boy from Osaka who stood up to Senkichi undaunted. Leaving their laughter behind him, Toyota hurried across the bridge.

Once on the other side, however, he began to feel uneasy. He had never set foot in Komori before, despite the promise to visit his friend, and he had no idea whether Seitaro's home had escaped the fire or been burnt to the ground.

The track suddenly narrowed when he turned off the Takada road, but there was no other way. His destination seemed a forlorn and shadowy place, linked to the main road by this one narrow path.

But his courage returned when he was nearer the village and could see more clearly the damage it had suffered. All at once, he knew intuitively that Seitaro's home too had been burnt down; it was unlikely that he would be exempt in a disaster of this kind.

Then he caught sight of Koji. And there was Seitaro. Were they living in that building like a manure hut?

"You lost your home too, then, Sei?"

"Yes, only the shed escaped."

"Oh, it's a shed, is it?"

"What did you think it was?" Seitaro smiled awkwardly.

Toyota looked around him in wonder. He caught a whiff of a strange smell and noticed a large tub under the eaves. Inside, there was a substance like straw steeped in dirty water, the source of the unbearable smell.

"What sort of pickles are you making, Sei?" he asked, unable to hide his curiosity.

"Pickled *yo*."

"*Yo?*"

"The top bit of the straw," replied Seitaro giggling. "It's what we use for making the upper sides of sandals."

"And I thought it was pickles! I asked though because it's got such a strong smell."

"It does?"

It was Toyota's turn to giggle.

"The *yo's* too yellow to use straight from the straw," continued Seitaro. "So we leave it in water rice has been washed in, and it turns whiter."

"You have to put up with the smell, then. Like when you use crap for manure. It's worth the stink."

"Ha, ha . . . You're right there. That's why my mother and grandmother take such care of this tub. I don't like it, though. It smells like stale piss."

Fudé had been working among the debris, but when Koji told her of Toyota's arrival, she came hurrying over. "What a surprise. You're the boy from Shimana, aren't you? How nice of you to come and see us when things are in this awful state," and she bowed politely to him.

Toyota was rather disconcerted. "My mother told me to give these to Koji," he lied, holding out the parcel of millet cakes.

Fudé looked overwhelmed as she took them. "You really shouldn't have gone to such trouble, on top of your kindness to the children at New Year's."

Toyota started. But Fudé, who had no reason to disbelieve him, took the cakes at once to the shrine as an offering. The little bell there tinkled as she struck it.

Toyota turned aside, conscience-stricken, and his eyes met Seitaro's, which were laughing as if to say "You can't fool me, Toyo."

Seitaro had indeed guessed the truth. He knew Toyota's mother would never dream of letting him visit Komori; Toyota must have successfully deceived her as to where he was going, believing it his duty to do so. As for the millet cakes, no doubt they were intended for a certain boy from a good family in Sakata, and not for the likes of those Komori brats.

"Don't you want to meet Kiyo and Shige, Toyo? Their homes were burnt down, so they're at the temple."

As if nothing were wrong, Seitaro set off through the fire-ravaged village. He too found it hard to face his mother, whom they had deceived.

IV

The destruction caused by the fire was heartbreaking—but then, so were the houses that still remained. Lines of rags hung under their lopsided eaves, a fetid smell clung to them and they echoed with the crying of young children.

Toyota noticed a tiled roof on which the upper sides of straw sandals were laid out in rows. Had they accidentally been drenched last night when people were trying to put out the fire?

"They always dry them like that," remarked Seitaro, observing his puzzled expression.

"Why do they dry them?"

"They have to as soon as they come out of the fumigator."

"The fumigator?"

"The stove where they're fumigated with sulphur. They leave the sandals in there overnight and the sulphur bleaches them."

"It's poisonous, isn't it? I bet it stinks."

"I'll say. It makes you choke if you're not careful."

"Where do they keep the stove?"

"They set it up in a corner of the shed."

A man who was on the roof must have heard their voices, as he suddenly looked down. Toyota could not see his expression, since the lower half of his face was hidden by a towel, but the man appeared to recognize Seitaro.

"What a time we had of it last night," he called out in a deep voice. He reminded Toyota of a freshly picked burdock; there was the same firm, upright quality about him.

"That man's good at everything. He can take sandals out of the

fumigator faster than anybody else. He just puts a towel over his
nose and mouth and whips them out like greased lightning. He can
do a thousand pairs in under twenty minutes. He seems to enjoy it."

"A thousand pairs?"

"Yes, they cover the whole roof."

"What hard work."

"Mm, and it stinks too," said Seitaro, looking back at the roof.
In the spring sunlight, the rows of gleaming white sandals looked
like a brilliant floral pattern.

"Now I know why it smells in Komori, Sei," Toyota said quietly.

"You mean it's not us *eta?*" chuckled Seitaro.

"No." Toyota could not help giggling either. "All the work you do
is so smelly, it's not surprising."

"Sandal-making's got nothing on glue-making, though. That's
really smelly when they're boiling down the cowhide and bones."

"Do you do that here as well?"

"Yes. They make it over on the other side of Komori, but all the
people that work there are from here."

Toyota remembered the large glue wholesalers in Kyuhojimachi
in Osaka. The owner was reputed to be one of the wealthiest men even
in that commercial district, and he employed many clerks, although
from the front, the building had always looked as quiet as a private
house. At the time, Toyota had been uninterested in such a business.
He knew gelatin was refined from glue but had never stopped to think
about its uses. He had simply come to the conclusion that glue and
gelatin must be valuable substances, since the wholesaler was so rich.
Now, however, he realized how vital both were to industry; and here
they were, being produced in Komori. Naturally, the unbearable smell
of glue-making clung to those involved in the work. Senkichi Sayama
and his friends were always saying the *eta* stank, but they did not know
there was a good reason for it.

Glancing up, he blinked at the green of a *kaya* tree. It was massive,
ponderously confronting the sky.

"This is our temple, An'yoji, Toyo. The ones that lost their homes
in the fire have been staying here. Kiyo's family and Shige's and lots
of others."

At Seitaro's words, Toyota realized they were at the back of the
temple and that the great *kaya* tree towered within its compound.
Following the earthen wall that enclosed it, they came to the stone

steps leading up to the main gates and a row of familiar faces. Most of the Komori children were gathered there.

They had been making as much noise as a nestful of young sparrows, but silence suddenly descended on them as all eyes turned to Toyota. He came to a halt, feeling like a trespasser.

"Shigé," cried Koji, who had followed them there, and ran up the steps. Shigemi was standing in the shadow of the open gates, carrying a child on her back, her youngest brother, Tomizo, who was two. As his head was absurdly big for his age, he had been nicknamed "Daimonja," after the large-headed doll. He was now fast asleep, his head drooping against his sister's shoulder.

Koji ran round to face Shigemi. "Where's Také?"

"I don't know! I don't know!" Shigemi screamed wildly, turning her back on him.

Koji blushed. Shigemi's show of fury frightened him, besides which, he was embarrassed, since nobody had ever roared at him like that before, not even at school.

Seitaro marched straight up to Shigemi. "School starts tomorrow, so Koji wants to lend Také his books, Shige," he said soothingly.

Shigemi wheeled round, glared at Seitaro, and then turned her back on him too. "Také isn't going to school."

"You bet he isn't. He's off to the police station," said Takematsu, a boy in the fifth grade. "Také isn't going to school," he added, mimicking Shigemi's tone of voice exactly.

Quick as a flash, she charged at him. Tomizo started howling. Takematsu grabbed her hair and Seitaro tried to pull him away from her.

"Stop fighting, you two. Can't you see there's somebody from another village watching?" said Kiyokazu coolly. Once again, everyone's gaze fell on Toyota.

"Yes, it doesn't do any good fighting." Seitaro looked around with a sad smile.

"But it was that Hachimero who started it. She hit me first. She's always the one that makes trouble round here. And now that little idiot Také's gone and started a fire and burnt all our homes down. And instead of saying sorry, she's throwing her weight around again. We oughta give her a good thrashing, that's what we oughta do," said Takematsu with vehement hatred, at the same time, retreating a pace or two.

"But nobody really knows how the fire started yet. They say it was Také, but nobody saw him, did they? And what about the matches you buy by the measure? We use them at home—I bet you all do, too—and they sometimes catch light by themselves. Maybe that's what happened at Také's. Maybe one of them matches caught light when nobody was around."

For a moment, there was silence. What Seitaro had suggested was quite possible. Everybody knew the danger of the matches sold loose by the measure, at two sen a *sho*.* Although they were easy to light against the corner of the stove, there was always the risk of natural friction causing them to ignite unexpectedly, and notices warning against their use were constantly being circulated to Komori from the Sakata *mura* police substation. It made no difference, however, and these matches continued to be found in Komori homes, being slightly less expensive than the sort packaged in attractive boxes.

"But Sei," said Takematsu, stepping forward again after a moment's hesitation, "I still think Hachimero's family's in the wrong, because even if one of them matches did catch light by itself, it wouldn't start a big fire if you put it out right away. They'd all gone out and left Také on his own, though, and that's why it turned into something awful."

"But it's the ones that come round here selling them dangerous matches that's to blame," roared a girl called Hatsue, a close friend of Shigemi's. "They always say it's two sen a *sho* but you can have two *sho* for three sen, and try and get you to buy twice as much as you want so you're even more likely to have a fire."

"What d'you mean, Shichimero!" Fusakichi scowled threateningly, since his father earned his living by peddling these matches.

Despite Fusakichi's angry expression, everybody laughed to hear him call Hatsue "Shichimero," a name he had coined from Shigemi's "Hachimero."*

Fusakichi could not help smiling himself. "Well, I give up if you think it's wrong to try and get people to buy your matches because they're cheap. This Shichimero's too much for me."

"And Hachimero's too much for me. On top of burning my home down, she goes and hits me." Takematsu rubbed his head comically, provoking more shrieks of laughter.

Meanwhile, inside the main hall of the temple, the so-called meeting was in an uproar, the clamor of the grown-ups rivaling that of their children. Tosaku Nagai and his wife, in whose house the fire had first broken out, were not present, having gone with Také to appear at the Takada police station. Oishi, Také's grandmother, was there, however, sitting in a corner among the victims of the disaster, whose resentment over the loss of their homes was naturally focused on her.

True to her name, which meant "stone," Oishi remained firmly silent; there was nothing else she could do. Leaving Také to look after "Daimonja," all the members of the family went out every day to try and earn something; and how else could they possibly survive, she would have liked to retort to those who now criticized them.

Nui, her mouth drawn down, was sitting next to Oishi. Her thoughts wandered to and fro: there was nothing they could do about the loss of their home, but what was it going to cost to build another; look at the way Seitaro had handed her everything in the purse in the childish belief that even fifty sen would help in an emergency; Koji worried about things twice as much as other people, so anxious to lend Také his schoolbooks. A sigh welled up inside her but she stifled it and sat there silently, her large masculine hands resting in her lap.

In the afternoon, Ino Grandfather came rushing over to see them in their makeshift home, alarmed by rumors of the fire, and in the evening three other relatives arrived. They were all reassuring, promising to help in whatever way they could with the building of a new house. Later, Nui returned from An'yoji.

"Také and his parents are back from the police."

"Then he will be coming to school with us tomorrow."

Cheerfully Koji wrapped up his first-year books under the lamp. Seitaro watched him silently, knowing that Také and Shigemi, and Kiyokazu and Takematsu would all miss school the next day. He smiled sadly: at this rate, the flag with five stripes would be Komori's forever.

He said nothing though. Instead, he crunched the millet cake Fudé handed to him.

It was one of the cakes Toyota had brought, and it had a sharp, gingery taste.

V

It was the morning of April 1. As he was about to cross Ohashi Bridge over the Katsuragi, Seitaro suddenly looked round to see a

row of docile faces. But the faces of the children who were missing
were the ones that caught his eye: Takematsu, Fusakichi, Shinji;
Kiyokazu and his sister Harue; Shigemi and her brother Yasuo; and,
as expected, Také.

"Can't be helped after a fire like that," he whispered to himself,
to justify their absence; but, ironically, he winced at the same time—a
stinking fire, that *eta* fire.

He raised the village flag; a gesture of the utmost defiance against
the feeling of inferiority that threatened to crush him.

As soon as they passed through the school gates, all the Komori
children gravitated to a corner of the playground where there was a
great pile of stone and timber. A crowd had already gathered there,
and, from the chatter that was going on, it seemed that four new
classrooms, including a sewing room with fitted mats, were to be built
on the south side of the old schoolhouse.

"But that'll mean we'll have too many classrooms, won't it?"

"No, it won't. One's going to be for singing."

"Yes, all the other schools have separate singing and sewing rooms."

"And a nice visitors' room, too."

"We ought to have one here."

"We'll never have a nice school, though, with that Komori lot
here."

"That's right. They were poor good-for-nothings to start with,
but now that they've gone and lost everything in that fire, all they can
think about is building their own homes. Can you imagine them
giving any money to the school?"

"But they should've taken care not to start a fire. Imagine letting
something like that happen. They're hopeless."

There were guffaws as Shigeo Iwase comically raised his hands
to his head in despair.

Holding the flag, Seitaro quietly bore the raucous laughter. Their
plight was indeed "hopeless"; all the more so because it was a village
such as Komori that had suffered the fire.

Yet for onlookers such as Shigeo, it was no more than a joke. They
expected an *eta* village like Komori to be stricken with poverty and
disaster: it was the natural fate of the *eta;* just as it was the will of the
kami and an irreversible social law that the highest born should have
wealth and power.

Seitaro spotted Mr. Egawa coming through the gates and ran toward the school entrance, the flag fluttering out behind him. By the flag-stand, he met the teacher changing into his indoor shoes.

"Your home was burned down, too, wasn't it, Hatanaka?"

"Yes, it was."

"You must have been frightened."

"Yes."

"Is your family all right?"

"Yes."

"Where are you living now?"

"In the shed."

"That must be uncomfortable."

"We'll soon build a fine house."

"Good. I hope to see it soon then. Bear up, Hatanaka, and work hard at school."

Seitaro nodded, beaming with joy. He was his cheerful self again, as if these few kind words had made up for everything they had lost in the fire. Maybe Mr. Egawa would be in charge of his grade that year; the thought made him want to shout at the top of his voice and run around and around the playground until he was breathless.

After the opening ceremony to mark the beginning of the school year, Seitaro peeped into the sixth-grade classroom and saw the newly appointed teacher, Mr. Aojima, standing there. Nearby were Senkichi Sayama and Shigeo Iwase, who had apparently been called in to wipe the teacher's desk.

Seitaro's dream was shattered: the sixth-grade teacher was to be Saburo Aojima, who had recently graduated from teachers' training school.

Presently the bell rang for classes to begin. Seitaro and the others sat down in the same order as in the fifth grade. Mr. Aojima opened the register. The children's names, boys before girls, were listed by village, beginning with Sakata, then Hongawa, Shimana, Azuchi, and lastly Komori. The first was Senkichi Sayama, the oldest of the boys.

There was only one absentee until Mr. Aojima reached Komori, and then the number quickly rose to eight.

"What, are they all absent?" he said, staring at the class. "Kiyokazu Shimura." Again he looked round. There was no reply. "This won't do at all."

Seitaro waited nervously; his name was next. In a high, strained voice, Mr. Aojima called out, "Seitaro Hatanaka."

That instant, four or five children burst out laughing and Seitaro was not quick enough to answer.

With a shrug as if to say "I expect he's absent, too," Mr. Aojima passed on to the next name. "Yozo Samita."

Nobody laughed this time. They had all fallen silent, obviously aware of what had happened.

Mr. Aojima seemed to sense from the atmosphere in the classroom that Yozo was present and called his name again. But Yozo did not answer.

The teacher flushed slightly. "Yozo Samita."

Still no reply.

Senkichi Sayama stood up. "Hatanaka's present, too, sir, but he won't answer."

A glint appeared in Mr. Aojima's eyes. They seemed to Seitaro to pierce him alone and he could not help glaring back.

"Seitaro Hatanaka." The teacher's caustic voice had dropped. Seitaro hunched his shoulders to fend off that low voice.

"Why don't you answer, Hatanaka?"

The teacher now held Seitaro in his gaze, knowing instinctively which boy he was in spite of the silence.

What would happen next? All the children waited with bated breath.

Then, Shigeo yelled out, "The fire's made him dumb."

"I see." Mr. Aojima gave a faint smile, "And has the fire also made Yozo Samita dumb?"

He turned over the page of the register. As Yozo was the last boy, he began calling the girls' names.

Only one of the seven girls listed under Komori was present. This was Makié Minami, and, as if by arrangement with Seitaro and Yozo, she did not answer either when her name was read out.

"There's going to be trouble," Toyota thought to himself anxiously in the back row.

"Good." Mr. Aojima closed the register. His upper lip was twitching. What would he do? Would he start shouting at them?

However, the teacher merely dismissed the class, a cold expression on his face.

"What's wrong, Sei?" asked Toyota, running up as Seitaro left the classroom.

"Nothing special."

"Why didn't you answer?"

"Can't you guess?"

"I s'pose so, but you'll be the loser, Sei, if you put his back up right from the start."

Seitaro ran to a corner of the playground, dragging his friend along with him.

"You said I shouldn't put his back up," he panted, "but he hated me from the start. So I hate him too. Just as much as he hates me."

"Too bad then. It'll be tough, though."

"It's tough anyway for an *eta*," Seitaro almost blurted out.

The children lined up in their village groups and then marched out of the school gates, led by the group with the best attendance rate.

"Don't miss school tomorrow," Toyota reminded his friend, once outside the gates.

Seitaro thumped his chest heroically, displaying his resolve.

As they were crossing the Ohashi Bridge, Yozo Samita started giggling.

"What's up?" asked Seitaro, giggling too for some reason.

"Makié didn't answer either, and I was wondering if she would or not. I thought she was very brave today."

"Of course I didn't," retorted Makié, unsmiling. "The teacher treated Komori different from the rest. Look how his voice changed when he called out Sei's name. That's why everybody laughed. I wouldn't answer a stupid teacher like that, not if he called our names a hundred times. And I won't answer from now on either. I don't care what he says, I'll pretend I don't understand."

Seitaro felt a wave of relief: so the unpleasant prejudice he sensed in the teacher's attitude had not been his imagination. At the same time, however, this made him despondent.

"He's not a teacher, he's a 'bitterguts,'" joked Yozo mischievously.

"Hee, hee . . . Bitterguts—that's a good one." Makie looked mollified. And Seitaro guffawed.

"Bitterguts" was the local name for a *tanago*, a small freshwater fish with unexpectedly bitter-tasting entrails. Mr. Aojima too was a bitterguts, despite his pale good looks.

Yozo picked up a pebble and threw it into the ditch. Spring flowers bloomed along its banks, and in the bottom lived *tanago,* which he was trying to hit; although what he was really aiming at of course was the small, pale face of Old Bitterguts.

At school, next day, there was pandemonium during the first hour as the children changed their places. Seitaro, Yozo, and Makie alone were as quiet as mice. Even in the classroom there was "Komori," and none of the other children would want to sit there. Indeed, when everyone had finished, Seitaro found himself surrounded by the same empty desks as before.

The second lesson was taken up with the purchase of new textbooks; Senkichi and Shigeo acting as sales assistants. The books cost fifty-three sen altogether and were heavy to carry.

During the third lesson, the timetable was altered. After that, Mr. Aojima announced, a tense expression on his face, "The rest of the day will be devoted to spring cleaning the school. Tomorrow—Saturday—is a holiday. Can anyone tell me why?"

Several hands went up but even though Seitaro's was not among them, the teacher called upon him to answer.

"Drat," he whispered to himself. Out loud he said, pausing deliberately after every word, "It's the anniversary of the Emperor Jinmu."

"Correct. And why is it held on this particular day?"

"It's the day he died," volunteered Shigeo.

"Toyota Matsuzaki, tell us about the Emperor Jinmu's eastern expedition."

To the other children this sounded rather difficult, but Toyota replied without faltering, repeating everything he had learned in history: how the Emperor Jinmu left Mount Takachiho in Hyuga and passed through Naniwa and Kii, and about the crow Yata-no-karasu that was sent to guide him into the land of Yamato; and how, on an expedition to overthrow Nagasune-hiko and his followers, a golden kite came and perched on the Emperor's bow, blinding the villains.

Mr. Aojima looked very pleased. "Well remembered, Matsuzaki. Now, since tomorrow is the anniversary of this revered emperor, who was the founder of our great empire, I hope you will all go and worship at his tomb. And even better if you also worship at the Kashiwara Shrine. Can anybody tell me why there is a shrine there?"

"Because that's where the Emperor Jinmu was enthroned." This time it was Senkichi who answered. His mother came from Kumé, a village near the Kashiwara Shrine, and he went over there four or five times a year. He always played soldiers behind the shrine; an ideal spot with its hill, pond, and wood.

Mr. Aojima leaned forward over his desk. "Hands up, all those who will be going to worship at the Emperor Jinmu's tomb."

More than half the boys in the class raised their hands.

Seitaro stared at them absent-mindedly, lost in thought; he was pondering over the Emperor Jinmu's tomb. His aunt lived nearby in a village called Michi, on the northwest side of Unebi Hill.

She was Fudé's elder sister and had left her home in Ino to go and live there when she married. She had four children, and the youngest daughter was the same age as Seitaro. Fudé had taken him to Michi once on a visit, and he could still remember the steep hillside behind the house where there was a hut, its door wide open, beside a protruding rock. He had been too young then to notice how many houses there were in the village but the smoke rising from them seemed to curl around and around the hill endlessly, and he had retained an impression of a desolate place. It was after all an *eta* village.

Was it not strange, though, to think that one of these detested *eta* villages should be found on Unebi Hill, where there was an imperial tomb?

More to the point, why did the *eta* have to be detested in the first place? Why did they have to meet with such prejudice and contempt? Were they really so dreadful?

"Sir!" he cried out desperately. He suddenly wanted to hurl himself head-on at all the questions looming before him.

"Yes?" Mr. Aojima flinched as if caught off guard. "What is it, Hatanaka?"

"I want to know something, sir."

"What about?"

"About the villains."

"The villains? Oh, you mean to do with Nagasune-hiko, on the Emperor Jinmu's eastern expedition."

"Yes. What had they done wrong?"

"They rose against the Emperor. I thought Matsuzaki had explained all that perfectly well."

"I don't mean that, sir. I want to know what they'd done wrong."

"And I've just told you, they defied the Emperor. Only villains defy those in authority, those we look up to and revere; and that has always been so, throughout history. Do you understand?" Mr. Aojima barked out the last words as if they were an order. He looked round the class, "Do you all understand?"

"Yes, we do, sir," answered Senkichi, assuming the role of class representative. Seitaro felt the blood rushing to his head in rebellion. But at that moment, a chair was pushed back with a clatter as somebody in the back row stood up.

"I don't understand, sir."

It was Toyota. The girls sniggered; he still had a marked Osaka accent that at times such as this sounded very funny.

Mr. Aojima could not help grinning either. "What is it you don't understand, Matsuzaki?"

"Well, I don't see why the Emperor Jinmu bothered to go all that way from Hyuga to the land of Yamato when there were all those villains there, like Nagasune-hiko and the Shiki brothers. Japan's a big country and he could have gone somewhere else where there weren't any bad people."

"Ha, ha, ha . . . What funny things you come out with, Matsuzaki. The Emperor Jinmu embarked on his eastern expedition because this area of Yamato was then the best place from which to rule Japan."

"And Nagasune-hiko got there first, didn't he?"

"Yes, I suppose he did. Nagasune-hiko was a scoundrel and so he tried to resist the Emperor Jinmu, the descendant of the Sun Goddess, Amaterasu."

"I wonder why?"

"Well that's because he was a scoundrel."

"But he was still Japanese, wasn't he? And the other side was a *kami*. That's what I don't see—why did a *kami* have to defeat Nagasune-hiko in a battle?"

"It was the divine decree of the Sun Goddess that her descendants should rule over the Rich Reed-Plain of Yamato forever. But Nagasune-hiko tried his utmost to resist this by military force. And that is why such a scoundrel had to be overthrown. Now do you understand?"

"No, I don't," Toyota felt like saying. And Seitaro wanted to yell, "That's a load of rubbish. Why would a *kami* come down here from heaven?" But the bell rang, putting an end to the debate.

Mr. Aojima bowed to the pupils with military-style formality and hastened out of the classroom.

VI

"Do you think Také'll come to school tomorrow, Seitaro?" asked Koji, sitting under the lamp.

"Poor little Také. He does nothing but cry all day. Why don't you both try and cheer him up a bit and take him along to school with you?" said Fudé, a quiver in her voice, clattering the dishes as she washed up in the narrow makeshift kitchen.

"Tosaku's an odd fellow an' no mistake," said Nui, in a tone of strong disapproval. It was rumored that Tosaku Nagai was mistreating his son at every opportunity for having brought disaster on them with his prank. Moreover, he now refused to speak to his neighbors unless absolutely necessary, which was another source of grievance to victims of the fire such as herself.

Fudé too was tempted to censure Tosaku for his behavior. With all the frustration of the daily discomforts she had to endure, she could not help feeling bitter now about the fire, despite having managed at first to console herself with the thought that it was "fate."

Nevertheless, she and Nui were feeling a little more comfortable at last. Her father had come over from Ino with a carpenter both yesterday and today, and laid down floorboards and then tatami mats in a corner of the shed, making the semblance of a room there.

After tidying up the kitchen area, Fudé wiped her wet hands and peered under the lamp at Koji, who was curled up over a book. Seitaro was wrapping up his textbooks for the next day.

"Do you know who your teacher is yet, Koji?"

"The Headmaster."

"Imagine the Headmaster taking the second grade. Who have you got then, Seitaro?"

"A new teacher," he replied, without looking up.

"What's he called?"

"Bitterguts." Seitaro tied the ends of the wrapper as tight as he could.

"You shouldn't call him that. You'll be in for a scolding if he finds out."

"He looks just like a bitterguts, though."

"Ah, ha, ha . . . I can just see him. I bet he's pale-looking and hard to figure out—you can't tell if he's kind, or strict, or what," Nui declared loudly.

As if drawn by the sound of her voice, Kané Shimura, Kiyokazu's mother, pushed aside the straw mat hanging down over the entrance and peered in at the room with its tatami.

"Goodness, you've got a fine house now, haven't you?"

Like the other victims of the fire, her family had already built a shed among the debris of their former home, and smoke was now rising again three times a day from the stove they had set up under the overhanging thatched eaves.

It was little short of a miracle the way they all had survived the disaster without harm to mind or body, continuing to light their fires and draw their water as usual, even though their few possessions had been reduced to ashes. Perhaps there was a natural resilience in people; or was it that the bleakness of their own lives, of having to bathe and defecate out of doors, had fostered a particular toughness of spirit?

"Yes, we're lucky," said Nui, making room for Kané to sit down. "We've got a proper floor to sleep on from tonight. Now there's no excuse not to live to a ripe old age. Been a good experience, I suppose." She laughed.

"Yes, you really appreciate the comfort of tatami when you have to do without it. It's not much fun making do with a thin mat on the ground. Well, I'll just sit down with you for a few moments," and Kané knelt down slowly.

"But it's lucky it happened when it did, with summer ahead of us. Imagine if it had been autumn—that really would've been a wasp on a tear-stained face."

"Ah, ha, ha . . . If there's a wasp on your tear-stained face, things can't be that bad. No wasp'd sting our face."

Seitaro and Koji hooted at this remark of Kané's.

Fudé chuckled too and then said, "That's very true. Seitaro's always being ticked off at school, but like the wasp it's better than not being ticked off at all."

"Of course it is. The worst thing is when even the wasp won't sting you. Kiyokazu says he won't go back to school because he doesn't like being ticked off by the teacher. But me and his dad want him to start again tomorrow. We've both had a hard time of it not being able to read and we don't want our son facing the same difficulties. But it's only natural for parents to feel like that. I can't figure out a man like Tosaku that'd send all three of his daughters into service. And going on the funny way he does, telling us to thrash the kid if we've got any complaints, seeing as he was the one who started the fire. I mean to say, how could any grown person thrash such a little boy? What it boils down to is that Tosaku doesn't want to lose any money over it. Také may've started the fire, but a child's prank is his parents' responsibility. It's only right and proper for Tosaku to sell his land and repay us for all we've lost.''

"Has Shigé gone into service as well?"

Nui seemed to speak so slowly after Kané's torrent of words, but, for that reason, Seitaro was all the more stunned by what she said. The daughters in question were Natsu, Toku, and then Shigemi; Tosaku's other children were all sons.

"Has Shigé gone to Osaka?" Fudé asked anxiously.

"I expect so. They say the oldest girl's going to be a nurse and Shigé a nursemaid, but what sort of nursing that'll turn out to be, your guess is as good as mine. And Tosaku's going to build a fine, four-roomed house with a tiled roof with the advance he gets on the three girls—downright scandalous, I call it."

"Takes all types, I must say," Nui responded.

"It does indeed. Now Sei, don't forget to take Kiyo to school with you tomorrow. I've scraped together the money for his books."

Kané left, and, in the silence that followed, they suddenly heard the sound of frogs croaking.

Seitaro flopped down onto the tatami and glared into space. Different faces appeared, one after another: Mr. Otori, the Headmaster; Mr. Egawa; Old Bitterguts; Senkichi and Shigeo; Toyota and Kiyokazu; and lastly, Shigemi.

"Don't let it get you down, Shigé, even if things are tough. Anyway, it wouldn't be any fun if you came to school this year, with Old Bitterguts in charge of us. You're better off working in Osaka," he said silently, expecting her to nod in agreement; but all at once, Shigemi's face crumpled. Seitaro too was on the verge of tears. He thrashed his arms about in the air, with a meaningless cry.

"You'll catch cold, Seitaro, dropping off like that," said Nui, tapping him on the shoulder.

"I didn't drop off."

"I thought you just talked in your sleep. I'd lay out the mattress and go to bed if I was you. You've got to be fresh tomorrow to work hard at school."

However, Seitaro was not sleepy. Neither was Koji; he was worrying about what Auntie Kané had said.

"I wonder if Také'll come to school tomorrow."

"Course he will. The teacher'll come looking for him if he starts missing school in the first grade."

"Won't the teacher come looking for Shigé, then?"

"Won't make any difference if he does. Her dad's made her leave."

"Poor Shigé."

"Mm," murmured Seitaro vaguely.

Shigemi's name cropped up again next morning when Kiyokazu mentioned her, to Seitaro's surprise.

"I saw Shigé go off to Osaka yesterday. She was in hemp-soled sandals and went with a lady not from round here. She looked so miserable. Just shows, even a Hachimero's scared of going to a strange place."

Seitaro merely grunted evasively, as he had done last night.

Shigemi's little brother, Také, walked hand-in-hand with Koji all the way to school, but, when they reached the gates, he suddenly broke free and ran off.

Yozo, who was at the back of the line of children, promptly caught him. "You mustn't run away, Také."

"Let go, let go!" Také wriggled and squirmed, a look of terror in his eyes.

"You can't go back when you've only just got here."

"I'm scared."

"There's nothing to be scared of. If anybody's unkind to you, I'll punch them."

"I want to go home . . ." and Také burst into tears, much to the others' dismay.

Children from Sakata and Shimana looked on from a safe distance, as if keeping clear of a piece of dirt. Také was now sobbing wildly and, in his stained kimono and filthy apron, he looked a very strange

sight to them. The most appropriate name for such an odd creature
was *eta*. The children exchanged meaningful glances:

"He's an *eta*."

"That's why he looks so dirty."

"Only an *eta*'d howl like that."

Of course, there were some who sighed inwardly, feeling sorry
for Také, but even they had not the slightest intention of comforting
or looking after him. Had they not been taught that to be born an
eta was a matter of karma, determined by the deeds of a previous
existence and beyond man's power to alter? Therefore, although
they might sympathize in secret with the *eta*, they were convinced
that nothing could be done to improve their sorry lot. After all, it
was the same for commoners like themselves; none of them could
ever belong to the Imperial Family, however much they might wish
to do so.

But why was that *eta* kid howling so much? It was very strange;
he sounded frightened, terror-stricken even. What could he possibly
be so scared of?

This was also a mystery to the other Komori children. They kept
trying to comfort him, "There's nothing to be scared of. Nothing
at all."

But Také was scared. He was terrified of the gleaming glass windows and the figures he glimpsed through them, in those foreign-
looking clothes. They were exactly like the foreign clothes and glass
windows he had seen when his father had taken him to Takada police
station, the morning after the fire.

Several frightening policemen had been there and a fat one, with
a particularly large mustache, had said to him, "Now, I want you to
tell us how you started the fire. And no lies, mind you, or you'll be tied
up. How did you light the match?"

Také said not a word, overcome with fear. His father cuffed him
on the top of his head.

"I didn't tell you to hit him." The man with the mustache threw
an angry glance at Tosaku out of the corner of his eye, and then
addressed Také once more, "You struck the match on the stove, didn't
you?"

"Mm," Také nodded.

"Then you lit the straw?"

"Mm," he nodded again.

"It was fun watching it burn, wasn't it?"

"Mm."

"Well done. You've answered like a good boy," and the man with the mustache gave him a whole packet of rice crackers. Také sobbed as he clasped the packet; and sobbed all the way home, without eating a single cracker.

He cried countless times afterwards as well. He could not help it; he would suddenly see those glass windows and foreign-looking clothes. But each time, his father would cuff him on the head—"Little bastard, starting that fire." Then Také would howl even louder, fear turning to rage; his body almost buckled with resentment.

He had struck a match and had lit some straw. It had been fun watching it burn. But he had never dreamt it would start a great fire.

He had lit the straw in the stove, put some broad beans in a pan on top and parched them, stirring them round and round with his chopsticks.

"Daimonja" Tomizo had been whimpering fretfully from hunger, but he stopped as soon as Také had begun cooking the beans, and crawled backward and forward by the stove.

Také dutifully crushed the beans with his teeth before giving them to Tomizo; and, naturally, he had a few himself.

All at once, he noticed some puffs of smoke coming from the bundle of straw in the corner by the stove. He pushed the straw away in surprise and immediately, flames leapt up into the air.

He ran to the well and drew some water. But there was no bucket in which to carry it and the fire spread rapidly while he was searching for one. In the end, all he could do was flee.

Také thought that he would be in for a terrible beating if his father discovered he had been parching beans. "*Eta* sweets," people from other villages rudely called them; but in Komori they were indeed relished as much as real sweets made from syrup, and hunger had driven him to cook and eat some in secret.

As he hid trembling under the raised floor of An'yoji, he had made up his mind that he must not tell a soul about the beans. He did not feel guilty about having taken them; it was simply that he feared the beating he would receive.

"Isn't he like Shigemi Nagai?" commented one of the children, who stood round some way off.

"He's Hachimero's brother," said another.

"He's the one that started the fire."

"What's the use of a little hoodlum like that coming to school?"

"Go home, troublemaker, go home!"

A stone flew through the air. At once the flag Seitaro was carrying swayed violently.

"You beasts!"

The girls ran off screaming.

"Teacher, the *eta* are making trouble again," they cried, as they ran.

"They're waving their flag about and making trouble."

In the midst of the noise and confusion, Také stopped howling. He wiped his eyes and runny nose with the back of his hand. In his own childish way, he had grasped the situation and could not go on crying anymore: from that day on, he would be labeled an *eta* kid, the young hoodlum who started the fire.

VII

Instead of sweet nectar, the Chinese milk vetch had now started to adorn itself with pods, slender as threads of silk, inside of which new life was ripening day by day.

Not to be outdone, the rape plant was also nurturing new life, its seedpods lined up regularly from the top to the bottom of the stem.

According to the old calendar, last night was *hachiju-hachi-ya*—the eighty-eighth night since the beginning of spring—and today, May 3, the sky had the look of summer.

Fudé was crouched over the rice seedbed. Satisfied, she whispered to herself, "Yes, that's fine."

The seeds were about to sprout. The good weather helped, but the bed was also wet enough and had been manured correctly. Fudé calculated what sort of crop they could expect in the autumn. She was always impatient for the harvest, but this year, in particular, there was the added burden of building a new house, and she desperately wanted a good crop—an extra five to seven *sho* a quarter-acre, if possible.

"Morning."

It was Tosaku's wife, Sayo. She came toward Fudé, rustling the grass on the ridge between the fields. No doubt she too had come straight out to look at the seedbed without stopping to wash. It was vital to ensure that the beds were under the right amount of water for the next day or two, and nobody who grew rice had time to spare in the morning for washing or eating breakfast.

Sayo splashed her face in the ditch by the bed, using her apron as a towel. The apron was filthy, its striped pattern no longer visible; but despite this she looked refreshed.

"I was thinking of coming round to say how grateful I am. That young rascal of mine's settled down at school now thanks to you."

Fudé hesitated, slightly unsure of how to react: it still took very little to upset people in Komori, though they were gradually beginning to behave normally to each other again, a month having now elapsed since the fire.

However, Sayo continued pleasantly enough, "Yes, it's all thanks to your Koji. Také doesn't mind going to school a bit now with Koji always ready to stick up for him if any of the others are unkind."

Fudé had guessed as much. Children were continually jeering at Také both in Komori and at school—"Firebug, firebug!" they shouted. It was no more than a game to them, but each time he heard it Také winced. Aware of this, Koji would flare up on his behalf. A smile came to Fudé's lips as she pictured his expression then.

Sayo was the first to stand up. Walking along by the ditch, she said, "Yesterday, Také told us the teacher ticked his slate. I asked what he wrote and he laughed and pointed at me. His dad had a look and do you know what, he'd gone and written my name. Would you believe it, when all I ever do is box his ears. I never make a fuss of him, you know. Not that I don't like the kid. I know I was mad when he got up to that dreadful prank, and gave him the rough side of my tongue all right, but now, I can't help feeling I was a bit hard on him."

Sayo rubbed her eyes; they looked sore at the best of times but they were even redder now.

Fudé too felt the sting of tears welling up.

"You'll laugh I bet, but I've a hunch Také's going to like school as much as Koji. I know he started the fire, but he didn't do it on purpose, did he, and it's downright unkind the way they keep shouting 'Firebug, firebug.' But that's people for you. They're the same to me, too—'She's the mother of that brat who started the fire,' they say. You don't know how awful it is . . . Anyway, I know it sounds silly, but it's nice to think that maybe Také'll come back with another big tick on his slate."

"Yes, I'm just the same. I get all excited one minute and worried the next, wondering how the children will look when they get back from school."

They both fell silent; there would be no end to their tale of woe if they said any more. Their sufferings were such that the only thing to do was to push them quietly aside and keep them hidden.

The grasses growing by the ditch rustled gently beneath their bare feet.

That day, however, neither Také's first-grade class nor Koji's second were using their books or slates. The pupils were all stark naked and three teachers were measuring their height, weight, and chests.

Some of the girls had started to cry, upset at having to take their clothes off, but the boys were even more full of beans than usual, thoroughly enjoying the novelty of their nakedness.

Seitaro's sixth-grade class also had a physical examination in the afternoon, but the children did not frisk about like those in the lower forms. The girls in particular grew very quiet when Mr. Aojima told them; some started to worry about their dirty underwear; others were ashamed of their budding breasts, as if they were evil.

"Shall we strip down to our drawers, sir?" asked Senkichi Sayama. Knowing they would be examined in the order of the register, he started undoing his sash as soon as they lined up in the corridor outside the examination room.

"That's right. Strip down to your drawers. You can't be weighed correctly in kimono."

"What about the ones that aren't wearing drawers?" asked Shigeo Iwase, also undoing his sash.

"There can't be any sixth graders without drawers, surely," Mr. Aojima sniggered.

"Yes, there are."

"Who?"

"The kids from Komori. They never wear drawers. Ha, ha, ha . . ."

"Ha, ha. The things you know, Iwase."

"I'll tell you something else, sir. They can't crap and piss at the same time because of not wearing drawers."

"Can't they?"

"No, they can't. You ask them."

"Is that true?" Mr. Aojima's gaze fell on Seitaro.

"Rubbish!" To say any more would be a waste of words. Seitaro tore off his clothes.

Some of the children gasped, others stared wide-eyed and Toyota Matsuzaki grinned broadly: Seitaro was in a pair of white cotton drawers—the most effective reply he could make.

"Look, Hatanaka's in drawers, isn't he? He may be from Komori, but really!" Mr. Aojima sounded as if he were trying to appease Seitaro.

However, Seitaro also took off his drawers.

Immediately, there was uproar; all the children tried to undress the fastest. And many from other villages besides Komori were without underpants.

"Everybody take off your drawers. You get beaten if you wear them for an army medical," cried Toyota, untying the fastening of his own calico ones. He ran to the examination room with Seitaro.

First their weight and height were measured, and then their chests. Mr. Egawa, who was in charge of the latter, beamed as he passed the tape measure round Seitaro. "You're a fine, strapping lad, Hatanaka."

Seitaro felt the teacher's smile touch something deep inside him.

"You'd certainly pass the army medical with flying colors."

Finally, Mr. Egawa tapped his back. Although he had no cough, a tear trickled down Seitaro's cheek.

VIII

Clouds were gathering far away to the south, in the direction of Yoshino. They billowed up into mountains, which then changed into monsters. The monsters advanced northward toward the center of the basin.

"We're in for a heavy shower this evening," said Nui, with conviction.

"The rice'll be ruined if it doesn't rain soon." Fudé was so impatient for the shower that her face wore an unusually discontented expression.

A curtain of rain hid Unebi Hill, and in no time it was beating down on their heads with the force of a waterfall.

Nui could not stop laughing. Nor could Fudé conceal her delight.

Seitaro and Koji stuck their heads out of the back door and were hit by the downpour. There was a clap of thunder and a streak of lightning, not that it scared them in the slightest. Let the lightning flash, the thunder growl, and the rain come down in torrents!

Their grandmother had been out of sorts for at least the last twenty days. Their mother had also grown increasingly quiet and appeared to have completely forgotten the subject of the new house they were to build, which she had talked of constantly until they transplanted the rice seedlings. For since then, there had been no rain to speak of and the paddy was now dry and cracked, and the new rice shoots seemed about to wither. A shower at such a critical time as this was truly a godsend.

"You know what they say, 'an evening shower, three days.' It's bound to rain again if you get a shower in the evening. We'll have a good crop yet," said Nui presently, as she watched the clouds move away northwestward.

Not wanting to waste a moment, Fudé was busy doing *yokiri,* although she had the feeling there was some other chore she should be tackling. Then she caught sight of Tosaku and his wife running along the footpath between the paddies on the outskirts of the village.

"Oh, of course," and she ran to the well to grab a bucket.

"Don't bother, Fudé," said Nui gently. "I'm sure the paddy's wet enough now."

"But it's a good idea to give it some more, even one extra bucketful. And now the soil's damp, it'll hold the water better. Sayo and her husband have gone running to their field."

"I'll help, Mom," said Seitaro, overhearing them, and he rushed out barefoot.

"All right, give it two or three bucketfuls. I'll be getting supper ready. We'll have something special to celebrate the rain."

In her heart, though, Nui knew it would not make much difference, however many bucketfuls they scraped up. Another farmer only had to set up a waterwheel further along the irrigation ditch, lifting all the water into his own paddy, and the fight would be lost. And there were several Sakata farmers with waterwheels who owned fields near the ones they and Tosaku cultivated. The odds were against them, no matter how hard they struggled.

Nevertheless, she did at least want to cook something special this evening to celebrate the rainfall and to make an offering at the family shrine. She went out to the patch at the back where there was a fine array of all kinds of vegetables: eggplants, pumpkins, kidney beans, corn, taros, and sweet potatoes. It was still too early for most of them, apart from the eggplants and kidney beans, but that meant there was all the more to look forward to in the autumn. Then she would pull up taros, dig up potatoes . . .

Nui suddenly realized her apron was bulging with beans and eggplants. Koji, who had been helping her pick them, stopped and gazed around him.

"Didn't there used to be a house here a long time ago, Gran?" he asked.

"Yes, about the time your father was born," she replied, supporting the heavy apron with her right hand.

"Where do the people who lived here live now?"

"Osaka, or so they say."

"What are they doing there?"

"I wonder. If they're in Osaka, that is. I haven't set eyes on them for thirty years."

"But why did they go to Osaka? Was their house burnt down?"

"No, it was because they were so hard up, though I s'pose it comes to the same thing."

"Oh."

"That's why folks have to work hard. You can't stay in the place you were born if you're stone broke."

"But Gran, Osaka's a nice place. I like Osaka. And I like Kyoto even better."

"Ha, ha, ha . . . How do you know when you've never been there?"

"But it says so in the books. Osaka and Kyoto and Tokyo are full of nice things."

"I should think they are with all them big shots there."

"Komori's not up to much, is it, Gran?"

"I wouldn't say that. You can do very well even in Komori if you work hard enough at school. That's why me and your mother'd like to send you to middle school. We've been thinking about it and decided we can't build that new house. It'd take all the money we've got and then we couldn't afford to send you to school. You want to go there like Master Hidé, don't you, Koji?"

"Yes, I do." He wanted to add, "But the middle-school students'd probably pick on me and shout '*Eta, eta.*' That's what they did to Master Hidé. I wonder why Komori's *eta*, Gran."

Unable to speak of such things, he ran off to hide in the middle of a thick clump of corn. The leaves rustled, spilling raindrops onto his collar.

"Look, there's a rainbow, Koji."

Nui's spirits rose. The welcome shower had not only revived the parched rice but given her fresh hope.

"Where? Where?" Koji peered out from the shelter of the rows of corn.

To the east, beyond the Katsuragi, a rainbow curved in a wide arc from Unebi Hill right over Miminashi Hill.

"What a marvel it is," sighed Nui. There were no words to describe the grandeur of nature.

Fudé was frantically scooping up water that had collected in the ditch when she too caught sight of the seven-colored arch and cried out, "Oh, there's a rainbow. Isn't it marvelous!"

Seitaro put down his bucket. "It looks as if it starts at Michi where Auntie lives."

"So it does."

"There's nothing so marvelous about it though, Mom. It's only sunlight catching the moisture in the air."

"I still think it's marvelous. Look at those colors, they're like nothing else."

"They say a rainbow in the evening brings twenty days of dry weather," butted in Tosaku, who had been scraping the bottom of the ditch with his bucket. "It'll be blazing again tomorrow, you'll see. I don't know why you're praising the damned rainbow."

"Fancy swearing at a rainbow," and Sayo went off into peals of laughter.

Fudé knew why Tosaku was in such a bad mood: there was less rainwater in the ditch than he had expected, and he was not at all pleased at having to share even that with the Hatanakas.

Fudé crawled out of the ditch. "But they also say 'an evening shower, three days,' Mr. Nagai, so you never know, it may rain again tomorrow."

"I dare say it would, if luck was with us, but it certainly ain't this year. Our houses are burnt down, the fields are parched—things are going from bad to worse.''

''That's enough of your miserable talk. He's a real wet blanket, Fudé. It always puts him in a bad mood if anybody's happy. He has to go and spoil it. Nobody knows what the weather'll do tomorrow, anyway; we should just be grateful for rain today, however little,'' said Sayo, a conciliatory expression on her face.

Fudé listened with a smile, but at heart she felt uneasy, as if they were living under a curse. Twenty days of dry weather—things were going from bad to worse—yes, that was probably how it would be in such a disastrous year as this, when even their house had burnt down.

''I'll catch you lots of mudfish tomorrow, Mom, if there's another shower and the stream starts flowing again,'' said Seitaro cheerfully, on the way home. ''I can soon catch masses with a trap.''

But his promise was in vain. There was no shower the next day, or the following, or the one after that. It looked as if the winner was not ''an evening shower, three days'' but ''an evening rainbow, twenty days dry weather.''

IX

By the end of July, all the irrigation ponds in the Nara basin had dried up and the freshwater mussel shells lay pathetically agape. A puddle of water remained in the bottom of some conical-shaped ponds, but evidently not enough for the fish, judging by the pale bodies of roach and *tanago* floating there.

The belts of hot sand now traversing the basin were only rivers in name. Maybe there was also a drought in the mountainous area of Yoshino, which had sometimes recorded the highest rainfall in Japan. Or was the Yoshino watershed perversely supplying the Totsu and Kitayama rivers and irrigating the Kumano area of Kii?

The farmers began to lose their faith in nature, exasperated by the drought. But one group still had a last resort: the artesian well in a corner of their land, from which they could draw water by means of a long pole, or sweep, with a bucket attached.

Nui and Fudé had such a well, complete with sweep, for their sole use, on the half-acre of land they rented. Normally, they kept it covered with a stout lid, over which they spread soil and grew crops, but in times of drought they used it for irrigation, mounting the sweep on a support. Of course, there was a higher rent for land with an artesian well, as much as ten bushels a quarter-acre, which was about what Nui and Fudé had to pay.

In the midst of their troubles it was a comfort to find that the sweep, bucket, and support had survived the fire and were safely stored away up in the rafters of the shed. On Sunday, July 25, they asked their neighbor Hirokichi Shimura to help them open the well.

Seitaro and Koji lent a hand in drawing the water. Their job was to pull down the end of the sweep. There was often a heavy stone at the end acting as a counterweight, but this only made it harder to lower the bucket, and it was in fact easier to have a lighter stone and then raise it by hand—in other words, to have a human counter-weight, a role that usually fell to children.

In spite of going to such lengths to obtain water, the soil remained as dry as a bone, the cracks in the paddy swallowing up one bucketful after another. But Fudé continued to wield the bucket briskly until Nui took over; they simply could not afford to stop while there was any water left in the well.

Seitaro and Koji shouted and sang as they strained at the sweep, thoroughly enjoying the novelty of the situation.

"You'll have to stick at it, mind you," said Fudé, when it was her turn to take a rest. "We'll have to carry on with this watering every day until the end of *doyo** if there's no rain."

"Don't worry. I'll work the sweep all during the summer holidays." Seitaro was in fine fettle. The school holidays began the next day, five days earlier than usual.

Fudé laughed. "That's more than I'm prepared to do. We'll die of starvation if we have to water the paddy by hand all summer. We've got to have some rain by the end of *doyo* at the latest . . ."

"Yes, we won't save the crop just watering it like this. We've got to have some rain, even if it's only an evening shower," added Nui. Their desperate struggle to water the paddy from the well was only a stopgap measure after all, and without proper rainfall the autumn harvest would certainly be ruined.

When it was his turn to rest, Koji began gleefully kneading some earth. The bucket had brought up many greenish lumps of mud, which were ideal for modeling. He fashioned a cow and a horse, and then a dog and a rabbit, lining them up in a row. The rabbit's long ears soon dried and dropped off.

Fudé had brought along some rice balls for both the "early snack" at ten o'clock and the afternoon one at three. After the latter, Seitaro eagerly seized a lump of mud as well. "I'm going to make a man," he announced.

The gush of water from under the ground had grown weaker and Nui and Fudé were sitting on the ridge, resting.

"No, it's no good. A face is too difficult to do. I can't get the shape of the head right, either," he said dispiritedly. After a while though, he managed to produce something resembling a man.

Fudé stared at the figure with its narrow forehead and giggled. "It looks like a monkey with its mouth sticking out like that and such a small head."

"No, it's a man all right. It reminds me of Tosaku," praised Nui.

Seitaro started molding another figure.

"I think I'll try." Fudé grabbed some mud. Nui too reached for a lump, and in no time, they were both busy fashioning whatever shape took their fancy . . .

All thought of the drought and ruined harvest vanished from their minds. A gentle smile softened their faces as cares faded away at the sight of a single leaf, the ginkgo leaf their fingers had given life to . . . A feeling of content stole over them.

It was short-lived however.

"Mrs. Hatanaka," came the voice of Tosaku. "All working yourselves to the bone, I see."

Clad in nothing but a loincloth—and that was loose—his body was burnt the shade of copper.

"Come over here into the shade. You must be hot." Nui moved her knees. The one spot of shade was provided by an oiled-paper umbrella.

"Ha, ha . . . I don't give a damn about the heat; it's the water shortage that's hurting."

"We're all in the same boat, you know."

"Ah, now that's where you're wrong. It wouldn't be so bad if we were in the same boat."

Fudé was startled. Nui was tense; she knew what he was driving at.

Tosaku stood there stiffly, arms folded, and then said, "Now be reasonable, Mrs. Hatanaka. I only want to use the well once every three days."

"That's all right by us but . . . "

"We farmers've got to stick together."

There was silence.

"It's no good you thinking it doesn't matter about anybody else just so long as you've got water."

"But we're tenant farmers. We can't say yes without talking it over with the landlord, Mr. Sayama."

"You're just making excuses."

"Well, Tosaku, why don't you go and talk it over with Mr. Sayama yourself this evening? You can use the well tomorrow if he agrees."

"Do you think I'd be here now if it'd do any good talking to him? That old skinflint'd begrudge me even one bucketful. Now listen here, Mrs. Hatanaka, and you too, Fudé; half the water from this well has seeped in from my land and that's all I want to draw." With this parting shot, Tosaku stalked off.

"The heat must've gone to his head, Fudé."

"Yes, I've never heard anything like it. Of all the crazy things . . ." Fudé spat on the ground and seized the rod at the end of the sweep from which the bucket hung. There was the reassuring splash of the bucket hitting water; the well had filled up again.

Seitaro threw away his lump of clay and grabbed the rope dangling from the other end of the pole.

An evening breeze had sprung up when the well ran dry again.

"It's a good time to stop. I bet you're both worn out. We'll call it a day," said Fudé, and took the bucket off the sweep; it would be foolish to leave that behind.

"Shall I carry it for you, Mom?" Seitaro offered, but Fudé shouldered it herself.

"You've both got somebody to see on your way home, haven't you?"

"Hee, hee . . . How do you know?"

"Well, I don't," said Nui, with a smile.

"Master Hidé's meant to be coming home today from his school in Kyoto. I wonder if he's really back."

Fudé came to a sudden halt and pointed at the rice leaves. "Seitaro, Koji, look."

Now, as the sun set, the leaves that had been dark and crinkled all day were unfurled, quivering in the slight breeze. The rice was still alive.

Tosaku's crop, by contrast, was in a critical state, standing rigidly, the leaves wrinkled up.

"That settles it. We must carry on with this watering until it rains, come what may. So you both be ready to work the sweep again tomorrow."

"Yes, we will, we will," called back Seitaro and Koji, as they ran. The roof of An'yoji rose before them.

X

"Is Master Hidé back?" asked Nui.

"Yeah, he's back," replied Seitaro.

"He gave us these," said Koji, holding up a spray of oleander.

"What lovely flowers. Why don't you make an offering of them?" Nui opened the doors of the family shrine; it was the twenty-fifth, the anniversary of her husband's death.

"How is Master Hidé?" asked Fudé.

"Fine. He looks as if he's put on a bit of weight."

"There's lots of good things to eat in Kyoto, I expect."

But it was not only the food, Seitaro thought; it was because in Kyoto there were no students to sneer at him for being an *eta,* as there had been at Unebi Middle School. Not that he had asked Hideaki of course; he had not needed to, he had sensed as much the minute he set eyes on him.

He was standing beneath the oleander. Its crimson flowers looked darker in the twilight, but Hidéaki's light summer kimono was a jubilant white. And one glance at that crisply starched, white kimono had told Seitaro all he wanted to know.

"Come over and see us if it rains, Master Hidé," he said.

"It soon will, Sei. They're going to hold torchlight processions all over the place to pray for rain," Hidéaki had replied, with a little smile.

Fudé burnt a pile of broad bean shells as they sipped their supper of gruel under the eaves. A sulphur-yellow smoke rose from the shells, driving away the mosquitoes, which were particularly vicious at the height of summer.

"Look, it's cloudy again this evening. Gran was right. She said the evenings are cloudy in a drought," cried Seitaro, putting down his chopsticks, more impressed with Nui's fund of natural wisdom than the menace of a prolonged dry spell.

They all stepped out from under the eaves. The sky above was overcast, as if rain was imminent.

"Weather's a funny thing. The sun'll be beating down again by nine o'clock tomorrow morning, you see if it ain't."

Nui sounded more cheerful than she had of late. She felt calmer, no longer gazing up at the sky in anxiety and frustration, wondering if it would rain the next day, or the day after. In fact, she had no time to spare to fret over the drought, now that it was so advanced; besides which, it was a comfort to know that at least they had the artesian well. She derived a certain satisfaction from this knowledge, feeling a sense of superiority over those who did not possess such a last resort.

Fudé was no different. "I wonder what they'll do over at Tosaku's," she thought, and, picturing the worried faces of Tosaku and his wife, said to Nui lightheartedly, "We'll just have to stick it out. This fine weather can't go on forever, can it? Same as it never goes on raining forever."

The next morning, she rose before four, and by half past five the family was ready to set off.

A waterpot in one hand, Koji ran ahead, trampling down the grass on the ridge. It was wet with dew, belying the continuous dry weather.

"If it wasn't for all this worry about water, I'd say there's nothing nicer than a summer morning," remarked Nui, who was following him.

"The mountains are enjoying it. Still fast asleep," laughed Fudé behind her. Mounts Katsuragi, Kongo, Nijo, Shigi, and Ikoma lay hidden in the thick morning haze, as if they were slumbering peacefully.

Seitaro, who brought up the rear, began singing, marching along in time.

At the outset of the Gempei War
Came the battle of Fujikawa.
Over fifty thousand Heiké troops,
Startled by waterfowl on the wing,
Fled in the night, forgetting their weapons.

Once more the Heiké were put to rout
At Kurikaradani, in Etchu,
When Yoshinaka drove cattle toward them,
With flaming brands tied to their horns.

Lastly, the great sea battle
Of Dannoura in Nagato.
Amid stormy waves of red and white flags,
The famed Nasu-no-Yoichi shot down the fan.

This was the "Gempei Song," which Mr. Egawa had taught them
when he was their third-grade teacher, accompanying them rather
clumsily on the organ. Seitaro could still hear that organ whenever
he sang the song even now. It made him want to call out to the
teacher; although at this hour of the morning he would probably be
asleep, like Mount Katsuragi or Mount Kongo.

"At the outset of the Gempei War," Fudé sang to herself, having
picked up the words of the first verse. "I wonder why the Genji and
Heiké fought all those terrible battles though," she reflected. "I'm sure
they weren't in any danger of starving. I know both sides wanted to
grab all the power for themselves, but they were fellow countrymen.
They didn't have to kill each other." The feuding between the two
rival clans was naturally incomprehensible to her, since she was
having to fight a drought together with her children on the front of
starvation.

Koji ran straight up to the well and began searching for something
eagerly, forgetting to put down the waterpot.

"What's up, Koji?" asked Nui, sensing that something was wrong.

"The cow I made yesterday isn't here anymore. The horse and
the dog aren't either."

"They've all run away, have they? That's because you made them
so well. You're a second Left-Handed Jingoro."* Nui chuckled at
her own joke.

The next moment, she was staring about her in amazement: it
was all too clear from the signs around the well that somebody had

been drawing water there only a few minutes ago. "I bet I know who!" and, sure enough, when she looked at Tosaku's paddy she found the soil there dark with moisture, spots of dew on the rice leaves.

"Fudé, something awful's happened!"

Fudé ran up and peered into the well; only two feet of water at the most remained where there should have been at least six or seven. "So somebody has been drawing our water. Do you know, last night I dreamed the well was empty, Mother, and it's come true. What are we going to do?"

"What can we do? He's a desperate man. We'll just have to sit back and watch. Mind you, he'll get *his* in the end. He'll ruin his health stealing water every night."

"Who is it?" Seitaro lowered his voice, "Také's dad?"

Nui wagged her finger at him disapprovingly. "You mustn't say things like that."

Seitaro guffawed, overcome with mirth at the thought of how much braver the night water-thief was than the Heiké troops, who had been so startled by some birds that they dropped their weapons and ran away. All the same, who could have done the job of pulling down the sweep? Surely not a first-grader like Také, or his brother Yasuo, still only in the fourth grade. Even such a harsh father as Tosaku would not drive his own children to work at night, would he?

Seitaro stared down at the ground, his expression now serious. Then he caught sight of a lump of clay near his feet.

"I know what happened!" he cried excitedly. "Koji's cow and horse and dog and rabbit got trampled to death by the water-thief. This lump's the man's head I made."

Koji picked up the squashed horse. "They aren't dead really, Seitaro. They just fainted 'cause they were trodden on. I'll bring them back to life again."

"Kneading them with water?"

Koji giggled in reply.

Fudé attached the bucket to the pole and began drawing water without delay. Seitaro pulled down the sweep by himself while Koji moistened the dried-up clay figures in a trickle from the bucket. Soon he was completely absorbed in kneading them.

The haze cleared and the mountains in the west shimmered a deep blue, while a cow, a horse, a dog, and a rabbit all lined up on the grassy ridge.

"You'd better watch out, Koji, or they'll run off to play," teased Nui mischievously.

But Koji did not laugh, nor did he reply; he was far too busy talking to the animals that had come back to life. There were so many fairy stories to tell; and then he also had to tell them about the shells he had sent back to the sea, and about Master Hidé, and Nanaé and Také, too.

XI

For five mornings in a row, they found the well undisturbed.

"It looks as if the water-thief's given up. He must have found it about as good as water on a hot stone in a drought like this," remarked Nui, on the fifth morning, as she lowered the bucket into the abundant supply that had collected overnight.

Fudé felt depressed. Everybody knew what a zealous farmer Tosaku was; the situation must be hopeless indeed for him to have given up. And had she not noticed the previous day how many well sweeps were now standing idle? Their owners had probably decided that it was a waste of effort to carry on watering the paddies by hand.

Nevertheless, Fudé and her family labored on until evening, resting occasionally when they reached the bottom of the well. Yet most of the rice plants showed little sign of reviving, their leaves still wrinkled up even when it was time to go home.

"We may be in for a famine. All this watering doesn't seem to make a scrap of difference," sighed Nui.

Famine—Koji had never heard that word before but he sensed it had some frightening connection with death. Over supper, he remembered it again.

"What'll we eat if there's a famine, Gran?"

"It isn't a famine if there's food about, silly." Seitaro laughed loudly, painstakingly scooping up the grains of rice in his gruel.

"That's right. It's not a real famine if there's any food. But Koji's right too. You've got to eat something to stay alive, even in a famine."

Fudé dexterously ladled some rice from the gruel into Koji's bowl.

"They say tens of thousands died in the Tenmei Famine, though that was more than a hundred years ago now," Nui remarked, after a few moments. "People lived on straw for the most part—rice bran or cornstalks, if they were lucky. But they didn't even have straw in places like Edo and Osaka. Masses died there. Round Oshu way they all took to begging, and they say there was nothing but skulls by the roadside in the end. There was no way ordinary folk could escape death, even if they did have a little bit of money, because the price of food just went on soaring."

"Do the rich have food then even in a famine?" Koji asked.

Seitaro laughed again. "The rich are so rich they can always afford to buy rice whatever it costs. Besides, they've got storehouses stuffed full of it. So they can sell it and make even more."

"Very true," said Fudé, sweat trickling down from her temples.

Koji could not understand this at all. He had sensed that a famine was something dreadful, connected with death, and yet here they all were talking about people selling rice during it and making money. If that was so, how could it be a famine? Weren't people meant to be helpless at such a time? Yet it seemed that the rich still had money and rice even when ordinary people no longer had either. But why were some people rich and others so poor in the first place? Who had started dividing them up like that?

Suddenly Koji remembered the story "Our Father" that he had read at Nanaé's that spring. There had been rich and poor people in the Father's country as well to begin with, and the Father himself had suffered great hardship when he was little. Despised as the son of a gatekeeper, he had often known what it was to go hungry. But, in his own childish way, he had grieved and grown angry until eventually he made up his mind to spend his life trying to get rid of such differences between people. And he was successful. Now there were no longer any haughty kings or ministers leading a life of luxury; or generals or field marshals decorated with medals for killing people in battle; or cunning merchants taking advantage of others' misfortunes and selling their goods at a higher price. Everyone in the land worked as equals and none was better off than others. Children could learn whatever they wanted, and there were certainly no *eta* among them, nor any children who would call others that!

"Have you finished, Koji? There's some more if you want." Fudé gave the pan a stir with the ladle, noticing Koji tightly gripping his empty bowl.

"No, I've had enough." Koji put down his bowl and licked the palms of his hands; his broken blisters, which were dreadfully sore, did not hurt so much then.

"Seitaro and Koji'll be collapsing if we don't get some rain soon." Nui peered at Koji's hands. Her own were chafed as well between the fingers, since the water in the field well contained mineral salts that irritated the skin.

A few moments later, Kané appeared, trying to drive away the mosquitoes around her legs with a fan. "Hasn't it been boiling all day?" she said.

"Beats me why there's no letup in this fine weather," replied Nui, fanning herself about the knees too. "I don't know about the rice, but we folk have just about had all we can take."

Kané laughed. "I'm sure you'll all stick it out till it rains, the way you're working at that watering."

"But we're fighting a losing battle. It'd be better if we'd given up right from the start." Nui was really beginning to feel dispirited.

"Once you've started, there's no turning back, though. Just keep going another five or six days. What with all the processions everywhere, it's bound to rain by then."

Seitaro and Koji knew about the torchlight processions that had been held for the last few days, not only in nearby villages but even the more distant ones toward the mountains. Sometimes they could be seen flickering in the darkness rather eerily, like will-o'-the-wisps.

"And by the way, did you know that Tosaku's down with the ague?" From the way Kané leaned forward, this was obviously going to be the talking point of the evening.

"Eh! That's the first I've heard of it," exclaimed Nui.

"They say it's dangerous if you get it for the first time when you're over forty," Fudé remarked.

"It's a punishment for being so greedy. Do you know, he's been drawing water from other people's wells at night and carrying it to his own paddy. We all think a harmful mosquito must've stung him then and given him the ague."

"How awful," Nui shuddered; the harmful mosquito must have been lurking near the well.

"There's no doubt about it, the Sun sees everything and knows what's right and what's wrong."

This remark irritated Seitaro. He started to poke fun at Kané. "It'd be a help if the Sun'd realize that the paddy's scorched and we're wearing ourselves out watering it by hand."

"The Sun knows what's for the best, Sei. I'm sure the drought's for some purpose."

"There's not much point in holding those processions to pray for rain then, is there?"

"Ha, ha, ha . . . You're an argumentative young rascal, aren't you!" laughed Kané, making light of it all.

The next day, on their way back from watering the paddy, they spotted some clouds in the blood-red sunset.

"They're thunderclouds. Maybe it's going to rain tonight." There was a quiver of excitement in Fudé's voice.

"Yes, and if it doesn't tonight, I bet it will tomorrow. What a blessing. It's the end of all our struggles." Nui could almost feel the drops of rain splashing down on her head.

They found Kané waiting for them when they reached home, and, without a word of greeting, she said, "Osaka's on fire. D'you see them clouds? It's no ordinary fire neither; they say it's been burning since morning. The old man heard about it at work."

In that case it was certainly true, since Hirokichi's work as a carrier took him to Osaka every day.

For one moment, Nui and Fudé relived the terror they had experienced when their house burned down. Then this gave way to a feeling of despair: they had not seen thunderclouds after all. They were numbed; their legs felt like jelly.

Presently, they all settled down to a gloomy supper.

As soon as it was over, Seitaro and Koji ran eagerly outside, wanting to watch the fire from the banks of the Katsuragi.

"Don't be late," was all that Nui said.

"Don't hurt yourselves," was the only warning Fudé gave.

Not that they need have bothered, since they soon returned.

"I shouldn't think it was much fun to watch, was it? It's not a local fire, after all," said Fudé, and Seitaro and Koji looked at each other.

They had found a crowd from Sakata gathered on the east bank of the river, all talking at the top of their voices, expressly to be overheard, it seemed.

"It started in Osaka this morning and it's still blazing. It's far bigger than that *eta* fire."

"It may be bigger, but at least it doesn't stink."

"It's an offering for rain to end the Yamato drought."

"Yes, it's bound to rain tomorrow or the day after."

"But what a waste to send rain to those *eta*."

There were loud roars of laughter.

Seitaro and Koji, as well as Kiyokazu and Yozo, who had come with them, ran back down the bank, stooping low.

There was not a proper downpour in the basin until nine days later. The *doyo* season was over by then, and it was time for the ears of rice to shoot, but most of the crop had already withered. Even so, official notices appeared in the villages announcing a holiday in celebration of the rain.

Komori also decided to have a half-day holiday, and Seitaro and Koji were to be seen climbing the stone steps to An'yoji, together with Kiyokazu and Yozo. The oleander still had many crimson flowers nestling among its thick foliage; while the luxuriance of the broad-leaved banana plant made it hard to imagine there had ever been a drought. The four boys could not help beaming, they felt so carefree.

"Good to see you. Come in."

Hidéaki ushered them into the cool corridor of the priest's living quarters, where there was both a chess and a go set. They were all skilled hands at board games. At school, they would draw the board on the ground outside and play with big and little stones, but today they had both the board and the pieces. "Right, then, how about a game?"

However, they also wanted to listen to Hidéaki. He was looking through a great many newspapers and remarked, "I know earthquakes, thunder, fire, and your father are said to be the most frightening things, but I think fire's the worst. Do you know, 11,365 houses were gutted in the Osaka fire."

Eleven thousand, three hundred and sixty-five houses . . . that was like forty villages the size of Sakata being burnt down.

"The damage was worse because the fire was in the north part of the city, where there are all sorts of important buildings—the Osaka Court of Appeal, the Osaka District Court, North Osaka Ward Office, the Meteorological Station, the Prefectural Industrial Experiment Station, the Commercial Exhibit Center. They think it must have amounted to about fifteen million yen altogether."

Fifteen million yen . . . No, it was impossible to work out how many silver fifty-sen pieces that would be.

"Lots and lots of measurefuls, I expect," Koji thought to himself.

"The fire was all the harder to put out because of the long drought they've been having in Osaka, too. It went on burning for twenty-four hours, starting at four in the morning on the thirty-first, right until the morning of the first. It must have been like a burning hell. Much more terrifying than an earthquake or thunder."

They all nodded in agreement.

"Anyway, new homes will soon be springing up to replace the ones that were lost. Apparently, the Forestry Bureau of the Ministry of Agriculture and Commerce is going to supply the timber, and the banks and insurance companies will be putting up the money. And it says in the newspapers that officials from the Imperial Household have also been over there and donated twelve thousand yen from the Privy Purse."

"What on earth's a Privy Purse?" asked Yozo, slapping his knees like a grown-up.

"The Privy Purse is the money the Imperial Household has to spend. It's like the Emperor's pocket money."

"Twelve thousand yen in pocket money! The Emperor must be terribly rich." Yozo looked envious.

"You can say that again. The Imperial Household's wealthier than anybody else in Japan."

"I wonder how they got so much money," said Seitaro.

"On the market, I bet," said Kiyokazu, lining up the pieces on the chessboard. "My dad says there's a place in Dojima in Osaka where you can play the market. They buy and sell things like rice and company shares there and they all make a bundle out of it. The Emperor's got lots of shares too, and that's how he's made so much money. And he's got loads of mountains and fields as well. Twelve thousand yen's just chicken feed!"

"Then why didn't they give us in Komori something from the Privy Purse when we had a fire? The teacher told us that the Emperor's the father of the nation and the Empress is the mother. If that's so, they should've given something to Komori, because we're the children of the nation, too."

"But the Emperor probably hates Komori, Sei. Look at the way our Old Bitterguts hates us. He's never ever given any of us an 'A'; we just get bad marks all the time." Yozo picked up a chess piece, ready to play against Kiyokazu.

"Do you want a game, Sei?" asked Hidéaki, turning to Seitaro.

"Yeah," and Seitaro slapped a black stone down on the go-board.

Hidéaki's high-bridged nose tautened as he plunked down a white stone. Then he and Seitaro looked at each other silently.

"Nobody comes to help us, not even when there's a famine. They all hate Komori so they never come and visit us," thought Koji, sitting beside them. "Except Toyo. He comes to see us . . ."

After the equinox there were often wet days, as if the rain was trying to make up for its forgetfulness in the summer; and autumn set in early. On November 4, Fudé and Nui reaped the harvest.

The landlord, Keizo Sayama, strutted backwards and forwards on the ridge between the paddies. He expected the harvest to yield only about four bushels a quarter-acre this year and had decided to divide the crop as it stood in the field, fearing that otherwise the Hatanakas might try and keep it all for their own consumption. Accordingly, he had brought along two of his men to reap his share.

It was very hard for Nui and Fudé to see the meager rice crop being divided in this way, and their hearts ached when they thought of the blistered palms of Koji and Seitaro. But their position was too weak for them to protest; to do so would inevitably mean losing the land they rented.

The field looked more starkly empty than usual after reaping, since there was no need to hang the brittle sheaves over racks to dry.

"This time last year the Grand Maneuvers were just beginning," thought Nui and Fudé, feeling as if it were only yesterday. But a whole year had passed since then, and, at Sakata Primary School, the ceremony to mark the Emperor's Birthday had been held the previous day. Today, too, there was another ceremony, but this time a piece of black cloth was hanging from the national flag in the hall. It was the state funeral of Hirobumi Ito.

Why had Hirobumi Ito, former Resident-General of Korea and President of the Privy Council, been shot by a Korean nationalist, An Jung-geun, in Harbin? Why had An Jung-geun felt he had to kill Hirobumi?

"His Excellency, Hirobumi Ito, one of His Imperial Majesty's senior statesmen, and the mainstay of our nation, has been shot by a villain called An Jung-geun . . ." declared Mr. Otori, the Head-master, his eyes flashing with indignation.

Seitaro started at the word "villain." He thought of what Old

Bitterguts had said in class recently: "Only villains defy those in authority, those we look up to and revere; and that has always been so, throughout history."

And that was why An Jung-geun too was a villain. Deploring Japan's annexation of Korea, he had dared to turn against the former Resident-General!

Together with the rest of the school, Seitaro stood in silence facing eastward, the direction of Tokyo, where the state funeral was being held in Hibiya Park.

XII

The rice leaves rustled as Koji eagerly kneaded the earth.

"I'm working it with my feet," cried Seitaro, who had plunged up to his knees in mud. "It's a lot better than using your hands."

"Koji, look what I've made," called his mother, a little way off. He looked up and saw a row of three large water jars.

"Let's fill them up with water, Fudé," said his grandmother delightedly.

"That's what I made them for," his mother replied in a shrill voice. "If we fill them right up, we'll be fine, even if we get a bad drought."

Then she rushed over to the well and seized the sweep rod to lower the bucket. Koji ran up and grabbed the rope at the other end. The sun beat down on his head. It was hot, terribly hot. He felt thirsty. Water. He was dying for a drink of water.

"Water . . ."

"Do you want some water?"

Koji woke up at the sound of his mother's voice. He had been dreaming; all the same, he did feel thirsty.

Fudé tilted the waterpot very slightly. "Only drink a little, Koji. You've got the measles."

He nodded docilely as he lay there.

"Nanaé in Ino got measles last New Year's, didn't she Mom? It's my turn this year."

"Do you remember that?"

"I wonder if hers was as bad as mine."

"I expect so. Measles always makes you feel awful. I can still remember when I got it. I had lots of bad dreams and I cried several times."

"I just had a dream, too. You were drawing water from the well and I was pulling down the sweep. It was so hot I was dying for a drink. That's why I called out 'water.' ''

"Poor little boy," thought Fudé, but she said nothing, stroking his head instead. His forehead was burning.

Koji's face lit up as his mother's hand caressed him. "You made some lovely things in my dream."

"What were they?"

"Water jars. Three big ones."

Fudé laughed. "What a funny thing to make."

"You said, 'If we fill them right up, we'll be fine, even if we get a bad drought,' so that's why I was working the sweep."

Again Fudé almost blurted out "poor little boy." She stroked his head once more.

"Mom," Koji called faintly, rubbing his red spotty cheek against his mother's hand . . . He did not really mind having measles, even though it was supposed to be serious; on the contrary, he could not have felt more contented yesterday and today with his mother constantly by his side.

The clitter-clatter of clogs could be heard.

"I'm back!" Pushing aside the straw-mat screen hanging in the entrance, Seitaro appeared, dressed in his *haori*.

"Hello." Fudé turned round.

"How's Koji?"

"Much better. We've been having a chat."

"What about?"

"A dream he had."

"Is that all! Here's something you'll like a lot better, Koji," and Seitaro pressed a tangerine into both of his hands.

"So they gave out tangerines at school this year as well, did they?" said Fudé, looking impressed.

"Course they did. It was the New Year's Day ceremony."

"All the same, I thought they'd probably stop giving them out, seeing as Sakata has just decided there have got to be cuts all around for the next five years."

"Well, they didn't cut down on the ceremony. We sang 'May Our Sovereign's Reign' and 'A New Year Has Dawned,' and the Headmaster put on his white gloves and read the Imperial Rescript on Education, same as usual. So they had to hand out the tangerines too."

"You are funny, Seitaro," Fudé laughed, Koji joining in.

"It's true though," said Seitaro, untying his *haori*. "And you know what, Mom, they've made a fine Imperial Portrait Room at school, too. Do you know what an Imperial Portrait Room is?"

"Yes, it's a room where they keep a photograph of the Emperor."

"Have you ever seen one?"

"No, I haven't."

"I haven't seen inside either. You can't go near it, because it's down a special corridor and there's this great big door there. And none of us is ever allowed in the corridor. Only the pupils with top marks for deportment can do the cleaning there."

Fudé felt a pang on hearing this: the Komori pupils were treated differently, even when it came to cleaning the school. It was like the army Grand Maneuvers, when no soldiers had been quartered in their homes. Not that it stopped their men being dragged off to fight in time of war; many had already been killed in battle, and many more would surely die in the future . . .

It was nearly lunch time. Seitaro, who had eaten nothing since his bowl of gruel at breakfast, was no doubt starving. Fudé stepped down into the kitchen, where she added some water to the leftovers from the gruel and began chopping up some radishes and greens.

A narrow strip of paper, like an amulet, was stuck on one of the worm-eaten pillars there, and the following words had been printed on it with a woodblock:

> There must be cuts all around throughout
> Sakata *mura* for the next five years.
>> December, 1909

The reason for such a measure was, of course, the poor harvest. Nevertheless, there were some landowners in the district who still had a considerable store of rice left from the harvest of 1908. But the same notice was also to be found posted up on their imposing entrance gates.

As Fudé was lighting the stove fire, she heard Koji ask in a low voice, "Has Master Hidé come back?"

"No, not yet," Seitaro answered quietly.

"I wonder when he'll be back."

"Mm, I wonder."

"The winter holidays'll soon be over."

"Maybe he won't be back till spring."

"Why not?"

"Because he's got a lot of studying to do."

"Hm," snorted Koji.

"Oh, I've got it!" cried Seitaro with a chuckle. "He heard about the all-round cuts and decided not to come back at New Year's to save the train fare."

He had to joke to hide the unaccountable concern he felt about Hidéaki, as well as disappointment that he had not returned; he had been looking forward to seeing him again for such a long time.

Fudé lifted the pan of boiling gruel off the stove. "It's ready, Seitaro. What about you, Koji? Will you try a little?"

"I don't want any." Koji turned over on his front, and, as if making an offering, placed both tangerines carefully on the *haori* that lay folded by his pillow; he did not feel like eating anything yet, even such a treat as these.

"If only Master Hidé'd come back, Koji would brighten up in no time. What can have happened to him?" said Fudé crossly, convinced that Hidéaki was the very person Koji needed to see now that he was off his food; her children's faces always lit up at the mention of his name.

She had never stopped to think why they were so attracted to him, however. And Seitaro kept this a secret. He would never have dreamed of telling either her or his grandmother that he had talked about a subject like *eta* with Hidéaki; he could not, even if he had wanted to.

Koji was the same. He could talk freely to Hidéaki about whatever occurred to him; and Hidéaki for his part was always willing to explain anything. It was he who had told him that all the relatives of people in Komori were *eta* too, as well as the story about the primary school teacher, Ushimatsu Segawa, who had such a hard time because of being one that eventually he went to America. Koji had made up his mind that this year he would find out in detail from Hidéaki why there were *eta* at all. If people became beggars through being lazy, then how did they become *eta?*

When Seitaro had finished his gruel, he sat down on a mat beside his mother, near the face of his sleeping brother.

"I'll help you make some sandals, Mom. I can't manage the hemp-soled ones, but I can do these." He reached for some bamboo-sheath.

"Don't waste your time," said Fudé quietly, in a strange tone of voice; there was anger, despair, even ridicule in it.

"Why not?" exclaimed Seitaro loudly. "I can earn some money too, can't I?"

"Don't talk so silly. Who'd buy the sort of sandals you make?"

"Well, I'll never get any better if I don't try."

"It doesn't matter. You'd do better to get on with your school-work. If you start doing sandal-making, you'll regret it the rest of your life."

"Then why do you spend all your time doing it?"

"Because I'm too stupid to do anything else. But there's nothing to stop you and Koji doing well for yourselves if you study hard at school."

Seitaro fell silent, knowing that no amount of studying would alter the fact that they were *eta*.

"All right, then; I'll split some bamboo-sheath for you, as there isn't any *yokiri* to do." He shifted his position slightly and began splitting bamboo.

Fudé no longer wove the upper sides of hemp-soled sandals. The straw from which they were made had been ruined by the drought and it was too expensive to buy in supplies from other areas that had not been affected. Instead, she now made sandals of bamboo-sheath, a material easy to come by. The one drawback was that the whole-saler paid a mere eight rin a pair for them, which meant that a day's work brought in only five or six sen at the most, when the cost of materials had been deducted. Nui had therefore undertaken to peddle them herself, and today she had set out again early in the morning.

Fudé and Seitaro knew only too well what a hard job it was.

One *shin* five *shin* a pair. Down to one *shin*.

Eta hag. Dirty old hag.

Nui would wince at the ugly taunts. But she would bear them silently, her large mouth drawn down at the corners . . .

"Gran!" Seitaro cried out inside; and his large mouth, so like his grandmother's, was also drawn down.

XIII

"You know Master Hidé, the priest's son."

Seitaro awoke with a start at the sound of his grandmother's voice. Unaware of this but taking care to speak quietly, Nui continued, "Okuni told me he's changed schools again."

Okuni was Yozo Samita's grandmother and Nui's peddling companion. She knew more about Hidéaki than anybody else, since she lived near An'yoji and was sometimes asked to help there when services were being held.

Fudé raised her eyebrows. "Eh! So that's why he didn't come back for the winter holidays."

"Yes, it must be. This time it's Tokyo, so he can't very well pop home for a short visit."

"Why has he gone all the way to Tokyo?"

"It seems this teacher came to work at his school and recognized him. 'Oh, so you think nobody knows where you're from, do you?' he says, 'Well, we'll soon see about that.' So Master Hidé said he was going to give up middle school altogether and the priest was so worried he made him change to a school in Tokyo."

Fudé said nothing. Seitaro opened his eyes a crack, troubled by his mother's silence. She was sitting under the lamp, absorbed in sandal-making; no doubt strongly affected by this news. Opposite her, his grandmother was also weaving bamboo-sheath, as might be expected. The habit of working at night had become so ingrained in her over the years that she could not break it now, however tired she might be after a day spent peddling.

"Poor boy." Nui finished off a sandal, pulling the warp tight with a sharp tug. "How unlucky bumping into a teacher who recognized him. He must've thought he was safe in a school in Kyoto."

"We must keep it a secret from Seitaro and Koji."

"You don't have to tell me that. Imagine how upset Seitaro'd be if he got wind of it. He'd lose heart straightaway and start thinking there's no point in studying if you're from Komori, I know he would."

"But that's just what he is beginning to feel, Mother. I've been keeping an eye on him and you know he doesn't get all excited about soldiers anymore the way he used to, and as for his school work, well he looks as if he couldn't care less about it. He seems to have got low marks for everything again in his second-term report—I can't think what he's doing at school every day."

"It's all very well to say that, Fudé, but things haven't been easy for Seitaro either you know. What with the drought, he hasn't been able to get on quietly with his studies since spring. If you ask me, we'd better hurry up and build some sort of home as soon as possible to help him settle down again."

"Yes, that's what I've been thinking. You know those government bonds we've got; well, maybe we ought to sell them and build a house. They said we could always sell them for 250 yen."

"Yes, if that's what you want to do, Fudé; I think it'd be for the best myself. I mean, we can't keep the family shrine in a place like this forever, can we? Only thing is, we won't be able to send Koji to middle school then, if he wants to go, and that does seem a pity."

"It can't be helped though, the way things have turned out. And it'd be even worse if we did send him there and the same sort of thing happened to him as to Master Hidé. After all, we couldn't then send him to another school in Tokyo, could we?" and Fudé gave a slight smile.

It struck eleven. Seitaro crawled further down into bed. "Damned teacher!" The mattress muffled his cry and all that Fudé and Nui heard was the night wind.

The third term began the next day, Friday, January 7. In the morning, as she wrapped a cotton flannel scarf round Koji's neck, Fudé said lightheartedly, "Now work hard. Master Hidé's bound to come back at the end of March so you've got to be ready with your school certificates to show him you were both top of your class."

"But our Old Bitterguts only likes the girls. They get all the good marks and there's none left for me," retorted Seitaro jokingly, although he was speaking the truth. The favoritism Mr. Aojima showed toward one or two girls was already attracting attention.

At the start of the first lesson, the atmosphere in the classroom underwent a sudden change.

"You've all got a new friend from today. This is Hisako Aikawa," Mr. Aojima announced, in a strangely pompous tone.

The little girl he was introducing had long hair hanging down her back. Over her kimono, she wore a purple jacket with a chrysanthemum pattern. No doubt she was dressed up in her best clothes for her first day at a new school, but, even so, she was strikingly beautiful.

Seitaro swallowed, wondering where she lived. Then he heard the others whispering:

"She lives in Sakata."

"Her dad's at Sakata substation."

"She's learning the *koto*."*

"She's very clever."

Now he understood. Recently there had been a changeover of staff

at the police substations, and Hisako's father must be the new policeman in Sakata.

Hisako was given a desk in the back row, next to Kinu Miyajima,
which was a particularly good place, even for one of the new classrooms. On a fine day, it was flooded with sunlight, a bright circle
dancing on the ceiling from the water in the inkstone-well.

"Old Bitterguts'll soon forget all about Kinu Miyajima," said Yozo
Samita, on the way home.

"Anybody can see that," remarked Makié Minami. "I just happened to look round and there he was winding Hisako's hair round
his hand with this smile on his face. I bet it felt nice 'cause she doesn't
have any lice in it. Ee, hee, hee . . ."

"Old Bitterguts'll make her his wife. Ha, ha, ha . . ." Kiyokazu
Shimura was bent double with laughter.

"He will, he will. Old Bitterguts'll do all right for himself and
make her his wife. Ah, ha, ha . . ."

"Ooh, how funny."

Yozo and Kiyokazu fell against each other.

"Idiots," said Seitaro coldly.

"Why are we idiots?" Yozo answered back sharply, a smile still
lingering on his face.

"Saying things like that. It's stupid," snapped Seitaro.

"What things?"

"What you just said."

"I didn't say anything that stupid."

"Sei's in Old Bitterguts' good books these days," chipped in Kiyokazu. "So it makes him cross if we're rude about him."

Linking arms with Yozo, he ran off, with Makié Minami not far
behind.

Seitaro felt suddenly drained both mentally and physically. What
Yozo had said about Old Bitterguts making Hisako his wife was not
really stupid at all, it was all too likely; one day they might well
marry. But for that very reason, he did not like to hear it spoken of.
He hated Yozo even more than Old Bitterguts, for blurting it out.
And he could have knocked Kiyokazu flying when he roared with
laughter like that.

The usual strong westerly was blowing and his nose started to run.
As he swallowed, he saw Hisako's face again.

XIV

It was the first history lesson of the third term. Mr. Aojima barked out Kiyokazu Shimura's name.

"Repeat the first of the five articles of the Imperial Charter Oath."

Kiyokazu was silent, lifting his hand to the back of his head as if to say that, try as he might, he just could not remember.

Two or three children burst out laughing, confident perhaps of knowing the answer.

"What, you've forgotten? Or didn't you take the trouble to learn them in the first place, as you were meant to do during the winter holidays?"

"I've forgotten them," replied Kiyokazu, hanging his head.

"Have you? Well, it can't be helped then, I suppose. But don't just sit there, boy, stand up when you reply."

"I've forgotten them, sir," repeated Kiyokazu brightly, looking relieved.

"Then let's try Yozo Samita."

"I've forgotten them too," Yozo replied spiritedly.

"What do you mean, 'I've forgotten them too' . . ."

But Mr. Aojima suddenly stopped pursuing Yozo as his gaze fell on Seitaro. "What about you, Hatanaka? Have you forgotten them too?"

Seitaro hesitated. While he would have liked to pretend that he had forgotten, he was afraid of the teacher's sharp tongue; he could imagine him saying with a sneer, "What a hopeless bunch they are, these Komori children."

He stood up and began reciting in a loud voice: "Assemblies shall be widely established and all measures of government decided by public discussion. All classes, both high and low, shall unite in vigorously carrying out the administration of affairs of state. Civil and military officials, as well as the common people, shall be allowed to realize their aspirations so that there may be no discontent. Evil . . ."

"I see, you know them all do you, Hatanaka?"

"Yes."

"I'm most impressed. Well, then, continue."

"Evil customs of the past shall be abandoned and everything based

on universal principles of justice. Knowledge shall be sought throughout the world, thereby strengthening the foundations of Imperial
rule."

"Well done. Can anybody else remember all five of the articles?"
The teacher looked around the classroom but not a hand was
raised.

"That's very poor. Hatanaka's beaten the lot of you, hasn't he?
He appears to be the only one to fully appreciate the benefits of the
Meiji Restoration. Anyway, in accordance with the wishes of His
Imperial Majesty, as expressed in the five articles of this most valuable
Charter Oath, the new Meiji government decided to completely
reform the misguided administration of the Tokugawa shogunate.
Remember, you learned all about it at the end of the second term.
Toyota Matsuzaki, tell us about the rule of the Tokugawa shogunate."

"Yes, sir. During the Tokugawa period, the samurai lorded it over
everybody and killed innocent people."

"What else?"

"They made the farmers pay heavy taxes."

"Very good, indeed. So the new Meiji government was established
and the four classes were all made equal. During the Tokugawa period, people had been divided into four classes—samurai, farmers,
artisans, and traders—and farmers could not talk to samurai on an
equal footing. But now, we are all equal. And that is why Hisako is
studying here with us today, even though her family are called *shizoku*,
which means they were originally samurai. Do you all understand?"

Instead of replying, everybody turned round to look at Hisako, who
sat with her head bent. She did not like being stared at, whatever the
reason.

"Now, having abolished the classes of samurai, farmer, artisan,
and trader, His Imperial Majesty also graciously permitted the
eta and the *hinin** to join the ranks of the commoners in August 1871.
They are now known as 'new commoners,' since that is what they
are, and there are said to be about 400,000 of them altogether in the
country."

There was the sound of stifled laughter.

Seitaro felt as if he were suffocating. New. New commoners—
these words had always made him wince as much as the word *eta*—
sometimes more so—but now he realized that they were not simply

a malicious insult, they were an official name, with historical significance. It was unbearable. On top of the indignity of being *eta,* there was this humiliation as well. And it was all the Emperor's doing.

"Sir." Toyota Matsuzaki suddenly stood up.

"What, another question? You've always got something to ask, haven't you?"

"It's only because I want to know the answer. Sir, you said the four classes in Japan were all made equal, but I don't think that's right."

"What do you mean?"

"Japan's still divided into four classes—the Imperial family, the nobility, the *shizoku,* and the commoners."

"Of course, it is. The Imperial family and the nobility are different. When I said the four classes were made equal, I meant that the people were no longer divided into different ranks, that is, into samurai, farmers, artisans, and traders."

"But aren't the Imperial family and the nobility the people, too?"

"No, they are not. They are either the relatives of the Emperor or closely connected with His Majesty."

"But they're all Japanese, aren't they?"

"That is perfectly obvious. And that is why it states in the Charter Oath that 'all classes, both high and low, shall unite in vigorously carrying out the administration of affairs of state.' Which means that the Imperial family, the nobility, and the common people shall all join together in thinking about and carrying out the government of Japan. Do you see now?"

"I don't know why, but it's still not too clear," said Toyota, pretending to scratch his head as he sat down.

Everybody laughed out loud. Toyota's mocking attitude toward the teacher gave them a certain feeling of liberation and, in fact, they were "not too clear" about the Restoration, the return to Imperial rule, and the peerage system, either.

That day, it was the turn of the Komori group to clean the lavatories.

"Sei's definitely a bit different from the rest of us. How did he manage to remember all them difficult words?" said Kiyokazu, obviously feeling that it was more normal to be like himself and forget them. He was talking about the five articles of the Charter Oath.

As he scrubbed the urinal drain with a long-handled brush, Yozo added, "It's too hard for me. I'd better try and learn one, though, in case we get it in the exam. How did it go, Sei?"

"I wouldn't bother," replied Seitaro, emptying a bucket of water.

"Why not?"

"It's a waste of time."

"Why?"

"Yes, I would like to hear the reason too."

Mr. Aojima had come near the lavatories without their realizing it. Bucket in hand, Seitaro stared back at the teacher.

"Put the bucket down."

He did as he was told.

"Now, would you mind telling me why it is a waste of time learning the five articles of the Charter Oath?"

Silence.

"Can't you tell me why?"

He could; but the teacher would never understand; not only that, he would almost certainly hit him. Even so, he ought to tell him. Yes, and he would too. He would tell him all right!

In a flash, Seitaro made up his mind.

"We're new commoners, sir. Nothing's going to change that, even if we do know all five articles of the Oath by heart."

"Do you dislike being a new commoner so much then? Would you rather still be an *eta?* His Imperial Majesty has most graciously condescended to raise you all to the rank of new commoner and yet you feel no gratitude whatsoever, do you? Well, let that be a lesson to you!"

A blow landed on Seitaro's shoulder. He staggered and fell down on top of the bucket.

"I'm sorry, Sei," Yozo apologized, as they went out of the school gates.

"Why? You haven't done anything."

"But it's all my fault because I asked you to tell me one of them."

"No, it isn't."

"He wanted to hit Sei anyway 'cause we're new commoners and *eta,*" said Kiyokazu. "Look at the way we even have to do the cleaning separate from the others, all because they've got the gall to say it's dirty wringing out their floor cloths in the same bucket as us. Well, I'll be damned if I'll go to their rotten school anymore. That stinking teacher Bitterguts!"

On Ohashi Bridge, they all shouted out together, "Stinking Teacher Bitterguts!"

But Mount Kongo remained the same shade of mauve as before. Facing the mountain, the three of them took a deep breath.

XV

> We hate Miss Swanky,
> Miss Swanky,
> Miss Swanky,
> Look at that bun
> Stuck on top of her head,
> Silly old Miss Swanky.

The children chanted as they sheltered by the riverbank from the biting wind of a February morning. Most of them were sixth-grade boys and they were led by Senkichi Sayama.

After a few moments of raucous laughter, they began again, but this time as quietly as possible.

> We hate Aojima,
> Aojima, Aojima,
> Sugino's the one we like
> Even though he's darker,
> Poor old Aojima.

This was greeted by more guffaws from the surrounding group; and naturally, Seitaro, who was one of them, joined in. He was not surprised that Senkichi should want to lead the chanting, even if he had not made up the jingle himself; after all, he must find Mr. Aojima's recent coolness very galling after having been the teacher's pet at the beginning of the school year.

But who had made up the chant? Mr. Sugino, the fourth-grade teacher, was a middle-school graduate, ranking below Mr. Aojima. He was dark-complexioned and good at painting. And whenever any of the girls from Sakata, Azuchi, and Shimana got together to weave cotton cloth at home, or when they went out to work as seamstresses during the slack season of farming, his name was sure to crop up in the gossip—a fact that Seitaro might not have known but that Senkichi and Toyota had been aware of for a long time. With greater relish than Seitaro could possibly imagine, therefore, they began to chant again meaningfully.

> We hate Aojima,
> Aojima, Aojima . . .

After they had been through it a third time, Senkichi said, "I'll teach you another one now. You'll soon pick it up," and he began chanting slowly.

> We hate Miss Aikawa,
> Aikawa, Aikawa.
> First they were samurai,
> Now just policemen,
> Poor old Miss Aikawa.

"The ending of this one's 'poor old' too, isn't it?" checked Shigeo Iwase.

"Yeah. Because Hisako Aikawa's family used to be samurai and boss everybody about but now her dad's only a policeman. And that's nothing to brag about. Only little kids and good-for-nothings look up to policemen. Honest. When a policeman comes to our house, you should see him bowing and scraping."

Everybody nodded in agreement and began chanting. But there were no guffaws this time when they had finished. It made them feel rather awkward to think that Hisako might be listening somewhere in the playground.

In fact, Hisako *was* listening. As soon as she reached her desk in the classroom, she bent her head and burst into tears.

"It's that song," Seitaro guessed, inadvertently looking round at her.

"Hatanaka!" Mr. Aojima's voice barked out at once.

Seitaro was not the only one to have turned around, however; at least ten others were craning their necks to stare at Hisako.

"It's always me that gets the blame," he thought, although without any particular sadness or annoyance now that he only had about a month left at school. He opened his book composedly for the ethics lesson.

After standing by Hisako's desk for a while, listening to her tale of woe, Mr. Aojima hurried back to the teacher's dais. "Close your books, everyone. We're having a test today."

"Not a test," somebody whispered despondently, and everyone's heart sank. The atmosphere in the classroom suddenly felt close and oppressive.

Presently, the pupils at the end of each row handed out paper to the others. Mr. Aojima wrote two lines on the blackboard:

Ethics Test
Write down the five articles of the Charter Oath.

"Sir, do we have to use the proper characters?" asked Toyota, without standing up.

"Well that would be ideal, of course, but I'll allow you to use *kana* since the characters are so difficult. You will receive ten marks if you can write all five articles, two marks for only one. And anybody who cannot do even one will fail to graduate."

"We won't really fail, will we, sir?" asked Toyota again.

"You most certainly will if you get a zero in ethics, and that's a fact."

"But sir, it's just a test, isn't it? Tests are different from exams. Only the one result counts for exams, like the middle-school entrance exam, but the marks for a test are added to the rest of the term's work before going in our reports. That's what you told us, sir."

"Yes, that's right, that's right." Two or three others cried out in support.

"That is quite correct. But if you cannot answer such an important question at all, the rest of your term's work is bound to be unsatisfactory. And how can you possibly say that you have completed your compulsory education if you do not even know the five articles of the Imperial Charter Oath? Remember, you are about to graduate. Now, try your best."

There was not much point in trying, however, for those who had not memorized any of the five articles. Secretly, they envied Seitaro, who was without doubt the hero of the moment.

Yozo waited until the teacher was not looking and then peered over at Seitaro's desk; he might be able to figure out one of the articles if he could catch a glimpse of a few words.

But Seitaro was only drawing countless lines on his answer sheet. And at last, the bell rang.

Yozo could not muster enough courage to ask him why he had not written anything. He suddenly felt afraid, aware of something in Seitaro he could not understand.

School was finishing for the day when Seitaro, Toyota, Senkichi, and Shigeo were told to remain behind. At first, they stood in the corridor rather shamefacedly, as they waited for the girls to finish cleaning the classroom, but presently Toyota remarked, "Imagine Sei being kept in too, when he didn't sing the 'We Hate' song— poor old Hatanaka."

"Oh, very good," laughed Senkichi, applauding Toyota's wit.

"I bet that wretch Hisako went and blabbed he was singing with us. You lay into her good an' proper tomorrow, Sei," said Shigeo, in a tone of righteous indignation.

Seitaro knew this was not the reason, however. A moment later, the others realized it too, when Mr. Aojima came out of the staff room and, after ordering them to line up in front of his desk, added, "Not you, Hatanaka, I'll deal with you later."

Then he continued: "Right, I hear you have made up a fine song. How does it go—first they were samurai, now something or other? Come along, sing it to me."

Shigeo started giggling, at which Toyota and Senkichi also sniggered.

"Didn't you hear me? I told you to sing it."

"But it's not the sort of song you can sing in a classroom. We're very sorry, sir. We won't ever sing it again."

"You've a smooth tongue, Matsuzaki. Well, if you promise not to sing it ever again?"

"Yes, we promise."

"Then hurry home. And apologize to Hisako tomorrow."

Senkichi and Shigeo did as they were told and ran straight out of the school without looking back.

"Go on, Matsuzaki, you too," ordered Mr. Aojima, frowning at Toyota, who was standing in the corridor.

"I'm waiting for Sei."

"Why? You live in opposite directions."

"I need to talk to him about something."

"You can talk to him tomorrow. Hatanaka won't be going home for a good while yet."

Toyota went out of the building and then walked round to stand beneath the classroom window.

"Do you know why you have been kept in, Hatanaka?" asked Mr. Aojima, in a low, tense voice.

"No, I don't." Seitaro shook his head.

"You don't? Are you quite sure?"

"Yes."

"What's the meaning of this then, you impudent boy?" The teacher thrust a sheet of paper under Seitaro's nose. "What do you mean by not writing a single word in today's test when you've already shown you know the answer perfectly well? Have you absolutely no respect at all for our most sacred Charter Oath? Or are you simply trying to make a fool of me? Well, which is it?"

Seitaro said nothing.

"What a warped nature you have. You're a disgrace to your father's name."

Seitaro stared at the lowest button on the teacher's jacket.

"Look up. Your father died honorably in battle in the Russo-Japanese War. How he must be weeping now over your utter lack of filial respect and loyalty!"

Crash! Seitaro was knocked flying, overturning a desk. As he hit the ground, something exploded inside him.

How dare he talk about loyalty!

And filial respect.

And *eta*.

And new commoners.

Seitaro's hands swept the floor as if he were swimming. Then he pushed himself up to a crawling position and very slowly rose to his feet.

Everything looked quite different, as if a long period of time had elapsed. He felt several inches taller.

"Right, go home."

Mr. Aojima retreated onto the teacher's dais: the boy who had got up from the floor looked singularly big.

Seitaro hastened down the cold corridor; Toyota was bound to be waiting for him somewhere, he thought.

XVI

"The list of sixth-grade results was completed yesterday, ahead of any other grade's," Mr. Aojima announced, with the flicker of a smile.

The pupils looked at each other, trying to guess which one of them would have the honor of representing the class at the graduation ceremony and answering the speech of congratulation from the rest of the school.

"Two pupils have failed," continued the teacher.

Everybody stared at him, with a chill feeling of suspense.

Halfway across Ohashi Bridge, on their way home, Kiyokazu said, "I bet I failed. I missed nearly all the tests in the third term."

Yozo balanced his bundle of books on his head. "If I get to the other side without dropping it, I've passed. If I don't, I've failed."

In spite of all his pains, the bundle fell off when he had almost reached the other side.

"Drat!" He kicked it. "I don't want to go to school anymore."

"It's me that's failed really." Seitaro came to a halt and looked down at the riverbed. The sand there was dry and white and he suddenly wanted to walk over it making a crunching sound.

"You fail? Don't be silly," flared up Kiyokazu, as if he were being teased.

"You don't know about it, but Bitterguts hates me more than anybody else in our class. Ask Yo, he knows."

"Do you, Yo?"

Yozo laughed evasively. Secretly, he thought that Seitaro might well have failed, as a punishment for handing in a blank answer sheet for the ethics test.

"I wish I could get a peep at that list of results." Kiyokazu looked back toward the school.

"It wouldn't change anything even if you did," said Seitaro.

"I'd feel better if I knew, though."

"What, even if you'd failed."

"Yes. And it'd give Dad time to get used to the idea if I told him now."

"But it's too difficult. How could you manage to get a look at the list?"

"I could try when there aren't any teachers about."

"That's no good. They're always about," cried Yozo, waving his hands.

"Then I'll have to find a way when we're cleaning the staff room tomorrow."

"You've got a nerve, Kiyo." Seitaro threw a pebble at the riverbed. That evening, Nui complained of feeling tired from her peddling.

"You can take it easy from now on, Gran, I'll soon be going out to work," said Seitaro, massaging her shoulders for her.

Nui started. "Aren't you going on to the higher elementary school?"

"No. I've got a feeling I'm going to fail this year."

"Ha, ha, ha . . . That's a chicken-hearted thing to say. Only last year you was talking about becoming a fine soldier."

"I was just a kid then and didn't know any better."

A cold shiver ran down Nui's spine and Fudé looked up in surprise.

"I don't care if I do fail, Gran. I'd rather work than go to school anyway."

"But what sort of work do you want to do?"

"Oh, anything. Farming, or making shoes, it doesn't matter."

Nui stifled a sigh and Fudé swallowed her tears. They both realized that Seitaro now knew clearly what he was.

The next day, Seitaro was ordered once again to remain behind after school, this time, together with Senkichi Sayama and Toyota Matsuzaki.

Toyota was not in the least perturbed. "I bet it's about something nice today, Sei. Maybe Mr. Aojima'll tell you to try the middle-school exam, too." Both he and Senkichi were among those who were going to take the entrance examination, and only recently they had submitted their applications. Seitaro felt sure, however, that he was being kept behind for an entirely different reason, although what it was he could not imagine.

Presently, the three of them were called into the reception room.

Toyota nudged Seitaro and whispered, "You see, it is something nice this time."

Then Mr. Egawa also arrived and a smile appeared on Seitaro's face.

"Now, you must tell us the truth, Hatanaka," said Mr. Egawa, sitting down beside Mr. Aojima.

"I wonder what's up," thought Seitaro, looking from one teacher to the other.

"Do you know what this is?" Mr. Aojima drew out a large book from under the table.

It was the Record of Sixth-Grade Results, with its cover of thick Mino paper. Thinking he must have failed after all, Seitaro's legs began to shake.

Mr. Aojima grabbed him by the shoulder. "Was it you?"

"Have I failed?" Seitaro could not stop his voice trembling.

"Of course, you have. Now, when did you steal it? If you don't tell the truth . . ." In his excitement, Mr. Aojima broke off in mid-sentence.

"Hatanaka, was it you who stole the record of results? You must answer truthfully."

Resting his folded hands on the table, Mr. Egawa stared intently at Seitaro, for whom all this was completely bewildering. What was he meant to have stolen? Somebody it seemed had taken the record of results, but then, why was it there in front of him? Or did they mean somebody had stolen a look at it? Kiyokazu had talked seriously about doing just that on the way home yesterday; but it hardly seemed likely he had found the opportunity. And if not, what was all the fuss about?

Confused and uncertain, he could only stand there looking blank.

Suddenly, Senkichi Sayama spoke up. "I took it."

"What! You took it?"

"Yes, I just wanted a quick look. It was yesterday, when I was cleaning the staff room."

"Do you mean you took it home and then brought it back again?" Mr. Aojima steadied his trembling body against the edge of the table.

"So you were the one, Sayama, who changed the results here and there." Mr. Egawa turned over the pages of the record.

Senkichi nodded.

"But why did you do it?"

"I just wanted to know soon who was going to be class representative and who'd failed."

"Yes, I understand that, but why did you alter the results—not only your own but even Hatanaka's and Matsuzaki's?"

"Undoubtedly, he thought he'd be found out if he only altered his own. Little wretch!" Mr. Aojima started boxing Senkichi's ears.

"We don't need to resort to violence, do we, Mr. Aojima?" said Mr. Egawa quietly.

Senkichi edged toward him. "I only altered the ones that didn't seem fair. Sei had three 'E's, so I changed them to 'A's because that's what they ought to be. And Toyo's were wrong too. He's the one that ought to be class representative."

"All the same, Sayama, you're the one who's being unfair. A teacher has his own way of looking at things and his own opinion as to what marks he should give. And thanks to your giving him those 'A's, Hatanaka was thought to be the culprit for a while, wasn't he? Anyway, you've had the honesty to own up, so you haven't caused Hatanaka or Matsuzaki too much trouble."

Mr. Egawa turned to Mr. Aojima. "I'm sure it would be all right if they went home now. We can deal with the rest of the matter later."

He opened the door and Seitaro dashed straight out. His legs felt like jelly, as if he were in the middle of a disturbing dream.

A few days later, Seitaro heard a rumor at school that Senkichi's father—the most influential man in Sakata—had come dressed up in formal *haori* and *hakama* to apologize for his son's misconduct. Nobody seemed to know exactly what Senkichi had done wrong, and Seitaro and Toyota had naturally decided to keep it a strict secret. All at once, they felt closer to him.

Before they knew it, the graduation ceremony was upon them.

"Kinu Miyajima? A girl, class representative?" Seitaro heard several boys say disappointedly on the day.

"That Old Bitterguts was lying when he said two of us had failed. And here's me been worrying about nothing. What a waste of time," said Kiyokazu, sounding delighted nevertheless as he rolled up his graduation certificate.

"Goodbye, Sei." Toyota waved to Seitaro in front of the school gates.

"Goodbye, Toyo."

Seitaro walked backwards for a while. He could see the long sleeves of Hisako's kimono; Senkichi's new hat . . .

"Goodbye, everybody."

But this time he could not say it out loud. The words sank inside him and settled there heavily. It was March 28, 1910, and Seitaro was twelve years old. The winter crop of barley had grown to its full height and the new life of spring was burgeoning throughout the basin.

4

Crickets

Early June—with the rainy season at hand, the sun was now as fierce as at the height of summer.

In the area drained by the Katsuragi, the winter barley had been harvested, and, here and there, the glint of watery paddy fields could be seen. Within the next fortnight, the broad beans, Chinese milk vetch, and wheat would have completely disappeared and all the arable land transformed into paddies for the main rice crop.

Both nature and man in the Yamato basin seemed impatient to make up for the damage caused by last year's drought.

On Monday, June 6, the Komori children, Koji among them, were on their way to school, the morning sun beating down on them. With nothing but thin gruel inside them, they felt the heat, and the forehead of every boy and girl was damp. If they quickened their pace in the slightest, their tummies rumbled and they were soon bathed in sweat. Not only this particular morning, either; their gruel-filled tummies always rumbled when they ran.

Presently, they passed through the school gates and clustered in a corner of the playground, like chickens driven there. Since April, the school rules had changed, and pupils were no longer free to enter the classrooms until lessons began, which meant standing about clutching their bundle of books, waiting for the bell.

In fact, though, the lower grades, a few timid girls, and the children from Komori were the only ones to continue zealously clasping their books. The fifth- and sixth-grade boys from Sakata and Shimana had taken over most of the playground and were running about playing baseball, a game that had suddenly become popular.

It was fun to watch, and sometimes the Komori children would imitate them when they got home from school, playing in the narrow roadside. The teams consisted of both boys and girls, and they used a girl's handball, made of thread wound round a wick, and either the flat of their hands or sometimes a wooden pestle for a bat. Even with these, the game was so much fun that they were always sorry when it grew dark; but how much more thrilling it would have been to whack the ball with a real bat.

Now, they looked on with a broad grin, cheering the teams silently. Smack . . . The ball came rolling toward them and Takeshi quickly grabbed it.

"Oi!" roared one of the basemen, running up and giving Takeshi a kick.

"Get over there, you lot, you're in the way," shouted the boy acting as referee, in a grown-up tone of command.

The Komori children said nothing; nor did they show any sign of moving: they were putting up as strong a show of resistance as they knew how simply by remaining where they were.

"You've got some nerve!"

"It'll serve you right if you get hit."

With these parting retorts, the Sakata and Shimana boys ran off.

The Komori children waited anxiously for the bell. Why was it so late in ringing? Koji could tell that it was from the position of the sun.

"Perhaps the District Governor's coming," he thought, and his heart gave a thump.

After a while, however, the bell rang as usual near the main entrance facing the courtyard. Three minutes later, all grades from the first to the sixth were lined up in the playground ready for morning assembly. The teachers filed out of the staff room, and, with Miss Hatsu Kashiwagi in the lead and the Headmaster, Mr. Otori, bringing up the rear, they proceeded to the corridor of the old schoolhouse. It was like a veranda, directly overlooking the playground, and they always stood in a row there for assembly.

Holding himself bolt upright, the Headmaster glared round at the pupils, and Koji guessed at once there was something afoot, and that it was not at all pleasant, either. Maybe the Komori group was in for a severe scolding; at which thought he realized that most of the ones in the upper grades were absent . . . His heart missed a beat again.

When Mr. Egawa gave the word, they all turned toward the Imperial Portrait Room and made a deep bow, after which, there were deep breathing exercises. Then all that remained was for the grades to march to their respective classrooms.

The pupils picked up the bundle of books at their feet and waited for the order, "Quick, march." But, unexpectedly, Mr. Egawa stiffened and shouted, "Stand to attention!"

The children stared round them wide-eyed, wondering if there were some mistake.

"Boys and girls, today I have a most terrible announcement to make!"

Koji did not know the word "anguish," and yet that was what he sensed in the Headmaster's voice. Something quite out of the ordinary had obviously occurred.

"I feel sure you all remember how Marquis Hirobumi Ito was killed on October 26 last year, when he was shot by a Korean scoundrel at Harbin station. His state funeral took place on November 4, the day after the Emperor's Birthday; we also held a ceremony to mark the occasion, didn't we? Well, the wicked An Jung-geun was executed this year on March 26, exactly five months after the event; a fitting end for Marquis Ito's evil assassin."

Koji shivered, suddenly wanting to urinate.

Execution. He knew what that meant: it was the most frightening, the most horrible thing in the world. The shock of it had made him want to pass water; not that he realized that was the reason of course. He grew red in the face and squeezed his thighs together, embarrassed by such an urge at a time like this.

Managing to control himself for the present, he began to wonder why Mr. Otori should have decided to mention the execution today, June 6, when it had taken place on March 26. Maybe another young man like An Jung-geun had turned up somewhere in Korea. Yes, that must be it, or there would be no reason for bringing up the subject now.

Koji craned his neck and stared at Mr. Otori. As if in response, the Headmaster stopped biting his lip and continued: "However, something a hundred times, a thousand times worse than the assassination of Marquis Ito has now happened, and here in our own country."

He paused and bit his lip again.

Koji felt increasingly certain that a second An Jung-geun had indeed appeared; although he did not find the idea as "terrible" as the

Headmaster apparently did. Execution seemed far more ghastly than one person shooting another.

It was unbearably hot, though. He could see lice crawling about in the hair of the girl in front of him. Were they enjoying the scorching sunshine or trying to find shelter from it? Five, ten, fifteen . . . There were too many to count.

"Boys and girls, what has happened is as dreadful as if we had lost the sun. We could not live even one day without the sun. The whole world would be in darkness and we could not possibly survive.

"Nevertheless, some wretches far more wicked than An Jung-geun have actually sought to plunge this nation of ours into darkness.

"Of course, they have been caught—seven of them altogether. They had made a bomb and intended to plunge us all into darkness by throwing it at His Imperial Majesty, our most revered Sovereign, whom we look up to as to the sun.

"What a wicked idea! What a sordid plot! What a despicable act! Marquis Ito's assassin was Korean, but this time the villains are all Japanese.

"Boys and girls, this is indeed a most tragic, frightful, and contemptible affair. An unpardonable disgrace to His Imperial Majesty.

"With the deepest respect, we, the sixty million citizens of this nation, look up to His Majesty as our father, and His Majesty graciously looks upon us, His subjects, as His children. There is not another country in the world to compare with ours. It is because of the uniqueness of our nation, in other words, the august virtue of His Imperial Majesty, that we won such great victories in the wars with China and Russia. And we consider it an honor and our duty to be ready to fight and lay down our lives at any time for His Majesty.

"It was utterly insane to plot to throw a bomb at His Majesty the Emperor, a crime against Heaven, to try and plunge the Great Japanese Empire into darkness and our sixty million citizens into the direst misery."

Were these seven people then insane? Even though the Headmaster's speech was difficult and there were some points he could not grasp at all, Koji realized that something terrible really had happened and that it concerned the Emperor.

The Emperor was a *kami*—or so they were taught at school. And a *kami* was not only easily offended but quick to mete out dreadful punishments. That was why the shrines to the *kami* were always so splendid and well-kept; and why the Emperor's photograph was enshrined in the Imperial Portrait Room off a corridor nobody was allowed to use; and why the Headmaster had to dress up in such a smart Western-style suit and spotless white gloves whenever he took the photograph out. It made Koji shudder to think of the awful punishment lying in store for those who dared to throw a bomb at this vengeful *kami*-Emperor.

But was what the Headmaster said true, and would the world be plunged into darkness if a bomb was thrown at the Emperor? Would the sun now beating down on him suddenly disappear if the Emperor were killed like Marquis Hirobumi Ito? But surely, a bomb could not kill the Emperor if he were a *kami*. Was it not odd to talk about a *kami* being killed like that?

Koji glanced around at the others. They seemed to be paying little attention to the Headmaster's speech, judging by their vacant expressions. It was so terribly hot they were obviously longing to go inside, to the classroom.

However, the Headmaster had not yet finished his report on the "unpardonable disgrace to His Imperial Majesty."

"Boys and girls, as I told you all a few moments ago, all seven of the villains have been arrested, and there is no doubt about it, their ideas are completely insane. It seems they have been discontented with the state of society for a long time and aimed to overturn the present order of things at the first opportunity. They decided that the quickest way of achieving their objective was to eliminate the Emperor, who is like the sun to us, the very heart of our nation. And that is why they plotted to throw a bomb at His Majesty.

"They also declared that war is wrong, daring to voice opposition to the Sino-Japanese and Russo-Japanese Wars. What a flagrant act of disloyalty—to oppose the Imperial edict ordering us to take up arms against Russia."

Koji felt a shock as if he had run smack into something.

War was wrong! They were against war! Never had he dreamt for one moment that there might be people here in Japan who would say that. And what would the country be like now if everybody had done as they said and opposed the wars? There was no way of knowing the answer of course, but of one thing he was sure: without the Russo-Japanese War, his father, with his *banko* head, would still be alive and well. And if his father were alive, then his brother might have gone on to the higher elementary school instead of starting an apprenticeship in Osaka.

Koji had known for some time now that Seitaro would be going to Osaka to serve an apprenticeship as soon as the rice had been transplanted.

Wiping away a trickle of sweat, he dried his hand on his kimono.

"Boys and girls, these scoundrels not only opposed the war, they had other ideas even more dreadful; ideas that would be the ruin of our society. They sought to deprive people of their wealth, to take away their money. They thought that since all men are equal, money too should be distributed equally among us. But then, of course, nobody would bother to work at all. It would lead to chaos, every man for himself. This terrible group are known as anarchists and their ringleader is Shusui Kotoku, whose given name is Denjiro."

Deep inside, Koji gave a cry of understanding. Although he had no idea what "anarchist" meant, not to mention the other difficult words, it was as clear as daylight to him what Shusui Kotoku, given-name-Denjiro, had sought to do.

Shusui Kotoku, given-name-Denjiro, had tried to do what that father did; the one in the story "Our Father," which he had read the spring before last at his grandfather's in Ino. He had wanted to share all the food so that there would be plenty for the hungry children of Komori, whose parents were always poor despite their hard work.

The Headmaster kept saying how wrong such ideas were, but was it right for the people of Komori to remain poor *eta?* The teachers said the Emperor was the father of the people, but the father in the story had only come to be called that because he had worked so tirelessly for the happiness of everyone in the land. However, it seemed that the Emperor had ordered the arrest of Shusui Kotoku and his followers, which must mean they were going to be punished.

Imagine being ready to punish somebody for a little thing like not wearing gloves when they carried your photograph. What a frightening person. But that sort of person was a *kami*, not a "Father," because it was the job of a *kami* to punish people . . .

The ground at his feet was whirling round and round. Suddenly, he was no longer bathed in sweat and he felt cold about the shoulders. Instinctively, he crouched down. The very same moment, something dark flopped to the ground with a thud right in front of him.

"Oh! Také . . ." Koji cried out, immediately straightening up again.

Miss Kashiwagi came rushing over in her indoor sandals and picked up Takeshi, who was in her class.

"At ease!" shouted Mr. Egawa, in a flustered voice.

At once, all the children crouched down as if about to collapse. Wide-eyed and open-mouthed, they watched Takeshi Nagai being borne away in Miss Kashiwagi's arms; he made not a sound, his dark legs dangling down against the teacher's purple *hakama*.

"Maybe he's dead," said a little girl from Komori. Nobody answered, as none of them knew what had happened.

Cold drops of sweat trickled down under Koji's arms. It was frightening to think of Také dying, but so was the thought of him dead. Even so, Koji was envious: Také seemed much luckier than himself, being carried off in Miss Kashiwagi's arms like that.

II

"The hedge is fragrant with flowers . . ."

Miss Kashiwagi sang, accompanying herself on the organ. It was strange the effect her voice had on Koji; it seemed to stroke his back with a touch neither too hard nor too soft. He did not know why it had this effect; he had never even thought about it, awareness of such things not yet having awakened in him.

"And already the cuckoo is here . . ."

Miss Kashiwagi only taught his singing class.

"With its hushed, secret call . . ."

The teacher made them practice it again.

"With its hushed, secret call . . ."

Koji sang opening his mouth as wide as he could.

A gentle breeze blew in from the window. It teased the stray locks of Miss Kashiwagi's fashionable chignon, brushing them against her cheek.

Také had not died. At the end of the first lesson, he was chatting with everybody again as if nothing had happened, although slightly more subdued than usual. Koji now felt as if Také had come off the loser, while he himself had gained; but again, he did not know why, nor did he even think about it.

"Summer has come . . ."

This time they sang without stopping.

"The hedge is fragrant with flowers
And already the cuckoo is here . . ."

But there was another song mingled with it in Koji's throat.

"Shusui Kotoku, given-name-Denjiro."

A song branded on his memory that morning, together with the heat of the sun-scorched playground. It was surprising how well it went with the tune he had made up.

"Shusui Kotoku, given-name-Denjiro."

He could sing it any way he wanted; fast or slow; high or low. And nobody realized he was singing it at all. What fun. Even the teacher did not know; though that was rather a pity . . .

Koji stared at Miss Kashiwagi, and, as he did so, the lightly powdered face of the teacher gave way to another; a reddish face with a long, white beard. It was that of an old man, although it had a certain youthfulness. It was Shusui Kotoku, given-name-Denjiro, and he was smiling, about where Miss Kashiwagi's nose was. He was staring back at him and smiling.

"Can anybody sing it by themselves?" Miss Kashiwagi peered over the top of the organ.

Machié Sugimoto raised her hand, much to Koji's relief. While confident of being able to hold his own against anyone with arithmetic or reading, the girls were much better at singing; especially Machié, who completely outshone him.

"The hedge is fragrant with flowers . . ."

Machié sang exactly in time with the organ.

"Will anybody else have a go?"

This time, nobody raised their hand; there was not much chance of sounding tuneful after Machié.

"Koji Hatanaka, let's hear you."

Koji had no choice but to stand up, whether he could sing or not. However, there was no need to worry because Miss Kashiwagi not only played the accompaniment but sang along with him as well.

"The hedge is fragrant with flowers . . ."

Koji was pleased with himself, thinking he sang surprisingly well. He sat down with a glow of satisfaction just as the bell rang for the end of the fourth lesson.

Miss Kashiwagi closed the organ and returned to the teacher's dais. But she did not dismiss the class as usual. They sensed she had something to tell them.

"Children, I . . ." She flushed slightly. "I'm afraid I must say goodbye to you all." She folded her hands over the front pleats of her *hakama*.

What did she mean? Was she going away? Yes, she must be. But why was she going away in the middle of the first term? That was not fair. Koji looked down.

"You were the first class I made friends with when I came to this school. You were all in the first grade then, and it was my first year as a teacher too. That is why I feel particularly concerned about you all and hope you will keep well and happy and continue to work hard after I've left."

She paused for a moment and then dismissed them. Koji looked down, trying hard not to cry. He felt sure the teacher had chosen to sing with him as a way of saying goodbye.

"The hedge is fragrant with flowers . . ." His Komori friends crooned jokingly as they left the school, and they were still singing when they crossed Ohashi Bridge; they obviously could not care less that the teacher was going away.

"Idiots!" Koji muttered angrily to himself. But then he suddenly realized it was lucky they were, since it would never occur to them to wonder why Miss Kashiwagi should have chosen to sing with him.

At supper, that evening, he remarked as casually as possible, "Miss Kashiwagi's going away."

"Eh!" exclaimed Seitaro. "What school's she going to?"

"I don't know."

"Maybe she's going to get married," suggested Fudé, with a little smile.

"Yes, that'll be it," said Nui, confidently.

"But teachers don't get married, do they?" asked Koji, in disbelief.

"Of course, they do." Nui tried not to laugh. "She may be a teacher but she's still a girl."

"Yes, a girl's got to get married, teacher, young lady, or whatever." Fudé's smile faded and her expression grew serious.

"Why?" pestered Koji.

"You wouldn't understand yet, Koji. And when you're older, you'll understand by yourself."

"Sounds funny to me."

Koji felt irritated, but not because he thought his mother and grandmother were talking nonsense; rather, it was the obvious truth of what they were saying that made it all so confusing.

Intending to thresh the barley that evening, Fudé and Nui went out to the shed after supper and lit the lamp there. Seitaro and Koji were left facing each other in the bare-looking room. The new house had finally been built a year after the fire, and they had moved in at the end of May. But it still was not properly furnished yet, tatami having been laid only in the bedroom; and even these were the old mats from the shed. In the remaining two rooms there were merely loose mats of coarsely woven straw on the floor.

Seitaro threw himself down on one. "Gosh, I'm worn out with all that harrowing today. Farming's terribly hard work. I really have to take my hat off to Mom and Gran for the way they've kept at it all these years."

When the winter crop of wheat and barley had been harvested, the fields were flooded and then harrowed to break up the clods of earth and produce a smooth mud in readiness for the transplanting of the rice seedlings. But harrowing was backbreaking work, as could be seen from the state of any farmer afterwards, completely bespattered in mud from head to foot.

Seitaro was obviously exhausted and ready for bed after helping his mother and grandmother all day. Nevertheless, Koji felt that he must at least tell him about that "Shusui Kotoku, given-name-Denjiro." He wondered where to start and was at a loss as how best to explain.

"If only he'd read "Our Father" it'd be easy," he thought, worried that Seitaro would not really understand about Shusui Kotoku, given-name-Denjiro, without having read the story, and not feeling at all confident of being able to give a clear account of such a difficult matter.

"What'd happen if the Emperor died, Seitaro?" he asked at last.

Seitaro started giggling at the unexpectedness of such a question. "First, Miss Kashiwagi, and now the Emperor!"

"No really, Seitaro, is it true it'd go all dark if the Emperor died?"

Seitaro stopped laughing. Koji was looking down at him with a troubled expression, as if he were about to burst into tears.

He sat up. "No, if the Emperor died, his son the Crown Prince'd take over and be emperor. It wouldn't go all dark really, that's just a story."

"Even if the Emperor was killed by a bomb?"

"A bomb! Why on earth would the Emperor be killed by a bomb?"

"Somebody made one."

"Aren't you mixing it up with the shooting of Marquis Hirobumi Ito a while ago?"

"No, I'm not. That was An Jung-geun."

"That's it. How did you remember? I guess your memory's much better than mine."

"Course I remember. The Headmaster was only talking about it today."

"Why was he talking about that again? It happened last year."

"Because this time, some people tried to kill the Emperor with a bomb."

"A bomb! The Emperor!"

"Mm."

"You're making it up?"

"No, it's true. The Headmaster said there were seven of them and they'd all been arrested."

"Seven?"

After a moment's pause, Seitaro whispered again, "Seven?" feeling both, "only seven?" and, "as many as seven?"

"Did he tell you their names?"

"Just one."

"What was it?"

"Shusui Kotoku, given-name-Denjiro."

"Shusui Kotoku, given-name-Denjiro?"

"Yeah. His real name's Denjiro Kotoku and Shusui must be his pen name. D'you remember Toyo told us that Sazanami Iwaya's* real name is Sueo and that Sazanami's just a pen name. Well, it's the same as that."

"There's not much you don't know, is there? But why did Shusui Kotoku and those other people want to kill the Emperor? Didn't the Headmaster tell you?"

"Yes. He said the man called Kotoku was against war because he thought it was wrong."

"So that's it. It makes sense now. The Emperor's always ready to go to war because he's the Supreme Commander of the Army and the Navy, as well as the Army Commander-in-Chief.''

"And he said that they ought to share the rich people's money because otherwise it wasn't fair to poor people.''

"That makes it even clearer. The Emperor's richer than anybody else. Look at the way he handed out twelve thousand yen of his pocket money when there was that fire in Osaka. So that's why they made a bomb . . . But they didn't stand a chance. The police and the troops are all the Emperor's men. They were bound to be caught straightaway and executed.''

Buriburi! Buriburi! They could hear the grain pattering down as their mother and grandmother stripped the ears of barley.

"I bet it's all in the newspapers.'' Seitaro clasped his hands behind his head.

The newspapers. Fancy that . . . And then Koji thought of Hidéaki, who was probably reading those same newspapers somewhere. Toyo might be too; and even if he was not, he would certainly have learnt about Shusui Kotoku, given-name-Denjiro, at middle school . . .

Naturally, neither he nor Seitaro was conscious of the great flow of history, but, as they lay there with their ears to the floor, they felt as if they could hear a rumbling in the distance.

III

July 2 was *hangesho*—the eleventh day after the summer solstice. The early ripening variety of rice had taken firm root and the leaves were already beginning to darken.

"Looks as if the weather's going to be all right this year.''

For no particular reason, they all felt hopeful. And Seitaro too seemed in the best of spirits. His uncle Yuji from Ino was taking him to Osaka that morning.

"When'll you be coming back again, Seitaro?'' asked Koji.

Seitaro stretched out his arms, in their narrow-sleeved kimono. "I'll be back when I've got wide sleeves. And I bet I won't need tucks in the shoulders by then, either.''

Koji grinned at the thought of his brother in a fine, wide-sleeved kimono; until it occurred to him what a long time it would be before that were possible, and the smile died on his lips.

Seitaro was going to be apprenticed to a rice dealer—the ideal place for a Frogfish, according to his mother and grandmother, since he would at least be able to eat his fill there. Once he had left, however, they could think of nothing for the next few days but that figure in the white summer kimono with the crosshatch pattern, which they had made specially for the start of his apprenticeship.

Koji did not have any news of Miss Kashiwagi until the end of July. The teacher, whose surname had changed to Hayakawa, sent a letter addressed to the whole school, and for two days it was stuck up in the corridor outside the sewing room. Koji went to have a look many times, but there was always a group of pupils from the upper grades clustered around it, and so he could not read it at leisure. But he did manage to memorize five or six lines: "When the children are tired of swimming, they sit on a big rock drying their backs in the sun like little turtles. I think of you all whenever I see them and wish that you could swim in the Yoshino River too. The water is so clear you can see right to the bottom."

It seemed that Miss Kashiwagi had married into a family living in a village near the Yoshino, many miles to the south of Sakata.

"The hedge is fragrant with flowers . . ."

Her successor, Miss Takano, taught Koji's class the second and third verses of this song. The daughter of a landowner in Shimana, Miss Takano wore a maroon-colored *hakama,* and, although she had a lovely voice, Koji was afraid of her because she hardly ever smiled. Besides, she always seemed to give the Komori children a wide berth whenever she passed them. Koji did not mention her at all to his mother and grandmother. Nor did he tell them about Miss Kashiwagi's letter, or the fact that her name had changed to Hayakawa; and he would not have breathed a word about the time he sang with her.

"You've been out of sorts ever since Seitaro left, haven't you, Koji? Never mind, you'll soon get over it."

Nui supplied such a plausible reason for his unusual quietness that Koji himself believed it.

There were thunderstorms from time to time this summer, unlike the previous year, and the rice grew at a satisfactory rate. Tosaku Nagai's family, who had managed to survive somehow through the winter and spring by peddling sandals like beggars, were now looking forward cheerfully to a decent supply of rice again in the autumn. Only Takeshi was still out of sorts, trembling every day. He was not sick; it was simply that Officer Aikawa came to patrol the village once a day without fail, stomping around in his heavy boots.

He usually walked his beat after one o'clock in the afternoon and Takeshi would run and hide in the shed at Koji's then, pretending he had come to play. The new house hid the shed from the main track through the village.

Koji always joined him there, feeling sorry for Také, who had been so terrified of the police ever since the fire, although, in fact, he was not overfond of the Officer's shoes and sabre either.

And Koji and Takeshi were not the only ones to hide from Officer Aikawa; most of the young children in Komori held their breath in fear and trembling as he went by. "If you don't stop that blubbering, the Officer will be round here," their parents roared at them countless times every day. They could not even cry in peace, although they had reason enough to want to.

"I'm hungry!" "I want some money for a slate pencil!" But their wishes were never granted. Instead, some would be scolded, others hit, and all would end up in tears; and then there would be the threat of an angry visit from the Officer. On top of everything else, this summer they had been told they would be arrested on the spot if found without any clothes on. So the only thing to do was to hide from this policeman, who frightened them even more than the thunder that their mothers said came to take away their navels.

However, their parents could not hide; and while they found it hard to suddenly abandon the habit of going around half-naked in the middle of summer, it was even harder to have to pay a fine of ten sen. Therefore, there was always a mad rush to pull on some sort of proper clothing whenever they caught sight of Officer Aikawa's white uniform.

Dress was not the only thing they had to be careful about. A woman could not leave a needle in her hair without risking a fine; and surprisingly, women still often popped one in their chignon instead of in a pincushion when they were sewing. This was not a matter the police could overlook, since it might easily cause injury, and their mission was surely to protect the life and property of their fellow citizens.

It was commonly held, however, that they were so strict about needles because women had been known to fatally injure men with them. But, whatever the reason, such a fine was undoubtedly a great blow for the woman concerned.

At first, Officer Aikawa had usually passed through Komori without stopping on his daily beat, but after a while he took to calling in at people's homes to give them the following sort of guidance:

> You must brush your teeth every morning.
>
> Comb your hair and remove the lice every morning.
>
> Each member of the family must use a separate towel to prevent the spread of trachoma.
>
> Both men and women must always do up their sashes before going out.
>
> Do not go out at night unless absolutely necessary.
>
> Do not defecate in the countryside.
>
> Take strict precautions against fire.
>
> Do not indulge in idle gossip.

Their neighbor on the north side, Kané Shimura, who had a liking for "idle gossip," was undeterred and dropped in at Koji's home as usual when she had a few moments to spare. According to her, Tosaku Nagai's two eldest daughters had sunk into a life of shame, and, with the money he received for them, Tosaku had built a new house, about eighteen feet by thirty feet.

Although Koji did not understand what she meant by a "life of shame," he thought it sounded a hard kind of apprenticeship.

Kané also told them how Kiyokazu was learning to make shoes at a shop in Osaka. Seitaro too would be better off in a shoe shop instead of with a rice dealer, she added, because even country folk would be wearing shoes before long.

After the 210th Day,* it was no longer so unbearably hot that they wanted to go around half-naked, and they were released from the threat of a fine. Instead, there was the problem of baths: whereas in summer they could always warm a tubful of water in the sun, now there was no alternative but to find the means to kindle a fire.

Fortunately, in their neighborhood, there was the custom of visiting each other's homes for a bath. Of course, without anywhere to wash, this merely consisted of wallowing like a frog in a tub of water, but, even so, the pleasure of a hot soak soon brought over all the neighbors.

One evening in the middle of September, Koji's family heated up a bath. Hirokichi came round early with his wife, Kané, but maintained a gloomy silence while the other neighbors were still there. At last, at about ten o'clock, they all left and his eyes lit up immediately.

"I've got rather an interesting bit of news for you tonight. You know the way the Officer's taken to coming 'round here every day; well, there's a good reason for it, all right. It seems there's been this terrible intrigue. A group of educated fellows is behind it. They started up something called the anarchist party at the beginning of the summer."

"Gracious, an intrigue?" chimed in Kané, who had not heard about it until now.

Hirokichi grinned. "You know what an intrigue is, do you?"

"Ha, ha . . . Course I do. If I was having it off with another man behind your back, that'd be an intrigue, wouldn't it?"

"Er, yes, I s'pose it would. Anyway, this particular intrigue is a bit more serious. You see, these fellas didn't care for the way the present government's handling things, and, more important, they didn't care for the Emperor, so they made this bomb to kill him."

"Kill the Emperor?" interrupted Kané again.

"That's right. You can always find another minister or general, so there wouldn't be any point in killing somebody like that, but there's only one Emperor."

"They must've been nabbed by now, though, seeing as everybody knows all about it."

"Yes. I heard the last four or five were nabbed only the other day in Osaka."

"You mean to say there was even some of 'em in Osaka?"

"Yes. That's why the police are looking round here, too. They think there may still be a few hiding in these parts. Imagine it, big shots like that in a village like Komori. That'd be something to tell the grandchildren for generations."

"Wouldn't it," Nui seemed to sigh.

"Anyway, the police net stretches right across the whole country these days. But even they can't go peering into people's homes without a good reason. That's why they go on the way they do—you mustn't go about without any clothes on, have you got rid of your lice, have you washed—when all the time they've just come to have a sniff around. 'Dogs' we call 'em, and there couldn't be a better name for them, could there? Ha, ha, ha . . .''

"Downright frightening, I call it," said Kané. "Here I was thinking the Officer really had come 'round to complain about the lice, not knowing any better."

"So did we," agreed Fudé. "We haven't a clue what's going on in the world. It's because we don't get out and about much and don't have any newspapers. Only thing we can be sure of is that we'll never know what it is to have a full stomach . . . Anyway, things being as they are, let us know if you hear anything else. I expect they'll try the fellows they caught and . . .''

"That's right," interrupted Hirokichi. "They'll get a stiff sentence with Taro Katsura, the prime minister, him being a general and the Emperor's right-hand man. That's what everybody's whispering Osaka way—they have to whisper it or else they'd be nabbed too. And mind you don't go mentioning it to anybody else."

"As if we would. But it takes all sorts, doesn't it? Only a while back there was that man that couldn't believe his good luck when he found the Emperor's crap on Miminashi Hill, and now there's folk trying to kill His Majesty with a bomb . . . I can't make head or tail of it."

But it did not particularly bother Kané whether she understood or not, and presently she and Hirokichi returned to their hovel.

Koji, who had been sitting with his back to the lamp, now turned to face it. The light from it seemed yellower than usual, and the faces of his mother and grandmother looked dreadfully gaunt.

He was in a quandary: should he tell them about Shusui Kotoku, given-name-Denjiro, or not? He had been holding his breath, in case Uncle Hirokichi mentioned the name, wanting to hear it one moment and not the next; too nervous even to face the lamp.

In the end, he decided to keep it a secret. He woke up three times that night; and each time, heard the crickets' melancholy cry.

IV

"I dreamed of Seitaro last night."

Fudé and Koji pricked up their ears at once, as Nui hardly ever talked about dreams.

"It was in the evening and I was busy with something or other, when all of a sudden I heard this voice say hello. It was Seitaro home again. And bless me, if he wasn't wearing a kimono with proper wide sleeves. So I said to him, 'Well, you've got your wide-sleeved kimono, then. Before you went away, you said you'd be back when you'd got one.' And he says, 'Yes, I've become a salesclerk, so it's wide sleeves from now on,' and he held out his arms to show me."

Koji heard the cry of joy that welled up in his mother's throat. She was making rice cakes for the "Sickle Offering." The freshly boiled rice was still very hot and Koji was fanning it to cool it, while Nui exercised her skill at making the bean paste—it was no easy matter judging the salty taste.

"But would you believe it," she continued. "The sleeves had a slit in them edged with red silk. I was taken aback, I can tell you, and I said to him, 'That's a woman's kimono, Seitaro. Why ever have you come back dressed up like that? You'll be the laughingstock of the village.' Then he replied, looking so serious, 'But Gran, it's the latest thing in Osaka.' And funnily enough, I was that impressed I thought to myself, 'Yes, there's no place like Osaka.' Just goes to show you how stupid dreams are." Nui laughed scornfully as if to dismiss her own stupidity for talking about them.

"But don't you think it means he's settled down now in Osaka, seeing as he came back in something that's so fashionable there?" Fudé suggested, with such earnestness that Nui stopped laughing.

"Yes, he'll 'ave been gone five months soon," she replied gravely. "I expect he's quite good at finding his way around by now."

"I wonder if he dreams of us, too?" Koji began fanning his mother's face and she blinked.

"Maybe he'll dream of rice cakes tonight. Remember, we couldn't make any for the 'Sickle Offering' last year because of the drought. We're certainly making up for it this year, though. I bet they can smell them even in Osaka."

"I'll make them smell them even better," and Koji began fanning the steam vigorously northwestward.

The savory bean-paste cakes were soon ready and three plates of them were placed on a small table: one for Seitaro, one for the sickles used in the harvest, and one for the family shrine.

"Seitaro'd probably turn up his nose at these savory cakes, but why don't we have one, as it's the 'Sickle Offering.'" Nui opened her

large mouth and laughed, sounding quite untroubled, although
secretly she felt anxious about Seitaro now that the cold weather was
setting in. She was longing for a letter from him, despite maintaining
that no news was good news whenever Fudé grumbled about his
not having written.

However, they were not entirely without news of Seitaro's apprenticeship. Uncle Yuji in Ino apparently visited his employer when he
went to Osaka on business and had already written twice to say that
Seitaro was fine and working hard. The day before yesterday too,
another card had arrived announcing that he would bring more news
when he visited them in the near future to help pack the rice.

Perhaps it was Nui's impatience for this visit that was the reason for
her unexpected dream. Although Yuji had written "in the near
future," it would be quite a while yet before he came over, since the
rice not only had to be reaped, but hung over racks, threshed, dried,
and husked before it could be packed into sacks.

The "Sickle Offering" cakes were not so much delicious as life
itself to them, after having warded off starvation for so many months
with cheap Nanking rice, wheat flour, and rice bran. The rice was a
living substance, and each mouthful they gobbled up went rushing
down into their stomachs.

"We farmers are quite something," said Nui presently, with a
satisfied burp. "They say the Emperor can't eat any of the first crop
till the Niiname-sai.* Not like us; we can eat as many cakes of it as
we like."

"Too true," agreed Fudé.

Only a small part of the half-acre they rented was used to grow the
earliest variety of rice. Yesterday, it had been husked, and this evening,
turned into cakes, which required some ingenuity, since it was not the
glutinous variety usually used. But Fudé had cleverly contrived to
produce a sticky texture by adding some finely chopped taro.

The Niiname-sai festival was four days later. Koji was overjoyed
because it meant "a whole day's holiday," without any ceremony at
school, unlike the Three Great Festivals. Moreover, by a lucky stroke
of fate, a card from Seitaro arrived at midday.

The original message on the back had been brushed out with jet
black ink and another written over it in pencil, which could only be
read if the card was held at a slant; then the characters shone silver
and showed up surprisingly clearly.

Nui was spreading out unhusked rice to dry in the back vegetable garden when she heard about the card.

"He must've written it a hundred times or more, judging by how black it is," she said, half laughing, half choked with tears.

"Isn't his writing small?" Fudé pulled off the towel covering her head and started to read it slowly out loud.

Dear Gran, Mom, and Koji,

I hope you are all keeping well. You will be pleased to hear that I am getting used to the work now. I started learning the abacus in the evening at the beginning of November. I am also learning a lot about rice, but it is very difficult and there is still a lot I do not know.

I am sending Koji a magazine somebody gave me. I am very busy and I do not have time to read magazines. Please take care of yourselves because the weather will soon be turning cold. Goodbye.

For a while, the three of them were silent, each wrapped up in their own thoughts.

"He said he's sending Koji a book. Should get here by tomorrow or the day after," Fudé remarked at last.

"I'm glad he's learning the abacus," Nui added.

"I wonder if the rice business is as difficult as he says it is."

"Well, you've got to learn to tell one grade from another and then there's the market . . . It's bad enough for folk like us that get down in the mud to grow the stuff, but I expect them dealers 'ave got their own set of problems." Nui threw back her head and laughed.

"I s'pose you're right," replied Fudé. "We'll have more than mud to worry about ourselves though this year, Mother," she added meaningfully.

Nui nodded. "You mean the tenant farmers' scourge?"

She was referring to the Rice Inspection System. Hitherto, inspection had been undertaken by trade associations of rice dealers and had not affected individual tenant farmers at all, whose only obligation was to pay the rice due as rent in the presence of the landlord. Of course, some landlords had collected more than their fair share, insisting the rice be weighed over and over again on the pretext that they were getting short measure; but such disputes were considered a private matter between landlord and tenant, and settled accordingly. This year, however, the system of inspection had come under the control of the prefectural government, and, at the same time, extended to cover both the rice paid as rent as well as that produced for sale by owner-farmers. Moreover, first of all, there was to be an inspection of the straw sacks in which the rice was packed; at present, the biggest headache for Nui and Fudé. The sacks had to be a specified weight, and so from now on they would have to scrutinize the quality of the straw and weigh it before making even the round lids at either end, to which they had never given a moment's thought before. And when this first hurdle had been surmounted, there would be the second even harder one awaiting them; to cross which . . . Nui crouched down on the mat to examine the unhusked rice: no, it was not nearly dry enough yet.

Koji was affected by the anxiety of his mother and grandmother, and whenever he heard them talking about the rice inspection, he thought of Officer Aikawa; for some reason, he had imagined that the Officer would accompany the rice inspector and still could not quite rid himself of this notion. But now, his thoughts turned to something of more immediate concern and his face broke into a smile. He took the card from his mother and read it to himself again and again. There were a few characters that he did not know, but he managed to work them out by remembering what his mother had read, and he could also decipher most of the address on the front: c/o Yasui Store, 57 Tamatsukuri-machi, Higashi-ku, Osaka.

That night, he slept with the card by his pillow, hoping to dream of Seitaro. Instead, he dreamed of Master Hidé; and he was deep in conversation with someone else and never once looked in Koji's direction. But by the next morning he had forgotten all about it. He threw the card up in the air, telling himself that if it landed black side up the magazine would arrive that day; and that was indeed the way it landed.

V

They had laid down a mat in the narrow *doma*, and Nui was twining rope there while Fudé wove straw sacks. A circular had informed them that the first inspection of the empty sacks would take place on December 1, and the second on December 15, which meant that they still had some time; but they both wanted to finish this worrying task as quickly as possible to be free to concentrate on their night work of sandal-making again.

Koji had been sitting quietly by the chaff fire of the brazier since before supper. His longed-for magazine had arrived, and, well aware that he was now lost to the world, Fudé had left him undisturbed, apart from calling him to the evening meal. By nine o'clock, however, she could no longer remain silent:

"Hadn't you better finish it tomorrow, Koji?"

"Yes, you won't have anything to look forward to if you read it all in one go," agreed Nui.

"Mm." Koji closed the magazine. "D'you know what a pass is, Gran?"

"A pass? You mean over a mountain?"

"Yes. Do you know where it is?"

"Well, there's lots of them. If you're heading for Kawachi, there's Takenouchi Pass, Jusan Pass, and Kuragari Pass. And then there's Awara Pass and Namida Pass over Yoshino way, and maybe two or three others besides."

"Have you ever gone over a pass, Gran?"

"Can't say as I have, but Hirokichi next door crosses one on the way to Osaka."

"The other side of the pass . . ."

"There's Kawachi," explained Nui, with a patient smile.

But Koji was no longer paying attention. He jumped into bed muttering to himself, "the other side of the pass, the other side of the pass."

There was a story called "The Autumn Pass" in the boys' magazine Seitaro had sent, and the hero of the story, Yokichi Ohara, had said, "The other side of the pass, there's the place I come from. And, it's . . ."

At first, Koji had thought it was about a faraway place. Yokichi was fourteen and the tucks in the shoulder of his kimono had only just been let out when he began traveling from place to place peddling knickknacks, which he carried on his back. Everybody was amazed at how hard he worked, and, since he never haggled unpleasantly with his customers, after a while they began to look forward to seeing him, remembering how many times a year he came round.

By the time he was a young man of nineteen, Yokichi had saved enough money to be able to stop peddling and set up a store in the town. Many families offered him their daughter's hand in marriage, but he refused them all. He had set his heart on marrying a girl who had been working for the past five years at an inn at the foot of the pass.

She was called Kayo, and it was rumored that the innkeeper and his wife felt sorry for her because she had no close family, and they treated her with particular kindness. One day, Yokichi told the innkeeper of his love for Kayo.

The innkeeper was delighted, and said that he would like to give Kayo away as his own daughter. Then Yokichi decided to cross the pass and return home to tell his parents the happy news.

"Why not take Kayo with you so you can show her your home and introduce her to your parents and brothers and sisters?" suggested the innkeeper.

This was what Yokichi wished too, and he made up his mind to help Kayo over the steep pass.

It was autumn when they set out, and the colors of the wooded slopes seemed lovelier to them than any flowers.

On reaching the top of the pass, they rested their weary legs for a while, and then they were about to start the descent when Yokichi suddenly stopped dead in his tracks. "What is it?" asked Kayo, in great concern, and Yokichi replied, "There is something I've been hiding. The other side of the pass, there's the place I come from. And, it's an *eta* village."

Kayo hid her face against Yokichi's breast and wept, and through her tears, she said, "But I'm an *eta*, too."

"The Autumn Pass" was no longer a story about somewhere far off. Koji could picture Yokichi's face; he could hear Kayo's tearful voice, and see the autumn colors, and the two figures moving away as they climbed down, side by side, toward the village bathed in evening sunlight . . . How odd, though: they now seemed to be walking toward him; and the young man was Seitaro.

"If Seitaro masters the trade so as he can run a store in Osaka, I can die in peace," he heard Nui say.

"I hope he learns the trade soon as well. It won't be for a good while yet, though."

"Four or five years go by quick enough. Look at Shinkichi, it's already seven years."

Koji gulped in surprise: his father had been dead for seven years. He had often heard his mother and grandmother talk about how they would like to distribute gifts to their neighbors on the seventh anniversary of his death, and now he suddenly realized that that would be on December 3, in nine days' time.

Then, out of the blue, he heard the words "Shusui Kotoku, given-name-Denjiro." They had been lying hidden, unspoken by anybody since September; but tonight they had returned, together with the *banko*-headed father who had died in the war. And what was more, Shusui Kotoku, given-name-Denjiro, did have a white beard.

"Have you finished that magazine yet?" his mother asked, three days later, and although he did not think there was much likelihood of her wishing to read it, he lied to be on the safe side. "I've lent it to a friend," he replied. He did not want her to read "The Autumn Pass," nor to be responsible for her reading it, either.

Unaware of this, Fudé continued, "Well, that's all right, I suppose, but make sure you take good care of it, seeing that Seitaro's gone to all the trouble of sending it. Then maybe he'll send you some more."

Koji almost cut out "The Autumn Pass," but, as he gazed at the illustration of Kayo weeping on Yokichi's breast, he changed his mind. In her hemp-soled sandals, Kayo somehow looked a little like "Hachimero" Shigemi, who had gone to Osaka.

On the seventh anniversary of Shinkichi's death, Nui and Fudé asked the priest from An'yoji to recite sutras, and they gave each of their neighbors a plate on which were arranged two dumplings from the offering. Koji took the plates round, repeating the same message fifteen times:

"Today is the seventh anniversary of my father's death. Please accept this small gift in his memory."

After faltering a little at the first two or three houses, he could soon rattle it off with confidence.

"It's not seven years already, is it? My, how time flies," replied one woman, deeply moved.

"It's a nice plate," said another, turning it over to look at the back.

At Takeshi's house, Také and his brothers Yasuo and Tomizo began squabbling over the two dumplings until their mother Sayo boxed their ears.

That evening, Fudé took up her sewing needle instead of doing the usual work with straw. The cold weather would soon be upon them, and for the next two or three nights she would have to patch up their clothes, such as they were.

Nui sat warming her hands over the brazier, something she rarely did. "Well, we can rest easy now at any rate," she remarked, sounding as if a load was off her mind.

Fudé felt equally relieved. Although the plates were cheap at eight sen each, it had cost one yen twenty sen to buy fifteen, the cost of almost half a bushel of unpolished rice—which, for people like themselves who lived on gruel the year round, was an expense they felt in their bellies. Yet they had undertaken it unhesitatingly. Apart from the question of making an offering to the dead, there was after all their obligation to the neighbors; and, in the neighborhood, it was felt to be only right and proper for the bereaved family to do as much for a Fallen Hero such as Shinkichi.

"The next one'll be the thirteenth anniversary," blurted out Fudé after a moment's pause. "I suppose we'll have to do something a bit better for that, Mother."

"Yes, everybody splashes out for the thirteenth. But don't start worrying yourself about it, Fudé. Seitaro'll be nineteen by then. I'm sure he'll help with it."

"You're right, he will be nineteen." Fudé gave a little smile, as if the nineteen-year-old Seitaro was standing there before her.

Koji silently watched the fire in the brazier. He was thinking about Yokichi in the story. He was nineteen when he revealed to Kayo that he was born in the *eta* village on the other side of the pass. Would Seitaro, too, when he was nineteen, tell somebody that he came from the *eta* village of Komori?

"I'm going to burn that magazine," he resolved. He liked Yokichi and Kayo, but hated the story. It somehow seemed to be saying, "And you're an *eta*, too, you know, Koji"; although it was hard to understand why for a third-grader like himself.

The next day, he took advantage of the fire lit for a bath and threw the magazine into the flames.

VI

Koji was already on holiday when Uncle Yuji from Ino came over to help with the packing of the rice toward the end of December.

"We'd better run it through the *mangoku* again to be on the safe side.

Depends on the person of course, but them inspectors are terrible stick-lers as a rule," he said, examining the unpolished rice in the baskets.

Fudé immediately set about getting things ready, and presently the rice started to roll down the screen of the *mangoku,* an apparatus for sifting out faulty grains. The angle of the screen could be adjusted, altering the rate at which grains fell through it, and naturally Fudé and Nui wanted to keep these to a minimum. But, on the other hand, if they did not sift the rice strictly enough it would not pass the inspection, which meant that the landlord would not accept it as rent. Sadly, they had no choice therefore but to set the *mangoku* at a gentle tilt and close their eyes to the amount falling through.

"Can't be helped the way things are at present. You'd better keep what's under the *mangoku* for yourselves," Uncle Yuji tried to console them as he watched the steady stream falling through the screen.

"That'll be all that's left for us if we sift it this thorough," remarked Fudé.

"Yes, but like I said, you've just got to grin and bear it with things the way they are. They thought up this rice inspection for the benefit of the rich, so it's obvious that those who grow the stuff are going to suffer."

"Yes, the landowners are doing all right for themselves. Whoever it was that worked it out certainly made sure it'd help them."

"And they say the ones that play the rice market are smiling, too. They can see the quality of rice getting better every year."

"The more I think about that rice market, Yuji, the funnier it seems. I could understand it if they were buying and selling real rice you eat, but they're just gambling, buying and selling rice they haven't really bought and sold—futures they call it, don't they—and doing well out of it, I'm sure."

"That's right. It's what you call speculating."

"Then playing the market's no more than gambling, is it?"

"It's the biggest gamble of the lot."

"But I thought it was wrong to gamble."

"It is if it's on a small scale, but not on a large scale with things like stocks and shares and rice, where you've got the Stock Exchange and the Rice Exchange. There's all sorts of complicated laws surrounding it then. It's quite something."

"Was it the same in the old days?"

"Well, the other day, Mr. Yasui in Osaka was telling me the rice market goes back to the time of the shogunate, and it started off in Osaka, too."

"Well, I never. And Mr. Yasui should know, I suppose," said Nui, who was measuring the rice with a 30-pint vessel as it gushed from the mouth of the *mangoku*.

"You see, Osaka was the biggest city in Japan in the early days of the Tokugawa shogunate," continued Uncle Yuji, packing the rice into sacks. "It had a population of about 400,000 and they sold more rice there than anywhere else. And the daimyo* got to know that Osaka was the place to sell, so they all set up warehouses there, where they sent the rice from their estates. They got their agents to handle it for them, and they say there were as many as five hundred of these warehouses by the time of the third shogun. And by then, they'd found out it was better to get the merchants to do the selling rather than the samurai. And eventually, with all the merchants getting together every day to buy and sell, they set up a market, which was the start of the rice market as we know it."

"Then they bought and sold real rice in those days?"

"No, as a matter of fact, they didn't. They seem to have been even more reckless then than they are today. What happened was this: the daimyo issued vouchers that by rights could be exchanged for rice. In fact, though, they all had trouble making ends meet on their estates, so they raised money by issuing sham vouchers. They'd pretend there was rice in their warehouses when there wasn't, counting on the tax rice they'd be getting the following year. They couldn't have got by without cheating, living off the fat of the land the way they were—not only the house of the shogun but all the daimyo and samurai as well. The rice merchants did all right out of it. They competed with each other, using these vouchers, and they made money through the fluctuations in price. Some of them got rich overnight by cornering the market and forcing up the price. But anyway, they'd issue so many sham vouchers that people would get suspicious and realize in the end that the goods were lacking. Then the price of rice'd shoot up until the poor couldn't afford it anymore, and there'd be riots, with people smashing and burning down the mansions of the rich."

"It's always the rascals that come out on top in this world," said Nui with a sad smile; she could not help feeling how ridiculously honest they were, carefully measuring out half a bushel of rice into each sack.

"So we're working ourselves to the bone growing rice all for the sake of a bunch of gamblers," and Fudé too smiled bitterly. She had always thought that society was far too complex for people like themselves to understand; that the State was something remote, a subject not even to be mentioned inadvertently, much less discussed; yet now she had the impression of being able to see it clearly in its true colors.

Uncle Yuji laughed, as if it were funny. "Everything in this world's a gamble. Take war, for instance: the Battle of Sekigahara was just a gamble between Toyotomi and Tokugawa, and so was the last war between Japan and Russia. Same thing with us farmers. There we are every year, out gambling in the open air with them fields."

"What about that business? I s'pose that was a gamble, too." Nui pulled the strickle smartly toward her, neatly leveling off the rice in the measure.

"What do you mean 'that business'?" asked Uncle Yuji. Struck by Nui's deftness, he thought to himself, "And that comes of years of practice."

"You know, somebody or other made a bomb to try and do the Emperor in."

"Ah, I've got you now," he nodded; "How did you know about that, Gran?"

"Ha, ha . . . The man next door told us. During the summer he was working as a carrier, traveling to Osaka, and came back with all sorts of stories. Now he's got a job with a charcoal-burner over Yoshino way and we don't hear anything interesting anymore."

"Really? Well, I don't know much about it myself, but it seems they've arrested twenty-six so far."

"That many. It's a frightening business."

"Yes, it certainly was frightening what they plotted. Did you know there was a woman among them?"

"A woman? How dreadful!"

"They say she's about thirty, the wife of the ringleader."

"But whatever made them think of such a thing?"

"I'm sure they had their reasons, which we wouldn't understand. There's no getting away from it, though; it's playing for high stakes to try and do in the Emperor—quite something if you win, but if you don't, you pay for it with your head. And it's rumored that the death sentence will be handed down for those twenty-six too in the next few days, seeing as they're being tried for treason, the most serious offense of the lot. Not that it'll make any difference to us whatever happens. We're never any better off no matter who's emperor or shogun."

Did he mean that? Koji glanced at his uncle's face. He had been listening intently to the grown-ups' conversation while holding the funnel steady at the mouth of the sack, as his uncle poured in the rice.

Unaware, his uncle said as if to humor him, "It's not very interesting is it, Koji, all this difficult grown-ups' talk?"

"Yes, it is," he retorted defiantly.

"Oh, you think so, do you?" His uncle looked down at him, "Did you understand it then?"

"Yes, I know all about it. The Headmaster told us at school."

"The Headmaster told you about a thing like that? Well, I'll be! He must've been shocked, all right. But it's enough to shock anybody. I mean, they were trying to kill the Emperor with a bomb."

"But that man didn't do it because he wanted to be emperor himself, Uncle."

His uncle tried to laugh but could not; and Nui and Fudé were the same: they had never dreamed they would hear Koji's opinion on such a subject.

"He said that war's wrong and the Emperor's no good because he wants to make wars."

"Did he really?" Fudé blurted out.

"Yes, the Headmaster told us. And he wanted to share the rich people's money with poor people."

"Sounds an odd sort." Nui gripped the strickle tightly.

"That's what they call 'dangerous ideas' these days. They disagree with the doings of the Emperor and the powers that be, that's why. But in this world the strong get fat by preying on the weak. That's the way things are, and it's about as much use as throwing straws against the wind for one or two hundred people to try and change it. It's all very well to talk the way they do about sharing the money of the rich with the poor, but can you imagine the rich agreeing? It's just a pipe dream."

Nui and Fudé were silent.

"So we'd better make a good job of this rice and try and get the best grade we can. There's a difference of about thirty or forty sen a sack between one grade and another."

Once more, Nui and Fudé turned their gaze toward the *mangoku* and watched the rice trickling down it and the rice falling through.

The weak sun shining on the eaves of the shed felt chilly to them all.

VII

"They say you get a better grade if you entertain him nicely with saké and some delicacies," Fudé and Nui heard it rumored; but it was in connection with another village and they did not think it would apply to Komori. Hideo Ogaki, the thirty-one-year-old owner-farmer from Shimana who was the rice inspector, would probably never have come near Komori even for a pee if it had not been for the office he held. And he had not drunk even one cup of tea when he inspected everybody's empty straw sacks in the grounds of An'yoji in December.

Nevertheless, on the day of the rice inspection, Fudé swept and cleaned and gave the kettle a special polish in case he should want some tea.

Inspector Ogaki eventually arrived in the afternoon, attired in a brown striped *haori,* serge *hakama,* a deerstalker cap, and black lace-up boots.

"Dear, oh dear, what a path," and he stamped the mud off his boots in the entrance. The frozen ground was thawing, and all the tracks through Komori were in a terrible state; the dirty water flowing from the densely packed houses made it worse, and here and there it was as muddy as a paddy field.

"We're very much obliged to you coming out in such cold weather." Simultaneously, Nui and Fudé removed the towels from their heads.

Inspector Ogaki marched straight through the *doma* and out of the back door. He peered into the shed, "How many sacks?"

"There's eleven-and-a-half here that we're taking round as rent . . "

"Right, hurry up and weigh them."

Each sack had to be weighed separately, and, with Nui's help, Fudé hoisted them, one after another, onto the 165-pound balance she had borrowed for the occasion. This sounded easy enough but was in reality a backbreaking task for the two of them, since the sacks of rice weighed over 140 pounds each.

Inspector Ogaki leisurely wrote the weight on the labels. Then he took out the metal scoop he had brought with him and sullenly thrust it into the belly of first one sack and then another, at the sight of which, Nui and Fudé felt a pang in their own bellies.

"All the same variety, I suppose?" he said, when he had examined the eleven sacks.

"Yes, all 'Shinriki' . . ."

"And just the one field?"

"Yes, one-half-acre belonging to Mr. Sayama," replied Nui, mentioning the size as most of the paddies in that area were a quarter of an acre.

The inspector began stamping his seal on the sacks, producing big black circles the size of balls of charcoal.

"What grade are we getting?" asked Fudé, tense with apprehension.

The inspector cast a sidelong glance at her. A smile, half-ironic, half-roguish, played about his lips and finely trimmed mustache— look and you'll see, won't you, it seemed to say.

Thump, thump. Two black circles. Grade two. A wave of relief swept over Nui and Fudé. Had not Yuji said as he left, "I reckon it's bound to be second grade"?

But, oh dear, the next sack had three circles. And the next had three. And the next. They looked at each other. It was absurd: how could the same variety of rice receive two different grades, they thought, grinding their teeth.

At last, Fudé could bear it no longer. "Excuse me, Inspector, but what's the reason for this?"

"Reason for what?"

"All the sacks are the same variety."

"I'm well aware of that."

"Then why are some grade two and others grade . . ."

The inspector grinned. "Shall I make them all the same grade?" he said slowly.

Fudé was struck dumb: obviously he was thinking of lowering the grade two, since it was easier to add a circle than delete one. And how could they possibly curry favor with him to do otherwise, without the necessary saké and delicacies to offer him?

"I'm sorry, I shouldn't have mentioned it," and Fudé bowed in apology, her legs trembling.

"I take it then you're quite happy. Frankly, they should all be grade three, you know. It's well dried, I grant you, but there's a high percentage of husks here. Anyway, I realize it must've been hard for you women preparing all this rice by yourselves, so I've let you have three, at grade two. Fatherly love you might say. Ha, ha, ha."

"It's very kind of you." Nui hurried back to the *doma* to fill the teapot with hot water from the kettle.

"Don't bother, Grandma. I don't want to start having cups of tea with people or next thing I'll be feeling sorry for them and handing out favors. Strict fairness and impartiality in all things, that's my motto."

He went out of the front entrance.

It was then that Fudé realized Koji had been standing in the corner of the shed all the time, watching. Now he ran out after the inspector, evidently intending to watch at other houses as well.

"How children like anything out of the ordinary." She smiled wistfully and stared round at the rows of sacks. Three grade two and eight grade three. Despite what he had said about letting them have the grade two as a favor, she was left with a bad taste in her mouth, as if they had been duped.

"Let's take the rent round as soon as we can, Mother," she said with a frown. "I can't bear the sight of these sacks after that shameful inspection. How on earth can he tell what the rice is like, glancing at a tiny bit of it like that. We're the ones that know best, we grew it. Rambling on about dryness and husks, he thinks he can make fools of us just because it's Komori."

But Nui knew that once they gave vent to their indignation, there would be no end to it. She tried to calm Fudé. "I know, but what can you do? We couldn't start fighting over it, not even if it was grade four."

"There's a fight!" cried Koji, rushing in.

"A fight?" Instinctively, they both leapt to their feet and peered outside.

Two or three people passed by and disappeared around the corner opposite, as Kané came running up.

"What a to-do! Tosaku's gone and hit the inspector . . . The inspector's down on the ground," she managed to gasp. She had not actually witnessed it herself but had soon got wind of the news and rushed over to tell them. "I don't know what's got into him, turning violent again like that . . ."

Fudé was not in the least surprised, however.

"He's a good-for-nothing, that Tosaku," Kané continued, in a tone of obvious disapproval. "He may not like the grade he gets, but there's no getting away from it, the man's a proper, qualified inspector. Tosaku's heading for a spell of hard labor if you ask me."

For the next few days, they heard all sorts of stories: according to one, when Tosaku saw his rice being stamped grades four and five, even though he had been telling everybody that it would be grade three at the worst, he picked up a pole and, without a word, beat the inspector over the head with it; while another had it that he flared up when told the rice was not dry enough, and went for the inspector—he'd show him all right! And some claimed that far from trying to stop her husband, Sayo had joined in too, although others said that was nonsense.

There was only one rumor with any apparent truth in it; namely, that the quarter-acre field Tosaku had owned had reverted this year to being tenant land. Both Nui and Fudé knew only too well how many years he had toiled to make that quarter of an acre his own; and yet he had only been allowed to enjoy the pleasures of ownership a mere five or six years before the field was once more registered as being held in tenancy. Small wonder then, after such a cruel setback, that he should have reacted violently on finding himself treated as a Komori tenant farmer. Even so, the majority of people in Komori only scoffed at him for being a "prize fool."

And like a "prize fool," Tosaku was locked up in Takada Police Station for a week, on the charge of assaulting Inspector Ogaki. At the end of January, however, he crossed Ohashi Bridge over the Katsuragi, pulling a cart laden with the rice due as rent. Koji and his friends were on their way to school at the time.

"We'll push; we'll push it for you," they cried, gathering round, and proceeded to push the cart up the slope.

"Ah, ha, ha! Ah, ha, ha . . ."

Instead of thanking them, Tosaku opened his mouth wide and guffawed, his breath flickering in the air like white smoke. Koji helped push as far as the school gates, his back drenched with sweat.

The first lesson that day was reading. Koji's back felt cold after sweating so much, but he soon forgot it when the teacher, Mr. Ikuta, pointed to him. He braced himself and began reading aloud.

Firstly, loyalty comes before all other virtues, for great is our debt to the Emperor and to the State.

Secondly, let us remember how much we owe our parents and treat them with love and respect.

Thirdly, let us live in harmony with our brothers and sisters, as branches that grow from the same trunk.

Fourthly, let us always encourage one another to do good and avoid evil.

Fifthly, to be truthful is the first thing that children must learn. Let us always be on our guard against telling lies.

"Right, thank you. Well read."

Mr. Ikuta, the oldest member of staff, was already quite bald on top; yet his salary was the second lowest, Koji had heard. He was rather fond of the teacher, all the same.

" 'Firstly, loyalty comes before all other virtues . . .' We must all be unwavering in our loyalty to the Emperor. After all, it is thanks to His Imperial Majesty that we are able to lead the happy lives we do. Our debt to the Emperor and to the State is great indeed—as great as Mount Fuji, you might say."

Koji did not understand what was meant by the word "debt," and he was even more confused to hear that it was as great as Mount Fuji. But he felt he had better remember what the teacher was saying and repeated over and over to himself, "Our debt to the Emperor and the State is great indeed—as great as Mount Fuji."

"However," Mr. Ikuta's tone suddenly grew more forceful, "recently, some scoundrels plotted to throw a bomb at His Imperial Majesty, as the Headmaster told you. But they were all caught and three days ago twelve of them were executed."

Koji felt the blood rush to his head, followed by a singing in his ears.

"The remaining fourteen have been sentenced to imprisonment with hard labor and will be locked up for the rest of their lives. In fact, they should all have been executed, but they were spared at the gracious request of His Majesty. So you see, you must all study hard and do your best to be loyal subjects."

"That's a lot of rot, you stupid, stupid teacher," Koji cried silently.

All he could see was a scratch on his desk, which seemed to grow larger.

" 'Secondly, let us remember how much we owe our parents . . .' Your debt to your father and mother is deeper than the sea and so you . . .''

"My father's dead. How can I be a good son to him?" Koji protested again to himself.

" 'Thirdly, let us live in harmony with our brothers and sisters . . .' You must all be nice to your brothers and sisters because . . .''

"Idiot, how can I, when my brother's gone away to Osaka to be an apprentice? Everything in this reader's a lie!"

As tears stung his chapped cheeks, he could no longer see the scratch on his desk.

VIII

Out we step gaily in the fresh morning breeze,
Leaving our school far behind us;
Even the garden birds seem to share
The excitement of the school outing.
We march bravely, voices lifted in song . . .

They were setting off in high spirits on a fresh May morning, as in the song they were singing. The school outing had had to be abandoned the previous year, owing to the drastic cuts adopted after the drought. This year, however, no sooner had the spring term begun than plans were made, and today the whole school was going on an excursion.

Each grade was heading for a different place, naturally, none so far that any great expense was involved. There was only a small train fare for the fifth and sixth grades, off to Horyuji temple and Nara, respectively; and Koji's fourth-grade class needed no more than a packed lunch and new pair of straw sandals, since they were visiting Taimadera temple, within walking distance. Even so, three of the nine boys from Komori had dropped out of the trip.

The previous day, Koji had seen his friend Genji being boxed on the ears by his mother—"If you think you're going on some outing, you'd better think again"—and his own head had ached as if he were the one being hit. But there was no time now to dwell on such things, and he appeared to have completely forgotten as he sang along with the others.

> Come, there are flowers to pick in the meadow
> And rocks to find on the hillside;
> Let us seize this chance to see for ourselves
> All we have learnt in the classroom.
> A solitary pine by the seashore
> Would be a fine scene to paint.

They had sung the School Outing Song a number of times when they saw, ahead of them, a scene that really would have made a fine painting. Although not a pine tree by the shore, it was of such loveliness they could not help crying out.

"Look! A pagoda!"

"I can see two!"

Far from striking a lofty pose, the pagodas nestled peacefully in the forest, with Mount Nijo behind them, perhaps smiling secretly to themselves at the sound of the approaching footsteps. The children could not wait to reach them.

The path began to climb gently towards the village of Taima and Koji suddenly remembered the story "Taima no Kehaya," which had been in his third-grade reader. According to this story, Taima no Kehaya was exceedingly strong, but since it led him to brag and behave in an unruly fashion, the Emperor sent his vassal, Nomi no Sukuné, to wrestle with him, and Kehaya was kicked to death.

There was an illustration in the reader of him being kicked to the ground, which showed him as a man with a very long, shaggy beard. Koji had decided, therefore, that the word *kehaya*, which was in *kana*, must be written with the characters *ke* and *haya* that meant "hairy"; but the teacher said it was simply the man's name and that he came from Yamato. Perhaps, then, he was born in the village they were now approaching.

Koji was afraid of asking, though, in case his friends and the teacher laughed at him. But eventually, curiosity got the better of him, and, as luck would have it, Mr. Sugino happened to be walking nearby.

"Please, sir, did Taima no Kehaya come from that Taima?" he blurted out, turning red.

"Yes, that's right." The teacher smiled the way he did when

pleased by a question. "Well spotted, Hatanaka. There's a place there said to be where he lived."

"Is that story true then, sir?"

"Did Kehaya and Nomi no Sukuné really wrestle together?"

"Was Nomi no Sukuné a real person, too?"

Mr. Sugino found himself besieged with questions. He was in charge of Koji's fourth-grade class and was the leader of today's excursion. Since the graduation of Seitaro's class, nobody had chanted "We hate Aojima, Aojima, Aojima, Sugino's the one we like, even though he's darker, poor old Aojima"; nevertheless, Mr. Sugino was as popular as ever, both within and outside the school.

Blinking, as if rather taken aback, he said, "Nomi no Sukuné is an important figure in the history of our country, as you'll see when you start learning the subject in the fifth grade. Up until his day, whenever somebody of high rank died—such as the Emperor or Empress—large numbers of their attendants had had to sacrifice their lives also. But Nomi no Sukuné said that this was too harsh and he made clay dolls to bury round the dead person instead. The dolls are known as *haniwa*. At that time, it was a very bold thing for him to do, and the Emperor conferred on him the title of Haji no Muraji."

However, the children were more interested in the Nomi no Sukuné who had kicked Taima no Kehaya to death; and Koji was no exception.

"Please, sir, why did Nomi no Sukuné go and kill Taima no Kehaya when they were only wrestling?" he asked, blushing again.

"He was a bad man, wasn't he, sir, killing somebody in a wrestling match," added another boy near them, looking at the teacher.

"They've forgotten what they read in class already, haven't they, sir?" butted in Hisao Ogaki, the son of the rice inspector. "The Emperor ordered Nomi no Sukuné to wrestle with Kehaya because he was up to no good. It was a fight to see who'd come out on top, so it didn't matter if he kicked him to death, did it, sir?"

"Well, no, I suppose not."

"The Emperor then was the same as His Imperial Majesty today, and they always put the bad men to death in the end. Nothing wrong with that." Grinning triumphantly, Hisao slipped past Koji.

Koji looked down and blushed even redder: not from shame at being accused of forgetting what they read in class—he could remember all the readers right from the first-grade one—but because it grieved and angered him deeply that something he secretly cherished, unknown to anyone, should be mocked and insulted so unjustly. According to Hisao's way of thinking, there was nothing wrong at all with the Emperor having Shusui Kotoku, given-name-Denjiro, executed.

How was it, though, that the Emperor was free to kill as many as he liked of the people he considered bad? Who had arranged things like that?

Of course: the Emperor and his chosen followers must have got together and arranged it. And Nomi no Sukuné must have been one of the chosen followers of the Emperor of his day . . .

The "Nomi no Sukuné" illustration he had seen in the reader unfurled life-size before him. But the next moment, it changed and there was Inspector Ogaki, in *hakama* and lace-up boots, while the bearded face of Taima no Kehaya, who had been kicked to the ground, became that of Také's father, Tosaku Nagai, who suddenly sprang up from the page.

"Aah!" At the sound of loud shrieks, Koji came to himself with a start. His friends were making the most tremendous din, not only excited at having arrived but startled and delighted by the two monstrous figures of the Nio, the guardian gods towering on either side of the gates to the temple precinct.

The teacher took off his gray felt hat. "We'll stop here for a short rest. Now, the object of today's outing is, as it says in the song you've been singing, to see for yourselves, discover for yourselves the things you usually only learn about in the classroom. And remember, if there's anything you want to know, go ahead, and ask. I'm sure the Abbot here will tell you about the pagodas and all the other treasures a little later on."

He mopped his brow with a handkerchief.

Machié Sugimoto sidled up to him. "Please, sir, why are the Nio angry and making such horrible faces?" she asked.

"If they were laughing, they wouldn't be Nio, would they, stupid," retorted Hisao at once, at which several others guffawed.

Mr. Sugino stuffed his handkerchief into his pocket. "The Nio aren't really angry, they just look as if they are because they're so big and strong. Together they're called Kongo Rikishi, which means the strongest in the world—this one here with his mouth wide open is Kongo, and that one with his mouth tight shut is Rikishi."

"But they're nothing much, are they, sir, even though they're so strong? They're only the temple's watchmen," Hisao commented again.

The teacher laughed. "Hey, careful. The Nio will scold you, talking like that." He paused and then added in his classroom voice, "The Nio are the divine guardians of the Buddhist faith."

The children received this in silence. Not one of them understood what he meant, and, naturally, Koji too was mystified.

It turned out that at close quarters there was something rather oppressive about the pagodas, which before had seemed to nestle so peacefully in the forest; and Koji even felt a strange sort of fear. The teacher said they were built to store the sacred remains of the Buddha. Were the Buddha's remains the same as those of a dead person, he wondered.

In the Mandala Hall, an old priest with a face the color of brown wrapping paper unrolled a cloth with a complicated pattern, which he said was the Blessed Mandala. Although he talked at length about its history, Koji found it hard to see why the cloth was "blessed."

And so did the other children: as was evident from the way they sat staring vacantly into space with their mouths hanging open, or glancing restlessly about them, or digging each other in the ribs.

Only among the girls were there a few faces expressing wonder at the mystery of the mandala. The majority, however, were more fascinated by the mother-of-pearl balustrade. Their mothers and elder sisters had ornamental hairpins and combs inlaid with similar mother-of-pearl, and they knew how expensive these were.

Koji felt very irritated: it was too much to be expected to believe a story like the one the priest had just related. It was about Lady Chujo and how, when she began weaving thread from a lotus, hundreds of Buddhas suddenly appeared and, lo and behold, she found the finished Mandala of Paradise on her loom. He had already read in his fourth-grade ethics book about the man who became rich by cashing in on people's faith in the *kami*. The man would place a *gohei** in a jar in which he had hidden a mudfish, and, when the fish moved the *gohei*, would pretend it was a sign of the *kami's* presence in the jar. But he could not see why the man's claim that the *gohei* was moved by the *kami* was any more far-fetched than all the priest's stories about the mandala.

He looked around at the teacher and was perplexed to see him listening with an air of respect, his hands neatly folded in his lap. Only a short while ago, at the gates with the Nio, he had said that they had come here today to discover for themselves what they usually learnt about in the classroom. If that were so, why were they now quietly listening to all the tales and superstition surrounding the mandala? Or was it that such miraculous happenings did not surprise the teacher in a splendid temple like this, built long ago by a member of the Imperial family?

Koji had listened attentively while the priest gave a detailed account of how Taimadera temple was originally built on the west side of Mount Nijo in Kawachi province, by Prince Maroko, the younger brother of Prince Shotoku, who built Horyuji temple, and how it was moved to its present location during the reign of the Emperor Tenmu. But he was mystified as to why Prince Shotoku and Prince Maroko should have wanted to build such impressive temples. Were there no poor people like themselves in those days, who could scarcely afford even gruel?

Temples were not surprisingly a strange puzzle to a little boy like Koji, who could not be expected to understand such things as *kuyo* and *ho-on*.*

When they left Taimadera it was almost noon.

"We'll eat our picnic at Sekkoji," said Mr. Sugino, setting off at the head of the file of children. Sekkoji temple, a few hundred yards to the north of Taimadera, was noted for its azaleas and commanded a view of the whole Yamato basin.

They found the azaleas in full bloom, and the children ran around them delightedly; the flowers looked welcoming somehow in the tiny temple garden.

"Can you all spot your own villages?" The teacher stood on tiptoe at the edge of the temple precinct. From there, the two chimneys of the Dai Nihon cotton mill seemed close enough to touch.

"See that pond by the chimney, that's in our village."

"Look, there's Unebi Hill over there."

"And this one's Miminashi."

"There's Mount Miwa behind it."

"You can see our school really clearly."

Koji stared silently at the pagodas of Taimadera. He had found them oppressive and disturbing close up, but now, seen from a distance, they had a dreamlike beauty.

The children began unpacking their lunches. Koji chose a spot on the west side of the precinct, overlooking Mount Nijo. He could not bring himself to sit on the east side, facing the chimneys of the cotton mill, because he dreaded somebody remarking, "Look, there's Komori, the *eta* village."

Before he knew it, the other Komori children had gathered round. The six of them dove into their boiled barley-and-rice balls that they had all brought as if by arrangement.

Hisao and his friends, the group to their right, began sharing out their rice balls wrapped in dried seaweed or fried bean curd. Noticing them, Matsukichi Katsura went rushing over, clutching a large bamboo-sheath package in both hands.

"Sushi! Delicious fish sushi! Who'll try some sushi?"

He sounded like a tradesman hawking his wares and was greeted with howls of laughter, which, as he was a natural comedian, only egged him on. "Sushi! Delicious sushi!" he began crying again.

But that moment, Hisao Ogaki jeered witheringly, "A cremator's sushi stinks!"

Matsukichi paled visibly and dropped his bamboo-sheath package.

In a flash, Koji charged up to Hisao as if about to attack him. "Say that again, Ogaki." His icy tone surprised even him.

Hisao glared back menacingly but then ran off, without a word, toward the priest's living quarters, where the teacher was to be found.

Koji's friends gazed at him in wonder as if they had witnessed a miracle. They had never seen this side of him before; and neither had Koji himself.

The fish from the sushi Matsukichi had dropped gleamed like mother-of-pearl among the red azaleas.

IX

Koji knew that a cremator was somebody who burnt corpses and dug graves. Although Matsukichi Katsura's family was now counted among the wealthier of Shimana (they even had a whitewashed rice storehouse), it was said that formerly they had been cremators, living in a corner of the cemetery shared by Azuchi and Shimana. Koji had learnt this by chance only recently, when he overheard some of the older pupils talking about it at school.

But what right did that give Hisao to say that Matsukichi's sushi stank, he thought to himself over and over again with rising anger. Not that he had any intention of telling his mother and grandmother about it; they would only start worrying in case someone had said something similar to him.

Fortunately, when he arrived home there was a magazine from Seitaro awaiting him; the sixth to arrive since last autumn. "Snow White," a fairy story from another country, had been serialized in the last two issues, and this month's carried the final installment. It ended happily with the Prince marrying Snow White, and the Queen, Snow White's stepmother, who was so jealous of her beauty that she had tried to kill her four times, was finally unmasked. She was made to put on a pair of red-hot clogs and she danced about wildly until she dropped dead.

Koji had certainly enjoyed the story, particularly the part where the mirror spoke, but tonight as he finished it he suddenly wanted to retch at the cruelty of the Queen's death.

At the same time, he was struck by the similarity between Snow White and Lady Chujo of Taima. Lady Chujo was the daughter of a minister, but she had been abandoned by her stepmother, Teruhi-nomae, on Mount Hibari in Yamato. She was rescued by a servant, narrowly escaping death. It was true that while Snow White married the Prince, Lady Chujo retired to a temple and wove the Mandala of Paradise with thread from a lotus; but, in both cases, the most marvelous good fortune awaited these young ladies of noble birth, even though their real mothers had died and their stepmothers tormented them. And, in the future too, happiness undoubtedly awaited others like them. How different from the story of Yokichi and Kayo he had read in the same magazine. Despite having worked hard and saved enough to marry, they could not help weeping bitterly when they reached the mountain pass overlooking Yokichi's village.

Koji closed the magazine with a bang.

"Koji, why have you left two rice balls?" asked Fudé, from the sink.

He had pounced on the magazine as soon as he arrived home and left his packed lunch lying in the doorway, leading inside from the *doma*.

"What a waste. A nice lunch like that. Well, I'm sure we'll enjoy them, if you don't want them," added Nui, changing the position of the lamp for supper.

"Yes, you two have them. A present from me," Koji answered, trying to sound cheerful in case they guessed something had happened at Sekkoji.

"You must be starving though, walking all that way on one rice ball. Are you sure you're not getting sick?" Fudé asked again.

"No, I'm fine. A friend brought something special and he shared it with me."

"Oh, I see. What was it?"

"Sushi. Sushi with fish."

"Goodness, what a treat. Which friend was this?"

"The rice inspector's son," Koji lied on the spur of the moment; Hisao Ogaki's name sprang to mind not unnaturally, considering his close connection with the sushi.

Fudé smiled as if satisfied, and Nui said delightedly, "How nice. I wouldn't mind trying a piece of fish sushi myself one day. They say it's very tasty."

"Maybe after the transplanting," suggested Fudé, feeling that it might even be possible by then, as it was two months off.

Nui, however, suffered no such delusions and dismissed the whole idea with a loud guffaw.

Throughout May and June, the weather was normal for the time of year, and by the beginning of July most of the wheat and barley had been harvested. Nui and Fudé were hoping that Seitaro might return home for the Festival of the Dead on August 15, as it was now a year since he had left. Instead, in the middle of August, they received a letter from him. It gave them a great deal of pleasure, nevertheless, since it clearly showed how much he had grown up.

> I've been away from home a year and a month now. Doesn't time fly? Uncle Yuji came to see me the other day and told me that you are all well. I'm fine too and eating as much as ever, you'll be pleased to know. Talking of which, I hear this year's crop is coming along nicely. That is good news. It'd be terrible to have to water the field by hand from the well again, wouldn't it?
>
> The crop may be doing well, but at the moment the market price for rice seems to be going up all the time. Today's price for medium quality reached eighteen sen five rin a *sho* in Osaka. And they say that by next month it'll go above twenty sen. All the dealers are buying up as much as they can, and not just in

Osaka, either. Even in Tokyo, all the wholesalers are trying to corner the market. It seems the government has ordered everybody to stop dealing in futures, but my master says that that will only push the price up even more.

I don't expect you know much about futures, do you? I've only just begun to understand it a little myself. It's nothing but gambling with rice really. You can make a fortune at it if you're lucky, but you can be ruined, too, if you're not. And when the price keeps going up like it is now, those that are well off with rice to sell do all right, but it's terribly hard for people who have to buy it for food. These days there's great demand for Nanking rice in Osaka, and I bet that's what everybody's buying in Komori as well. What about you? There are all sorts of different kinds of Nanking rice and some are tastier than others. The sort we had at home with the blue and red grains and the funny smell is called Chiang-hsi, and my master told me it doesn't taste any good because it's fast-ripening with two crops a year.

Things are much easier for the dealers this year because the rice has been inspected and there's hardly any chaff or stones mixed in. They say the inspection's going to be even stricter from now on. That's all right for a dealer's apprentice like me, but it's not so good for you.

There are lots of other even more interesting things to tell you, but I can't write about them all in a letter. If I can get time off to come home for New Year's, I'll tell you then.

I don't suppose there's electric lighting in Komori yet, is there? It's a pity because it would make your night work a lot easier and Koji could get on with his homework better, too.

Let me know if you hear any news of Master Hidé, won't you? Well, that's all for this evening. Goodbye.

Nui waited until Fudé had finished reading aloud, then she took the letter. As her eyes wandered over the writing she could not understand, she remarked, "Seitaro's done very well, I must say, to learn all that about the rice trade. And you're doing well too, aren't you, Koji? We may not have them electric lights yet, but there you are studying away every night. You write and tell Seitaro."

"Yes, he has done well," nodded Fudé. Koji's average marks for the first term were an outstanding 98.5 percent.

But Koji did not feel much satisfaction in being the object of such praise. Ever since the day of the outing to Taimadera, he had been determined to work as hard as he could, but not because he enjoyed studying—he simply wanted to beat Hisao Ogaki. And yet his mother and grandmother, unaware of this, were now singing his praises as if he were some sort of prodigy.

"I will write to Seitaro, Gran, and I'll tell him all about you and Mom." Although he said it half-jokingly, he had already made up his mind to write and tell Seitaro the village and school news.

However, when he came to actually starting, he found that letter-writing was no easy matter, and, before he knew it, three or four days had slipped by and there were only two left of the summer holidays. That afternoon, Toyota Matsuzaki suddenly appeared in the open gateway wearing a black-and-white middle-school uniform.

"It's the young gentleman from Shimana, isn't it?" Fudé cried shrilly; and both Nui and Koji, too, were startled.

"Please come in. I'm afraid everything's in rather a mess." Fudé pushed away the worktable and stepped down into the *doma* to greet Toyota.

"I hope I'm not disturbing you," he said, bowing in a grown-up way. But the next moment, he looked more like his old self as he flashed a grin at Koji.

"I've brought these over for Koji. I'm starting middle school in Osaka in September." He undid his cloth wrapper in the doorway leading in from the *doma;* there were five books inside.

"Then you're moving to Osaka?"

"Yes."

"Well, I never . . . That's nice for us, because you'll be able to go and see Seitaro."

"Er, as a matter of fact, I was wondering if you could tell me whereabouts he is . . ."

"You mean he hasn't written to you at all?"

"And when you're such good friends . . ." Nui sounded shocked at Seitaro's apparent thoughtlessness.

Toyota twisted the wrapper as if it were rope, obviously not knowing what to say.

How could Seitaro write though, Koji thought to himself, when Toyota's mother had only permitted their friendship because she thought him the son of Mr. Sayama in Sakata. If a letter arrived from the rice shop in Osaka where he was apprenticed and she were to learn the truth, it would only get Toyota into trouble; which must be why Toyota himself had not tried to find out Seitaro's address before now.

However, now that he was returning to Osaka, he would be able to meet him whenever he liked.

"Seitaro sent us this letter." Koji put it down in front of Toyota.

"Do you mind if I have a look?" he asked, picking it up.

"No, please read it. It's all about what he's doing now." A look of pride flickered across Fudé's face.

"Doesn't he write well. He's a real grind," Toyota praised warmly before he had read even half of it. Familiar with the city rice polishers, he could vividly picture Seitaro with his eyebrows and eyelashes white with dust, his work-clothes smeared with bran.

Presently, drawing a notebook from his pocket, he jotted down the name of the shop.

"When are you off to Osaka?"

"Tomorrow, or the day after."

"You'll be happier there, I'm sure."

He was silent.

"Well, I don't suppose we'll be seeing you again for a while."

Another pause.

"Please remember us to your mother."

"Goodbye." Toyota stepped outside, looking much redder than when he had arrived.

"I'll see him off," muttered Koji of his own accord, and went out after him.

"Come as far as that Ohashi Bridge, Ko."

As Toyota put an arm round his shoulders, Koji felt a thrill of joy.

"You know the letter you just showed me, the bit about Master Hidé, does he mean Hidéaki Murakami?"

"Yes. Master Hidé's father's the priest and their surname's Murakami."

"Well, he's studying painting at an art school in Tokyo."

"How do you know that?"

"Teiichi, Sen's older brother—you know, Sen over in Sakata—well, Teiichi entered the same art school this year and bumped into

Master Hidé. He says he's terribly good at painting, so maybe he'll end up a famous artist one day.''

Koji was too upset to consider such a remote possibility. All he could think of was how Master Hidé must have looked when he came face to face with Teiichi.

He knew they had both been in the same grade until middle school, and, surely, there was nobody Hidéaki could have wanted to meet less. Yet, that was just what had happened.

"I think you're lucky, Ko."

Koji looked up at Toyota, wondering what he meant.

"Your mother's a really nice person."

He stared at him, still puzzled.

"If you want to know the truth, my mother's going away."

What did he mean by "going away"?

"I'm going to stay at my father's when I start school. I don't want to go to Osaka, but there's nothing I can do about it. The one good thing is that Sei'll be there. Anyway, thanks for seeing me off. Good-bye.''

Koji felt a wave of sorrow.

"Bye, Toyo." He came to a halt at the edge of the bridge.

Thunderclouds over Unebi Hill were slowly moving eastward.

5

Sleet

I

All the farmers in Komori received better grades for their rice in 1911: some said it was because Tosaku Nagai had beaten Inspector Hideo Ogaki the year before, while others, feeling renewed bitterness toward the inspector, insisted that this year the grades were right and that last year they had been too low.

Fudé and Nui fared slightly better with five sacks grade two and five grade three. However, neither of them thought it any fairer. On the contrary, they grew increasingly skeptical, wondering how there could be a difference of quality in the same variety of rice, harvested from the same field.

Fudé suddenly nodded to herself as she saw their rice being divided: people too were stamped different grades, and that was what made it possible for there to be an *eta* subgrade like themselves. Naturally, it was not something she could or would talk about, but this only made her ponder the more. If it was in the interests of the landowners and speculators to grade rice, she mused, then it must be in somebody's interests for people to be graded as well . . . That moment, Inspector Ogaki unexpectedly spoke to Koji, who had been watching him.

"Are you Koji?"

"Mm." Koji involuntarily took a little step backward.

"You're doing very well at school, I hear," the inspector continued, putting his tools away in a bag.

Koji stared at him, wondering what lay behind this remark.

The inspector shifted his gaze to Fudé and Nui, looking from one to the other. "My boy's very impressed with the way young Koji here always knows the answer. Take that change of government

231

a while back, he was the only one who remembered the name of the former prime minister.''

"Was he really?'' asked Nui. She had no idea what he was talking about.

Neither had Fudé; but the event was still fresh in Koji's memory. It had happened at the opening ceremony on the first day of the second term.

"Boys and girls, there has been a change of government and the new prime minister is named Kinmochi Saionji,'' Mr. Otori announced. "You must always be sure to remember the name of the prime minister at least.''

Then he asked them the name of the last prime minister.

Not a hand was raised, even though the whole school was assembled in the hall.

"Come on, put up your hand, anybody who knows,'' Mr. Aojima urged the sixth graders, of whom he was in charge. But still nobody responded.

"Right then, I will . . .'' Koji made up his mind and raised his hand.

"Can you tell us, Koji Hatanaka?'' A glimmer of a smile appeared in the Headmaster's eyes as his gaze fell on him.

"Yes; Taro Katsura.''

Somebody sniggered. Koji knew it was Hisao Ogaki; and in a flash he guessed why: he must have thought of their classmate, Matsukichi, whose surname was also Katsura, and been tickled at the contrast between a prime minister and a cremator's son.

As Koji left the hall, several sixth-grade boys slipped by shouting "Taro Katsura.'' They were jeering at him of course, and he suddenly felt wobbly at the knees. He bit his lip, regaining control of himself, but he could feel trickles of cold sweat under his arms.

As soon as he arrived home, he began doing *yokiri* by himself, though nobody had asked him. The older boys' taunts of "Taro Katsura'' continued to echo in his ears, but he also felt a fierce pride in having been able to outstrip them and answer the question; and what gave him the greatest satisfaction of all was the thought that Taro Katsura was no longer prime minister. It was last September, exactly a year ago, that he had first heard the name from Hirokichi Shimura next door: "They'll get a stiff sentence with Taro Katsura as prime minister, him being a general and the Emperor's right-hand man. That's what everybody's whispering Osaka way—they have to whisper it or else they'd be nabbed too . . ."

And Hirokichi had been proven right: Shusui Kotoku, given-name-Denjiro, and the others were executed. All the same, Taro Katsura, the man responsible for their execution, was no longer prime minister.

"Go on, you sixth graders, say what you like. Taro Katsura, *eta*—go on, anything you like," Koji roared to himself, over and over again, as he sat buried in straw in a corner of the shed.

The cold dampness under his arms had dried and his forehead was bathed in the healthy sweat of work. Not knowing the reason for his industry, Fudé and Nui stopped work to marvel at the amount of stalks he had cut.

The bag of tools over his shoulder, Inspector Ogaki picked up his brown gloves, which were lying on one of the sacks.

"A boy like that has a bright future ahead of him." He licked his upper lip with its thin mustache.

"What's so bright about it?" Nui laughed loudly, dismissing the hollow compliment.

"No, really. It's not like the old days now, you know. You ought to send him to middle school."

"Middle school? You must be joking." Fudé also brushed his words aside with a laugh. Both she and Nui found his flattery particularly unpleasant. Unlike the previous year, they saw him off without bothering to offer him any tea.

Nui was pleased, however, that Koji had been praised, as she showed that evening when she spread out a square piece of cloth before him. "Here's a new wrapper for your books," she said.

Koji touched it. The material was fine and soft and would make a much better wrapper than his old cotton one.

"You didn't buy it for me, did you, Gran?"

"Yes, I did. It's double-width calico, so it'll make a nice wrapper when I've hemmed the edges."

Koji was in no doubt about that. He was very taken with its deep turquoise color. He pulled it toward him and popped it over his head.

"Ha, ha, ha . . . You like it that much, do you, Koji?" Nui laughed, tapping him on the head.

Koji stared at the lamp through the fine turquoise cloth; it made everything look blurred and magical.

"I'll hem it for you," and Fudé whisked it off.

Koji rubbed his eyes. Then he scratched his head, smiling wistfully; for a few seconds, beneath the turquoise calico, he had come face to face with Miss Kashiwagi after all this time.

She was wearing the same purple *hakama* and white *tabi*, with their high instep. Her kimono was striped, black and green, and she carried a bundle wrapped in a turquoise material; her left hand, which gripped the bundle, was plump and pink.

"Look, miss, my wrapper's the same color as yours."

That moment, his mother pulled the cloth off his head, and Miss Kashiwagi vanished without saying anything. But he had a feeling that if they could have stayed like that a little longer, she would have asked, "Have you done all your homework for the winter holidays, Koji?" And he would have answered truthfully, "I don't want to do that homework, miss."

"That homework" was a composition on the subject of "My Home." He had picked up his pencil countless times during the holidays and tried to tackle it as he had his other writing and drawing homework. Yesterday, in particular, he had been determined to finish it at all costs and had licked his pencil feverishly until the lead made him feel sick. But the composition had progressed no further than "My home is . . ."—at which point he came unstuck. He felt that he ought to begin with the statement, "My home is in Komori," to explain where he lived, but he could not bring himself to write that last word.

His heart had sunk at the thought of the new term the next day; if only somebody would realize that even though he had not done the composition, it was not for want of trying; if only somebody would understand how hard it was for him to write on such a subject. Then, who should have suddenly appeared beneath the turquoise cloth but Miss Kashiwagi—and now she had gone, too.

"Have you got all your homework done, Koji?" asked Fudé, quickly finishing the hemming.

Taken aback, he managed to reply without much hesitation, "Yes, I have," and then made the lie worse by adding, "I did it ages ago."

"Just like him." Nui laughed as if Fudé's concern was needless.

"I know, but I thought I'd ask, seeing as he's got such a nice wrapper now for his books. Anyway, it makes you feel sort of responsible, doesn't it, when an outsider like the inspector starts praising him."

She folded the turquoise wrapper neatly in four and, reaching over, popped it on Koji's head.

"Thank you." He ducked his head mischievously. The wrapper slid off and fell onto his knees, still folded. Grabbing it, he stood up and went over to the corner of the room where his school things were already wrapped in the old striped cloth. In the gloom, he rewrapped them in the new one.

Fudé peered across. "Let your grandmother see how it looks when you've wrapped your things up."

Koji lifted up the bundle but put it down again in the dark corner almost at once, feeling uncomfortable about the missing homework, even though his mother and grandmother could not possibly know about it.

All the same, it would be no use telling the teacher at school that he had forgotten the composition; he would simply be told to bring it the following day. And his marks for the third term would obviously suffer if he did not hand it in at all.

"If only Sei had come back in the holidays . . ." he thought, knowing that his brother had been far and away the best at composition in his class. Suddenly, a hole appeared in the wall in front of him and there was Seitaro's face looking through.

"That's it!" he cried out loudly and carried the bundle over to the lamp.

"Goodness, you aren't going to do some study now, are you?" said Fudé, turning up the wick of the lamp.

"Yes, I mustn't let the rice inspector's son get ahead," he replied, half jokingly.

Deftly, he undid the wrapper, and, resting a sheet of straw paper on his reader, began writing his composition.

I do not have a father. He died in battle in the war with Russia. He died on December 3, 1904, at a place called Shaho.

My grandmother will be sixty this year. Her hair is nearly white now. My mother will be thirty-six. Her hair is a bit reddish. My brother will be fourteen; but he is not living at home anymore. He is an apprentice at a rice shop in Osaka.

In the summer holidays, he wrote and told us he would come back at New Year's, but at the end of December he wrote again to tell us he'll be home on the 15th for Apprentices' Day. That is not long now. I can't wait to see him. My mother says she is sure he will be wearing a kimono with wide sleeves. My brother's nickname is Frogfish because of his big mouth. And I bet it is still just as big.

"What a funny composition," Koji whispered to himself as he read what he had written.

He gave a sigh of relief, as if he had been set free. The torture of this homework was over; and he had not needed to use the word 'Komori' anywhere . . .

He crawled happily into bed and there, looking down at him from the dimness of the ceiling, was Seitaro, his mouth as big as ever. He fell asleep, still lying face up.

II

The young man who came through the gates surrounded by a crowd of Sakata children went straight into the school and disappeared into the staff room. He was tall and looked slightly younger than Koji's teacher, Mr. Sugino. Who could he be, Koji wondered, and he was not the only curious one. The children were always intrigued whenever a grown-up came to the school; and more so than ever by this morning's visitor. He was so unusually well-dressed in his matching dark blue kimono and *haori* and his serge *hakama*. Maybe he had come to replace one of the teachers?

But they soon realized they were wrong.

"That's Mr. Sayama's son. He's at the school for painters in Tokyo," said the Sakata children, looking smug at being able to satisfy the others' curiosity.

None of them appeared surprised by this news, reasoning with a child's logic that a son of the landowner Mr. Sayama might very well go even as far away as Tokyo to study.

Only Koji's heart beat faster: so that was Senkichi's elder brother, Teiichi; the one who had news of Master Hidé, as Toyota Matsuzaki had told him last summer, before leaving for Osaka. He also knew that it was Teiichi who had made life unbearable for Master Hidé at Unebi Middle School, spreading it around that he was a Komori *eta* until eventually he was forced to move to another school in Kyoto. And perhaps Teiichi was now spreading the same rumor about him in Tokyo.

Suddenly he noticed that the window of the reception room, which faced the playground, was open. He could see the profiles of the Headmaster and Teiichi. The Headmaster was smiling and nodding repeatedly, as if trying to ingratiate himself with his visitor.

Koji felt envious; not sad because he and Master Hidé were *eta*, simply envious of the young man being welcomed in the reception room, who could look upon Sakata Primary School with affection as his old school.

Tucking his turquoise bundle under his arm, he ran across the playground, into the north wind. Almost at once, his nose began to hurt. He wiped away some tears with a bitter smile. Then he thought of Seitaro, who was due home tomorrow, and wondered if he too had not sometimes run round the playground like this, tears rolling down his cheeks.

It was raining the next day. "Would have to rain today of all days," grumbled Nui and Fudé, but Koji did not mind; Seitaro would come home whatever the weather.

At lunch time, he ran home, but Seitaro still had not arrived. "It's because of the rain." His mother and grandmother sounded as if they had almost given up hope and he felt cross with them as he munched one of the rice balls prepared for his brother.

"I bet he's home now," he thought excitedly, at the end of the afternoon lessons. But as he was about to leave the classroom, Mr. Sugino unexpectedly called him back.

"Stay behind, will you, Hatanaka. I want a word with you."

Although he had never been kept in after school for misbehavior, Koji could not help feeling anxious. He decided to wait by the shoe box to be out of the way of the pupils who were cleaning the classroom, but Mr. Sugino added, "We'll use the singing room, it's empty now."

What were they going to do there? Koji waited for the teacher outside the singing room, on the east side of the old building.

"Are you cold? You can have my hand-warmer if you like." Mr.

Sugino smiled at him. He was carrying some blue-lined paper on top of a writing-set box containing inkstone, ink, and brushes.

"No, I'm fine." Koji was itching to know what it was all about.

"You remember the composition you wrote during the holidays; well, I've decided to send it somewhere and I'd like you to copy it out nicely on this paper."

The teacher put the writing set down on a desk by the door and began grinding the ink himself.

"Why, sir?"

"Because it's imaginatively written."

"I didn't imagine it. It's all true."

"Yes, I know. It wouldn't be so good if it weren't. That's what I liked about it."

Was it really true though? After all, the word "Komori" had been left out. Koji's ears suddenly reddened.

The first two attempts were unsuccessful, but the third time, he managed to copy out the composition without a mistake.

"Well done."

Koji shook his head. Then he bowed and ran swiftly to the shoe box. Taking off his *tabi,* he stuffed them into the breast of his kimono.

"I wonder if Seitaro's really coming back," he thought, now more anxious than excited. Wanting to get home as fast as possible, he slung his bundle of books across his back and ran straight out of the school without even putting up his umbrella.

But when he stopped at the gates to put it up, he let out a gasp: the figure standing in the middle of Ohashi Bridge, looking toward him, was unmistakably that of his brother in a wide-sleeved kimono.

Too impatient to bother with the umbrella now, he sped on, still carrying it over his shoulder. He did not even call to his brother.

Neither did Seitaro call to him. When Koji ran up, he sheltered him with his umbrella and silently stared downstream . . . Then he took off his left glove.

"Here, put one on. It's wool. See how warm it is."

"I'm all right."

Koji tried to withdraw his hand, but Seitaro seized it and thrust on the glove.

"How is it?" He grinned for the first time.

"Nice and warm." Koji grinned back, rubbing his cheek with his gloved hand.

"D'you remember?"

Koji looked up at Seitaro inquiringly.

"That time we came here to let the shell tops go."

Koji was silent.

"You haven't forgotten?"

"No, I haven't." He shook his head very slightly; he did not dare shake it any more than that for fear of betraying his feelings and Seitaro laughing at him.

"Haven't you? I often think about it, too."

Koji wondered what his brother's expression was like then. He looked up. Seitaro was staring fixedly at a spot on the riverbed . . . Something there gleamed faintly; probably a bit of china. Koji also gazed silently at it, and gradually he began to fancy that the white fragment on the gray riverbed knew his brother's feelings better than anybody else, and would understand his own as well. They were too contradictory for teachers or friends to comprehend—the joyful-sad feeling, happy-empty; the way everything seemed somehow cruel. But the bit of china on the cold riverbed would know—of that, he felt sure.

"And d'you remember that evening when they held the Grand Maneuvers and we brought sweet potatoes here? Weren't the soldiers pleased?"

Of course he remembered; and he also remembered how Senkichi Sayama held his nose, scoffing at their "stinking *eta* potatoes," and how it eventually led to a fight with his brother.

"I'd have a quick run around the school playground if it was fine."

Did that mean Seitaro too looked on Sakata Primary School affectionately as his old school, even though he had suffered so much there with all the taunts of *"eta, eta"*?

"Come on, let's go home." Koji tugged at his brother's sleeve.

"All right . . . That's a nice wrapper you've been given, Koji. I'll bring you back a satchel next time. It's easier to carry."

They headed westward, still sharing Seitaro's umbrella; the rain, now turning to sleet, rustled against it.

"Have you seen Toyo?"

"Yeah. I saw him at New Year's. Things are tough for him, too."

"Is he going to middle school?"

"Course he is. His dad's well off, so he can go to any school he wants."

Seitaro had only had to look at Toyota to know that he was far from happy with the way things were at present; and with good reason, he thought. Although Toyota was still entered as illegitimate in the public register of families, it was now under the title of *shoshi*, which meant that he was recognized by his father. Accordingly, his surname had changed from his mother's, Matsuzaki, to Watanabe, that of his father; and, in an atmosphere so very different from that of the past, he could not help but feel humiliated at every turn, as if he were in some way responsible for what had happened. "You're better off than me, Sei," he said, and Seitaro had tried to smile. He knew it was no use protesting, since Toyota had no idea what it meant to be an *eta*.

As he and Koji stepped into the house, their eyes and noses were assailed by thick smoke billowing toward the open door from the stove fire Fudé had lit. Amid the smoke, Seitaro caught a whiff of miso-and-vegetable gruel, the dish he had ordered.

"You would have to be late today of all days, Koji. Seitaro was getting worried so he went to meet you," said Fudé, setting the trays for supper.

"The teacher kept me in to write out my composition," Koji replied, warming his wet feet in front of the stove.

"A composition? And did you do it?" Fudé suddenly looked pleased.

"Yes."

"What did you write about?"

"I wrote that my brother's nickname's Frogfish because of his big mouth."

Fudé laughed. "Get away with you. Whoever heard of a composition like that."

She did not believe him. As far as she was concerned, writing a composition meant describing things in as favorable a light as possible: brothers and sisters got on well together when in fact they did nothing but quarrel; a mother was fair-complexioned when really she was dark. And the idea of writing the plain truth—that one's brother actually did have a big mouth—was not so much absurd to him as inconceivable.

"Sounds a good composition to me," said Seitaro. "I'm still Frogfish, you know, and I can put away ten helpings if it's my favorite miso gruel."

Nui lit the lamp; usually she would not have dreamt of lighting it so early, but the rainy weather made it gloomy, and, besides, it was a special occasion with Seitaro home.

"Come and look, Koji, I've a present for you." Seitaro untied his wrapper beneath the lamp.

A little bashfully, Koji lifted the lid of the cardboard box and peered inside.

Nui had a look too. "What a lot of pencils. Goodness, paints as well."

A set of a dozen pencils; and a black tin of paints: how Seitaro had hankered after these when he was at school, and today, at long last, he had brought them home as a present for Koji.

"You can write as many compositions as you want now, Koji."

Koji kept opening and shutting the tin of paints, too embarrassed to say thank you properly.

"Now, how about some supper. Loosen your sash, Seitaro, and dig in."

Laughing, Fudé set Seitaro's tray in the place of honor. He sat before it very upright, legs tucked under him, knees together. And it was at the sight of those neat, square knees that Nui and Fudé realized a year and a half had gone by.

III

The earthenware brazier was too small for all four of them to warm their hands at the same time, and before long Hirokichi's were there as well. Fudé went to sit behind Koji.

"We got five sacks grade two and five grade three with this year's crop," she said, reaching over to warm her right hand. "But how you can sort the same variety of rice into two different grades beats me."

"It beats me, too," said Hirokichi. "I don't know what they're about. I bet if the inspector has a row with the missus before going out in the morning, he dishes out the worst grades for the rest of the day," and he guffawed.

"You're probably right. In our shop, they often say the grades just show how the inspector was feeling at the time. That's why the market price varies such a lot, even for the same grade of rice from the same area. If there was a clear difference between one grade and another, silly things like that wouldn't happen."

"Very true. Spoken like a real pro, Sei."

"Not yet. I'm still only an apprentice."

"Well, you know the saying, the shop boy near a temple chants sutras untaught."

"But, Seitaro, how can the inspection be worth all the time and money if the market price varies such a lot?" asked Nui.

"Well, if you have an inspection, Gran, the farmers put a lot more effort into fertilizing the soil properly, and transplanting and harvesting at the right time, to try and get the best grade they can, and so little by little the quality of the rice gets better."

"That's only good for them landowners and dealers though," said Hirokichi. "Not for the tenant farmers, nor the likes of us, who have to buy rice for food. The more hands it passes through, the more expensive it gets."

"That's right. It changes hands any number of times before ending up in the mouths of the townsfolk. Seven times at least, from the farmer to the middleman, the local wholesaler, the city wholesaler, the agent, the dealer that polishes it, and the retailer."

"There, what did I tell you? You're a real pro, Sei. And I bet you know why the price has been shooting up like it has. There's no way we can afford it at twenty sen a *sho* at the cheapest. All we eat is Nanking these days."

"It's probably some speculator trying to corner the market. They say that playing the market is just licensed gambling and that once you get addicted to it, you can't stop," Fudé remarked, with a smile.

"I'm still only an apprentice, so I don't know much about complicated things like why the price goes up, though the master did tell me a bit about it the other day. Polishers like us go to the rice market to buy our supplies. The ones who sell to us are the wholesalers, who handle rice on commission, buying it from the growing districts. Between the buyers and the sellers you've got the middlemen—they're like witnesses to the deal. Now, when it comes to deciding on a price, things aren't quite what you'd expect. The seller comes up with a figure of twenty yen say, and if a buyer calls out 'done' the sale's agreed. But what happens if nobody calls out? You'd expect the seller to lower the price ten or twenty sen, wouldn't you?"

"Of course, you would," agreed Hirokichi.

"Yes, but things are topsy-turvy these days, Uncle, and instead the seller usually puts up the price, to twenty yen fifty sen say, or twenty-one yen. Stiffening the price they call it, and when that happens the buyer can complain all he likes—'Oi, you said twenty yen just now. Come on, sell it to me for twenty yen'—but it doesn't make any difference, the seller won't listen. And that's the way the price is settled now."

"I don't get it. Why raise the price to twenty yen fifty sen, twenty-one yen, when there aren't any buyers at twenty yen?"

"It's because of the rice exchange. When prices are ruling high there, sellers get bullish and raise their prices by as much as one or two yen. At the moment, prices are shooting up and you can't buy if you're not quick enough. All the polishers are desperate, because you can't do business without any rice."

"I suppose this rice exchange you're on about is Dojima? So what we have to pay for the rice we eat is decided by the gambling that goes on at Dojima?"

"Yes, that's right."

"It's as if they're gambling with all of us, isn't it?"

"I've never heard of anything so stupid," added Fudé.

"But money's what makes the world go round these days. It's the ones who grab some, gambling or whatever, that come out on top. Look at all the rich merchants that were made barons last year— Hachirojiro Mitsui, Kichizaemon Sumitomo, Zen'emon Konoike, Denzaburo Fujita—there's the power of money for you. If I was you, Sei, I'd aim to become one of them professionals in the rice market and make a fortune."

Seitaro drew a paper handkerchief from his sleeve and blew his nose.

"No, I mean it, Sei." Hirokichi slapped his knees as he sat there cross-legged. "I may not have any education, but I get around a lot and I've picked up all sorts of information. Three or four years back, I was staying at this inn in Kawachi, and there was a fella there a bit out of the ordinary, and he told me that even in olden times you could always buy any title in this country so long as you had the money. Those that wanted one would cross mountains and seas with as much money as they could carry and come up to the capital. Some of them were unlucky, though, and didn't get their title because they were robbed on the way, or if they did make it to the capital a demon went and took their precious life. Anyway, at the time I thought it was just a good story this fella was telling me, but now I realize that's what really happened. Same with gents like Mitsui; it's the power of money that made them barons. And it's not only titles like baron. A priest gets himself a fine title if he gives money to Honganji,* and the more offerings you make to a temple, the better your death name. Like they say, money's the key to all doors. Ah, ha, ha . . ."

"Who is it that sells the titles, Uncle?"

Hirokichi had been enjoying the sound of his own voice, but at this question of Koji's his eyes opened wide with surprise, as if he had suddenly tripped over a stone; although a natural enough thing to ask, it was so unexpected.

"The government; always has been," he answered, with a sober expression. "And as the government's under the Emperor, I suppose you could say that His Majesty sells the titles. Must be the best business in the world. You're never going to run out of them no matter how many you sell."

"But who did the Emperor buy his emperor title from?"

"He didn't buy it. The Emperor picked up his title a long time ago at Kashiwara. And if my ancestors had done as well for themselves and been quick enough to pick up a title, or buy one, I wouldn't have to be working in the carrying trade like I am now. I mean, they even treat your crap like treasure if you're the Emperor."

They all roared. But when the laughter had subsided, they were left with a hollow feeling inside and a strange silence stole over them. Tick, tock—the pendulum of the clock swung back and forth in the empty quietness.

As soon as Hirokichi heard the clock strike nine, he went home. Fudé laid out the mattresses in the back room where the shrine was, arranging them so that they would sleep with their heads close together.

"Are you going back tomorrow, Seitaro?" asked Koji.

"Yeah, not till the afternoon though."

"You'll still be here when I get back from school, won't you?"

"You bet."

They lay down side by side in the same bed. The *banko* foot-warmer had only just been put in and it was not yet warm enough for them to stretch out their legs.

"I'm sure your apprenticeship has its hard side that you can't talk about, Seitaro, but stick to it."

"Don't worry, Gran, I will. But the trade has its interesting side too, you know. It's not as hard as all that, really."

Kneeling down, Nui patted the foot of his quilt. "When do you think you'll be home again?"

"When my apprenticeship's over, I suppose."

"That'll be next year, in the summer then."

"They don't usually let you come home at all during your apprenticeship."

"Are they all kind to you in the shop," asked Fudé, lowering the wick of the lamp.

"Yes, they're all nice . . . Next time, I'll be back in a fine *haori*."

Nui and Fudé pictured a *haori* tied with silk cords with gold rings at the end.

The next morning, there was a change of plans; Seitaro returned to Osaka with all speed at the news that a big fire had broken out there and was apparently still raging. "I'd say five or six thousand houses were burning, from the color of the sky," announced Hirokichi, who knew Osaka quite well. "Last time they had a fire, it was in the summer and it broke out in the north ward, so I bet it's the south ward this time, seeing as it's winter," he joked. Fudé and Nui prayed that he would be right, since Seitaro's employer lived in the east ward.

Hirokichi's joke proved correct, as they found out three days later when a pencil-written card arrived from Seitaro. "The fire started at a bathhouse in Nanba Shinchi, in the south ward, and more than 4,500 homes were burnt in ten hours," he wrote. Fudé guessed that after Apprentices' Day, he must be far too busy in the shop to find time to sit down and write a proper letter, and, besides, having been anxious about the fire, nothing could have given her greater pleasure than this hastily scrawled message of his.

IV

In April, there was a sudden increase in the number of visitors to Koji's home. The first to arrive was his grandfather from Ino, who brought a present of sponge cakes. "I wanted to see how much you'd grown, Koji," he said, but Koji felt sure that he must have another reason for hitching up his kimono and coming such a long way. Before he could discover what it might be, Grandad was getting ready to return home. He saw him off as far as Ohashi Bridge, where Grandad pressed a shiny silver fifty-sen piece into his hand.

"Nanaé still remembers the time you and Seitaro came over to see us, and she often talks about you, Koji. She's like you. She loves her books, and this year, she was top in her class. I know you'll both hit it off, but I suppose you can't come all the way over to Ino by yourself yet."

"No, I can't," Koji answered truthfully, although at the same time feeling regretful and a little ashamed. He had often found himself thinking, "I wish I could go over to Ino," "Shall I go?"—but he was afraid; afraid of going through Sakata and Soga and across the Asuka River all by himself. The idea of going with his mother frightened him too, for exactly the same reason it had frightened Seitaro: what would he do if they started shouting *eta* when he was with her? He broke out in a cold sweat at the mere thought of it. Three days later, Uncle Yuji visited them in the evening.

"You must come over to Ino, Koji. We're all looking forward to seeing you," he said, giving him a bright silver twenty-sen coin.

"I'll come over in the summer holidays," Koji replied, all at once feeling that by then he should be able to manage it.

On Saturday of the same week, his aunt from Michi arrived with her husband, Masukichi. They had not visited them since the fire three years ago, and by now Koji was in no doubt that something was afoot. That evening, his grandmother said: "Our family may be joined to the head family of the Shimuras, Koji, if things go as planned."

What did she mean "if things go as planned?" He turned to his mother.

Fudé gave a little smile. "Tsuya in Michi is a fine girl and she's your cousin, though you don't know her or even what she looks like, I dare say. Anyway, it looks as if she may be marrying into the head family of the Shimuras. And if she does, then we'll all be one big family."

"Gosh," Koji sighed in wonder—at least "wonder" was the only word that came near to describing what he felt. He was not merely interested or pleased by the news; there was something overwhelming about it.

"If it comes off, you and Sadao'll be like brothers," said Nui, sounding all the more delighted. "It'll be a help to you both, so you stay good friends and confide in each other."

He certainly had no objection to that. Sadao was his best friend, and the younger brother of Keiichi Shimura, Tsuya's prospective bridegroom. They were both in the same grade and, although Sadao's marks were on average slightly lower than his own, Koji envied him for always being best in arithmetic. In some ways he was rather similar to Seitaro and had quarreled with the boys in the upper grades on numerous occasions; it was always because he had been insulted as an *eta*, and the fight would end with his being made to stand in the corridor.

As Nui had said, it would be a help not only to be friends with him but also to belong to the same family. Yes, he thought, from now on, they could make a stand together whenever anybody sneered *eta*.

But why was Tsuya marrying into a family in Komori? Was it that she had no choice but to come to the *eta* village of Komori, being from the *eta* village of Michi? But would not that make Michi and Komori even more *eta?*

Despite his delight at the prospect of belonging to the same family as Sadao, the match seemed to Koji to leave behind an unexplained sediment.

The arrangements for Tsuya's marriage proceeded smoothly from the *o-miai*—the preliminary meeting of the couple—to the exchange of betrothal gifts, and it was finally decided to hold the wedding on April 21.

Nui and Fudé never seemed to tire of repeating, "It's a fine match," and Hirokichi Shimura and his wife, Kané, were no less thrilled— "From now on, we'll all be one happy family." This was quite true, for all the families in the village with the surname of Shimura came from the same line, having broken away in some previous generation to form a branch of the main house, or perhaps yet another branch from that one. Hirokichi and his wife were proud of their connection with the head family, since it was regarded as one of means in Komori, having not only farmed but been in the footwear trade as well for generations. Rumors flew thick and fast that the betrothal gift to the bride's family had been as much as 150 *ryo* to 200 *ryo*, some said—a further source of pride to Hirokichi and Kané.

On April 21, the day of the wedding, Fudé and Koji were invited as guests of the head family to accompany the groom's relatives as far as Takahashi Bridge, over the Soga River, to greet the bride.

Takahashi Bridge, a little further upstream from Shimana, was

about halfway between Michi and Komori, which was why it had
been chosen as the place where the party seeing off the bride and that
welcoming her should meet and exchange formal greetings.

Fortunately, April 21 was a Sunday. Koji and Sadao marched
ahead of everybody all the way, acting as guides for the grown-ups.
They chatted together about their private concerns, such as their
new class teacher, Mr. Aojima, and the other fifty-three boys and girls
in their class. Koji wanted to try telling Sadao some of his secrets,
too, now that they were related, but before he had the chance, they
arrived at Takahashi Bridge.

Across the river, they could see the bridal procession approaching
the opposite bank. The timing was perfect and the welcoming party
crossed the bridge joyfully and began exchanging the customary
greetings.

Koji looked at the bride. She was shielding herself from the glare
of the sun with a pale turquoise silk parasol, but he could still see her
face clearly; encased in thick white powder and painted with rouge,
it was the image of an Ichimatsu doll.

"I mustn't laugh," he thought, which of course made him want
to all the more, as if he were being tickled somewhere. Just then, the
go-between's rickshaw started moving, followed by the bride's. A
new team of carriers shouldered the two chests of drawers, the wicker
trunk, the oblong chest, and the cylindrical lacquer food box that
made up the bride's luggage, and set off across Takahashi Bridge
in fine fettle.

Koji and Sadao followed the procession over the bridge, and, on the
other side, they turned and looked back. The bride's party was lined
up on the bank opposite, Uncle Yuji in their midst.

Nobody spoke; nevertheless, Koji felt they were saying goodbye.
All desire to laugh left him, and he felt a lump in his throat.

"I'll tell you a good story later, Sada," he said, as they left Shimana
behind them. He had looked on Shimana as the first hurdle, afraid
that Hisao Ogaki's house might front on the road and that he would
come flying out and say something. But apparently this was not the
case as there was nobody resembling Hisao among the people who
rushed out, and from those, only complimentary remarks were heard
—"What a lovely bride," "Look at that fine luggage." Not one of
them commented that the bride was bound for Komori, or maybe
they did not realize it. At any rate, Koji felt a wave of relief.

"A story? That sounds interesting," Sadao responded cheerfully. "The way you like reading, I bet you know lots of good stories."

He suddenly looked back, and Koji knew that Shimana had been a hurdle for him, too.

They were now approaching the second hurdle of Sakata, and the pace of the procession quickened.

"*Essa-haiyoh!*" the porters chanted in unison, barking it out like a command.

Sakata was coming nearer and nearer.

"*Essa-haiyoh!*"

Surprisingly few people came running out in Sakata, and, as they passed the larger houses, the women merely opened the entrance gates a slit to peep at them. A few children were loitering near the shop by the school however. They began screaming, "*Misashi, misashi*"—"three poles, three poles"—by which they meant the two chests of drawers and the oblong chest strung to poles, luxurious items of luggage in that district, especially in Komori, where they had not been seen for years.

After crossing Ohashi Bridge, the bridal procession paused for a rest. A large crowd of people waiting to greet the bride, as well as onlookers, had already gathered on the outskirts of Komori.

Bo-oh!—the blare of the noon siren from the cotton mill swept northward over the rippling barley. The bride's rickshaw began moving slowly in the same direction.

V

"Here's a present from the bride, one for each of you children."

In front of the Shimuras' storehouse, Hirokichi undid the red tassels of the lacquer food box and lifted off the lid to reveal piles of *manju* buns. They were all sorts of different shapes—red and white chrysanthemums, yellow clams, and green bamboo shoots—and, at the sight of them, the children's mouths began to water. Most of them had never set eyes on such fine *manju* before.

"I want a red flower, Dad," and Harué held out her hand, unable to wait a moment longer.

"Right, here you are, then. Anybody else?" Hirokichi was in a generous mood.

"I want a red flower, too."

"I want a white one."

In a twinkling, seven or eight hands were outstretched.

"What do you want, Koji?" Hirokichi asked encouragingly.

"I'd like a clam."

"Ha, ha, ha . . . You like clams, do you? Dear, oh dear, what'll he come out with next!"

"What do you expect?" butted in Kané. "He's a boy, isn't he? A fine thing it'd be if he didn't like clams."

Everybody roared, including Hirokichi.

Koji at last saw the joke, and, without saying anything, walked away.

"Koji," called out Fudé from the veranda of the annex.

"Ko," Sadao also beckoned him.

"What?" he asked, although he had guessed already that Tsuya, the bride, must be resting there.

"He probably doesn't remember meeting you. He was only about four or five at the time . . ." Fudé broke off and seated him before the bride.

"So you're Koji, are you? Haven't you grown!" Her rouged lips looked a little severe, but as she spoke her face lit up in a smile. "You're like your mother," she added.

Koji did not know what to say. He could not help feeling awkward; it seemed so unnatural being addressed by the big Ichimatsu doll.

"You and Sadao will have to go over to Muné Hill in the summer," said Fudé.

"It's a lively place," said another lady, who appeared to be from Michi. She was attending the bride and had walked beside her rickshaw all the way. "Yes, and there's July 28, so don't forget to come over."

"Oh, let's go over there, Ko," said Sadao, his mind obviously made up.

Muné was the old name for Unebi Hill; not surprisingly, considering that the great mountain range of Yoshino spanning Mounts Sanjogataké, Shakadaké, and Dainichigataké, was known as the Muné Peaks. The name Unebi still had no associations for people like Fudé, but, at the mention of the word Muné, it was amazing how vividly she could picture the hill; even the way it changed according to season or weather.

Muné Hill was alive to her; probably because she had gradually become steeped in the legends surrounding it. According to one, it was the form of a woman for whom the male Miminashi Hill and Amanokagu Hill were both consumed with love, desperately vying with each other.

There was a shrine dedicated to the Empress Jingu on the summit, and the belief that it was a sacred place protecting women in childbirth drew the local villagers there every year on July 28. This custom may not have been particularly old, but the legend connected with sex undoubtedly dated back to a time before recorded history; and it was possible that people had already begun to settle in Michi then.

Or did the ancestors of the Michi villagers belong to a tribe brought there at a later date, after the Unebi imperial tombs had been built?

Buzz, buzz—two gadflies started to fly about outside the papered screen, illumined by the afternoon sun.

Fudé hurriedly rose to her feet, as if she had caught herself thinking something most inappropriate. Taking advantage of this, Koji and Sadao slipped outside.

"D'you want it, Ko?" asked Sadao, pulling something wrapped in paper from the breast of his kimono. It was a clam-shaped *manju*.

"Give me half."

"Here you are," and Sadao handed him half the bun. "Do you want to come to my nice sitting room?"

Koji stared at him questioningly.

Sadao ran into the rice storehouse. "In here."

Sheaves of straw were piled up in a corner like a staircase, and at the top was the one quiet spot in the whole house.

The two of them climbed up side by side. The sheaves were not very steady and swayed in places, but they were soon seated at the top, legs outstretched, eating their *manju*.

"Sada," said Koji presently.

"What?"

"Do you know what a pass is?"

"You mean the pass that goes over a mountain?"

"Yeah."

"Course I do. Haven't been over one though."

"It doesn't matter. You see, there was this girl called Kayo at an inn at the foot of the pass. The innkeeper had adopted her and she was a good hard-working girl."

"Is this the story then?"

"Yes. Anyway, Yokichi always stayed at the inn. He'd been a packman, going round all the villages, since he was thirteen."

"Oh."

"And when he was nineteen, he decided to marry the girl."

"Mm."

"He was a fine, hard-working young man, and Kayo was a nice quiet girl, and the innkeeper was very pleased and said he'd arrange the wedding. Then Yokichi decided he'd like to take Kayo to his home just once, so they climbed up the pass because it was on the other side."

"Oh."

"It was autumn and the colors of the woods were lovely . . ."

"Well, what happened?" Sadao was more interested in Yokichi and Kayo than the autumn colors.

Koji bit his lip, still faintly sweet from the *manju*.

"Go on, Ko, what happened?"

He remained silent for a while, stripes of light falling on him from a dormer window with vertical bars.

"Yokichi just stood there, stock-still. He couldn't go down the other side," he said at last.

"Why not?"

"Because he'd hidden something from Kayo."

Sadao swallowed. Uneasiness gripped him: could it be that . . .

"In the end, he said, 'There is something I've been hiding. The other side of the pass, there's the place I come from. And it's an *eta* village.'" Koji used the exact words of the story for the first time.

Sadao sat up and crossed his legs. "So that was it," he whispered.

"And Kayo cried and cried, and then she said, 'But I'm an *eta*, too.'"

The sound of lively clapping reached them. The celebration in the front living room was now in full swing, and obviously both hosts and guests were thoroughly enjoying themselves. They could no longer hear footsteps outside the storehouse; the women helpers, who had been dashing about so busily, and the children who had grown tired of playing, were probably all watching the merrymaking.

Koji and Sadao were breathing hard, as if they had fallen into a deep fissure in the ground.

"Is it a story?" Sadao asked after a while.

"Yes, it's called 'The Autumn Pass.' It was in a magazine my brother sent me."

"I'd like to read it, too."

"I don't have it anymore."

"Why not?"

"I burnt it in the fire for the bath."

"Why did you do that?"

" 'Cause I think it's horrible."

Sadao was taken aback.

"Don't you think it's horrible?"

"I just feel terribly sorry for Yokichi and Kayo," Sadao sounded as if he was fighting back tears.

"So do I. It always makes me want to cry thinking about how they must've felt climbing down that mountain path as it got dark."

"Then why do you still think it's horrible? That's really peculiar."

Koji did not know what to say: he himself could not fathom why he should feel such sympathy for Yokichi and Kayo and at the same time hate the story as much as he did.

He sat there clasping his knees tightly.

"Would you like it better if Kayo wasn't an *eta?*"

"No, I wouldn't."

"No, it would've been even worse for Yokichi then. She'd have said she didn't want to marry him anymore."

"You mean it's better for *eta* to stick to other *eta?*"

"I'm not saying it's better, but it can't be helped, can it?"

"Well, there'll always be *eta,* if you think like that. You know something, I hate being *eta* more than anything in the world."

"So do I."

"Then you've got to do something about it."

Sadao was silent.

"It's as if the story's saying *eta* are better off with other *eta.* That's what I hate about it. We aren't *eta* because we want to be. We don't even know what it means. We just put up with it because that's what they all call us. D'you know what it means, Sada?"

"No, I don't."

"Then why d'you say it can't be helped?"

Sadao was silent again.

"Why should *eta* be better off with other *eta?* We'll go on being *eta* forever if we think like that."

Koji had been quick to sense that what he experienced was unjust discrimination, disguised as the unalterable law of karma—although karma was still a word and a concept unfamiliar to him.

As they talked, Sadao suddenly felt as if the thick rope binding him hand and foot had severed somewhere, and that, with a little more effort, it would loosen and his limbs would be freed.

"Let's go together, Ko," he said.

"Yeah, together."

"Everywhere."

"Everywhere."

They put their arms round each other's shoulders.

Sadao stood up. "I'm going to fly."

Flapping his arms, he sprang off the straw staircase. Koji leapt after him and the bundles of straw collapsed in a heap.

The two of them exploded, covered in straw from head to foot. As he laughed, Sadao repeated to himself, "Let's go together, Ko. Everywhere."

VI

"I've brought you back something nice, Gran. Come on, eat it up straightaway."

Koji came bounding in and then suddenly lowered his eyes in embarrassment. Také's elder sister, Natsu, was sitting opposite Nui, under the smoky globe of the lamp, sobbing desperately. He pushed the box of food toward Nui and began undressing as fast as he could: twenty-year-old Natsu certainly would not want a child like him to see her crying, whatever the reason.

Nui laid out his mattress in the back room. "You turn in now, Koji; you've been rushing around since morning," she said, not really wanting him to hear her conversation with Natsu. All the same, as soon as he was in bed, Koji pricked up his ears.

"Look what Koji's brought back. Why don't you try a little? It's easier to keep down, if it's something a bit different."

Was Natsu sick then?

"No, I can't manage anything. I don't feel like eating anyway . . ."

"You won't keep your strength up if you go on like that."

"I don't care; I'd be happy to die."

Natsu began crying again, a sure sign she did not really mean it.

"You silly girl. What's the good of dying?"

"I can't bear to go on living. But before I die, I at least want you to know the truth, Grandma, then I'm sure I'll go straight to Paradise. I've learnt one thing all right—*eta* like us have absolutely nothing to live for."

Koji folded his hands on his chest. So that was what it was all about.

"There's nobody I can turn to. My parents wouldn't understand. They'd only get angry and call me a fool, being ditched like that."

Whoever could have ditched Natsu?

"I'm sure you know all about it, Grandma, but I stuck out that terrible service for three whole years without coming home even once, and all for the family's sake. Same thing with my sisters. Not that there weren't times I longed to come back, but what with the expense of the train fare and everything . . . Anyway, just when it looked like I'd be able to settle down at long last and have a home of my own like everybody else . . ."

Unfortunately, a fire had made this impossible, the big fire that had broken out in the new year on Apprentices' Day, Koji thought to himself—a conclusion he came to because it was immediately after it that Natsu had returned for the first time since going into service in Osaka three years previously, at the age of sixteen. Besides, somebody had said that the fire started in a public bathhouse near the small restaurant in Nanba Shinchi where she was in service, and that she had not only lost all her possessions but suffered burns as well.

Since then, Natsu had been coming and going between Komori and Osaka and, about a month ago, she had taken to visiting Nui and Fudé. Koji had caught snatches of these conversations, too, and he decided it must be true that she had suffered burns because she looked rather sickly.

This evening, however, he realized there was another reason for her sickliness.

"*Eta* like us have absolutely nothing to live for," she had said, weeping; which must mean that somebody in Osaka had accused her of being an *eta*.

"Why are we Komori folk *eta*, Grandma?" Natsu's voice sounded a little different, as if she were eating something. "It's enough to make you want to hate your parents, being born one. I mean, do you think he'd start talking about parting after all this time, if I was ordinary?

I know it sounds just like some affair, but in the beginning he was
so deeply in love with me."

"But, Natsu, what do you think would have happened if you'd told
him right at the start you were from Komori in Yamato?"

"Er, well . . ."

"You know, don't you?"

"No, I don't."

"It would have turned out the same, wouldn't it? He was bound to
break it off sooner or later."

"Do you mean we can only marry among ourselves?"

Koji's heart began to pound: what would his grandmother have to
say to that?

"Well, what's wrong with that? We don't have tails on our behinds
or horns on our heads, do we?" and she guffawed.

"No, and that's why I hate being called an *eta*. It's not as if we're
different in any way. I don't know why we are *eta*."

"Then do you think the Emperor and them generals and ministers
are different?"

"I don't suppose so. They eat and marry and have children and die
in the end, too, same as everybody else."

"Of course they do. But, at the same time, it's their lot in life to be
top dog and live in comfort, just as it's our lot to suffer as *eta*."

"I suppose it is. It makes you wonder, though, who first decided
who'd be what."

"A bad fellow an' no mistake. Ha, ha, ha . . ."

Their voices grew faint as Koji felt sleep stealing over him, down to
the tips of his toes.

He awoke at dawn the next morning, to the whispering of his
mother and grandmother.

"I feel sorry for poor Natsu, but what can you expect? He was
bound to find out sooner or later, no matter how hard she tried to
hide it."

"Course he was. And really it's much better for Natsu that it's
happened when it has. She'd have been living on her nerves all the
time in case he was about to find out."

"Trouble is she doesn't look at it like that. Ha, ha . . ."

"Mind you, fancy that woman going out of her way to tell him
Natsu was from Komori. She's from Azuchi, isn't she?"

"So they say. And she was in the same grade as Natsu."

"It just shows it's much safer for us to marry among ourselves. Look at Keiichi and Tsuya, they'll be happy together for the rest of their lives."

Pretending to be asleep, Koji was busy working out everything he had heard since the previous evening: it seemed that Natsu was about to marry somebody when this woman from Azuchi went and told the man that she was an *eta,* and so he broke off the engagement.

What he could not grasp was why his mother and grandmother should think it so much better that the whole thing had ended now, instead of Natsu continuing to hide the fact that she was an *eta.* If, as his grandmother had said the previous evening, it was a bad fellow who had made them *eta,* why should they go on accepting it forever? Or was there after all a reason for their being set apart from others, the way they were?

The mystery of being an *eta:* the one thing that neither riches nor learning could alter. Under the quilt, Koji felt this mysterious body of his as far as his hand could reach.

VII

"You're a nice quiet boy, Koji, not like that brother of yours. He was a real troublemaker in the school—stubborn, argumentative, always ready to pick a fight. And what's the use of such behavior? You only make yourself unpopular and ruin your chances of success, no matter how able you may be."

Koji reddened the first time Mr. Aojima spoke to him like this; but there was nothing he could do about it, he decided, and, as Seitaro's younger brother, it was inevitable that Mr. Aojima would grumble to him. Nevertheless, the second time it happened, he began to feel guilty toward Seitaro, as if he were to blame for the criticism of him.

The third time, he merely laughed scornfully to himself, "Idiot. You think he's argumentative? Don't you know my brother only tells the truth?"

It was half sleeting that day, and, as he looked down at the river-bed from Ohashi Bridge, the fragments of broken china there shouted back their support.

From then on, Mr. Aojima ceased mentioning Seitaro, as if he had forgotten about him. Naturally, he did not praise Koji, either, which

Koji much preferred, since it was far more painful to him to hear
the sneer of "Komori" behind the words of praise than to be dis-
paraged openly.

They were soon more than halfway through the first term, and despite the usual upsets with children crying and making others cry, no
incident was so serious that any were made to stand holding the
buckets, or the large abacus, as a punishment.

It was about this time that Koji and his friends heard that electric
lighting might be installed in Komori. They were overjoyed, even
though it was only a rumor.

"We'll study together every evening, Ko, when we get electricity,"
said Sadao, enthusiastically. He had begun to outshine the others
since moving up into the fifth grade, and was now bent on beating
Hisao Ogaki.

Koji was no less keen to study with him, knowing that, as far as
ability was concerned, Sadao was already the best in the class. When
they learnt about area, at the beginning of June, he was the only one
who could answer straightaway that a classroom 30 feet long by 24
feet wide was 720 square feet, or 40 mats if tatami was laid.

Unfortunately, little progress was made with regard to Komori's
electric lighting. It was proving difficult to find the required number
of households in favor: some thought that it would be wasted on poor
people like themselves who could only afford to use it sparingly; while,
according to others, it would certainly be convenient but not as
economical as oil lamps. Nevertheless, the ones who raised such objec-
tions were still interested in the idea of having electricity, unlike those
who could afford to buy no more than one *sho* of rice at a time, for
whom even oil lamps were out of the question.

Natsu disappeared from Komori shortly after people had begun to
shake their heads in disbelief over the price of polished rice, which had
risen to an unprecedented twenty-two sen a *sho*. She had been idling
away her time amid the tiresome gossip of the villagers, who speculated
that she must have either had a miscarriage or else induced one. Then,
one day, perhaps because she had grown strong enough to work
again, or could no longer bear to live off her family now that rice
was so expensive, she came to take her leave of Nui and Fudé, saying
that she was off to Osaka.

It turned out that the price of rice had not reached its peak at
twenty-two sen.

"It's terribly hot this summer . . ." began a letter from Seitaro sent on July 10. After asking about the state of the rice crop, it continued:

At Dojima, the buying price finally soared to a record twenty-three yen on July 1. My master's amazed and says he's never heard of anything like it. And the retail price for polished rice is now thirty sen a *sho* and looks as if it will go on rising. I don't know about anywhere else, but here we're selling grades three and four as grade two, and my master says it's this sort of thing that makes the trade interesting. Recently there was the case of a dealer who was delivering rice to a customer when a policeman stopped him to check the quantity and found there wasn't a full *to** there. When the dealer came to measure it again though, there was at least one *to* and the policeman said, 'There's no beating the tricks of a tradesman.' It will be a long time yet before I can get up to such clever tricks, though I don't think I could bring myself to when I think of the people who have to buy rice for food and of how expensive it's getting. Maybe I'm not really suited to business. But don't worry, I don't want to give up the work in this shop. By the way, I've been wondering how you are all managing these days now that foreign rice is at least twenty-two sen . . .

Although they ate gruel all year and every year, Nui and Fudé felt confident that they would somehow manage to survive until the autumn, which was why they wanted to have electric lighting installed if possible.

"Don't you have electricity in Komori yet, Ko?" asked Hisao Ogaki, one morning about ten days later. "They set up the electricity poles in Shimana yesterday. By the summer holidays, the lights'll be sparkling all right."

Koji's face remained expressionless, even though he did not feel so composed inside. And at assembly, he was excited by news of a different sort.

"His Majesty, the Emperor, is at this moment gravely ill, and throughout Japan all forms of entertainment, all public performances of music and dancing, have been canceled. You must all study quietly too. Remember, it would be an act of the greatest disloyalty to His Imperial Majesty for any of you to fight, or argue, or misbehave.

From this evening onward, you must go regularly to your village
shrine and pray that His Majesty may be restored to health. It is
your duty to your country to do so. Is that clear? All those who
understand, raise your hands."

At once, a forest of hands shot up among the upper grades and the
lower grades followed suit. It was an easy enough thing to do, but
Koji, who had started to raise his, suddenly lowered it.

From that day on there were lessons only in the morning, it now
being the hottest part of the summer, and Koji and his friends went
home at noon. The rice had already grown considerably, and it was
close and sultry walking back along the track through the lush paddies. They felt stifled, and their unlined kimonos were soon heavy
with sweat—the Komori children suffered as much in summer from
the heat as they did in winter when they shivered with cold.

"Right, split up now," ordered the sixth-grade leader of the group,
as soon as they had crossed Ohashi Bridge; it was far too hot to march
back in file behind their village flag.

The children ran off, wanting to get home as quickly as possible
and have a cold drink of water.

"I'll stop off at your place, Ko, for a drink," said Sadao, as he ran.
Koji's home was not far out of his way, and, at the water inspection in
spring, the supply in the Hatanakas' well had been certified as "good";
in Komori the number of such wells with good drinking water could
be counted on the fingers of one hand.

Fudé knew what was required as soon as she saw Sadao, and began
lowering the well bucket.

"It won't be long before Muné Hill now, Sadao," she said.

He looked at Koji without answering. "What shall we do?" Koji
knew he was trying to say, and then it occurred to him that the Muné
Hill festival would probably not be held that year.

"Will they still hold the Muné Hill festival if the Emperor dies,
Mom?"

Fudé lowered her voice as if afraid of somebody hearing. "What
are you on about, Koji? The Emperor's not going to die."

"Yes, he might. The Emperor's terribly ill. The Headmaster told
us so today, didn't he, Sada?"

"Yes, he did. He told us to start going to the village shrine from this
evening to pray the Emperor'll get better."

"Goodness, I wonder if it's true then?"

"I bet it is," said Nui behind her. "Emperor he may be, but he's still a man and men get sick and die. Anyway, he's getting on a bit now."

In fact, she knew the Emperor was sixty that year, being the same age herself, born in 1852.

"But we don't have to go and pray, do we, Gran, because there isn't a shrine in Komori?" asked Koji, wiping his wet mouth with his hand.

Nui shook her head. "No, I s'pose not. It'd be a bit odd going to the temple instead."*

This was such a funny idea Fudé could not help giggling.

On July 28, the day of the Muné Hill festival, prayers for the Emperor's recovery were said in all the shrines in the district. The one on Muné Hill was no exception, and, in the evening, Koji and Sadao could see lights moving about there, when they looked across from the first floor of Sadao's house; people seemed to be going to worship at the shrine carrying paper lanterns.

At assembly the following morning, the Headmaster, Mr. Otori, addressed the school standing stiffly at attention.

"Boys and girls, tens of thousands of His Majesty's subjects have gathered at Nijubashi in front of the Imperial Palace, and are praying for His Majesty's recovery day and night, pouring oil into the palm of their hands and burning a light there. Heaven will surely be moved by such devotion, and it will not be long before His Imperial Majesty's health shows signs of improvement. Truly, His Majesty's life is more precious than those of all His sixty million subjects put together. Therefore, all of you must pray with even greater fervor."

However, the children soon learned that the people at Nijubashi had offered these votive lights in their palms in vain. By the afternoon of July 30, rumor of the Emperor's death had reached even Komori. The following morning, the whole school hurriedly assembled in the hall.

Mr. Otori began sorrowfully:

"The devoted prayers of His Majesty's sixty million subjects were to no avail, and at forty-three minutes past midnight, on the morning of July 30, His Imperial Majesty, the Emperor, finally passed away. Our grief knows no bounds," and his voice quivered.

Koji remembered how, when he was in the third grade, the Headmaster had glared down at them during assembly in the playground and told them that Japan would be plunged into darkness if the

Emperor were to pass away. It was at the time of the arrest of Shusui
Kotoku, given-name-Denjiro. But today, the Headmaster made no
mention of Japan being plunged into darkness and continued in a
different tone.

"However, yesterday, His Imperial Highness, the Crown Prince,
ascended the throne, and we have now entered a new era named
Taisho. As ordained, the Imperial line shall prosper for as long as
Heaven and Earth shall endure. We must obey the final injunctions
of His Imperial Majesty, the Late Emperor, and with our Great
Empire of Japan, which is without equal in the world . . ."

He went on talking for over thirty minutes.

The children were stifling yawns, but they all woke up with a start
when the Headmaster said, "Starting today, everyone must wear a
badge of mourning. Anybody going out without one will be fined."

Mr. Kono, one of the teachers, showed them a piece of black cloth.
"As long as the mourning badge is made from black material like
this, it doesn't matter about the quality—either cotton or silk will do.
You tie it in a bow, thus, and pin it to the breast of your kimono, on
the left side. Or you tie it in a band round your left arm, when wearing
a Western-style suit," he explained, demonstrating.

The children's eyes sparkled, all trace of sleepiness having vanished.
They wanted to escape the monotony of the daily routine and pin the
black bow to their chests as soon as possible.

Koji too pressed his mother for some black material the instant he
reached home. Fudé split a black satin collar and made two bows for
him; one extra one in case the other was lost. But he then asked her to
pin it to his unlined white *kasuri* kimono, which had belonged to
Seitaro and was kept for best occasions.

Fudé smiled rather doubtfully. "What are you going to wear it for?
Muné Hill's over now," she teased.

"Ino of course," he flung back, in an unusually defiant tone.

"Ino?"

"Yes, Uncle's expecting me. I promised to go over in the summer
holidays."

"But you'll have to go on your own this time, Koji. Are you sure
you won't be afraid?"

He snorted, and Fudé sensed a certain contempt; "what's there to
be afraid of" he seemed to scoff.

"When are you thinking of going then?"

"Tomorrow," he replied decisively.

The next day, Fudé said to him as he washed his face by the well, "Tell them over at Ino that we will be getting electric lighting in Komori at long last. Everybody suddenly seems to have changed their mind since the Emperor died, and last night they agreed that at least we ought to have electricity here."

Instead of crying "hurray," Koji stretched himself out to his full height.

"Come on, taller!" urged the sky, which looked so much higher and wider than usual.

VIII

Despite the deep tucks at the waist and shoulders, which made him sweaty, Koji felt comfortable in his brother's old white kimono; and the fact that he could now wear the ordinary adult size showed how much he had grown both in height and breadth.

In Sakata, the national flag draped in black was displayed outside every house. The Sayama residence looked particularly impressive, with a brand-new flag on either side of the entrance gates, draped in what seemed to be black silk. Koji slowed down as he passed beneath these flags: he would not turn a hair even if he did come face to face with Senkichi or his elder brother, Teiichi, he whispered to himself; and he certainly could not care less if he met any of the children he knew at Sakata Primary School. Let them dare try and throw a stone or a bit of tile at him. Let them dare call him an *eta*. What was there to be scared of? The Emperor was dead, wasn't he? Yes, even the Emperor died. And all those generals and ministers and rich people would die, too, because they were all only human beings, every one of them . . .

Nevertheless, as soon as he reached the outskirts of Sakata, fear swept over him. He took to his heels and fled. It was the same stretch of road down which Seitaro had once fled, leaving him behind, and he now understood how his brother had felt. Despite all the bravado, Seitaro had been afraid of Sakata, as he was. Sakata was a wild animal that might pounce and dig its sharp claws into his heart at any time.

But the moment of real terror was not when one risked all and faced the wild animal; it was immediately after narrowly escaping its clutches; and that was why Koji suddenly took to his heels as soon as he was safely out of the village.

"Phew, I'm worn out." Once across Sogahashi Bridge, he deliberately heaved a deep sigh, ridiculing his own lack of pride in running away and, at the same time, wanting to acknowledge this side of himself.

For the next thirty minutes, he kept his eyes fixed on the road ahead and passed through several large villages, but they held no fear for him, as he knew no one there, nor did anyone know him.

He was now approaching Hayase.

"Buy ten-sen worth of *manju,* if they have any—they may not be making them as it's summer. If not, get a pound and a half of Matsukaze candy," his mother had said as he left. She was certainly thinking of the cake shop at Hayase, but he was loathe to go there. He could not forget the time he and Seitaro bought the present of *manju* and the shop lady asked twice, "Where are you boys off to?" Suppose he were asked the same thing today? Would he blush and be tongue-tied, like Seitaro, or would he answer back truthfully, "I'm off to Ino?"

Before he could make up his mind, he found himself at the shop. But he was taken aback when he peeped inside: there was not a cake in sight, only a jumble of empty boxes and bottles, covered in white dust.

He decided to walk straight on toward the main Nara road, instead of taking the turnoff by the shop to Ino. Although it was somewhat of a detour, he knew there were many houses along the main road and thought that there might be a shop among them selling *manju.* He remembered having walked that way with his mother two or three times before he started school. Once was certainly in summer, and there had been a stall selling goldfish under the trees by a shrine, just before the main road. While his mother rested by a pond there, he had stared untiringly at this stall, which had also sold little pale green glass bells that tinkled in the wind. He would have liked a swimming goldfish, of course, but not nearly as much as a wind bell. Yet he had said nothing, knowing that it would have been useless to clamor for one, as they were bound to be expensive.

And, as they left the shrine, Fudé remarked, "A goldfish soon dies and a wind bell soon cracks, Koji. There's no point in wasting money on things like that."

"I don't want one," he had replied.

Even now, though, he still hankered after both. Maybe there would be a goldfish stall today by that pond; it was only a faint hope, but he quickened his pace.

As he neared the precincts of the shrine, a sweet fragrant smell wafted toward him through the trees. His small nose twitched, and before long his mouth began to water and he felt sharp pangs of hunger.

"Oh, it's *taiyaki*."*

He put his hand into the breast of his kimono; his purse was safe. With a little smile, he ran up to the stall.

Evidently the man there had not been in business long, as all his utensils were brand-new. Six *taiyaki* were done; the fish-shaped cakes lined up in a row on the gleaming counter.

"Can I have some, please?" said Koji, putting his silver ten sen down on the edge of the counter.

"How many?" Bang; the man turned over the iron griddle and glanced at Koji, who stole a quick look back.

The man seemed about fifty. He was broad-shouldered, which made his face look small, or perhaps it was because of his overlong neck. He somewhat resembled Hirokichi Shimura, his eyes turning down at the corners in the same way.

"Ten-sen's worth," Koji replied, pushing the silver coin toward him.

"A whole ten-sen's worth? Give me a few moments then. They'll be done in a jiffy."

As he busily wielded the griddle, the man suddenly popped a cake in front of Koji, who sensed it was thrown in for good measure.

"Go on, try it. How is it?" he said, without a smile.

Koji took a large bite of the fish's head; the hot, sweet bean paste melted in his mouth and he squirmed with pleasure.

"Gosh, it's good."

"Good, is it?" the man said, again without smiling.

Two children came running round from the other side of the pond, followed by an old lady who looked like their grandmother.

"What's the use of trying to deceive them when there's such a nice smell coming from over here?" and the old lady laughed. She put a copper one sen down on the counter and picked up two cakes, giving one to each of her grandchildren.

The little girl, who seemed about three years old, rubbed her nose with the palm of her hand and started eating the fish from the tail end.

The little boy, of about six, watched his sister's mouth with a big grin, obviously crowing over the fact that in no time at all her fish would have completely disappeared while his own would still be whole.

"Shigé's just like her mother—give her something tasty and it's gone in a flash. Try and make it last a bit longer, Shigé. There's no point in Grandma buying you things if you're going to gobble them up so fast."

But the little girl calmly swallowed the last mouthful, together with her grandmother's scolding.

"Here you are, my lad, ten-sen's worth." The man put the *taiyaki* in two paper bags, ten in each.

"Goodness me, what a lot he's bought." The old lady stared at Koji openly.

He spread his wrapper on a tree stump beside the stall; the stump shone as if it had been polished, evidently having served as a seat for many years.

"Don't go and drop them now. Wrap them up good and tight," said the old lady, drawing near to him. "You're off somewhere, are you?"

"Mm."

"Isn't that nice. Have a little rest, though, before you go. It's nice and cool here. You don't know much about this spot, I dare say, as you're only passing through, but there was a temple here a long time ago where Kobo Daishi studied. And this pond is where Kobo Daishi waved his staff and water gushed out. It never dries up at all, you know, even in a long drought. And I'll tell you another strange thing. There are no frogs of any kind living here. It seems they were making such a noise with their croaking once when Kobo Daishi was trying to study that he got angry and cried, 'Be quiet, Frogs!' and, from that day to this, frogs have never come near the pond. Kobo Daishi certainly had amazing powers."

Koji silently tied the ends of the wrapper. From his history text book he knew that Kobo Daishi was the posthumous name of the monk Kukai, and that Kukai had studied in China and later founded Kongobuji temple on Mount Koya.

All the same, one thing puzzled him very much: why was it that so-called great men, like Kukai, or Prince Shotoku, or his brother Prince Maroko, always seemed to build enormous temples? Or was that the reason why even now people looked up to them with such respect?

"Take care of yourself."

Still with his hat on, Koji nodded to the old lady. The little girl stared at his fat bundle, sucking her thumb, while her brother nibbled his cake and threw a pebble into the pond. There was a faint plop, and widening ripples effaced the summer sky reflected there. A cicada, looking down on the scene from high above, broke into a shrill whine.

IX

"I expect you've forgotten who this is, Nanaé," said her mother, when Nanaé came running in from the well, having spotted the visitor's arrival.

"Yes, she won't remember him," added her grandfather.

Nanaé protested by drawing up her shoulders, sticking out her chin, and making a face. She was cross with her mother and grandfather as their unfair teasing had prevented her from flying toward her cousin with a cry of "Koji."

For a moment, Koji was at a loss, but then luckily he thought of his bundle and held it out. "Look what I've brought you, Nanaé."

She took the bundle and hugged it to her chest, smiling happily for the first time. He was surprised by how much she had grown, but when she smiled her dimpled face was exactly as he remembered.

Keizo drew some water from the well and Koji washed his face, hands, and feet, and then Nanaé's mother, Chié, brought out a fresh kimono for him.

"I hope you'll feel this is your home, too, Koji, and stay with us right through the summer holidays. Nanaé's been simply longing for you to come, chattering on about all the books you'll read to her.

But haven't you done well, coming all this way by yourself. Keizo's in higher school now, but he couldn't go over to my family's by himself yet."

Keizo grinned. He had now started higher elementary school, and the fact that he had never visited his mother's home by himself was because it was in the distant district of Yoshino, and even a grown-up would think twice before going so far.

However, presently, Koji learned that Keizo's elder brother, Ken'ichi, had been staying there since the end of July. According to Chié, he was in the second year at an agricultural and forestry college, and, since her family in Yoshino grew leaf tobacco, he himself had suggested that he should go and help them that summer to gain some practical experience. Koji thought he sounded very grown-up; but he could not help feeling a little amused at the same time when he thought of General Ken'ichi of three years ago, playing soldiers.

Uncle Yuji arrived home carrying a watermelon. From his damp breeches, it was obvious that he had been weeding in the paddy fields.

"Well, if it isn't Koji. Aren't you brave!" He rolled the watermelon along the veranda. "How's everyone at home? All well?"

"Fine. Oh, and Mom said to tell you Komori's going to get electricity, too." Koji hurriedly repeated his mother's message, which he had suddenly remembered.

"Electricity? That is good news." After a moment's pause, he continued, "Another twenty years, Koji, and there'll be trains running here as well. Once the world starts changing, there's no stopping it."

Koji had never seen a train—he had never had the opportunity— but he could imagine what it looked like because of illustrations in his textbook, and the larger pictures that hung on the school walls.

"I wish they'd start running soon. Then I could go to Yoshino and Osaka, and all over the place. I can't stand having to plod everywhere on foot," said Keizo, with great feeling.

"I know Keizo likes to pamper his brains, but he likes to pamper his feet even more," chuckled Uncle Yuji.

Judging by Keizo's pained smile, Koji guessed that the joke about pampering his brains was a hint that he did not study hard enough.

"I'll cool the watermelon," and Keizo ran over to the well with it, as if to escape his father's and grandfather's gaze.

"Are you going to pamper your mouth next?" said his mother, laughing.

"You bet. But I'm going to have some of those cakes first. I'm getting a bit hungry, so I could do with two or three."

"Food's the one thing you never forget about, not even when you're asleep."

"Yes, the thought of it haunts me day and night."

"Hee, hee . . . You certainly talk different since you started that higher school of yours. Look at those characteristics of mammals you were talking about, too—something about them being warm-blooded, viviparous, and suckling their young, wasn't it—anyway, it sounded very difficult."

Chié had inadvertently picked up the characteristic of mammals when Keizo was repeating them over and over again, trying to memorize them for a science test the previous day.

Keizo burst out laughing. "And the second characteristic of mammals is that the various organs of the body are more or less the same as those found in man . . ."

In response to the general merriment, Chié brought out the bag of *taiyaki* she had put away in the cupboard; Koji's grandfather had already placed the other bag before the family shrine, where even Keizo could not touch it.

"Now, share these with everybody," she said, as she prepared lunch.

Keizo counted the ten *taiyaki* cakes and gave Koji, Nanaé, and his grandfather two each, leaving one each for his father and mother and two for himself.

"Did you know, Koji, that mammals are creatures with warm bodies, which are born from their mother's womb and raised on their mother's milk?" said Uncle Yuji, filling his pipe with shredded tobacco. "Human beings, horses, cows, and dogs are all mammals. Fish are quite different, though. They hatch from eggs and their bodies are cold."

Koji listened in wonder.

"But Dad, these fish Ko brought us are warm like mammals." Keizo guffawed and then stuffed the *taiyaki* into his wide-open mouth, head first.

"Ho, ho . . . The only thing Keizo's any good at is cracking silly jokes." Putting down his pipe for a moment, Uncle Yuji bit into the *taiyaki's* head.

With their savory smell and sweet bean-paste filling, the cakes slipped down their throats in one gulp.

Keizo was about to start on his second when he began sniffing it. Koji watched him, afraid that it smelt sour.

Keizo continued sniffing the *taiyaki* and then picked it up gingerly by the tail, as if it were unclean. "It smells too good," he said.

"How can it be too good?" retorted Koji.

"Because you shouldn't overdo things. Like they say, better too little than too much. And these smell so good it makes me uneasy. Where did you buy them, Ko?"

"This side of Hayase. The cake shop at Hayase was shut so I came the long way round, by the shrine with the 'Kobo' pond. There was a man cooking them there so I bought some."

"What did he look like?"

"He was tall and thin."

"With a long neck like Rokurokkubi?"

Koji faltered; the man certainly did have a long neck.

"Stupid boy!" roared his grandfather, quite unexpectedly.

Koji was startled, thinking he must be shouting at him for having bought *taiyaki* from the man with the long neck.

But the next moment, he realized that it was Keizo who was being rebuked, as his grandfather added, with a sad smile, "I'll eat them all if you're so worried. You really are being silly, Keizo."

"Here you are then, Grandad, I don't want it. Ugh, it's horrible." Keizo handed the *taiyaki* to his grandfather as if he were throwing it away.

"I don't want mine, either," and Nanaé thrust her half-eaten cake at her father.

"Give them all to me, then. You won't find such tasty *taiyaki* even in Osaka." Uncle Yuji laughed heartily and ate up Keizo's as well.

"Don't take any notice of Keizo's silly talk, Koji," said Chié, soothingly, as she busied herself preparing his lunch tray.

Koji decided there must be some story about the man with the long neck: perhaps it was rumored among Keizo's friends that his neck really did stretch and shrink at night, like the monster Rokurokkubi; or perhaps he was an *eta* and Keizo and Nanaé shared their schoolmates' prejudice against him for that reason, not realizing that they themselves were the same.

He did not particularly enjoy the meal with white rice made specially for him, partly because of the two cakes he had eaten before it. For the rest of the day, he avoided the subject of the *taiyaki*.

That night, however, as they lay under the mosquito net in the back room, Keizo remarked, "I know what Mom said, Ko, but she doesn't like eating Rokurokkubi's *taiyaki* any more than we do. It makes her uneasy 'cause they're too good. Grandad's getting on now, so it doesn't worry him. It doesn't put him off like it does us. And when I tell you why, Ko, you won't want to buy *taiyaki* from that man ever again, either. He's a cremator."

It was fortunate they were in the gloom of the mosquito net, as Koji felt the color drain from his face.

His grandfather, who had lain down beside him saying, "I'm going to sleep next to Koji tonight," now cleared his throat. "That's enough of that," Koji felt he was scolding.

But Keizo continued, "D'you know what a cremator is, Ko? It's somebody who looks after a cemetery and digs graves and burns dead bodies. Rokurokkubi's called Tetsu the Cremator, and he lives in the cemetery right next to our school. It's enormous and they've built a fine crematorium there. And you know why his *taiyaki* smell so good? 'Cause he takes the oil that comes out of the dead bodies in the crematorium and uses that. He wouldn't get such a delicious smell if he used ordinary oil."

To Keizo's annoyance, Koji sniffed skeptically.

"D'you think I'm kidding? Well, I'm not. It's true, every word."

"But you've never seen him take the oil, have you?" Koji said fiercely.

"Of course, I haven't. Nobody has, because he takes it in secret."

"Then how d'you know he does?"

"Everybody says so, and, besides, there's that smell. It's so good it must be human oil."

"Is that why the bean paste's so sweet then?"

Koji intended this to sound witheringly sarcastic, but Keizo took it quite literally and replied with a certain excitement, "No, he puts powder from the bones in the bean paste."

"Get away with you. Imagine believing such twaddle. It's nothing but malicious gossip, isn't it, Koji?" declared Grandad emphatically.

Keizo fell silent in spite of himself, and stared up at the blue mosquito-netted ceiling. He was the first to drop off.

Koji could not sleep at all: he saw the faces of Fudé and Nui and Seitaro, and then the Ichimatsu-doll bride, Tsuya; and all the while, it seemed to him his grandfather was whispering over and over again, "Poor Tetsu. He's got no idea that people dislike him and don't want his *taiyaki* because he's a cremator. He goes on thinking they'll sell if he makes them tastier. That's why he only uses good quality sugar, and the very best sesame-seed oil on the griddle to give a nice smell. But people don't realize that. They just go on talking about human oil and powdered bones, saying all sorts of unkind things. He can't win—they pick on him because his *taiyaki* are so delicious, but you can bet that if they were as tasteless and dirty as they usually are, they'd only say, 'Well, what do you expect from a cremator?' Poor Tetsu, he's got no idea that people dislike him and don't want his *taiyaki* because he's a cremator . . ."

A mosquito began murmuring the same thing . . . Before long, Koji had fallen asleep. The mosquito continued to buzz round his ears persistently.

X

The low story between the ground and first floors of the house was divided into a storeroom and a room laid with tatami, in which Keizo had placed his desk by the window. He only sat at this desk in the mornings.

"Know ye, Our subjects:

"Our Imperial Ancestors have founded Our Empire on a basis broad and everlasting, and have deeply and firmly implanted virtue . . ."

One of the pieces of homework he had been set for the summer holidays was to read "with reverence" every morning the Imperial Rescript on Education, which he was now doing in a loud voice. Not content with this, he went on to read the Imperial Rescript of 1908 as well, partly to impress Koji. But having memorized both, Koji did not appear in the least impressed; in fact, from the moment he entered the room, his attention had been caught by some magazines lined up on a shelf.

"Can I have a look at them, Kei?"

Keizo laughed. "Do you like magazines? I can't stand them myself. They're nothing but a pack of lies."

Nevertheless, he climbed onto his desk and brought them down. Apparently, it was his brother who had collected them, judging by the name "Ken'ichi Minemura" written on the back cover.

"Here's some goodies for you, Ko. They should keep you busy four or five days."

There was no doubt about that; and Koji licked his lips at the prospect. Then he started, as his gaze fell on one of them. He stole a glance at Keizo; but he seemed interested in neither the magazines nor Koji, and, leaving his schoolbooks where they were on his desk, ran off downstairs, singing.

Koji picked up the magazine. He could not forget that cover, showing a boy with a broad grin on his face, gripping a tennis racket. "The Autumn Pass" was toward the back, and he found himself turning over the pages, as if being driven to do so. He could not find it. He looked again, but still without success.

"How funny," he whispered, and went back to the list of contents. "The Autumn Pass" was listed, as he had thought. He tried finding the page number that was given but it was missing; the story had obviously been cut out.

His heart was pounding. Everything suddenly grew hazy and he felt his own body was about to fade away. He wanted to go straight home to his mother.

"Koji."

It was Nanaé. She had a white ribbon in her hair.

"What's the matter?" She looked at him suspiciously. "How long are you going to stay with us?"

"Not long," he managed to reply at last in a hoarse voice.

"Oh, why not? Why won't you stay?" She sat down beside him. "Gran'll miss me."

"Honest?"

"Yes. And so will Mom."

"You're fibbing. You won't stay because you're cross because I said I didn't want my *taiyaki* yesterday."

Koji was taken aback.

"That's why, isn't it, Koji?"

"No, it isn't. I'd forgotten all about it."

"Why won't you stay then? I've got something I want you to tell me." She gave him a push with her body.

"What about? Arithmetic? Reading?"

"No, nothing like that."

"What then?"

"Um . . ."

Nanaé's face paled slightly. Koji grew uneasy. To hide this, he waved his arms about in the air comically, crying, "Lord of Heaven, purify and save us."

Nanaé burst out laughing, seeing the joke at once. It was a prayer of the Tenrikyo, a sect that was becoming popular then, and it was the craze in all the schools to come out with it in fun as soon as anybody looked at all upset.

"Um . . ." Nanaé began falteringly again, when she had stopped laughing, and blushed a little this time. Then she looked up and stared at Koji, as if she had made up her mind at last.

"How are babies born?" she asked.

He could not have been more dumbfounded if he had suddenly found himself abandoned in a desert. It was such a simple question, yet, at the same time, unimaginably complicated, about something that was familiar, yet as remote as the sky above.

"Is there a baby inside my tummy?" she asked again.

"Lord of Heaven, purify and save us" was no longer any use: Koji himself was now the one who faltered, at a loss for words and in need of help.

"Koji, do you think there's a tiny baby like my finger inside my tummy?"

He grew increasingly disconcerted; something enormous was hurtling down toward him with alarming speed. Finally, he threw caution to the winds and confronted it.

"Don't be silly, how could there be!"

"Are you sure? Are you sure there isn't?"

"Yes, I'm positive!"

"Thank goodness, I was so scared there was."

"Silly thing."

"Well, I was scared, so there."

"Why?"

Nanaé slapped him on the back four or five times, until her palm tingled.

"Ooh, that feels good. Go on, hit me again." He gesticulated like an old man to try and make her laugh.

But Nanaé did not laugh. She blew hard on her tingling palm and

said, "If there had been a baby in my tummy, it would have come
out in the end, wouldn't it? And it'd be an *eta*. That's what scared
me."

So that was it. Koji blinked and his mouth twitched; he could
neither cry nor speak. Although he had often thought about what
he was, it had never occurred to him before that this "*eta*-ness" was
inside a mother's tummy. And yet it must be, if all the children born
in an *eta* village were *eta*. No wonder then that a little girl like Nanaé
should worry about it.

But what was this "*eta*-ness" anyway?

"Did you know we're all *eta*, Koji—my family, and yours, and Auntie's over in Michi? I hate this '*eta*' thing more than anything in the
world."

He was silent.

"I wonder what it is. Tell me what *eta* is, Koji." A tear trickled
down to her dimple, and she hurriedly brushed it away with the back
of her hand.

"I don't know. You'd better ask Grandad."

"Don't be stupid."

Nanaé glared at him. Then, as if talking to a younger brother, she
said, "I can't do that, Koji. If I talked about it with Grandad, or
Mommy, they'd know that's what everybody calls me at school and
it'd worry them. But so long as I keep quiet as if nothing's the matter,
they're happy because they think I haven't found out about it."

Koji could not argue with this; he felt equally protective toward
his own mother and grandmother. And so did Seitaro; however
bitter his experience in the world outside, he never breathed a word
of it at home.

"Koji, don't go back yet."

Nanaé put her hand on his knee.

"No, I won't."

He gave her hand a squeeze, as a promise. It felt soft and surprisingly cool.

XI

"You certainly stayed a good long time. Did you enjoy yourself?"

"Did you have lots of nice things to eat?"

"I bet Nanaé and Keizo have grown."

Nui and Fudé plied Koji with questions when he returned from Ino after five days' absence.

He went through all the meals he had been treated to there; and told them about the interesting magazines he had read; and how his grandfather took him shopping one day to a nearby town, and bought him a writing brush and some ink. Finally, he showed them the silver fifty-sen coin he had been given as he left.

"Well, you're having a good time this summer holiday, and that's for sure." Nui and Fudé were both clearly delighted, but, while gratified at having successfully hidden the things that would have upset them, Koji could not help feeling disappointed that they had not noticed at all and were so easily pleased.

There was no doubt, however, that he was having a good time this summer. First and foremost, there was no fear of a drought. Although there was little rainfall in the central area of the basin, the Katsuragi and Soga rivers were swollen, a sign that there were occasional downpours in the mountains upstream. Therefore, he was not kept busy helping to water the paddy and was mostly free to do as he wished, apart from the daily chores. Then, with the help of his friend Sadao Shimura, he found he was able to quickly finish the homework set for the holidays. And, last but not least, at the end of August they began installing electric lighting; not only that, but on the very same day a picture arrived of Seitaro and Toyota, side by side.

"It's the spitting image of them," said Nui, at least thirty times.

It was a small photograph showing Seitaro in a cloth cap and Toyota in a middle-school one. They were both about the same height, but, with his lips pressed together in a grimace, Seitaro's mouth looked twice as big as his friend's; in which respect, it was an exact likeness of him.

"Do you remember seeing me off as far as Ohashi Bridge last summer, Koji? That was a year ago now and I've changed a lot since then, though you probably could not tell how. But I'm still as well as ever and don't worry because Sei is fine too and working even harder."

This was the message Toyota had written in a neat hand on the card that also arrived. It gave Koji as much pleasure as the photograph and that night, he suddenly realized he could remember every word of it.

On the first day of the second term, he put the photograph of Seitaro and Toyota inside his reader before setting off for school.

"Know who they are?" he asked, bringing it out to show Hisao Ogaki as soon as he arrived.

"Oh, a photograph, is it?" said Hisao, rather scornfully, staring hard at the faces nevertheless.

Others noticed and crowded round, clamoring for a look.

"Goodness, it's Master Toyo!" cried Machié Sugimoto, as if she had made an unexpected discovery.

"Yes, imagine you remembering him."

"Course she remembers. He was living near her up until last year," said Hisao, prodding Machié.

Taking no notice, she touched the edge of the photograph. "So he really is going to school in Osaka."

"She likes him, doesn't she?" Hisao laughed, looking round at the others, five or six of whom guffawed obediently.

"Stop making fun of me!"

Machié blushed and Hisao and his friends laughed mockingly again.

Koji put the photograph away crestfallen, feeling he had made a hopeless blunder.

At morning assembly, Mr. Otori, the Headmaster, announced to the school:

"It has been decided that His Majesty the late Emperor shall be known henceforth as Emperor Meiji. The Imperial Funeral will be held on September 13, and all pupils, from the third grade upward, will pay their last respects to Emperor Meiji in the school hall at midnight on that day. You must all be accompanied by a member of your family then. The ceremony begins at 10 P.M. Is that clear?"

"Oh, how funny, coming to school at night." Whispers could be heard as soon as the Headmaster finished speaking.

Koji felt even more dejected; he could not imagine either his mother or grandmother coming to the school.

When he arrived home he duly reported the news, however.

"The Headmaster said there's going to be a ceremony at night on the thirteenth, and we've got to go with somebody from our family. Do you want to go, Mom?"

"It must be the Emperor's funeral," Fudé guessed at once.

"The Emperor's funeral? But only big shots go to them ceremonies. It wouldn't do for the likes of us to turn up," said Nui quietly; and Koji knew that, as he had foreseen, neither of them intended to go.

Nevertheless, on September 13, the national flag draped in black was displayed outside every door in Komori. There was one in front of Koji's house, too, a piece of black cloth wrapped round the new finial on the flagstaff. Most families had bought their flag reluctantly only the previous evening because of a rumor that the policeman from the local substation would be coming round to look for "disloyal citizens."

Shortly after nine o'clock, the Komori children lined up and set off for school. The crescent moon was already sinking, and it was pitch black. Only a local official accompanied them, and the older pupils carried lanterns and guided the younger ones.

Although the school hall was dimly lit, Koji had no difficulty in spotting Inspector Ogaki's neat mustache. There were about fifty or sixty grown-ups, all of them men, and they continued talking to each other in whispers throughout the Headmaster's lengthy speech.

All at once, Mr. Egawa gave the order "Turn right!"—and the pupils, who had been lined up facing toward the west, turned eastward, the direction of the capital. The next moment, the hall was plunged into darkness as lamps and candles were blown out, and the "silent tribute" began. There was not a sound, nor a voice to be heard.

In the hushed gloom, Koji started and held his breath: a hand was squeezing his.

Was it a prank? It must be. But who was it? The hand still had not let go. It felt like a girl's.

Of course. It was Machié Sugimoto. Surely she was the one standing next to him.

He squeezed the hand back as hard as he could. His was gently squeezed in return . . .

He felt a pain in his chest, as if he were suffocating, and yet he gripped the hand still tighter. "Face front!" came the order just then, and the hand slipped back into the darkness.

Lamps were lit again and candles began to burn. The ceremony of worship to mark the Imperial Funeral was over. Fathers began frantically calling their children and the hall was soon in an uproar. "Hisao, Hisao," cried Inspector Ogaki over and over again, waving his lantern.

As Koji made his way toward the exit, pushing and being pushed, he looked at Machié Sugimoto. She too looked at him. Then she gave a little smile—or at least, so it seemed to him. But the next moment,

she melted into the blackness of the corridor. He fell forward as somebody shoved him from behind.

At home, Nui and Fudé were still up, doing their night work.

"We thought we'd carry on till you got back," said Fudé, coming
out of the workroom. She bolted the sliding door. "There's some
gruel left. How about a bowl before you turn in? You must be
hungry."

He was, but he did not want to eat anything; all he wanted to do
was to crawl under the mosquito net as soon as possible.

"I think I'll have some myself before turning in. Not much point
in doing night work if it makes me this hungry," Fudé laughed, helping herself to the gruel.

"I bet you're sleepy, staying up so late," said Nui, when she laid
her pillow beside Koji's. He did not reply; not out of sleepiness,
but because he felt so wide awake. He knew why, but he could not
tell her, nor did he want to tell his mother: it seemed better to hide
the exciting incident of the hand, just as he always concealed the
cruel, wounding taunts of *eta*.

The clock struck one. He still was not drowsy in the least. His whole
body felt as light as air, as if he were made of some new substance.

6

A White Umbrella

I

That morning, the mid-season rice seemed to know the weather was favorable for the bearing of its fruit, and put forth its flower heads from their sheath.

"Oh, the rice is in flower!" Koji gazed at the flowers intently. They were the palest yellow—almost too pale for a flower. The stamens surrounding the pistils were quivering imperceptibly, issuing clouds of pollen secretly yet with all their might, while the pistils had an air of quiet self-importance, as though aware of the significance of their role.

"It's just like they taught us in science," he thought, his heart quickening with pleasure, as if he had begun to understand the secret of the universe. Craning his neck, he surveyed the paddies as far as he could see: both the flowering mid-season rice and the early variety now hastening to ripen looked utterly content.

"Ho-i!" he suddenly shouted.

"What's up?" Sadao looked around him. "Are you calling that man over there?" he asked, referring to a man who was hurrying toward Takada.

"Yes, I thought he was my uncle from Ino, but he's not," Koji managed to lie; he could not have explained what had prompted him to cry out like that to nobody in particular.

Before long, the Komori children were approaching Ohashi Bridge. Koji crossed it so often that he usually did so without thinking, but today he was conscious of it as a bridge. On the other side lay school, and Machié Sugimoto was probably waiting there already . . .

They were returning to school after two days' absence: yesterday

280

was a Sunday, and the day before that had been a holiday, following the late-night ceremony to mark the Imperial Funeral.

As they started over the bridge, Sadao remarked, as if he had only just noticed, "You've got a fine badge on, Ko."

Koji reddened slightly.

"Did you buy it?"

"Yeah."

"When?"

"Yesterday."

He was speaking the truth this time. The mourning badge everybody had to wear for one year from July 31 had turned into a commercial product, and, since August, all sorts had appeared on the market. Some were large, some were small, and all had a safety-pin fastening. He had wanted one for a long time. But he had hesitated to buy another while those his mother had made were still serviceable, continuing to wear them even when they had grown shabby. Then, yesterday evening, his longing had finally got the better of him and he ran to the shop in front of the school. There were three different kinds for sale—one sen, one sen five rin, and two sen—and he had chosen the most expensive.

He hid it from his mother and grandmother, knowing full well they would grumble at him if they saw it—"Why waste your money on one of them badges, you silly boy," they would say. Nevertheless, Sadao had drawn attention to it, although for a different reason.

Koji grew redder with embarrassment, as if his innermost feelings were on display. He himself saw only too clearly that the two-sen badge was nothing more than a piece of frippery.

"I bet the Head tells us to put on another mourning badge today," said Sadao, unable to perceive these secrets of his friend. "He's crazy about Nogi." He laughed sarcastically.

"You can say that again," agreed Koji. "And he's such an old waterworks I bet he starts blubbering when he talks about him."

"Nogi? D'you mean General Nogi?" Magoichi Otaké, the sixth grader shouldering the village flag, drew closer to Sadao.

"That's right."

"What's happened to him then?"

"He's committed *seppuku*."*

"*Seppuku?* Was it in the newspapers?"

"Yeah."

"Must be true then."

"It's true all right. And his wife died with him."

"What, by *seppuku?*"

"No. She stabbed herself in the throat with a dagger."

Magoichi gulped; and so did several others. The shock of it took their breath away.

"But why did General Nogi go and do a thing like that?" asked Magoichi again, expressing the incredulity they all felt. Their image of him through the pictures they had seen was of a general with a plumed helmet, chest ablaze with medals, sitting astride a magnificent horse and barking out orders, a hero who could dominate the largest army. That was why the stronghold of Port Arthur, said to be impregnable, had fallen, and why the meeting with the Russian general Stoessel in Shuishihying was mentioned in their school readers.

It was completely baffling that such a general, the most distinguished of the day, should have decided to take his life and commit *seppuku*.

"It's because Emperor Meiji's died. Dad says it probably upset him a lot because he was one of the Emperor's favorites."

"What, does the Emperor have favorites as well?" Magoichi looked disbelieving; but Koji was not surprised. He had noticed that people in what they called "upper circles" close to the Emperor were always making trouble of some sort, whether it was the execution of Shusui Kotoku, given-name-Denjiro, or the changes of government that took place with bewildering frequency. He did not really understand why, but, all the same, he found it very unpleasant that men with both wealth and influence should get on with each other so much worse than those who had to bear the burden of poverty.

That moment, the school bell rang unexpectedly for morning assembly. It startled Koji and his friends, who had come to a halt at the end of the bridge and were deep in conversation about General Nogi. They raced through the school gates, the group from Shimana behind them. Assembly was ten minutes earlier than usual.

"Phew, I'm all tired out."

Machié Sugimoto slipped into the fifth-grade class, gasping. She plunked her bundle down at her feet, patting her chest repeatedly. Koji thought that maybe she was trying to signal to him. He stared at her, and she looked back at him and gave a bright smile. But the same moment, Hisao Ogaki reached over from behind and gave her hair a tug. Most of the fifth-grade girls wore their hair up, coiled into a bun, and, apart from Machié, only three others had it hanging loose down their back; of these, Machié's was the longest.

She turned round and glared at Hisao accusingly.

"Hee, hee. Machié's only got to run a second and she's all tuckered out," remarked Hisao, as if for Koji's benefit.

"You don't need to worry about me, you know," retorted Machié, turning her back on him.

Hisao laughed. "She wants somebody else to worry about her, doesn't she, Hatanaka? Know who it is? . . ."

"Idiot! You idiot!"

Machié need not have bothered to interrupt him, however.

"Attention!"

The signal for assembly to begin effectively silenced Hisao. As Sadao and Koji had forecast, Mr. Otori began at once in a tearful voice: "Boys and girls, as no doubt some of you have heard already at home, on the thirteenth, General Nogi and his wife sacrificed their lives just as the coffin of Emperor Meiji was being borne across Nijubashi.

"No common suicide this: it was the supreme act of *junshi*. General Nogi and his wife committed ritual suicide in order to follow Emperor Meiji in death as they had in life.

"As commander of the Third Army, General Nogi captured Port Arthur during the Russo-Japanese War. Port Arthur was a stronghold reputed to be impregnable, and heavy losses were sustained on both sides, including the general's two sons.

"After this campaign, General Nogi resolved to die by his own hand to atone for the loss of so many of his men. However, Emperor Meiji said to him, 'Nogi, your life is in Our charge,' and, deeply moved, he bowed to His Imperial Majesty's gracious wish. But when Emperor Meiji passed away this summer, the general decided that now indeed the time had come to sacrifice his own life. What a shining example he set for us of the way the Japanese Warrior Code should be followed. This is the poem that he left behind:

> I hasten to follow my Lord,
> Who has passed from this fleeting world.
> I hasten. . . to follow . . . my . . ."

The Headmaster's voice broke as he tried to repeat General Nogi's last poem, and the tears literally rolled down his cheeks.

"Oh, the Head's started to blubber," thought Koji, a strong desire to laugh welling up inside him; their forecast had proved accurate.

Sadao too kept opening and closing his hand, trying hard to suppress his mirth. But eventually, he could no longer control himself, and, looking down, he let out a snigger. This at once triggered off explosions from several others.

Mr. Otori was known as "Old Downpour"; a harmless enough nickname, which had arisen because he tended to grow maudlin in his cups, as well as the fact that whenever he planned some special event, unaccountably, it never failed to pour with rain on the day. And now, true to this nickname of his, he was weeping, perhaps as a result of having downed some saké that morning, unable to bear the tragic news of General Nogi, whom he had long venerated. Whatever the reason, the pupils found it highly comical to see Old Downpour in such a tearful state.

However, Old Downpour suddenly underwent a transformation and thundered out, "What! You think General Nogi's suicide funny, do you!"

He leapt down among the rows of children as he roared, and seized Sadao and Koji by the scruff of the neck.

Crack! Koji saw blue sparks and Sadao felt a sharp pain shoot down his spine.

"Filthy little *eta* like you . . ."

As the Headmaster pressed down to bring the two boys' heads crashing together again, Koji bit his right hand.

"Aah," he groaned.

"Take that! And that!" Mr. Aojima beat Koji about the head with his fist.

"That's enough, Hatanaka. Let go."

It was Mr. Egawa's voice.

Picking up the bundle at his feet, Koji sped straight out of the school and up the bank of the Katsuragi, with Sadao at his heels. They crossed Ohashi Bridge.

"You're not going home now, are you, Ko?"

"Yes," he nodded and his eyes filled with tears.

"But your mom'll worry. She'll think you've been in a fight."

"I'll tell her what happened."

Koji put his hand to his forehead; there was a big lump there and he winced with pain when he touched it.

"That'll upset her even more."

Sadao was right. How could he possibly tell his mother that the Headmaster had called them "filthy little *eta?*" And yet if he did not, she would never understand why he had bitten him.

They climbed down to the riverbed. It was cool enough there to make them feel chilly. They walked slowly downstream.

"Ko, let's stay here today till school's over. Our moms won't know anything that way and they won't get upset."

"That's all right for today, but what about tomorrow?"

"We'll stay away tomorrow, too."

"And the day after?"

"Yes, and the day after. I'm not going back to school ever again. What's the use of all that learning anyway?"

"I'm leaving school, too."

Tears welled up in Koji's eyes again and spilled over. But as he tasted the salty wetness on his lips, he thought he heard a voice call sharply, "Oi, get back to school." He stood there looking around him and then said, "Sada, we've got to go to school. Come on, let's go back now."

"What are you on about! You just said you were leaving."

"I know. But I suddenly realized we'll be the losers if we leave now."

Sadao was silent.

"We can't let them get the better of us, can we?"

"No. You're right, Ko." Sadao's eyes filled with tears also.

They had to thrust aside this *eta* barrier to survive, and, to do so, they had to fight, and they needed weapons for that, one of which was learning.

They crawled up the riverbank on the school side, plumes of pampas grass stroking the bumps on their heads.

"Your head must be really hard, Sada. Look what a big lump I've got."

"Mine's much bigger than that. Your head must be as hard as a rock."

For both of them, their own swelling felt much larger than the other's looked.

"I'm sorry about it, Sada."

"I'm sorry about my head, too."

They burst out laughing and, feeling more cheerful, ran back together to the fifth-grade classroom.

A piece of chalk in his hand, Mr. Aojima stared at them open-mouthed.

II

"We don't need wild animals that bite the Headmaster in this school," roared Mr. Aojima from the teacher's dais.

Koji hesitated, not sure whether to advance or retreat, as the teacher seemed about to come flying down to box his ears.

"Hatanaka, Shimura, you must apologize."

It was Mr. Egawa. The boys realized he was worried about them and had come to the classroom on their behalf. But why did they have to apologize? That was not why they had decided to return.

Koji looked up at Mr. Egawa questioningly.

"I'm sure the Headmaster will pardon you if you say you are sorry. It does not matter what you have done, as long as you realize you were in the wrong and apologize. And don't be so stubborn and willful in the future. Now, I've apologized to Mr. Aojima for you, so go along with him to see the Headmaster and say you are sorry for what happened."

"Apologize," said Mr. Aojima, stepping down from the platform. "Not that you deserve to be forgiven, but as Mr. Egawa has spoken up for you, I'll take you along to the Headmaster for his pardon just this once. If you ever behave in such a way again though, you'll be expelled, whatever anybody says."

He put a hand on Koji's shoulder and gave him a shove, intending to send him scurrying before him to the staff room, where the Headmaster was.

Koji tucked his bundle of books under his arm and hurried along the corridor. Damn it! What was so special about General Nogi? Or the taking of Port Arthur? Didn't he know it was thanks to all those soldiers who died that they won the war? And his father had died, too!

Damn it! What was so special about the Emperor? Or dying by *junshi?* Everybody died in the end, didn't they?

How dare he call him a filthy *eta,* damn it! Stinking Headmaster.

Fortified with curses, Koji suddenly found himself standing before the Headmaster.

"All right, the matter's closed."

The Headmaster hastily withdrew his bandaged right hand.

"Go on, apologize." Mr. Aojima gave the back of Koji's head a push.

"You may consider the matter closed." The Headmaster lowered his gaze to the papers on his desk, apparently not wanting to look at the swelling on Koji's forehead.

"We really cannot apologize enough for such inexcusable behavior." Mr. Aojima bowed low, sticking out his behind, before sending Koji flying again with another shove. It was only then that Koji realized Sadao had been standing there in the staff-room doorway.

"Silly boy, you needn't have come."

Mr. Aojima went up to him and tapped him on the head, but not in anger. Sadao hunched up his shoulders and stuck out his tongue.

The crisis had passed.

On Monday, September 23, exactly a week later, the courtyard was buried in broken tiles from the roof of the old schoolhouse. A terrific storm had swept across the Yamato basin the previous night until dawn.

"I should think you were all frightened last night. Is your home all right, Hatanaka?" asked Mr. Egawa, who was working in his shirtsleeves, helping the fifth and sixth graders clear away the tiles.

"Some tiles fell off the roof, and the storehouse is leaning over."

"If that's all the damage, you're lucky. I expect houses were wrecked or washed away in other parts, and a lot of people killed too."

"I wonder what happened in Osaka."

"Osaka? I shouldn't think things are too bad there. Are you worried about your brother?"

"Yes."

"He'll be fine. He's not the sort to lie down and die. And you're a pretty tough fellow yourself, Koji." Mr. Egawa laughed.

"He's a frightening type all right. If you don't watch what you say he bites you," chipped in Hisao.

"Idiot," said Koji, dismissing this with a grin. He no longer considered Hisao a serious rival.

"And another thing, Hatanaka, the price of rice will go up after a storm like this so the dealers will do well out of it. Your brother will work all the harder. I feel sorry for the farmers, though. This year's crop destroyed in a night, and a bumper one, at that!"

"Only a teacher'd realize that," thought Koji; it would never have occurred to him that the price of rice would rise because of one night's storm.

Nevertheless, his mother and grandmother were probably now surveying the paddy with a sinking heart. Every year, they grew the mid- and late-season rice, which was long in the stalk and therefore suitable for their sandal-weaving. The late-season variety was at the critical stage when the ears were shooting, which meant that the damage would be all the greater.

Afternoon classes were canceled that day. The old school building was tilting over and emergency repairs had to be carried out.

"Wouldn't it be funny if the school had been wrecked or washed away too?"

"And them teachers killed."

"That stinking Headmaster should've sacrificed his life for old Nogi."

The Komori children shouted to each other as they crossed the turbid, swirling waters of the Katsuragi. It did them a world of good sometimes to spit out all the hatred and curses pent up inside them.

That evening, Koji asked anxiously if the storm had spoilt the crop, but instead of answering him, Fudé said, "Is it true you bit the Headmaster and hurt him, Koji?"

He could not deny it. But he was reluctant to simply admit it, since he still believed he had been fully justified in what he did.

Fudé continued in a tone of strong disapproval; "If it is, you must apologize. You know what they'll say in the other villages—it's because they act like that they live in Komori, only somebody from Komori'd do a thing like that—and it's not fair on the folk here, is it?"

"But Fudé, Koji's not the sort of boy to behave reckless like that without good reason," said Nui.

Koji thought her mouth looked even bigger than usual.

"That Headmaster wanted to bang our heads together, Sada's and mine," he said, moving closer to her.

"Why did he want to do that?"

"Because we laughed in assembly."

"Why was that?"

"Because he started crying like an old downpour all because Nogi went and sacrificed himself. Why should he cry about a thing like that? Nobody made Nogi do it, did they? He decided it by himself. But that old Headmaster was really blubbering about it. He's always going on about loyalty, and then he turns into an old downpour as soon as Nogi goes and kills himself. That's what made me and Sada laugh."

"There, you see, Koji had good reason to laugh. And the Headmaster shouldn't bang their heads together like that. We feel sorry for Nogi too, but it's different from the way our Shinkichi and the rest died. Not that I'm saying the Headmaster should be crying for them as well after all this time, just because he's crying for Nogi, but he might at least try not to hit Koji on the head."

"He didn't just bang our heads though, he dared to call us filthy *eta*," Koji thought, but he said nothing, secretly clenching his fist.

Fudé too remained silent for a while, affected by the mention of Shinkichi's name.

"I was thinking," she said presently, "what really would be terrible is if Koji came to dislike school because of a ridiculous thing like that. I dreamt about Shin again the other night and he told me that Koji at least must get a schooling, no matter how much of a struggle it is for us . . ."

"And that's why," Nui interrupted her, "we sit up every night working the way we do. You know, I haven't told anybody this, but I made a promise to myself when Shinkichi died in the war. I still don't know whether I'll be able to keep it or not, though."

"What did you promise, Gran?"

"Ha, ha . . . D'you want to know, Koji?"

"Yes. Tell me."

"Well, I made up my mind to outlive them."

"Who's them?"

"Guess. One of them was the same age as me and seeing as he's died already I've won there."

Did she mean Emperor Meiji? He was certainly the same age as her, and he was now dead.

"The other must still be living. I haven't heard any rumors of his death, and I'd be sure to if he had died. It'd be in all the newspapers."

"Who is it then?" Koji gave Nui's sleeve a sharp tug.

"Ha, ha, ha. Can't you guess? You could say they was Shinkichi's enemies, the pair of 'em." She paused before continuing, "Nogi, who's just died, was in command of the Third Army during the war. Well, Shinkichi was in the Second Army, under the command of General Oku and I won't rest easy till I've outlived him. Oku was born in 1846, so he's six years older than I am. It's not likely I'll be the first to go," and she laughed.

"Now see that you study hard at school, Koji, as your grandmother's going to live to such a ripe old age. It's all because I want to see you do well that I keep going and work hard to buy you your textbooks and exercise books, you know."

It must have been his grandmother, Koji thought, who called out sharply to him when he was walking along the riverbed, with a swollen forehead, swearing he would never set foot in school again. And with such mysterious powers, she would certainly outlive General Oku; after all, she had outlived the Emperor, had she not?

"I'm going to live to a ripe old age, too," said Fudé, who had been secretly wiping her eyes. "I won't be a burden to anybody as long as I carry on working . . . It makes you feel sorry for Nogi and his wife, though. *Junshi* it may be, but having to die by cutting open your own belly. Have you ever heard of anything so cruel?"

Neither she nor Nui could have explained that this was the heartless side of power, the tragedy of those who went in pursuit of it; nevertheless, they knew in their bones how much evil could come of a society that placed the authority of an emperor above all else.

Shinkichi had died in the war. Komori was an *eta* village. And tonight, too, they were weaving straw sandals, on a supper of gruel.

III

After the battering the rice crop had received from the storm, it seemed inevitable that the yield would be twenty percent less than usual. But there was little prospect of a reduction in rent for tenant farmers, since they had no means of bargaining with the landlords. To make matters worse, it seemed that the rice inspection was particularly stringent this year of all years, and grades were likely to be lower. Yet people in Komori felt themselves lucky when they heard about all the casualties from the storm in other areas, and how many houses had been wrecked or washed away—"We could be a lot worse off here in Komori," they thought. And it cheered them greatly when, at the beginning of October, the long-awaited electric lighting finally came into operation.

"You can grow as big as you like now, Koji, you'll never have to clean the globe again," teased Nui, his hands being rather too large already for the inside of the lamp globe.

Hirokichi Shimura's family was better off then than those who depended for their livelihood solely on the narrow piece of land they cultivated, and Kané could afford to buy a *to* of polished rice at a time. Kiyokazu, who was employed in an Osaka shoe shop, sent home a certain amount of money, and since May Hirokichi had been working on the Ikoma tunnel building site.

This was a scheme of the Osaka Electric Railway Company to link Osaka and Nara by the shortest route. The tunnel was to pass east-west through Mount Ikoma, which was 642 meters high, straddling Yamato and Kawachi provinces. Work had begun on it in June the previous year (1911) from both Yamato in the east and Kawachi in the west, and by this October more than half of it had been excavated. It was estimated that, at this rate, it would be finished by next summer, when it would be opened in grand style as the largest tunnel in the East.

Such a claim was no exaggeration on the part of local people. It was true that its length of about 11,000 feet was slightly less than that of Sasago Tunnel, but it was for a double-track, broad-gauge line, whereas Sasago Tunnel was only for a single-track, narrow-gauge one. Therefore, it could indeed be called the largest in the East, for which reason alone, work on it was proceeding at a feverish pace, day and night, the laborers drenched in greasy sweat in their effort to win the prize offered daily to whichever side, east or west, excavated the furthest.

Being a carrier by trade, Hirokichi had no experience with excavating work, but there were all sorts of other jobs on site, and the daily wages were far better than anything he could have earned traveling to and from Osaka. By a stroke of luck, Kané's family lived near Ikoma, and so he was able to stay over there.

Kané could not be numbered among the most industrious in Komori, but, with the recent improvement in their circumstances, she appeared to be feeling more energetic and announced she would go out to work as a day laborer that autumn, helping with the reaping and threshing. At the beginning of November, she actually set off for one of the farms in Shimana.

There were quite a few comparatively large farms in Shimana that hired many day laborers at the busiest times of the year. Komori was the source of supply for this seasonal work force, and Shohei Otaké acted as go-between.

Despite the enthusiasm with which she set out, Kané only stuck to the work for a mere three days.

"She's found out talking won't get the reaping and threshing done," said some, at a stroke disparaging both her lack of staying power and her glib tongue. But neither Nui nor Fudé had expected Kané, with her temperament, to last as a laborer in Shimana.

"I'd rather be sandal-making at home, even if I don't make that much," she said, when she came round for a bath. They did not pursue the matter; it was obvious from her manner what sort of treatment she had received. Besides, they were anxious not to talk about it in front of Koji.

Their vigilance was in vain, however, as he heard from friends at school how those who went to work in Shimana were treated. No matter which farm it was, they were always given hot water to drink in chipped cups, which were broken immediately afterwards and thrown away. Their daily wages were never directly handed to them but placed on the floor or the ground. Nor were they allowed to use the front entrance; if by chance they did, salt was sprinkled there at once to purify the house from the pollution of the *eta*.

Merely hearing about it was enough to make Koji grind his teeth. What a stinking place that Shimana was! No wonder Auntie Kané could not bear to work there, he thought. And yet, Komori people were still going there as laborers. They would probably continue to do so in future, too. They would eat dirt all for the sake of a few pints of rice. Treated like animals, they would carry on working without complaint, as if their only role in life was to endure. Then, other people would be increasingly convinced that they really were no better than animals and continue giving them hot water to drink in chipped cups, throwing their wages down on the ground, and sprinkling salt in the entrances they had passed through.

And this was true not only of Shimana.

"But Machié Sugimoto held hands with me. Why did she do that? She's from Shimana and I'm from Komori. What was she up to?"

Koji had asked himself this over and over again ever since Kané gave up working as a farm laborer. He could not find an answer though, and today, during the fifth-period singing lesson in the music room, he began asking himself the same thing once more.

"But Machié Sugimoto held hands with me. Why did she do that?"

Then, unexpectedly, the answer came wafting back with the tune Mr. Aojima was playing on the organ.

"She made a mistake."

"She couldn't have," he retorted, though without much conviction.

"Yes, she could. What do you expect when it was so dark?"

"Oh, I see what you mean," he whispered.

"Machié's from Shimana."

"I know."

"And you're from Komori."

"You don't have to tell me."

"Can you imagine somebody from Shimana holding hands with somebody from Komori?"

"No, of course not."

"In Shimana, they sprinkle salt after the likes of Komori."

"I know that."

"Machié and Hisao Ogaki have been friends a long time."

"Think I don't know?"

"You're a fool."

"Yes, I'm a fool."

"Going and buying a new mourning badge like that . . ."

Koji scowled at the badge on his chest. "What a useless thing!"

He was starting to undo its safety-pin fastening when Mr. Aojima peered over the top of the organ.

"Machié Sugimoto," he called out.

Machié was always asked to sing on her own during the lesson, and today seemed to be no exception. However, the teacher continued, "Name the boy you would like to sing with."

Everybody gasped in amazement. The teacher himself sometimes picked two or three to sing together, but never before had he asked one of the pupils to choose.

"When you have sung together, the boy will name another boy and then he in turn will choose the girl he would like to sing with."

Someone giggled.

"And when they have sung together, the girl will name another girl and then she will choose a boy to sing with. Do not choose anybody who has sung already, though. Now, you all understand the system, don't you?"

Not a voice of protest was heard; everyone was obviously longing to see who the others would pick, in particular, Machié Sugimoto, queen of the class. "She's bound to choose Hisao Ogaki," they thought, and tension mounted as they all waited.

"Koji Hatanaka," called out Machié.

The classroom buzzed.

"Right, step forward, Hatanaka."

Koji had no choice but to line up beside Machié and the organ. The song was one they had just learnt called "Kyoto."

> Flowers on Arashiyama,
> A moon in the River Katsura,
> Exotic colors and perfumes
> Not to be found elsewhere.
> Snowy Maruyama, Takao's scarlet maple,
> The holy water of Kamo,
> And the plum at Kitano . . .

When they had finished, Koji called out "Hisao Ogaki," and then fled back to his seat. He noticed the badge on his chest was crooked and pinned it straight.

"Machié chose me."

"Yes, she did."

"She sang with me."

"Yes, we were all listening."

"Machié held hands with me."

"Don't you think she mistook you for somebody else?"

"No, I don't!"

Koji looked up triumphantly and listened to Hisao and his partner; he did not think they sang very well.

It was Komori's turn to clean the classroom after school, but later, on their way home, Sakichi, another boy in the group, remarked, "Ko's lucky, isn't he?"

"Oh, he's brought that up," thought Koji, uncomfortably, but he feigned ignorance. "Why?" he asked.

"Don't you think so, Sada?" Sakichi turned to Sadao for confirmation. "Machié Sugimoto likes him, doesn't she?"

Sadao burst out laughing, obviously of a different opinion.

"Don't you think she does?" Sakichi sounded surprised.

"How do I know?"

"Well, she wouldn't have chosen him if she didn't, would she?"

"That's what you think. I don't see why it means she likes him though. I picked Aki, but I don't like her much."

Aki lived in Sakata. Her father, who sold bean curd when not doing farm work, had an opaque walleye, for which reason he was known as One-Eye. There was nothing Aki hated more than to meet him on her way to or from school.

Although Sakichi believed Sadao when he said he did not like Aki, he could not help wondering what had prompted him to choose her.

As if to answer him, Sadao continued, "You haven't had a turn yet, Saki, so you don't know. But d'you really think you'd choose somebody you liked in front of all the others, if it was your go?"

"No, I s'pose not." Sakichi blushed slightly.

"Well, that's why I picked Aki. Ha, ha, ha . . ."

"Poor old Aki. Ha, ha, ha."

Had Machié Sugimoto too felt shy of naming the boy she liked and chosen him instead? An *eta* like himself . . .

"Poor old Koji. Ha, ha, ha," Koji could not stop the cruel voice from whispering in his ear. Four or five crows flapped past overhead.

Most of the rice had now been reaped in the basin and the brilliance of the crimson clouds in the west augured a frost the next morning.

IV

"Frost-thaw": the pure white frost disappeared almost at once as if it had been wiped away; quickly, the sky over the basin grew leaden and only the faint yellow outline of the sun remained. On such a day, it was usually raining by afternoon.

Koji had the forethought to pick up an umbrella on his way out, while Sadao took the precaution of wearing clogs.

Most of the others walked with shoulders hunched, like injured chickens, the collars of their stained kimono feeling cold in the damp, strangely chill morning air. Nevertheless, every one of them was lighthearted. Today was Monday, December 23, and it was their last week at school before the winter holidays.

As soon as they passed through the school gates, Koji spotted Mr. Sugino writing in chalk on the notice board by the main entrance. It appeared to be something interesting, judging by the twelve or thirteen children already clustered around him.

"Let's go and have a look, Ko," said Sadao, who had noticed as well, and pulled Koji over to the board by the handle of his umbrella.

"On December 21, the third Katsura cabinet was formed."

The notice, written in Mr. Sugino's rather sloping hand, smote Koji like a stone. Others around him read it aloud with excitement, or to show off, making use of the *kana* beside the characters.

Prime Minister and Minister for	
Foreign Affairs	Taro Katsura
Minister for Home Affairs	Kanetaké Oura
Minister of Finance	Reijiro Wakatsuki
Minister of War	Yasutsuna Kigoshi
Minister of Justice	Itaru Matsumuro . . .

As the teacher wrote out the *kana* for the name of the last member of the cabinet, Makoto Saito, Minister of the Navy, one of the sixth graders asked him: "Does it mean there's a Katsura cabinet for the third time, sir?"

"That's right," said Mr. Sugino, getting down from the stool he had been standing on. "By the way, do you remember who the last prime minister was?"

Nobody replied.

"You haven't all forgotten already, have you? This won't do at all." The teacher gave a faint smile.

"I bet he knows, sir. He remembered the name of Taro Katsura that other time," and Hisao Ogaki pointed to Koji.

"You mean Hatanaka? Yes, I'm sure he remembers."

"I've forgotten," Koji answered at once, before Mr. Sugino had finished speaking. "Who'd tell you anyway," he thought, feeling a surge of revolt.

"Forgotten?" said the teacher, his head on one side. He laughed, "I'll have to tell you then. The last prime minister was Prince Kin-mochi Saionji, who had studied for many years in France."

"Sir, why does the cabinet keep on changing?" Hisao interjected again.

"There are all sorts of reasons, really."

"What sort of reasons?"

"Well, it's a bit complicated for you to understand, but, to put it as simply as I can, there have been some differences of opinion among the important people connected with the government, which have led to these continual crises. In the last Saionji cabinet, the Minister of War wanted to add two more divisions to the army, but the rest of the cabinet disagreed. Eventually, matters came to a head and the government had to resign."

"But what's wrong with the army getting more divisions?" asked Hisao, voicing the point that was troubling the others. As they had been instilled with the idea that the Japanese army, with its Imperial Commander-in-Chief, had greater valor and dignity than any other in the world, it seemed obvious to them that to enlarge it would only add to the nation's glory. Why then should the rest of the cabinet oppose it?

Mr. Sugino fiddled rather nervously with the chalk. "Two extra divisions would cost a vast amount, as much as building an enormous warship for the navy. It's out of the question with the state of the economy as it is at present, and the cabinet had no choice but to oppose it. But the army threatened that the War Minister would resign if their wishes weren't met and that is what happened in the end. It brought down the government because it was like one of the supporting beams of a house being taken away."

"But what's the new cabinet going to do about it, sir?" asked a sixth grader; again, something all the others were wondering.

"Yes, that's the question. It's hard to say," replied Mr. Sugino, walking away toward the corridor.

The children looked around at each other. This complicated talk of politics was of course beyond them, as the teacher had foretold. Nevertheless, they were urged to remember the names of all the cabinet ministers each time there was a change of government.

Koji tugged at Sadao's sleeve. "Let's go over there, Sada."

"All right." As he was pulled along, Sadao muttered to himself, "Iekado Shibata, Minister of Education."

"Why bother to remember that?"

"But in class old Aojima's bound to ask who's the Minister of Education. You wait and see. There'll be trouble if we don't remember his name and the Prime Minister's.''

"I'll say I don't know, anyway."

"Why?"

"I don't like that Taro Katsura."

Sadao chuckled delightedly; it struck him as very funny that Koji should say he did not like such a remote personage as the Prime Minister.

They had come to the toilets.

"And I thought you must look up to him a lot because you were the only one who knew his name that time," Sadao chattered on while urinating.

"Don't be stupid." Koji stood beside him and urinated too.

"My dad doesn't like Taro Katsura much either. Last night when he was reading the newspaper, he told my brother a bad lot had taken over the government," said Sadao, in a low voice, adjusting the front of his kimono.

Koji felt as if he had seen a ray of light. Sadao's father, who took a newspaper, would certainly know why the government kept changing, and might tell him a great deal if he asked, although, on the other hand, he might simply say it was not the sort of thing to discuss with a child. Sadao's father, Kunihachi, had the reputation of being more educated than anybody else in Komori—apart from the priest at An'yoji—but he kept himself very much to himself, not seeking to interfere in village affairs or to become district head.

The cold, gray, "frost-thaw" sky persisted, and, in the afternoon, it began to rain. By the end of the fifth lesson, water was gushing from the gutters facing the courtyard.

"Hisao," called Inspector Ogaki, from the exit near the classroom. Hisao ran over to him and his father handed him an umbrella.

"And here's yours, Machié," added the inspector, handing another to her.

"Oh, thank goodness. I was thinking I'd get soaked." Machié clasped the umbrella joyfully.

When he came out of the classroom, Koji took off his *tabi* and stuffed them into the breast of his kimono.

"It's Koji, isn't it?" came the voice of Inspector Ogaki above him.

"Mm."

"Have you got an umbrella?"

"Yes."

"Really?"

"Yes, I have. I thought it looked like rain this morning."

Koji removed his umbrella from the rack; a wooden tag with his name was tied to it.

"You see, Hisao, bright children are different, aren't they? Turning up in the morning properly prepared with an umbrella—there's an example for you," remarked Inspector Ogaki loudly. But he certainly was not scolding his son; on the contrary, he savored a pleasant feeling of superiority as he said it: the fate of these Komori children was so much more obvious when they were seen here at school instead of in their own village.

"It's rather sad though when you think about it. What's the use of being bright and working hard at school if you're from Komori?" he whispered to himself, as he passed through the school gates, knowing full well what it meant to be an *eta*. A faint smile played on his lips. Understandably: in a world where success was equated with thrusting aside and trampling down as many others as possible, it was undoubtedly a comfort to know there were people like those in Komori, who would never achieve anything all their life. Moreover, he himself need feel no personal responsibility whatsoever for their plight.

"You must have bad karma though to be born in a place like Komori—must have done something terrible in a previous life."

He gave another little smile, unaware of the sorcery of thought at work. Retribution for the wrongs committed in a past life: such a convenient notion made it all too easy to justify the cruel prejudice against the people of Komori. But this had never occurred to him; as far as he was concerned, Komori was Komori and would always remain so; and there was nothing anybody could do about it.

"D'you think Hisao's dad meant to lend you an umbrella when he asked if you'd got one?" said Sadao, putting a hand out to help Koji hold his. They had just crossed Ohashi Bridge and before them lay Komori, wreathed in its sash of mauve smoke.

Koji giggled. And so did Sadao, picturing Inspector Ogaki in his *haori* and lace-up boots, beaming smugly as he followed his son. Koji was imagining a similar scene, but there was one more person in it: beside Hisao walked a girl in white *tabi* and a sleeveless *haori*, or *donza*, with a floral pattern. On the umbrella she twirled from time to time over the shoulder of her *donza* gleamed blackly the characters "Machié Sugimoto, Shimana," painted with an umbrella-maker's thick brush.

Apart from Machié Sugimoto, only four or five others in Koji's class had an umbrella specially made for them.

He stared up at his own, a white oil-paper one. It was still new, and, if he asked, the umbrella-maker would probably paint on his name for him. But it was out of the question to think of having "Komori" painted on after it.

Damn everything! He suddenly wanted to curse. How he hated the word "Komori," which could not even be written on an umbrella; and how he hated "Shimana" too, which could. Even the flowery *donza* made him angry.

The rain, now mixed with sleet, beat against the umbrella.

V

"It's easy enough to say two million yen, but that's a hell of a lot of money, you know."

Hirokichi paused and looked round at the assembled company: Koji and Sadao; Sadao's parents and his brother, Keiichi; and his elder sister, Kikué, and Tsuya—who were coming in and out of the room. Having arrived home unexpectedly for New Year's, Hirokichi was calling on the head family not only to pay his respects but also because he wanted to tell them about his place of work.

"I'll say it's a lot of money—two hundred thousand ten-yen notes," and Sadao's father, Kunihachi, laughed with an exuberance unusual for him. He poured Hirokichi a cup of saké. "When people have money, they're certainly rolling in it."

"More than you can say for us," added Sadao's mother, Toyo, who was also in lively form.

"There may be rich folk about but it's not every day that somebody decides to spend two million on a tunnel," said Keiichi. He neither smoked nor drank but was gobbling up some fish poached in soy sauce. He would be twenty-three that year, although with his long face and hair cropped short, workman-fashion, he looked three or four years older—except, that is, when he laughed, revealing a fine set of white teeth, and then, on the contrary, he looked younger than his age.

"You're right there, Keiichi," agreed Hirokichi, delighted with this remark. He continued excitedly, "That's what impresses me, too. It's a venture that'll benefit the public, not like playing the market at Dojima. Just think, Osaka and Nara will be linked when it's finished. That Seishu Iwashita's a fine man."

He noticed the rapt expression on the faces of Sadao and Koji.

"Seishu Iwashita's the president of Kitahama Bank and the head of the Osaka Electric Railway Company," he explained. "It's all because of him they're building the Ikoma tunnel, and it's costing two million yen—that's quite something."

"When'll it be finished?" asked Sadao, stretching out his legs.

"They say by the end of August. And if it is, it'll have taken two years and two months. But I'd say it'll be finished before then at the rate we're going at present, especially when you think that more than seventy percent of it has already been excavated."

"How long will it be altogether?" asked Koji.

"Same as the height of Mount Fuji."

"Mount Fuji's 12,365 *shaku** high," muttered Koji, remembering how Mr. Sugino had told them once that the height of the mountain was the number of months in a year followed by the number of days.

"Eh! The Ikoma tunnel's the height of Mount Fuji?" Toyo looked very impressed. "But isn't it dangerous digging such a long way?"

"Well, you always get some that have accidents or get themselves killed in a stupid brawl, but the tunnel itself is one hundred percent safe. Them professors have surveyed it all good and proper, and the site foremen don't miss a thing. Besides, they put in a forest of props as they go—pine timbers, at least two feet thick. And more than half the stretch they've excavated is already lined with bricks. It's a fine piece of work. I'd like to take young Sada and young Koji here to see it."

"We wouldn't mind seeing it, either," Kunihachi grinned.

"Take one of the trains then when they start running, and have a good look. You'll find the bricks I carried with my own hands inside. Ha, ha, ha."

Koji understood now: Uncle Hirokichi's job was brick-carrying.

Hirokichi downed yet another cup of saké. "I must admit though, I felt a bit funny myself the first few times I went in the tunnel. Like I was being sucked further and further into it and I'd never come out again. But it was different when I saw it being lined with the bricks

I'd brought in myself, and before I knew it I'd really got to like it in there. But that's the way it goes, isn't it? That's why the real construction workers by trade don't turn a hair when they come to a dangerous spot or a tricky bit of rock.''

"My goodness, you couldn't do work like that for nothing, could you? I bet those workers are getting as much as fifty sen or thereabouts, aren't they?" Kunihachi asked.

"Fifty sen! You must be joking, Master. The foremen usually get forty-seven and the construction workers forty-two. The women only get about twenty.''

"Forty-two sen'll just about buy you two *sho*.''

Koji grasped that Toyo was talking about rice.

"It makes rice seem expensive,'' said Tsuya.

"No, it's the wages that's low,'' Keiichi corrected her.

"But that's about the going rate anywhere these days, Keiichi. All the workers seem happy enough with it and work hard, and they're highly skilled men from mines all over the country. With prize money being handed out every day, it's also a matter of pride with them to be on the winning side. I'm working on the east side, and right now, we're two hundred feet ahead of the west. Not that I get any prize money myself, seeing as I'm only one of the laborers, but it's nice all the same to be on the winning side. Ha, ha, ha.''

"It's money that makes the world go round, right enough,'' said Kunihachi.

"You can say that again. It's being able to play around with large sums like two million that makes Seishu Iwashita a great man. He'd be nothing if all he had was the body he was born with, like me.''

"You'd better take care of that body of yours, then, Hirokichi. For those who have to work for a living, their body is their one asset.''

"Not much of an asset, but I'll look after it though, as it's the only one I've got.''

Hirokichi began searching about in his *haramaki** and presently brought out a small cloth bag. Holding it in both hands, he raised it reverently to his head and then tucked it back inside his *haramaki* again.

"That's an amulet of the blessed Shoten-San. You'll never be troubled or come to any harm so long as you've always got it on you.'' He grinned, showing his yellow teeth.

"Who's Shoten-San?" asked Sadao, itching to have a look inside the bag.

Hirokichi placed his hand on his *haramaki.* "The deity they worship at Hozanji on Mount Ikoma. I've come to appreciate Shoten-San's divine protection, I can tell you, since going to work at the tunnel, and made up my mind to go and worship at the temple every month on the fifteenth. I don't know if it's true or not, but they say the deity's got the body of a human but the head of an elephant."

"What a funny *kami!*" Sadao and Koji both guffawed.

"Ah, ha ha . . . There's none funnier. It's a man and a woman embracing."

"Get away with you, Hirokichi," giggled Toyo, puckering her mouth as she always did when she laughed, to hide her buckteeth.

"It's the truth. If you don't believe me ask the Master here. He's the authority on everything."

"It isn't true, is it?" Toyo still looked disbelieving.

"Yes, it is. I've never actually seen it of course, but apparently it's one of the Buddhist guardian deities. The male god's a manifestation of a devil, and the female, the eleven-faced Goddess of Mercy, and because they're embracing, anybody who worships Shoten-San will be blessed with a happy marriage and children, and protected from sickness and robbery."

"Goodness. And can you see this funny-looking—what was it, a *kami* or a buddha—anyway, can you see it if you go and worship at Ikoma?"

"I shouldn't think so. It's one of what they call the "secret Buddhas," which means it's kept locked away in a shrine in the inner part of the temple."

"That makes it all the more blessed. There's no doubt about it, it's all thanks to Shoten-San that such a big construction job as this is going so well without any hitch at all."

Sadao and Koji exchanged glances: it was obvious that in Hirokichi's mind the two million yen had now been completely overshadowed by the funny, human-bodied, elephant-headed god.

"I'm sure it is, but has Kané told you that Komori's bought a fire-fighting pump for 120 yen?"

"Yes, I heard about it as soon as I got back last night. The missus is delighted, especially after all we've suffered from fire. And by all accounts, you've personally gone to a great deal of trouble over it,

Master. Thanks to you, somebody like myself can now work away from home with an easy mind. We'll be counting on that pump all right—fire's the one thing Shoten-San doesn't protect us against, you know."

Hirokichi turned to Sadao and Koji. "Have you ever seen the fire drill Downing-the-Lantern?"

"Yes," replied Sadao.

"Last spring, at school . . ." added Koji.

"Didn't you enjoy it?" Hirokichi looked disgruntled.

"Well, it wasn't that much fun." Sadao glanced at Koji, "It was a bit boring last year, wasn't it Ko, with nothing but other villages' pumps."

"It'll be fun this year though, now that Komori's taking part," said Toyo.

The Downing-the-Lantern, a fire-brigade practice that also tested the working order of the pumps, was held once a year. The villages of Sakata, Shimana, Hongawa, and Azuchi brought their pumps to the conduit in front of the school, where they competed with each other to be the first to bring down the suspended lantern and gain the winners' flag. For the past three years, it had gone to Sakata.

Needless to say, the contest generated great excitement among the children, stirring up their feelings of rivalry, and, on the day, there was all the hubbub of a festival as they cheered on their respective village teams.

Komori, however, had been unable to take part, not having a pump of its own, and, far from enjoying the contest, Koji and Sadao had felt only a sense of inferiority as they watched.

But this year . . . Already, they could hardly wait.

Hirokichi too squared his shoulders. "I know Sakata's always won before, but from now on, things are going to be a bit different. We're not going to let them get away with it again, are we? You show them, young General, and bring back the winners' flag. And be sure you cheer him on, young Ko and Sada. I'm counting on you."

Keiichi, the "young General," poured Hirokichi another cup of saké good-humoredly. "Don't worry; leave it to me. The flag's ours, as sure as Mount Ikoma's to the northwest of here," he laughed.

"Ha, ha . . . You've set my mind at rest. As sure as Mount Ikoma's to the northwest—very good, young General. Well, as I'm going back to work at that Mount Ikoma tomorrow, I'll be taking my leave of you, Master, and your good lady here."

There were tears in Hirokichi's eyes, not that the saké helped. He had enjoyed himself so much this New Year's he could have wept openly.

It was late in the evening before he eventually calmed down.

VI

"It's the fifteenth today, Ko."

"Yes, today's the fifteenth."

"No, I mean it's the *fifteenth* today."

Koji sensed a subtle difference of meaning, although they seemed to be talking about the same date.

"Got it?"

He was still puzzled.

"You know, to do with Uncle in the branch family."

He remembered then: Sadao was talking about Hirokichi Shimura, who had said he was going to worship Shoten-San every month without fail on the fifteenth.

"Yes, it was today, wasn't it?" He stared across toward Ikoma.

"I bet he's praying to Shoten-San right now to watch over him and help him make lots of money."

Sadao too looked toward Ikoma. The mountain rose in a gentle curve, like an eyebrow; above it, were three pale gray wisps of cloud, one just like a puff of smoke.

"You've got a good memory, Sada. I'd forgotten all about it."

"Shoten-San's such a funny *kami* I couldn't forget."

"I thought Shoten-San was a buddha, not a *kami*."

"Maybe. But what's the difference? They all punish us."

Koji gave a hoot of delight: that was exactly what he thought.

"It's true, Ko," Sadao insisted.

"I know." Koji's expression suddenly grew tense. "I hate all those *kami* and buddhas. Why do they let us stay *eta* when they're supposed to help people? And Shoten-San's just as bad. What's the use of helping people to have kids if they're going to be *eta* kids?"

His cousin Nanaé had been worrying about that during the last summer holidays when she said, her young face white with anxiety,

"If there had been a baby in my tummy, it'd have come out in the end, wouldn't it? And it'd be an *eta*. That's what scared me."

How could there be *kami* and buddhas when there was so much pain and suffering in the world and nothing at all was done about it?

"Hatanaka." He wheeled round at the sound of Mr. Egawa's voice.

"What are you and Shimura staring at?"

"Mount Ikoma," he replied.

"Mount Ikoma, eh? That's a pleasant thing to be looking at." Mr. Egawa laughed, his warm breath stroking the nape of Koji's neck.

"They're building a tunnel through Mount Ikoma, sir," said Sadao.

"Yes, I know."

"And somebody in our branch family's working over there."

"Really?"

"Yes, and he said the length of the tunnel is about the same as the height of Mount Fuji."

"That's very interesting. And is that why you and Hatanaka have developed this sudden interest in Mount Ikoma?"

Koji and Sadao looked at each other and grinned. They did not want to admit that really they had been thinking about Shoten-San, now that there were fifteen or sixteen others standing round the teacher.

"I was born in a village right at the foot of Mount Ikoma, you know," said Mr. Egawa, looking round at the children.

"And Mr. Egawa came to the neighboring village of Matsukawa when he got married," announced a girl in the sixth grade, as if introducing him.

The children all laughed, whether they knew this already or not; their image of a teacher as somebody frightening, stern, and unapproachable was dispelled instantly by the phrase "when he got married."

Mr. Egawa chuckled, too. Then he said, "I suppose you fifth and sixth graders have learnt about Nagasune-hiko in history?"

"Yes, we have," replied Machié Sugimoto.

"He was the strongest of the villains," added Hisao Ogaki.

"Well, Nagasune-hiko lived in Ikoma. He was the local chieftain."

"Are you descended from Nagasune-hiko then, sir?"

"I don't know. Maybe. Or maybe from Nigihayahi-no-mikoto, who killed Nagasune-hiko."

"Does that mean your family was living in Ikoma before Emperor Jinmu, sir?"

"I'm afraid I don't know that, either."

"But sir, was Mount Ikoma like it is now then?" Koji asked.

"I expect so."

"With lots of people living there?"

"There must have been. Otherwise Nagasune-hiko's forces wouldn't have been so strong."

"But what did they do?" This was a question always at the back of Koji's mind.

"Let's see. Well, first of all, they had to grow crops and go hunting for food. And then they also had to make their clothes and shoes, and all sorts of tools. They must have all worked very hard."

"Then the Emperor Jinmu came to attack them, as the *kami* ordered. Didn't he, sir?" said a sixth grader.

"If it's true," somebody remarked skeptically.

"It must be, it's in our textbook."

"You idiot," Koji silently rounded on the sixth grader. He could not attack him out loud: the story of how the Sun Goddess's descendants came down to earth to found the Imperial line and rule Japan was in their history book.

Koji and Sadao ran all the way home that day without a word. The bitter wind that blew down from Mount Kongo in midwinter chilled them to the marrow, despite their flannel shirts and padded coats; it was so cold it took their breath away if they tried to speak.

"It's freezing," Koji blurted out in relief, as he stepped inside. The living room door slid open.

"Koji." Seitaro grinned at him.

In his delight at this unexpected visitor, he scrambled up into the room on all fours.

"Haven't you got a scarf?"

Seitaro took off his own—a reddish-black one—and wrapped it round Koji's neck, a way of satisfying his urge to hug his brother.

"They've forbidden the boys in the fifth and sixth grades to wear them this winter."

He rubbed his chin against the scarf; the silk felt soft.

"I bet you think you're dreaming, Koji, seeing your brother all of a sudden . . ." Nui blinked. Seitaro's homecoming certainly seemed like a dream to her.

"Yes, . . . though I thought perhaps he might come home because it's Apprentices' Day today in Osaka."

In fact, as he ran across Ohashi Bridge, he had suddenly remembered standing there with Seitaro the previous year, staring down silently at the riverbed.

"It was very cold and half sleeting when Seitaro came back last year, too," said Fudé, wiping her eyes.

Seitaro warmed his hands over the brazier, cracking the joints of his fingers. "I didn't mean to come back so unexpectedly. I'd hoped to be wearing a *haori* like I said last year. But anyway, as I explained, when the master asked me to go with him to the temple this morning, I suddenly found myself over this way."

"What a stroke of luck, him letting you come home like this as well as visiting the temple."

"Well, I can't stay very long I'm afraid, as it's not a proper visit. If it was, I'd have brought you lots of presents, Gran."

"Don't be so silly," Nui chuckled, wiping her eyes like Fudé. Koji knew they were both crying for joy.

But which temple had Seitaro gone to with his master, he wondered. Before he had time to ask, Seitaro remarked, "The master's been a believer in Ikoma's Shoten-San for a long time."

"Ikoma's Shoten-San? I might've guessed." Koji tried not to laugh.

"What do you mean, you might've guessed?"

"Uncle opposite's the same."

"You mean Uncle Shimura?"

"Yes. Now he's working at the tunnel, he said he goes every month on the fifteenth to ask Shoten-San to watch over him. So me and Sada were looking at Mount Ikoma during break and wondering if he was praying to Shoten-San right then."

Seitaro was at a loss for words, but Fudé exclaimed, "Well, I never; what funny things you know, Koji," and she laughed.

"But Uncle was talking all about it over at Sada's, when he came back at New Year's. I was there listening."

"Talking of Sada, how's the bride, Tsuya?"

"Very happy, of course. The family's well-off and they're kind people, after all."

"I wonder if she'd recognize me?"

"I'm sure she would. She once said what a fine, strapping boy you were, being a Frogfish." Fudé stepped down into the *doma* laughing; she was going to cook him something special for dinner.

"Did you hear what sort of work Uncle Shimura's doing over at the tunnel, Koji?"

Seitaro helped himself to the crackers he had brought as a present, giving one to his brother.

"Brick-carrying, by all accounts," said Nui.

"I saw lots of carts loaded with bricks coming out of Oji station today. Maybe Uncle was among them."

"No, his job is to take the cartloads of bricks down the tunnel by truck."

"My word, you know all the details, don't you, Koji?" said Nui, admiringly. "But what an enormous construction job this Ikoma tunnel seems to be. You should've taken a look on your way here, Seitaro."

"I had a quick look from the outside. There were scores of women there breaking up rocks from the tunnel with a sledgehammer—they carry the bits back down the tunnel to use for concrete. And then, there were these machines called ventilators, throwing compressed air into the tunnel. They were making such a racket, it was like being in the middle of a battle. The master was dead impressed. He said Mr. Iwashita must be the bravest man in Japan—Mr. Iwashita's the boss of the Osaka Electric Railway Company that's excavating the tunnel. The master's bought a lot of their shares."

"He'll be stung then, if the tunnel's a flop," said Fudé, from the sink.

"Yes, but he stands to do very well if they do manage to finish it. The share price'll go up as well as the price of land. And the trains going to Nara through the tunnel will run just south of our shop."

"All the more reason for your master to worship Shoten-San then."

"I suppose so."

"Does it really do any good worshiping Shoten-San?"

Seitaro threw back his head and guffawed at Koji's question. "It depends; for some it does and for some it doesn't," he answered.

"What about Uncle Shimura?"

"I'm sure Shoten-San will listen to him, seeing as he's an honest man," said Nui, stepping down into the *doma* to help Fudé with the evening meal.

"Sada said the *kami* and the buddhas only punish us. That's why I wanted to laugh," Koji whispered, so that Fudé and Nui would not hear.

"He's right, too. The fact is, there aren't really any *kami* or buddhas, are there? There wouldn't be things like Komori if there were."

"They don't know about Komori in Osaka though, do they?"

"No. But all the same, Koji, just put Sakata *mura,* not Komori, when you write from now on. You can never tell, somebody might know about it."

"All right." Koji hung his head, feeling as if his brother had betrayed him. He knew how contradictory this was, since it usually made him happy to think of Seitaro living far away from Komori; and yet, it did not alter the fact that it was unpleasant to see him purposely trying to distance himself from it.

"Why don't you come to Osaka too when you leave school?"

He greeted this in silence.

"It's nice living in such a big place."

"But you've still got to hide you're from Komori, don't you?"

"Yes, so that's what I take care to do."

"I don't want to go to a place like that," thought Koji, crunching the biscuit to try and control his mounting anger and sadness. Seitaro reached across and laid a one-yen note on his knee.

"Instead of a present."

Although pleased with the money, Koji could not bring himself to thank his brother, sensing him slipping further and further away.

Seitaro set off for Osaka early the next morning in the icy wind that was still sweeping down from Mount Kongo.

7

The Oxcart

I

"They say it's coldest early on in January, but, my word, there's a bitter cold you only get later," said Nui, with a smile.

"Yes, there's cold and there's cold all right. Tonight I feel chilled to the bone," agreed Fudé, as if extolling the iciness of the weather.

Although it made their night work even harder, they both felt reassured by the very severity of nature, which allowed none of the prejudice, favoritism, and deception found in man. This evening, January 26, 1913, it was freezing everywhere without exception, not only down in the villages of Sakata, Shimana, and Azuchi, but also up among the peaks of Yoshino and Mounts Kongo and Katsuragi.

"You can go on studying if you want, Koji, but wouldn't you do better to turn in soon on such a cold night?" said Fudé, presently.

"All right." He quickly wrapped up his schoolbooks and tied the ends of the cloth, pulling them far tighter than necessary in an effort to keep warm.

Nui glanced up at the clock. "It's not eight yet. Still, why don't you bolt the door, Koji? Nobody'll be coming round on a night like this, and it might keep the cold away too."

"But Auntie opposite might come."

Fudé shook her head. "No, she'll be round at the head family's for a bath this evening."

The Shimuras—the head family—heated up a bath every third evening, an event that Kané never missed; and she was always welcome there, since, in return, she cleaned the bath for them afterwards.

"I'll go and bolt it then."

In the front entrance, they used only the papered screen door

311

during the day, but at night a wooden one was also slid across, usually when they had finished their work, although tonight it was so cold that Fudé had closed it immediately after supper.

Koji now reached up and bolted it. Almost at once, however, he unbolted it again and slowly slid back the heavy door.

Puzzled by the sounds she heard, Fudé called out, "What are you doing, Koji? Hurry up and close the door, it's cold."

"Good evening," called back an unexpected voice, and two lanterns crossed the threshold, followed by two pairs of leggings and straw sandals.

Fudé was seized by a sense of foreboding.

"Have you come from Ino?" she asked, hurriedly stepping down into the *doma*. She felt sure they were bringing news that Grandfather was on the verge of death or had already breathed his last.

"We're terribly sorry to trouble you at this late hour," said one of the visitors, bowing low in apology. "As a matter of fact, we're from Taki, and we're wondering where we can find Kané Shimura. We've knocked at her door several times but there's no reply, so we thought we'd better step over here and ask."

Taki was the village where Kané's family lived, and Fudé sighed with relief as the threat of personal misfortune lifted.

"If you'll lend me one of your lanterns, I'll run and get her for you," she said.

"Yes, you do that," said Nui, and promptly stepped down to the stove and began lighting a fire in order to offer the visitors hospitality on such a cold night.

"It's very good of you. Would you mind telling her that her brother has come over from Taki with a message for her."

"You're Kané's brother?" Fudé lifted up the curved-handled lantern and took a good look at him; his face did resemble Kané's, she thought.

"Yes, her younger brother, Kamezo. And this is my nephew, Masakichi."

"Then am I right in thinking you've come over with the sad news of your mother's passing? I guessed as much because I heard she was a ripe old age."

"It wouldn't be such sad news if it was the death of an old person, but I'm afraid the tunnel caved in today, just after three. About a hundred and fifty or sixty people were trapped, and nobody knows what's become of my brother-in-law. So I came straight over to fetch my sister.''

Fudé looked silently at the lantern. Nui stared into the stove. They were both too horrified to speak. Then, Nui shook off her shock and stood up.

"Fudé, it doesn't do for us to be shilly-shallying around here when a terrible thing like this has happened. Kamezo and his nephew had better go straight to the head family's and have a proper talk with them all there. And then they must get back to Ikoma as soon as possible or . . .'' She doused the stove fire with water.

Koji guessed that meant she was going to go with them to the head family's. He flung himself on her, a certain excitement mingled with his fear.

As soon as Nui and Fudé came in through the front entrance, Kané spotted them from the back door by the bathhouse, where she was getting dressed.

"Have you come over for a bath too, Fudé? You need a nice hot bath on a bitter night like this, don't you, or you won't get to sleep,'' she gabbed, hastily adjusting the front of her kimono. "You're just in time, a moment later and I'd have pulled the plug and then I wouldn't have been very popular, would I? Ha, ha, ha . . .''

But the next moment, the cheerful smile froze on her lips as she caught sight of Kamezo and Masakichi behind Nui. She crept nervously toward her brother.

"Has something happened?''

"The tunnel's caved in.''

Masakichi blew out his lantern with a puff; it sounded curiously loud in the large *doma*.

II

"It must've been just after three,'' Kamezo began impatiently, as he took off his sandals as invited. "I was unloading the bricks from Oji station, same as usual, when all of a sudden I heard this roaring sound, like a hurricane, coming from the direction of the mountain, and then there was this great rumbling in the ground. It sounded like the whole mountain was caving in and I took to my heels and fled, leaving the ox and cart behind. There'd been this awful rumor going around for a long time that sooner or later disaster'd strike and lots of people would get killed, as a punishment for spoiling Shoten-San's holy mountain. So I thought, 'That's it, it's happened!'

"All I wanted to do was get away, but my legs just wouldn't carry me very far. I suddenly noticed Masakichi beside me. 'It's terrible,' he said, 'Uncle from Komori's in the tunnel!' I ran to the company office but it was in uproar . . .

"Anyway, they say the tunnel's caved in about five or six hundred yards from the east entrance."

"How far back has it caved in from there?" asked Kunihachi.

"I'm afraid they still didn't know when we left. May only have been a few feet. On the other hand, it could be the whole length they'd dug—that'd be about four or five hundred yards. If that's the case, all the hundred and fifty or sixty people working in there will have been killed. Such a terrible thing doesn't bear thinking of! They're all believers in Shoten-San, too; they always wear those good-luck amulets."

"So does Hirokichi . . ." Kané blew her nose.

"Must have something to do with a person's fate, when you think about it. Masakichi here was pushing trucks in and out of the tunnel and he'd just come out when the rumbling began. But there was this foreman who'd been in the outside office till just before three and went into the tunnel only one minute before it happened."

"So that's fate, is it?" whispered Kunihachi, to nobody in particular.

"I escaped, and I don't even believe in Shoten-San," said Masakichi, looking down at his knees; he had been sitting hidden behind Kamezo.

"It's your fate," and Keiichi smiled at him. Masakichi looked about five or six years younger than himself.

"But it's funny to think that somebody like me escaped when all the believers were trapped."

"Don't talk nonsense! Just think how I'd feel if you was lying under them rocks as well."

There was a twinkle in Kamezo's eyes as he said this. It was strange, but the fact that a lucky survivor like Masakichi was not a believer in Shoten-San had broken the general mood of tension.

Kunihachi's wife rallied around and produced a late snack of "colored rice"—rice cooked in soy sauce—that was scalding hot and rather hard, being cooked so quickly. All the same, a hot meal was comforting on such a cold night, and even the hardness of the grains was somehow reassuring to them in their shock.

Naturally, Sadao and Koji joined the grown-ups. As he ate, Koji gave Sadao a look which said, "Good, isn't it?"

"Yes, it is," Sadao's eyes answered.

"The tunnel's caved in and lots of people have been buried alive, and Uncle Hirokichi's one of them."

"I know."

"It still tastes good though."

"Funny, isn't it?"

"I wonder what all the grown-ups are thinking?"

"They're probably thinking it tastes good, same as us."

"Yes, they're all having second helpings."

"Hee, hee, hee . . ." Eventually, Sadao giggled out loud.

So did Koji.

"Whatever are you laughing about, you silly children? I don't see anything funny at all," scolded Fudé, evidently afraid of what the others would think.

"What terrors children are . . ." Sadao's mother sounded embarrassed as well.

Koji and Sadao wanted to laugh all the more. They tried desperately to control themselves, but it only made matters worse. The tunnel had caved in; a hundred and fifty or sixty people had been buried alive; and yet here they all were, eating with obvious relish—Auntie Kané, Uncle Kamezo, Masakichi, each eating as heartily as the next. It was enough to make anyone laugh.

Koji awoke the following morning to find something covering his head. It was his mother's everyday kimono, which she must have thrown off in a hurry.

"Has Mom gone to Ikoma, Gran?" he asked, and, pushing it away, peered at Nui lying beside him. He remembered how last night, after the snack, the grown-ups had had a long discussion about going there.

"Yes." Nui turned toward him, scraping her wooden headrest. "I don't envy her, it's a long way. But you can't start complaining about things like the cold or the distance at a time like this. We've got a duty to Kané, now we're all one family."

But she made no mention of their feeling sorry for Uncle Hirokichi, trapped in the tunnel, or for Auntie Kané, and he suddenly wanted to press her further on the subject.

"Uncle didn't die in the tunnel, did he?"

"That I don't know. I don't want to repeat what we said last night, but it's all a matter of fate."

"What is fate, anyway?"

"Your lot in life—something you'll understand soon enough, Koji. And it's all to do with fate where you die."

Then was it also to do with fate where you were born? Did that mean you had to grin and bear it, even if it happened to be an *eta* village like Komori?

"What about Dad? Did he have to die in the war because of fate?"

"Your father, Koji, got caught up in that horrible spider's web called war. That's why I said what I did about outliving them. They're spiders, the lot of 'em."

"But you're caught, too, aren't you, Gran, in the spider's web of Komori?" he thought, but was too afraid to say it. He pulled Fudé's kimono back over his head and glared into the dark.

III

As they made their way to school, Sadao debated with himself how best to broach the subject of the Ikoma tunnel. It seemed a pity to simply announce to his friends that it had caved in when it was such a major disaster, but, on the other hand, he was itching to tell them as quickly as possible.

"Wasn't that meal late last night good, Ko?" he said loudly, so that everybody would hear.

"I'll say. Thanks a lot." A grin of delight at their secret spread across Koji's face.

Sure enough, the sixth grader Magoichi Otaké scowled at them with a mixture of envy and irritation. "What are you two going on about?"

"There was a terrible disaster last night, Mago. If you don't believe me, look over there." Sadao stood on tiptoe and pointed toward Ikoma.

"What's wrong with the sky over there?"

"Not the sky; Mount Ikoma. Can't you see it's sunk a bit on top?"

"Don't be ridiculous! Why would it sink, it's not a volcano?"

"But the tunnel caved in yesterday. It must have sunk a bit."

"You're kidding?"

"No, I'm not. It'll be in today's papers, won't it, Ko?"

"Yeah," nodded Koji, although it only took the word 'papers' to convince Magoichi. Together with the others, he stood staring toward Ikoma.

The mountain still rose in a gentle curve like that of an eyebrow, exactly as it had the previous day.

Presently, Magoichi whispered, "It does seem to have sunk a bit."

Sadao chuckled to himself in glee at the success of his prank.

As soon as they reached school, he tried the same trick on the other fifth graders.

"Look over there. Mount Ikoma's sunk a bit on top, hasn't it? It's terrible, the tunnel caved in yesterday, and a hundred and fifty or sixty people have been buried alive!"

"How awful! Have they all been killed?" The girls looked horror-stricken.

But the boys jeered at him for his ignorance. "Liar. The mountain wouldn't sink just because the tunnel's caved in." They were annoyed that he should have heard about the disaster before them.

"A hundred and fifty or sixty's nothing. Twice as many as that were killed in the coal mine disaster in Hokkaido," said Hisao, trying to belittle Sadao's news.

"I know as well as you about the gas explosions and all the people who were killed up in Hokkaido," retorted Sadao. "But that had nothing to do with us, did it? Not like Ikoma. Even somebody in our branch family's one of those that's been buried alive, and it'd be stupid to pretend not to care."

"You're the stupid one," snapped Hisao. "It doesn't bother me how many have been killed, there aren't any *eta* in my family. And it's only *eta* that work in places like mines and tunnels."

There was a ripple of laughter, acknowledging his victory.

With difficulty, Koji managed to fight back his tears. He did not want the others to think he was crying from vexation or sadness.

"Please don't die, Uncle. You mustn't die," he whispered through his hidden tears.

After school, on his way home with Sadao, he remembered and whispered again, "Please don't die, Uncle. You mustn't die."

Hisao and his friends seemed to think that anyone born an *eta* was naturally fated to meet a miserable end, whether in a tunnel or a mine, and if only Uncle Hirokichi would survive the disaster, it would show them how wrong they were.

IV

"Whatever's the matter, Koji? Leaving so much of your lunch . . ." Nui asked with unintentional sharpness, noticing that the lunch box he threw down sounded suspiciously heavy.

"I didn't feel hungry today after that nice meal we had late last night over at Sada's."

"Now then, you're just trying to pull the wool over my eyes. What you really mean is you didn't like what I gave you." Nui laughed, knowing perfectly well this was not the case, since, instead of the usual mixture of boiled rice and barley, she had given him what was left of the white rice specially prepared for Fudé before she set off for Ikoma—and not only that, but his favorite dried sardines as well.

All the same, he must have had some reason for leaving his lunch. She studied his face to see if he were getting sick, but he showed no signs of a temperature.

Koji looked up at the clock. "It's three, Gran."

"So it is. You must be hungry now. Why don't you have some of your lunch. I'll help you."

He fetched a pair of chopsticks from the sink and sat down beside her.

"I wonder what's happened to Uncle."

"Have you been worrying about that all day, Koji?"

"Yes."

"Is that why you didn't feel like your lunch?"

"Yes."

"He'll be all right if he's lucky; if not, he won't. All depends on fate."

Fate again: Koji suddenly lost his appetite.

Nui took a large mouthful. "White rice tastes nice even cold, not like barley and rice." She swallowed loudly.

"Can't we ever get the better of fate?" he asked, gripping his chopsticks.

"What was that?"

"I said, 'Can't we ever get the better of fate?' "

"Of course not."

"Is Komori fate too?"

"Well, to tell you the truth, we may resign ourselves to it as fate but deep down we're not really resigned to it, you know. It's just that if we didn't pretend to be, life'd be impossible."

Koji chewed a dried sardine; the guts had a faintly bitter taste.

"Another thing I've been thinking about all day today while I got on with my work. You know, we say it's fate when people get killed or wounded in a war, but war isn't something that just comes like a bolt from the blue, is it; it's all planned by somebody or other. Like I said this morning, Shinkichi got caught in a wicked spider's web."

"Try a sardine, Gran, they're good." Koji popped the rest of the sardine he had been nibbling into Nui's mouth.

"Same with Hirokichi," she added, savoring it with her tongue. "They'll go on about him being ill-fated if he dies. But it's got nothing to do with fate, and Shoten-San didn't destroy the tunnel, either. It caved in because they slipped up somewhere in the construction work."

"That's right." Koji suddenly leaned forward, greatly relieved. His grandmother was clearly saying that the railway company would be to blame if Uncle Hirokichi died in the tunnel; that it was not his fate as an *eta* to die like that.

"Ah, very tasty." Nui laid down her chopsticks.

"I'll wash up," and Koji stepped down to the sink. As he rinsed out the lunch box, he wondered what his mother was doing at that moment. The sight of Fudé's bowl on the shelf before him made him uneasy; he had a feeling that it would remain there untouched for another two or three days.

Fudé was then sweating her way up Mount Ikoma, certainly not something she had expected to do.

She and Kané had arrived at the east entrance of the tunnel shortly after nine that morning to find the workmen's hut that served as a resting place in an uproar, with all the relatives of the victims. Inside, they soon learned that the rescue operations had continued all night, but that it was still unknown whether the victims were alive or dead. Apparently, since dawn, one family after another had gone to climb the mountain to Hozanji temple, unable to bear the tension of waiting any longer.

"I know it's terrible to think of walking any further, but wouldn't you like to go and worship Shoten-San too, Kané? After all, Hirokichi seemed to be a great believer," suggested Kunihachi, with an encouraging expression.

"Go on, Auntie. Dad and me'll be here if anything happens," added Keiichi.

"I'll go with you, Kané," Fudé offered, not for form's sake, but because she thought it would help her to be away from the scene of the disaster for a while.

"I don't want to. What's the use, when Hirokichi was killed last night?" Kané replied, her face twisted in a smile.

Neither Kunihachi nor Fudé attempted to reason with her, both feeling that she would have to give up hope in the end, and that it was better for her to do so now rather than remain for hours in a state of suspense.

At noon, however, fresh news came in.

"We can hear the sound of moaning from where we've dug through."

"No doubt about it, there's some alive in there."

"We should be able to rescue them by this evening."

Kané, who had been quite calm until then, suddenly started trembling.

"Maybe he's alive. Yes, he is, I know he is. He must be, believing in Shoten-San the way he does. I must go and worship Shoten-San and pray they rescue him quick while he's still alive," she cried, as if she had taken leave of her senses.

She was not the only one to be so agitated. Everybody's joy knew no bounds now that the victims were apparently still alive, but, for that very reason, all were gripped by the new fear that the rescue operations might be too late.

And to escape this fear, Fudé and Kané were now climbing Mount Ikoma to Hozanji, where Shoten-San was enshrined.

The temple was said to be under a mile from the foot of the mountain, and the ancient path was hardly steep, but their legs ached all the same, having already walked such a long way.

"I'm sorry to be giving you so much trouble, Fudé," said Kané, as they drew near the stone steps leading up to the temple's main gateway. They were both panting hard as the path had suddenly steepened.

"Don't be silly," Fudé replied, with a smile, which was not merely from politeness; even an unbeliever like herself could not help but be struck by the beauty of the spot, and secretly she gazed about her greedily, wanting to make the most of the opportunity.

They passed through the main gateway and were approaching another flight of steps when a man came running up behind them. "You'd better hurry, ladies, we're in for a storm," he said. But the sky above was quite blue and they gazed up at it puzzled. All at once, the great cedars began groaning, and, the next moment, gray swirling clouds had obscured the blueness from sight.

Fudé and Kané hastily covered their heads with their shawls. A gust of wind mixed with snow that seemed bent on knocking them off their feet swept down from the top of the mountain.

When at last they ran under the eaves of the main temple building, they turned and looked at each other.

"Gave me quite a fright."

"I wondered what was happening."

Purple smoke rose from a large censer in front of them, and a sound like the soughing of a wind through the pines issued from the packed hall where sutras were being chanted.

Kané threw a nickel five-sen coin into the offertory chest and also bought two candles and a bundle of incense sticks.

"Thank you, Fudé," she said, when Fudé did likewise, and then she knelt down on the paving stones.

"You can go and worship inside, you know," said the old incense-seller, but Fudé knelt down there too, beside Kané,

"Look, blue sky again," the old man said presently, when they stood up. "We get these sudden snow flurries here on the mountain, even when the cherry trees are blossoming—it amazes folk who've never been here before. Myself, I see it as proof that Shoten-San exists. The wind and the snow are Shoten-San's breath, you might say."

"Very nicely put. I had the same sort of feeling myself, coming here to worship today. My husband's a believer in Shoten-San as well, you know. There's no danger at all, he said, when he went off to work in the tunnel. Then this terrible thing had to go and happen . . . But Shoten-San will save him. Don't you think so?"

"Of course he will! Nothing to worry about at all. Shoten-San wouldn't just sit back and let honest, hard-working men die like that. When you get down the mountain there'll be good news waiting for you, you'll see."

"You don't know what a relief it is to hear you say that. I'm much obliged to you," and Kané started down the steps. All trace of weariness seemed to have left her so that Fudé found it hard to keep up.

As soon as the temple precincts were behind them, the view suddenly opened out, and before long they could see whitewashed houses in the evening sun, here and there at the foot of the mountain.

"Only a few hundred yards more," exclaimed Kané excitedly, obviously convinced that good news awaited them.

The path now curved to the right, leading to the east entrance of the tunnel. Six or seven minutes and they would be back, if they hurried. Then, they heard a strange thudding noise.

Kané stopped dead in her tracks as if afraid. "Is it the wind, Fudé?"

The next second, she gasped.

People, people, people; more and more of them appearing over the ridge to their right. Fifty, seventy, over a hundred. Chests and shoulders naked, they came pounding up the mountainside toward them, drawing nearer with every second.

There was now no mistaking them: they were the victims who had just been released from the tunnel of death. And Hirokichi must be among them.

"Hirokichi! Hirokichi!" they cried, running toward the half-naked procession.

Beneath their sweatbands, the faces remained impassive. Some resembled Hirokichi, others did not; but none looked round.

"Hirokichi! Hirokichi!"

It was useless. The procession had moved past and was heading straight for Hozanji.

"He didn't have much luck, did he, Fudé? He worshiped Shoten-San same as the rest of 'em, but much good it did us." Kané put on the shawl she had been carrying.

"Don't talk like that," Fudé was about to protest, but suddenly changed her mind. With the evening breeze, a sense of futility swept over her tired body.

"He didn't have much luck, did he? He worshiped Shoten-San same as the rest of 'em, but much good it did us," Kané said again, at the same time the next day.

Fudé remained silent.

"It's not only Shoten-San he didn't have any luck with," remarked Kunihachi. "The company's not done you much good, either. You're not entitled to a thing from them because Hirokichi was only one of the temporary laborers. It'd be a different matter if he'd been one of the foremen or construction workers, though he worked the same as they did, and died in the tunnel with them too."

"But I'm sure he must be touched by the kindness you've all shown. And I couldn't ask for more than that." Kané began to sob loudly.

Hirokichi had been crushed by one of the supporting timbers that had toppled down like dominoes. He now lay, hands folded on his chest, in the single-shafted oxcart Kamezo had used to bring bricks from Oji station.

Ikoma gradually receded into the distance in the cold silence of twilight, which none broke, not even the ox.

V

"It was a fine way for Hirokichi to go. Like a soldier dying bravely in action," said Tosaku Nagai, at the wake; and no one disagreed with him.

Only Kané retorted defiantly to herself, "What's so fine about being crushed to death in a tunnel? You just think it serves him right, don't you?" Her anger helped to support her through the wake, and she managed not to cry in front of the others.

Kiyokazu too showed a self-possession that surprised Fudé and Kunihachi. He had returned home for his father's funeral from Osaka after an absence of three years and greeted everybody most correctly, making the appropriate distinctions between neighbors and relatives. His apprenticeship almost over and now an expert at soling shoes, he was beginning to acquire not only confidence with regard to work but social sense as well.

His younger sister, Harué, had grown beyond recognition in a year and a half and her face had an almost adult expression. The ladies of the neighborhood all stared at her in astonishment. She had left primary school at the end of the fifth grade and gone into service as a nanny with the family of a restaurant owner in Sakai. Now, however, she worked in the restaurant itself; one reason why she had let down the tucks in her kimono and wore a false piece in her hair at the front. She shed no tears in front of the others on her mother's instructions.

"Don't you start crying now." Kané had said. "All the crying in the world won't bring your dead father back, and it'll only please the neighbors. They come out with all them nice-sounding things about how sorry they are and all the rest of it, but at heart they're glad. They think it serves your dad right. And they can't wait for us to become beggars, either. But that's folk for you."

More than ten of her relatives, including her brother Kamezo, had come in their straw sandals all the way from Taki for the funeral, and people attending from other villages surrounded them to hear about the cave-in of the tunnel. It was true that the disaster—in which one hundred and fifty-three people had been suddenly trapped and nineteen of them killed—had none of the poignancy of, say, one of the old ballad-dramas about a lovers' suicide; but then the fascination of that uncanny, supernatural force, Shoten-San, more than made up for it.

"An hour or two soon pass by in the sunshine like this, where you can get a drink of water or a bite to eat whenever you want," said Kamezo. "But just think how long it'd seem, shut up in a pitch black hole in the ground. I heard about this fellow once that had such a frightening experience his hair turned snow-white overnight, and I can really believe it. If an hour can seem like a year, ten hours'd be like ten years—and that's long enough for your hair to go white.

"Anyway, the people trapped in the tunnel apparently prayed to Shoten-San like mad. They couldn't bear to be quiet even for a second, they was so scared they was going to die of starvation or be suffocated. Though I heard there was a few that got angry and said they didn't give a damn about Shoten-San anymore if a terrible thing like this could happen, even though they'd been believers.

"Then, twenty-four hours later, they were rescued. And, not surprisingly, those who came out of that hole went rushing straight off up the mountain to give thanks to Shoten-San. I happened to be standing near the tunnel at the time with Mr. Shimura and saw them. All blubbering like little kids they were . . . One of 'em had a dragon tattooed all over his back, and even he was crying and didn't mind who saw it.

"There was this one fella though, that went straight back to the workmen's hut and had a meal and went to sleep. 'I don't believe in them *kami* and buddhas and never have,' he says, 'and I'll be hanged if I'll go off to some temple now to give thanks when I haven't eaten a thing in twenty-four hours.' I don't know where he's from but I have to say I was amazed at his nerve."

"He's a fellow called Kusunoki, from Fukuoka. I know him well by sight, and I've chatted with him once or twice, too," remarked Masakichi.

"Well, he's certainly a bit different from the rest, isn't he? Talking like that, cool as a cucumber, when all the others was crying Shoten-San, Shoten-San, as if they'd taken leave of their senses. But you can't beat a young man for speaking his mind—and he doesn't look more than about twenty-one or -two.

"Which puts me in mind of another very pathetic character—Iseda, they say his name is, though on site, everybody calls him 'Bald Jizo.'*

"He's got this big bald patch, you see, over his right temple—must've had some sort of bad abscess there when he was little. Apparently, he'd have been passed as A-1 at his army physical if the one examining him hadn't lost his temper when even the army cap didn't hide the bald patch. 'You disloyal baldie' he shouted and stamped him only a 'B.'

"Well, he may have seemed disloyal to the examiner for all I know, but this baldie's a nice fellow who's mad about children. That's how he got the name Bald Jizo—he likes being called that himself.

"Anyway, Bald Jizo broke his left arm in the cave-in and he was so weak he could hardly speak when he came out. As soon as they'd treated him though, he was back in the tunnel again and he went on calling 'Tamé! Tamé!' for a day and a night.

"He and Tamé'd only just got married at New Year's and they were renting a farmer's house nearby. He's from a country district in Wakayama somewhere, but he doesn't seem to have any close relatives, as nobody came rushing over after the disaster.

"They still haven't found Tamé's body. She's probably lying under some big rock. But it was enough to make your blood run cold, though, to hear Bald Jizo calling her—like peering into hell, it was. You'd never sleep again if you'd heard that voice in the middle of the night.

"You'd think Shoten-San would understand better about things like that, especially as it's supposed to be a male and a female god embracing each other tenderly. Or perhaps Shoten-San was just plain jealous and wanted to torment Bald Jizo because he and his wife were so close. Ah, ha, ha!"

The people surrounding Kamezo laughed with him.

"So this young wife Tamé was working in the tunnel as well, was she?" asked one of them.

"Yes, she was washing bricks in there every day," answered Masakichi instead. "All the bricks to line the tunnel have to be washed first, you see.

"You wouldn't believe how many they use, what with the tunnel being forty-two feet high from floor to ceiling. And in places where the foundation's weak, they have to make the lining anything up to twelve bricks thick.

"There were about fifteen or sixteen bricklayers, all from Izumo—it seems that's the only place you can find bricklayers that can line tunnels—but three of 'em have been killed.

"And Bald Jizo's wife probably died with them, as she washed the bricks nearby. Not that they've found her yet. Uncle was killed not far from them too, but luckily they brought his body out the next day. By rights, I should've been killed as well because I worked with him every day. But I'd just gone outside when the tunnel caved in and so I escaped."

"You're very lucky. You must have great faith in Shoten-San," somebody remarked with a sigh.

"That's where you're wrong, he's no believer. He's never worshiped Shoten-San or Bishamon-San, or O-Ise-San or Inari-San, either." Kamezo looked at Masakichi and laughed again. Then a lively debate ensued as to whether in fact the gods existed or not.

"I don't know if there's any *kami* or buddhas in this world," Kamezo said presently, "but, to my mind, it's not a bad thing for people doing dangerous work, like on the tunnel, to believe in them, not if it gives them some peace of mind. And that's what the company thinks, too. They've encouraged the laborers to worship Shoten-San. But now the tunnel's caved in, with nineteen dead, the workers have all got the jitters. They think it's a sign that Shoten-San's angry, and nobody wants to go in the tunnel anymore. And when they do, the work doesn't go well because they're so worried Shoten-San's about to punish them again. It'll be the company that suffers in the long run. It's bound to take at least a year now to finish, in spite of what they said about six months.

"I heard that Osaka Railway shares fell from fifty yen to five yen the day after the cave-in, and by yesterday, they were worthless. And that's not the worst of it—the shareholders may be asked to pay up thirty-seven yen fifty sen a share if it takes a long time to repair the damage, or if it costs more than expected to excavate the remainder of the tunnel.

"The face value of the shares is fifty yen, you see, and only a quarter of it—twelve yen fifty sen—has been paid up so far. That's why it seems likely the shareholders will be called on to pay up the rest.

"People with money around here are pretty alarmed, I can tell you—they've all got masses of Osaka Railway shares, Ikoma being a local project. Can't be helped though. They were unlucky and their gamble didn't pay off; it's nobody's fault.

"The one with the biggest headache though is Mr. Iwashita, Osaka Railway's boss. I know he's a powerful man, but he's no match for Shoten-San. One more cave-in and Kitahama Bank could be finished too. And that'd be disastrous for Osaka businessmen—some of them would probably go under as well."

"Oh, Mom heard."

Koji suddenly noticed that Fudé was trying not to listen to Kamezo as she busied herself in the *doma*. Seitaro's master had stood to make a great deal from the rise in value of shares and land if the tunnel were a success. But now, on the contrary, they were talking about shareholders being faced with a heavy loss, and he knew his mother would already be imagining with horror the Yonoi rice shop having to close down and Seitaro having to return home.

But Seitaro would never come back to Komori, he thought to himself; even if they wanted him to, he would only turn his back on them and go even further away.

What would happen when he died though? Wouldn't he simply become an *eta* again, even if he had hidden it during his life? Or would the *eta* thing disappear? No, surely it wouldn't. Even dead, an *eta* must be an *eta*, just as the Emperor was still the Emperor.

"Uncle!" Koji cried silently, as he stood before Hirokichi's coffin, his hands joined respectfully. Tears welled up in his eyes. At that moment, what saddened him the most was not his sudden death in the tunnel but the fact that Hirokichi had been born in Komori and spent all his life there—and that so many others too would have to lead lives like his, stamped with the seal of *eta*.

On the way home from the cemetery of An'yoji, where Hirokichi's remains had been buried, Harué put her hand on Koji's shoulder.

"I'm sure that Dad was touched at you crying for him, Ko," she said.

He escaped her hand and ran away. He did not know what to reply; and besides, he felt rather shy at talking to a young lady with such a fashionable hairstyle.

The next day—Thursday—he and Sadao were scolded by their teacher, Mr. Aojima, for being absent from school without permission.

"What can you do with the likes of Komori? Things like regular attendance mean nothing to them, parents or children."

They said nothing. They knew they would simply be inviting another unpleasant rebuke if they tried to explain they had stayed away in order to go to Uncle Hirokichi's funeral, when they were not even directly related to him—"There, you see, those Komori . . ."

VI

There were two round white dumplings floating in the gruel for supper. Why were they having dumplings now? Not that it mattered, they were always a treat.

Peering into the pan, Koji ladled one into his bowl, filling it so full the hot gruel spilled over. "Ouch," he exclaimed, shifting the bowl to the other hand.

"There's no need to be in such a hurry. They're yours." Nui helped herself only to gruel and left the other dumpling floating in the pan. Fudé did the same. They both wanted Koji to have it.

He moved his bowl back into his left hand and very carefully sipped the gruel. The dumpling he kept until last; and then, being such an unexpected treat, it slipped down his throat in one swallow. Strangely enough, he preferred the slightly salty ones that were cooked in the gruel to the sweet ones filled with bean paste.

"Did you enjoy that?" Fudé smiled, glancing at him out of the corner of her eye. "Lucky you're a boy, isn't it? You wouldn't get one if you were a girl, no matter how much you begged."

"Why not?"

"Because they're Forty-Ninth-Day dumplings, of course. It'd spoil a girl's chances."*

That meant a girl would have difficulty in finding a husband, but boys did not have to find one and so they could eat as many dumplings as they liked, Koji reasoned.

Presently, he helped himself to the second one.

"They say time passes quicker after a death, but who'd believe it's Hiro's Forty-Ninth already," said Nui, drinking her gruel with a loud slurping noise.

Koji looked down into his bowl: so the dumplings were a Forty-Ninth-Day offering for Uncle Hirokichi. Then he worked it out in his head that today, March 15, really was the forty-ninth day since his death—it had been on Sunday, January 26, a date he would not soon forget.

"There's nothing sillier than folk though when you stop and think about it," Nui remarked again. "Spending our lives bickering and squabbling with each other, out for what we can get, when we're all going to finish up as dust when we die, every last one of us."

"Yes, and look at the silly things we fuss about, like girls can't eat Forty-Ninth-Day dumplings while boys can," Fudé laughed.

Yes, wasn't it stupid, thought Koji, seeing the funny side as well.

"That's right, doesn't make sense. Dumplings is dumplings, New Year's or Forty-Ninth-Day. But girls don't want to take any risks, do they? It's having to wait for some fellow to come along who wants to marry 'em that does it. It's all right for the men. They can go and ask for a girl's hand if they've taken a fancy to her." And Nui guffawed, in her usual resounding way.

This time Koji was not amused; something jarred in what his grandmother had said.

Unaware, she continued, "Lucky you're a boy, Koji, and don't have to worry about eating Forty-Ninth-Day dumplings." She was also hinting at his good fortune in being free to make advances to the girl he liked, and he blushed. But only for a second. The next moment, he paled: how could it be true that he was free to marry whoever he wished?

He stared down at his hand clasping the chopsticks; the hand Machié had found and gently squeezed in the darkness of the school hall, that night six months ago. It must have been a sign she liked him, and truly he liked Machié. Although rather ashamed to admit it, he knew she was the reason he looked forward so much to school, and was convinced that his feelings toward her would never change, not even when he had grown up.

Yet it was inconceivable to think of entering Machié's home and saying he would like to marry her. He was under no illusions that he would ever be received in Shimana as a fellow human being, even if he grew to be a fine young man six feet tall, with the strength and wit to earn a living.

Like a convex lens, his tears made the chopsticks he was holding look as thick as a pair of oven tongs.

"That was a nice supper," he said, putting them down.

"Don't you want any more?" Fudé asked, in surprise.

"No, I've had enough."

"But you've only had two bowlfuls."

"Yes, but I've had two dumplings as well."

"Well, as long as you're sure you're full. Seitaro never had less than five or six helpings when he was a fifth grader. 'I'm Frogfish,' he'd say."

Usually, the mention of "Frogfish" would have led to a chat about Seitaro and his doings, but tonight Koji got up straightaway.

"Machié held my hand. And I held hers. What's the use though, I'll never hold it again. I'm from Komori. An *eta*," he thought.

He turned his back on Fudé and Nui, and stared intently at his hand—work-roughened through stem-cutting, the nails overlong, it looked dirty even to him.

He rummaged in the sewing box in the corner of the room, and found a small pair of nail scissors. Snip. His thumbnail was brittle and made a sharp, cracking sound.

"What are you doing Koji! Stop it at once! You know it's unlucky to cut your nails at this time of night," scolded Nui; but he silently proceeded to cut the nail of his forefinger.

"Didn't you hear your grandmother, Koji?" said Fudé crossly.

Without replying, he cut the nails of his middle and ring fingers.

"All right, do them all then, but don't blame us if you cut yourself."

"I won't cut myself," he said, still with his back to them. "They only said it was unlucky because it used to be dark at night with just a lamp, and it was easy to hurt yourself. But it's different now that we've got electricity."

"I suppose you're right. There's no getting around you these days, Koji; you've got an answer for everything." Nui admitted defeat with good grace.

After a while, Koji turned round and held out his hands for his grandmother to see. "Look, Gran."

"What is it?" she asked, not understanding.

"Take a good look at them."

Nui looked at his face instead.

Dumbstruck, Fudé stared at him, clutching a pan lid.

"Grandad from Ino told me I'd got hands like yours."

"Like mine? Oh, he probably meant they're clumsy like mine."

"No, he didn't. He said I had nice handwriting because my fingers are long like yours. That's why he bought me a writing brush and some ink and told me to practice hard. I saw what he meant about the long fingers just now when I was cutting my nails."

If only it were true, thought Fudé, still eyeing him distrustfully. She could not help feeling that he was hiding something, that all the talk about long fingers was only pretense. Behind the outspread hands, he was really whispering to himself, "I'm an *eta,* a Four-Fingers, like Gran is."

She could imagine him saying, "They hold up four fingers, meaning us. 'You know,' they laugh, that Sakata and Shimana lot. They never talk about Komori, they just hold up four fingers and say 'you know' did this, and 'you know' did that. I can't stand seeing those four fingers, it's even worse than being called *eta* or 'new commoner.' It makes me go all wobbly at the knees. And why do they do it when I've got five fingers, same as everybody else? I counted them just now, one by one, as I cut my nails. The next time somebody holds up four fingers and says 'you know' to me, I'll cut my thumb right in front of him. It'll bleed and then he'll see I've got one."

In fact, Fudé herself had had such an experience.

"Not much chance of Fudé marrying well, what with 'you know.' Shame when she's so pretty."

Seeing the seamstress make the four-finger sign as she talked to her friends, Fudé immediately started cutting her thumbnail with her needlework scissors. One, two, three—slowly she went on to cut the nails of all ten fingers. The other seamstresses watched her hands with bated breath; there was something frightening about her deliberate movements, as if she might even cut her fingers, too.

Not long afterward, she came as a bride to the Hatanaka family. They were distant relatives, but the match had been difficult to arrange, as they were also the poorest. Yet Fudé herself had been in favor of it. She could still remember why: it was not despair over her Four-Fingers fate, but rather a feeling of wanting to try and corner that same fate in the depths of poverty. And her wish was granted, with a vengeance. She drew the hardest lot of all: Shinkichi's death in the war.

But the severity of it opened her eyes. Amid her yearning for Shinkichi, she reflected about the war, and about the Emperor, and came to realize that in a world ordered so irrationally that one perfectly ordinary human being could be held up as sacred, there was nothing to prevent the injustice of large numbers of working people being degraded like animals.

In other words, she understood that it was the weight of those such as the landlords, the wealthy, the aristocracy, and the Imperial Family bearing down on them that produced their pain as Four-Fingers, their misery as *eta*.

But such understanding did nothing to change things. Koji was following the same path she had trod, and he would continue to follow it in the future. And if not this evening, then surely one day, in tears, he would cut his nails, counting them as he did so, distressed enough even to cut his fingers.

Fudé was well aware that however many times one acknowledged the burden one shouldered, the weight of it only disappeared when one finally put it down. And, similarly, that their suffering would only cease when all the forces bearing down on them had been pushed aside. What was the use of knowing this, though? Knowledge alone was useless.

"Why don't you show off your fine handwriting in a letter to Seitaro?" Nui suggested presently, changing the position of the electric light. Fudé hurriedly began to clear away the supper things.

"But I've nothing special to tell him," replied Koji. Seitaro had stopped sending magazines recently, and there did not seem to be much reason to write.

"Nothing to tell him! Don't you think he'd like to know you've come top of your class again this year and you're going up to the sixth grade?"

"I don't know if I've come top or not, the closing ceremony's not for two weeks yet."

"Wait till after the ceremony, then. But drop him a line."

"I won't if I don't come top."

"Ha, ha . . . I don't know who else is going to."

"I don't think I will, Gran; I got low marks for deportment this year. I did bite the Headmaster, you know, and . . ."

"It doesn't matter if you're not top," said Fudé, from the sink.

Deportment has to do with dignity and the way one should behave; and since the teachers called the Komori children *eta,* looking on them as Four-Fingers little better than animals, it was no wonder that Koji's marks for this subject were low.

In her present mood, she thought it callous even to tell him to "try hard."

8

The First Cry

I

"The glee-am of the firefly," crooned Hisao Ogaki, as he wiped the windows of the classroom. "Sno-ow on the windowpane," sang four or five others in response. The closing ceremony was the next day, and there was a general feeling of excitement.

Hisao appeared particularly elated, surely a sign that the report card he had just received told him he had come first in class and would be the representative of the school at the closing ceremony.

"Yes, I bet that's it!" Koji whispered to himself, as he cleaned the floor on all fours. It was no more than he had expected, but, even so, resentment overcame him and his chin began to quiver. Hastily, he pushed his cloth straight across the floor.

Last night, he had sat down in front of Nui, bent over her night work as usual. "I won't need a packed lunch tomorrow," he had said.

"No, it'll be your last day in the fifth grade, won't it?" she answered, understanding at once.

Encouraged, he continued, "Yes, so do you think you could sew me a floor cloth, Gran, for the spring cleaning tomorrow?"

"I'll make as many as you want. Only takes a second."

From her basket of oddments, she brought out an old towel that, although rather grubby, seemed too good for a floor cloth.

"Now, thread a needle for me, Koji. I can't seem to manage it these days. Must be getting old." She placed her sewing box in front of him.

He found a long needle and deftly threaded it with some black cotton, remembering that Machié Sugimoto's white cloth had a zigzag stitch in black. It was more like a duster though than a floor cloth, and she always spread it beneath her inkstone.

In less than five minutes, Nui had finished it.

334

"How's that, Koji?"

"Fine, first-rate."

He was delighted with the cloth, with its leaf-stitch, and wished he could use it under his inkstone, as Machié did.

"Your marks for deportment'll shoot up if you put your back into the cleaning with a good floor cloth like that. You never know, you may be top yet," remarked Fudé.

"I'd better make two or three more, then," and Nui roared with laughter.

Koji giggled too, although at heart he felt unbearably sad. It was obvious what lay behind his mother's words, his grandmother's guffaws. They really wanted to say: "You're ashamed because you can't be top this year, Koji—you even seem to be worried about a floor cloth for school. But we know it's not because of laziness. We know your marks are as good as ever. It's just deportment you haven't done so well in because you bit the Headmaster. But there was a reason for that and we don't mind a bit you not being top. So keep your spirits up and put your back into the spring cleaning now with your new floor cloth."

A lump in his throat, he playfully raised the "first-class floor cloth" to his head in a gesture of thanks. He too had to hide his real thoughts.

Nui's leaf-stitch cloth did indeed turn out to be first-class. Soft to the touch, he could fold it in two, or four, or roll it up and use it like a scrubbing brush.

He knew, though, that however effectively he did the cleaning with it, there was not the slightest chance of improving his deportment marks. Not that it altered the fact that it was the fifth graders' responsibility to leave the classroom they were about to vacate looking as fresh as possible, and, sweating, he scrubbed the floor as if he alone were shouldering that responsibility. There was an ink stain about the size of a man's foot that was proving particularly stubborn.

"You'll never get rid of it, Ko, not even if you stay there rubbing at it all day. Why don't you give up?" he heard Sadao call down to him.

Sadao was cleaning the windows on the corridor side of the room. He had been watching Koji anxiously, wondering what he was thinking, since it looked as if Hisao Ogaki would be the one to represent the school that year.

"But look how black my cloth's got. That shows how much ink has come out already." Still on his knees, Koji spread out the floor cloth, now so dirty the leaf-stitch could no longer be seen.

Sadao grinned awkwardly, not knowing what to say.

"I'll rinse it and have one more go. That should get rid of most of it."

Koji stood up and looked round for the bucket. Luckily, it had just been brought back filled with fresh water. He ran over to it and plunged in his cloth.

"Oh, you idiot!"

"You stupid ass!"

A barrage of angry jeers smote him from all sides.

The room reeled before his eyes. He could have sunk through the floor with embarrassment: he must have inadvertently put his dirty cloth in the wrong bucket.

"What is it?" Sadao sprang down from the windowsill in surprise and peered across at the bucket, also afraid that Koji had unwittingly used the wrong one.

It was unmistakably that used for cleaning the classroom, however. The floor cloth was rising and sinking in the clear water and he could see nothing the matter at all.

"Hey, you lot, what's so stupid, then?" He glared at Yoichi and Choji.

Yoichi stuck out his elbows aggressively. "You're stupid yourself if you don't know."

"Know what?"

"That you're *eta,* stupid."

Sadao was taken aback.

"So don't go sticking your cloth in our bucket, see."

Silence.

"Because it makes the water stink if an *eta* rinses his floor cloth in it."

Several hooted at this, with one eye on Hisao, testing his reaction.

"So that's it," thought Koji, with a shudder of horror. It was all as clear as daylight to him now: the practice of cleaning the school on a rotating basis, village by village, was not without reason. He raised his right foot and gave the bucket a kick.

Crash! Clatter, clatter . . . It overturned, spilling the water.

"Teacher! The *eta* are making trouble again!"

Two or three girls ran shrieking down the corridor.

Koji picked up his dripping floor cloth; it looked like a drowned rat.

"Idiot, you idiot," cried Yoichi, leaping up onto the windowsill, while Choji fled from the classroom. They both thought he was about to throw it at them.

"Don't, Ko. You will be an idiot if you start a fight," said Sadao, gripping his arm tightly. Then, they heard the hard slap, slap, of leather sandals approaching.

"Right, which one's the troublemaker?"

"It's him, sir." Standing on the windowsill, Hisao pointed at Koji.

"It's you, is it? Very silly of you to start making trouble the day before the closing ceremony." Mr. Aojima stared at Koji, a slight smile on his face.

"I wasn't making trouble."

"Did you knock the bucket over by accident then?"

"No, I did it on purpose."

"Don't be ridiculous. How can you say you weren't making trouble if you did it on purpose?"

"He got angry, sir, and kicked it over just when I'd filled it up with fresh water," said Choji, edging toward the teacher.

Mr. Aojima gave him a little tap on the head. "There's no point in getting upset about it, he must be mad behaving like that. Why don't you wipe the water up instead? If you dilly-dally much longer, you'll be the last ones to finish cleaning your classroom."

"But sir, Hatanaka ought to wipe it up. He was the one that kicked the bucket over."

"Yes, and his cloth was in it, sir," added Yoichi, getting down from the windowsill and going over to stand by Choji. "We don't want to wipe it up, it's dirty."

"Don't be so silly. Of course, it's dirty if he's rinsed a floor cloth in it."

"Yes, but it's an *eta* floor cloth."

"You mustn't say things like that."

"But you wouldn't want to have a bath with an *eta,* would you, sir?"

"A bath is quite different from a bucket."

"It's not; it's the same. I can't wring my floor cloth out in the same bucket as an *eta,* I just can't."

Koji looked down; even so, the smug faces of Yoichi and the others stabbed at him like electric shocks.

"Right, if that's what you want, the *eta* will wipe up the *eta* water," he said to himself, throwing down his cloth and whipping off his *haori*.

Yoichi immediately disappeared behind Mr. Aojima, intending to use him as a shield. But instead of flying at him, Koji got down on all fours and began wiping the floor. Yoichi held his breath at this unexpected turn of events, all the more amazing since he was using not the floor cloth but his dark blue *kasuri*-weave coat.

Only five of the twenty or so boys in the fifth grade wore a *kasuri*-weave *haori* to school. Yoichi, unfortunately, was not one of them and always eyed them with envy. And now, here was Koji using the coveted *haori* as a floor cloth.

"Maybe he really has gone mad?" he thought and retreated to a corner of the classroom in fright.

"Hatanaka! Are you mad?" The teacher was plainly flustered.

The same moment, however, Sadao too got down on all fours and started wiping the floor, and it was his *haori* that he was using.

"Shimura, have you gone mad as well!" Mr. Aojima tugged from behind at Sadao's cotton sash.

"No, I haven't." Sadao resisted strongly, bracing his arms and legs.

"Then wipe it up with the floor cloth."

"I'd better not, an *eta* floor cloth's dirty," he answered back.

"I see. You're simply trying to provoke me, aren't you, with this absurd behavior."

Undeniably, there was some truth in this, but it certainly was not their only motive.

Still on all fours, Koji shook his head. "No, we're not."

"Then why are you behaving like this, you numbskull!"

He received a kick on the backside from the teacher's leather-sandaled foot. He fell forward, hitting his face on the floor. But the next second, he sprang to his feet like clockwork and rolled up his wet *haori*.

Sadao followed suit, rolling his up too and tucking it under his arm.

"What a pair of young rascals you are. Did you really imagine you'd frighten me with such behavior?"

Was the teacher then afraid of them, afraid of these *eta*? Yes, he must be; otherwise he would not have said that.

How puzzling though. Why should he be afraid of a pair of Komori

"rascals"? As a qualified teacher, a teachers'-training school graduate, he ranked above even Mr. Ikuta, who was in his forties, and it
was rumored that he belonged to a very influential family of landowners in the next *mura*. By comparison, Komori-born children, such
as they, were pathetic figures indeed, with less influence than a dog,
losers simply by virtue of being *eta*.

Koji looked down at the floor without moving. The part he had
wiped was strikingly clean but that meant his *haori* was all the dir-
tier.

His grandmother had first let him wear it one cold morning when it
was hailing, at the end of last year. "You can wear it to school from
now on. Not much point in leaving it stored away, you'll have grown
out of it soon. But take good care of it, though," she had said, and she
would certainly frown today when she saw how filthy it was. His
mother too presented problems. He could say he had been fighting
and fallen into a puddle, but the *haori* was in such a state she would
soon see through an excuse like that. He shrugged his shoulders: what
on earth was he going to do?

This gesture of his seemed to upset Mr. Aojima. "Stubborn little
wretch, aren't you! Haven't you even got the grace to say you are
sorry?"

He remained silent, his eyes still on the ground; why should he say
he was sorry?

"You're just like Seitaro. No, you're even stubborner. Seitaro was
unruly enough, but he didn't mean any harm by it, there was nothing
secretive about him. Not like you. There's something poisonous about
the way you behave, no childlike traits whatsoever. You're like a
snake, you nasty little boy. But you needn't imagine that snakes scare
me. You're very much mistaken if you think that."

Koji looked up slowly.

Snakes. He hated them as well. He only had to hear them rustling
through the grass to shudder. They were loathsome, frightening creatures and the sight of them made his flesh creep. Nevertheless, if he
did happen to come across one, he would start wondering where it
was going and sometimes even follow it, his heart pounding. What a
curious creature it was. And to think that Mr. Aojima detested him
in the same way, found him equally frightening and loathsome; to
think that for him there was no creature in the world so curious as the
eta.

Koji's mouth trembled. He pouted slightly. His eyebrows twitched and then deep furrows appeared between them.

"Oh, Ko's going to cry!" Sadao thought, hardly daring to breathe. A second or two passed. But he did not cry. Sadao gazed at him with increasing astonishment.

He was staring fixedly into space, as if looking far away across the distant heavens. His brow was very still now, as were his eyes and lips.

His expression was not one of sadness; there was no trace of anger or malevolence there. It was the face of someone who had been pushed to the very limits of endurance and could no longer even cry. Sadao felt afraid; Koji's look was unnerving.

Ah!—He suddenly squeezed the *haori* under his arm; he knew he had seen a face somewhere with exactly the same expression.

Of course. "Asura." It was the face of that boy with the six arms his father had told him was called "Asura."

Sadao's mother came from Nara, where her family had a large tanning business, and he had been fortunate enough to have countless opportunities to wander round the shrines and temples there. Naturally, he was not yet able to appreciate the architecture or Buddhist images, with their patina of history, but he loved playing with the deer in the park, clapping his hands over his ears at the boom of the bell by the Great Buddha, or running 'round and 'round the pillars of the Great Buddha Hall.

One image, however, had made a lasting impression on him surprisingly: "Asura," the boy with the furrowed brow, staring into the distance so intently.

And Koji's face now wore the selfsame expression as that old Buddhist statue. Sadao was alarmed.

"Ko!" he cried desperately. He sensed his friend slipping away to some far-off land and wanted to call him back.

Then his panic gave way to sorrow, and in tears he called Koji's name again twice.

"There's no need to cry, Shimura," said Mr. Aojima, pacing backward and forward after having been rooted to the spot. "You mustn't think I dislike you both. I'm talking to you like this for your own good. So as long as you both know you were in the wrong, we'll forget all about it. Now, I must warn you that if you don't attend the closing ceremony tomorrow you will not receive your fifth-grade certificate of study. And be sure you bring all those who've been absent, too. Is that understood?''

"Ye-es," answered Hisao and his chums.

"Right, we'll call it a day then. You may all go home."

Two or three jumped down from the windowsill with a thud.

"Ah, Machié Sugimoto, come to the staff room will you, I'd like to talk to you for a moment," the teacher called out, as Machié was about to leave the classroom.

"Maybe he wants to rehearse the speech for tomorrow with her," somebody remarked.

Was it going to be Machié Sugimoto this year who made the speech of congratulation on behalf of the school to the pupils who were leaving?

His brow still wrinkled, Koji watched her disappear down the corridor.

II

"Did something happen?"

His grandmother, who never missed a thing, was already eyeing the *haori* tucked under his arm with suspicion.

"I was too warm so I took it off," was the only excuse Koji could think of.

"Is it that warm out?" Fudé slid open the screen. "What a lovely day! I bet the horsetails are out already along the ditch."

He was saved; how lucky. He had never dreamt his mother would start talking about ditches and horsetails.

"Yes, they are, they're out," he cried, suppressing a desire to laugh. "Me and Sada were just about to pick some when I went and dropped my *haori* in the ditch."

"Is it wet?"

"Yes." He unrolled it since there was nothing to worry about now.

"Ha-hah, I bet you came across a snake there, Koji."

He stared at his grandmother in horror, feeling as if she could see right through him. But how could she know what had happened?

"Don't know why it is, but there's always been a lot of snakes by that ditch. Specially in early spring, they lie there coiled up without moving, even when you're almost on top of them. Gave me such a fright once I fell in." Nui laughed.

"In that case . . ." he thought, and proceeded to embellish his story with a snake.

"That's clever of you to guess, Gran. I didn't know it was there till I trod on it. I yelled and dropped my *haori*," he lied.

"I thought it must be something of the sort. I know you don't like snakes." Nui was pleased at her own perception.

"Snakes are hapless creatures when you think about it. Everybody hates them, though they don't do anything to deserve it," said Fudé, hanging the wet *haori* over the drying pole under the eaves.

"I feel sorry for 'em every time I see one. The priest told me once they've been living on this earth a lot longer than we folk have. Even so, when men came along, they wanted to get rid of them, and attacked and killed 'em whenever they set eyes on them. The snakes fought back as hard as they could at first, but, bit by bit, men got the upper hand. In the end, the snakes changed into the shape they've got now. Their revenge, you might say, changing into the shape their enemy hates the most.

"And the priest told me another story, too, that time, about a great snake that was the Lord of Yamato. It lived on Mount Miwa and was so long it wound 'round and 'round the mountain seven-and-a-half times. Anyway, I know they're only stories, but it makes you think we must have some close connection with them snakes."

"We certainly have, Gran. Only today somebody told me I was as nasty as a snake," thought Koji, wishing he could talk about it openly to his mother and grandmother; but they were precisely the ones in whom he could not confide. Without being aware of it, his brow grew furrowed again.

Fudé, who had fallen silent, suddenly started to grope around her where she was kneeling.

"Oh, I forgot, there's a letter from Seitaro," she said, producing it from under her hard cushion. "Here you are, read it. You're the one he seems most concerned about, though that's only to be expected, I suppose."

Koji guessed without seeing the letter that Seitaro was writing to find out his school results.

"I did get a low mark for deportment, Mom, and I'm not top. So there isn't much point in writing back to Seitaro," he said, taking the bull by the horns.

"It doesn't matter. He doesn't say anything about replying . . ."

He grabbed the letter and went outside, wanting to read it in secret.

It was three pages long and the first was addressed to his mother and grandmother. After the usual preliminaries about the weather, it continued:

> I was very shocked to hear that Uncle Shimura had been killed in the Ikoma tunnel disaster. It was an anxious time for my master as well. Even I felt uneasy. Share prices fell sharply, and it was rumored here that there was not much chance of them being able to repair the damage. But the tunnel has been repaired and surprisingly quickly. It only took one month instead of three as expected, and they're making rapid progress now with the construction work. It looks as if it will finally be opened next year in April. I've a feeling that something nice will happen about then, too. Anyway, you must both be sure and live to a ripe old age because one day I'm going to take you sightseeing in Osaka.

The next part was addressed to Koji.

> I always feel different in March, and I bet lots of others do, too. It's hard to describe, half-happy, half-dissatisfied. Maybe those that are top in their class every year just feel happy, but for the rest, like me, it's a time of year that really makes you feel peculiar. I can't explain it all in a letter, but I got into a lot of trouble at the end of my last year at school. Looking back on it now it seems rather funny, though at the time, three years ago, it was awful. I only managed to stick it out and graduate because luckily I had such a good friend in Toyo. But if he hadn't been there I'd have left school as a fifth grader and turned into a real little troublemaker. Toyo's still my best friend. He'll be starting his fourth year in middle school this year, but he hasn't changed at all really.
>
> I'm very glad you and Sadao seem to be such good friends. You start hating school if you're on your own. The second and third grades are all right, but when you get into the fifth and sixth, the teacher looks at you differently. He always seems to be hitting you for being rude. You get ticked off for nothing at all

until in the end you don't know what to do anymore. It helps
to have a friend then.

The other day, I read something that brought tears to my eyes.
It was in a school magazine Toyo showed me. It said, "The way
home is warm in winter and cool in summer," and it made me
think of Master Hidé. He hasn't been seen back in Komori once
since he left, and that's because for him the way home is freezing
cold in winter and scorching in summer. And to be honest, I
feel the same, except that I will come back.

Koji, why don't you go over to Ino during the spring holidays?
Look after yourself. Bye.

So Seitaro did not want to run away from Komori, or disown it,
despite what he had said about not putting it in the address when he
wrote. Seitaro was telling him that he would come back, even though
the way home was freezing cold in winter and scorching in summer.

"The glee-am of the firefly," he sang, as he returned to his mother's
side. He wanted her and his grandmother to know that he would be
going to tomorrow's closing ceremony head held high.

III

Lesson One. Mount Yoshino.

I know not
What lies beyond the mist
On Mount Yoshino.
As far as the eye can see
There are cherry blossoms . . ."

The voices of Koji and Sadao were animated. They were feeling
pleased with themselves. One reason was the "Sixth-Grade Curriculum
Guide" open before them. With it, they could prepare their lessons
or revise as they wished, able to unravel any difficult phrases or unfamiliar characters.

Today was the first day of the new school year, and a bookseller
from the town had come with textbooks, among which was this guide.
Only seven in their grade, including Koji and Sadao, had bought

a copy; the others would have given their eyeteeth for one, but at twenty-five sen it was too expensive, and all they could do was look on enviously. Koji and Sadao had been downcast as well at first, neither of them possessing twenty-five sen, until suddenly they realized that if they put their money together they could afford it.

The bookseller chuckled and remarked flatteringly, "You're a couple of bright young sparks. You've halved the price and you'll get on twice as fast studying together. You'll be top of the class!"

Sadao promptly lifted up the guide, with a little bow, and thanked him. The five or six others standing around, laughed meaningfully— "They want to be top, do they? Ha, ha, ha . . ."—but he and Koji pretended not to notice. They had every hope and confidence of doing well this year, since their teacher was to be the senior teacher, Mr. Egawa, which was what had prompted them to club together to buy the guide. It was worth studying hard for a teacher like Mr. Egawa, who, they were sure, would never be so prejudiced as to lower their deportment marks because they were from Komori, because they were *eta*.

They were not alone in trusting him; all the Komori pupils did. He never looked at them with disgust like Mr. Otori or Mr. Aojima; and it was amazing how different his way of calling out "Komori" was from the Headmaster's. To think he was to be their teacher for the whole year until they graduated. Right, they were going to study as never before!

"Haven't you ever wanted to go to Yoshino, Sada?" Koji asked all at once, when they had finished reading the first lesson parrot-fashion.

"No. Why should I? What about you?"

"I'd like to. That's where my aunt in Ino comes from. And you know that Miss Kashiwagi, well, she went to live there when she got married and . . ."

"Did she?" Sadao was impressed. He remembered Miss Kashiwagi had left to get married, but this was the first he had heard of her going to live in Yoshino. How did Koji know about it though?

As if in answer, Koji said, "I remember the letter she sent the school, about the children near her going swimming in the Yoshino River. It made me envious because we'd be fined if we swam in the Katsuragi. That's why it stuck in my memory."

Was that really the reason he had remembered all about Miss Kashiwagi?

"It's because you were her favorite," Sadao said, half teasing. Koji frowned, the same furrows appearing as on the occasion of the school spring cleaning.

"How funny. He looks so cross and I was only joking," thought Sadao.

"D'you know Shusui Kotoku, Sada?" Koji asked then.

"Yes," he answered automatically, and glanced at Koji. His father, Kunihachi, had once told him never to mention the name of Shusui Kotoku, which had had the opposite effect of fixing it firmly in his memory.

He stood his reader up like a screen and, lowering his voice, whispered in Koji's ear, "It's a secret, Ko, but Dad and my brother sometimes talk about him admiringly and say what a fine man he was. Dad gets mad, though, if I start listening. He says it's not the sort of talk for children's ears. So you won't ever show you're interested, will you, when you're round at my place?"

"No, I won't. But don't you like Shusui Kotoku too, Sada?"

"Yeah, I do."

"I like him a lot. He said it's wrong to fight wars, and there shouldn't be any rich or poor people in the world. And I bet he also said it's wrong the way they look up to the Emperor but down on us *eta*."

"Where did you hear all that?"

"Don't you remember that day the Head went on about the scoundrel called Shusui Kotoku, given-name-Denjiro, who plotted to throw a bomb at His Sacred Majesty, the Emperor? I liked the sound of him straightaway. I knew he'd done it to try and help the people that have a hard time of it because of being poor, or *eta*."

"Was that what happened? You've really got a good memory, Ko."

"I can remember everything about that day. The sun was beating down on the back of my neck, and Aki was standing in front of me, and I could see at least twenty lice crawling about in her hair. Then Také went as white as a sheet and fainted, and Miss Kashiwagi carried him away in her arms. And it was during singing later on the same day that Miss Kashiwagi said she was leaving."

As he spoke, Sadao found himself remembering, too.

"So you see, Yoshino makes me think of Miss Kashiwagi, and Miss Kashiwagi always makes me think of Shusui Kotoku."

"It hasn't got anything to do with being the teacher's pet, then?"

"Well, I know I was her favorite. She did get me the District Governor's Prize."

They both laughed, and there were tears in their eyes, although neither was sad. That moment, a strong smell assailed their noses: the smell of beef cooking. It invaded their empty tummies, which began rumbling hungrily.

"Sadao, Koji, hurry down. Supper's ready," called up Sadao's mother. Sadao led his friend downstairs.

IV

"It's a bit much, isn't it, getting you to buy my beef and then digging into it myself. Don't know what you must think of me," remarked Kané Shimura, in her pleasant-sounding voice.

She was seated with Kunihachi's family before a dish of beef they were cooking at the table. She had begun peddling beef shortly after Hirokichi's Forty-Ninth-Day, obtaining it, through Kunihachi's good offices, from a butcher's in Takada; and even though she was new to the trade, there was little fear of her making a loss. Today, Kunihachi's wife, Toyo, had been kind enough to buy the last two pounds or so and had invited her to share it with them into the bargain.

Toyo laughed, "Don't be silly, Kané. The more the merrier when you're cooking a dish at the table like this, with everybody keeping their eyes skinned, ready to get in quick as soon as a bit's done. Look at Sadao, hunting for all he's worth."

"Yes, I am, but all I keep finding is *konnyaku*,* not beef."

Uncharacteristically, Kunihachi threw his head back and guffawed.

"It can't be helped," said Toyo. "Beef shrivels up as it cooks. It's soon hard to find, even when you think you've done a lot."

"I'd better buy one *kan** next time, and then Sadao and the rest of you can feast to your heart's content. It isn't expensive really, when you look at the price of saké, and it's certainly tastier than anything else." Kunihachi too was very fond of beef.

"It's a funny thing, though, when you think about it. They never let me go in by the front entrance when I was working for them over in Shimana, but now that I'm selling beef, I swagger in the front way and nobody says a word. And nothing about the beef being unclean, seeing as it's from Komori, either. No, they're all peering inside my box, licking their lips. They're a perverse lot, there's no mistake.''

"People are perverse, Kané. Take this meal we're having. In the old days, they thought beef was so unclean you couldn't even cook it in a pan. But then with Meiji and the coming of Progress, suddenly, far from being unclean, it was the greatest delicacy. And imagine what an old fogey they'd think you today if you talked about it being unclean.''

"That they would. But what did they use, then, in the old days if they couldn't cook it in a pan?'' Toyo asked her husband doubtfully.

"A spade called a *suki*,'' replied Kunihachi, chewing a piece of meat. "The *suki* we use for digging ditches.''

Everyone put down their chopsticks at this unexpected answer.

Toyo was even more puzzled. "A *suki*? But how could they simmer beef on a flat *suki*? All the liquid'd run off.''

"They didn't simmer it in the old days, they grilled it. They couldn't use a brazier, though, because it would have meant throwing it away afterward, beef being unclean, so they lit a fire in the *doma*, stuck a *suki* over it, and, when it was hot enough, grilled the beef in a jiffy. They still call beef cooked at table *sukiyaki* in Osaka, as a reminder of the old days, though I suppose it's not very flattering to the beef.''

"It certainly isn't,'' agreed Toyo, eagerly taking up her chopsticks again. Kané and Keiichi and Tsuya, and Kikué, too, began eating, knowing there was nothing to be gained by standing on ceremony. Only Koji held back, his chopsticks somehow heavy.

Opinion had completely altered, and beef was no longer unclean but considered now a great delicacy in any household, to be cooked at the table in the living room, instead of on a spade over a fire in the *doma*. It was only when it came to the people who traded in beef that nothing had changed. But why did they still have to be shunned as *eta*, as Four-Fingers?

Uncle Kunihachi had said it was not very flattering to the beef to continue using the old name *sukiyaki*. How much worse then it was for them, unable to escape the humiliation of being known as *eta*, even though they fulfilled the Three Duties of a Japanese citizen* like everyone else.

Auntie Kané might go swaggering off to sell beef in Shimana and Azuchi, but even so, she would always be a Komori *eta*, wouldn't she? How could there be anything so absurd? How could Japan be called the leading nation of the world and allow such a state of affairs?

Seeing Koji deep in thought, Toyo decided he must be feeling shy and popped a large fatty piece of meat into his bowl. "Here's a tasty-looking bit for you, Ko."

"Let's see who can eat the most rice, Ko. That's only your second helping, isn't it? I'm on my third, and I can still eat two more," said Sadao, also trying to put him at ease.

But this merely made Koji feel even more dispirited. "I'm full already," he replied, quite unable to relax and enjoy himself.

"I'll treat Ko and Sadao to as much beef as they can eat tomorrow," said Keiichi.

Sadao was puzzled; his brother did not seem to be joking. "Is something nice going to happen then?" he asked.

"I'll say. We'll be celebrating Komori's victory. It's the Lantern-Downing tomorrow."

"We're counting on you, you know," said Kané. "My dead husband'll be cheering you on from the grave for all he's worth. So you've got to win."

"We will, we will. Leave it to us, Auntie. It'd be funny if we didn't, brawny guys like us, and with a first-rate brand-new pump."

"And a good beef dinner to give you energy in the bargain . . ." Toyo turned to her daughter-in-law, Tsuya. "You'd better eat as much as you can, too, dear. You never know, you might start tonight."

Tsuya hung her head and Koji realized vaguely that Toyo was talking about the possibility of her going into labor. Last April, she had looked as pretty as an Ichimatsu doll when she came as a bride from Michi, but now she was hollow-cheeked and her complexion sallow. Only the other day, his mother and grandmother had been discussing her and said, "It's bound to be a boy, judging by how haggard she looks." He wondered if they were right, feeling an urge to gaze at her.

"There's a lovely moon, Gran," he declared with fervor, when he got home.

Nui turned round. "Even the moon looks lovelier after a good dinner."

"What, you know already?"

"Of course, I do, a nice smell like that wafting across."

In fact, she and Fudé had heard all about it from Kané, who had returned shortly before him.

"Gosh, that beef was good," he said, guessing as much.

"I'll buy you some, too, one of these days, if you like it so much," Fudé remarked quietly.

He glanced at the calendar behind her. By the "1" of April 1 was a small "14," indicating the date (March 14) according to the old-style lunar calendar. No wonder the moon looked so beautiful; it would be full now.

"The fire drill Downing-the-Lantern's tomorrow," he said, and Fudé nodded.

"It'd be nice if we won," he added.

"We've got to win, and that's all there is to it. No use just talking about it." Nui changed her position in readiness for several more hours' work.

"What a marvel Gran is," he thought, inexplicably happy all at once, despite the feeling that he had been snubbed.

And so the new school year had an auspicious beginning.

V

Water from the Katsuragi was directed by means of a sluice gate into the irrigation channels that wound around the fields. In the spring, from the time the Chinese milk vetch flowered, these ditches were kept full, in preparation for the transplanting of the rice seedlings.

Today, the Sakata Mura Fire Brigade was going to make use of this water to check the working order of all the villages' fire-fighting pumps.

The second lesson at Sakata Primary School had just finished when the children noticed what was happening. With shrieks of "Waa, they're Downing-the-Lantern!" they ran to watch, raising clouds of dust like a whirlwind. Their excitement was only natural; even the grown-ups were more interested in the spectacle of the Lantern-Downing than the formal testing of equipment. And the winners' flag fluttering by Ohashi Bridge only served to heighten such interest. Resplendent with its scarlet cherry blossom on a purple ground, the flag would soon be gracing the shoulders of the champions; and, wanting them to be those of their own village team, the children began shouting frenziedly, at the top of their voices:

"Sakata, Sakataa-!"

"Azuchii-!"

"Come on, Shimana!"

"Show 'em, Hongawaa-!"

There were ripples of laughter and the sound of clapping.

In the midst of it all, Koji stood silent, biting his lip. He could not make a sound, as if a piece of rubber film sealed his voice. He braced himself to shout; but the word "Komori" stuck in his throat and only a sigh escaped like a rebuke.

"Idiot. What an idiot I am."

He could not even weep. Without warning, all the hoses pointed up toward their quarry, showing their contempt for him. The red paper lanterns atop the bamboo poles waited calmly. Keiichi was glaring at them, gripping the end of a hose.

It was at this tense moment that Sadao yelled out, "Keiichii-!" Simultaneously, there was a shrill blast from the whistle.

At once the five pumps groaned and silver whips of water sprang at the red quarry.

"Komorii-!"

The cry burst from Koji with the suddenness of an explosion.

"Komorii! Komorii-!"

Cries exploded from several others too; and, in their midst, one red lantern floated down like a falling blossom.

It was Komori's. Komori had won!

"Three cheers for Komori, hip, hip, hurray!"

The school and the riverbank resounded with cheers of triumph. Diving through them, one man charged up the bank to Ohashi Bridge. The next second, he had shouldered the winners' flag.

"Wait!"

"How dare you!"

"Give it back!"

"What, hand the winners' flag over to a bunch of *eta!*"

There was pandemonium: a confusion of howls and roars amidst a torrent of anger and hatred.

Most of the children ran back into the school screaming.

Koji and Sadao lingered where they were, in a daze. The man flew past them, the flag over his shoulder; and after him came a rush of Komori faces; followed by other faces.

The bell rang; the third lesson was about to begin. They looked at each other: should they go into class, or run after Keiichi into Sakata?

The next instant, they had made up their minds and they ran. They had to recapture the flag, snatched from them so unjustly, even if it meant risking life and limb.

The Sakata fire bell began clanging. "Hurry, hurry, it's the *eta*, they're rioting . . ." it rang out frantically.

"Hatanaka-a . . . Shimuraa . . ."

Mr. Egawa was coming after them.

"Hatanaka-a, wait . . ."

Koji ran on; Sadao ahead of him.

"Hey! I said wait . . ."

But they could not. Whatever the teacher might say, it was no time for waiting!

Koji had resolved to give Mr. Egawa no trouble at all during his last year at school; to put up with any sneers or insults from the other pupils, however difficult. But he had not bargained for the events of today. It was not simply the flag that the men of Komori surging into Sakata were risking their lives to regain: it was everything that had been wrested from them with equal injustice for generations.

Komori had triumphed in today's contest. Everybody must have seen and heard it. And the winners' flag went to the winning team; that was indisputable; it was the rule they had all agreed.

Yet Sakata and Shimana were now trying to break it; they already had broken it. Just as they had also been flouting other basic rules of man, with their long persecution of Komori.

"Don't think I don't know! Don't think I don't know it all!" Koji wanted to yell until his voice cracked, until teachers and pupils were deafened.

"Oi! This ain't no place for kids."

It was Tosaku Nagai and he barred the way, his long arms outstretched. They were standing before the residence of Keizo Sayama, landowner and Sakata Fire Brigade chief. The Komori crowd, Keiichi in their midst, were beating furiously on the closed entrance gates, behind which the flag was concealed, a fact Koji and Sadao grasped immediately.

"Why are you stopping us?"

Koji wanted to hurl himself against the gates, even once.

Tosaku shook his head. "Kids like you will get in the way. And you might get hurt if you hang around. Blood may flow. Now, clear off, the pair of you."

"I don't care if I get hurt," and Sadao wriggled out of Tosaku's grasp.

"Little fool."

But a shove from Keiichi sent him flying. "Go on, clear off. Look, the teacher's come after you, he's so worried."

Mr. Egawa had almost reached them.

Then they heard an angry roaring sound from the direction of Komori; and, the same moment, the gates suddenly swung open from the inside. Keiichi and the others surged through.

"You must leave the grown-ups to settle it. Come back to school now, both of you."

Mr. Egawa chose a route that brought them out on the north side of Sakata, not wanting them to come face to face with the Komori mob hastening over at the news of trouble.

As they came out of the village, they saw the school playground ahead. One of the classes was doing exercises there.

"There's nothing to worry about," Mr. Egawa said gently.

The lump in Koji's throat grew and he started to cry. Sadao too sobbed.

The Sakata fire bell had at last stopped ringing and the shrill blast of the cotton-mill siren floated calmly over their heads, signaling the hour of eleven.

In the evening, Koji learned that the winners' flag was to be burnt. It would be carried out at the foot of Ohashi Bridge, in the presence of the Mayor of Sakata, the Fire Brigade officer, the local policeman, and the Headmaster, among others.

Koji and Sadao had wanted at least to touch the flagstaff; but even this was denied them. To avoid further outbreaks of violence, nobody was to be allowed near the bridge when the flag was burnt, apart from the few chosen to attend.

They would certainly be able to see the smoke, however, from the second floor of Sadao's house, and they waited there in a mood of breathless expectation.

Soon, Kunihachi came up. "Well, have you seen any smoke yet?"

"No, not yet. Isn't it stupid, though, Dad, burning the flag. It hasn't done anything wrong, has it?" said Sadao, rather petulantly.

"I don't know; when you think about it, flags don't do much good if they make people fight like they did today."

Koji repeated this to himself. "Flags don't do much good if they make people fight like they did today."

"Look, they've lit it," yelled Sadao.

There was a faint brightness over the bridge. Little flames leapt up and people's shadows wriggled.

"Wa-a, wa-a-a," came a rending cry.

"My grandchild's born," whispered Kunihachi, and went downstairs.

"Ee, hee . . . Hee, hee, hee . . ." Sadao and Koji rolled about with laughter.

Then they heard hurried footsteps on the stairs again.

"Quick, both of you, go and tell Keiichi he's got a fine big son. D'you understand?" said Fudé, unable to hide her excitement. As Tsuya's aunt, she had been locked up in the annex—now turned into a delivery room—since noon.

"Ha, ha, ha . . . Ha, ha, ha . . ." They fell against each other in paroxysms; it was the only way they could express their feelings.

Presently, they were running along the path through the fields toward Ohashi Bridge. Now it was spring, the path had dried out to a whitish shade, and the scent of Chinese milk vetch filled the air. Koji drank it in, and then, suddenly, breathed out with a snort.

"You know what, Sada, the baby's naked."

"Ah, ha, ha . . . What d'you expect!"

"And it's got no name," he continued, in spite of being laughed at.

"Ha, ha, ha! You are funny, Ko. Everybody's like that when they're born."

"Yes. Everybody's got no name and everybody's naked when they're born, even the Emperor, even *eta*."

"Yeah!" Sadao gave a yell of triumph.

The full moon shone down on the basin as it rose over the neighboring province of Ise.*

Translator's Notes

General Note I have followed the Western practice of placing given name before family name. The final *e* of names such as Sué, Fudé, and Kané is always pronounced, as indicated by the accent. Thus, the author's name is pronounced "Soo-eh Soo-mee."

P. viii Burakumin, the modern term for outcasts, is the accepted abbreviation of *mikaiho burakumin,* or people (*min*) of unliberated (*mikaiho*) communities (*buraku*). In 1985, their number was officially put at 1,163, 372. Some estimates, however, put the figure as high as three million.

P. 1 The title is meant to indicate the passage of time because of the annual motion of the stars and the occurrence of frost every winter.

P. 7 There are two phonetic systems of writing Japanese, known as *kana,* in which each symbol represents a syllable. They are used in conjunction with Chinese characters. At school, children learn both the squarish *katakana* and the more cursive *hiragana* before embarking on the laborious task of memorizing characters.

P. 7 The word *eta,* meaning "much filth," is the name by which an outcast group in Japan was commonly known. Racially no different from other Japanese, they came to be considered hereditarily unclean because of the work they did, such as butchering and making leather goods. Their defilement was believed to be somehow communicable, like a germ, and during the Tokugawa period (1603–1868), in particular, they were kept strictly apart from the rest of society. In 1871, they were legally emancipated and the word *eta* is now taboo, having been replaced *burakumin,* (see note to p. viii). The *burakumin* number between one and three million, and discrimination against them still persists.

P. 9   Two mats is equal to about 36 ft², one mat being about 6 ft × 3 ft in size.

P. 11   Emperor Meiji's official birthday (November 3) is still a national holiday in Japan, now known as Culture Day. The birthdays of the Showa Emperor (April 29), now called Greenery Day, and of Emperor Akihito (December 23) are also national holidays.

P. 17   *Kasuri* is a type of cloth decorated with a "splashed pattern" produced by pre-dyeing sections of the yarn before weaving; it usually has a geometric pattern in white or light blue on an indigo ground.

P. 17   According to legend, Ninigi no Mikoto, grandson of the Sun Goddess, Amaterasu Omikami, alighted on this mountain when he descended from heaven to earth. Ninigi was supposedly the great-grandfather of the first emperor, Jinmu.

P. 23   Under the prewar Japanese education system, there was a compulsory six-year coeducational primary school course, followed by an optional two-year higher elementary course. After that, for boys there were academic middle schools leading to the higher schools and universities, and separate higher schools for girls. Students attended school five hours a day, six days a week, and this practice continues to the present day, although Saturdays are now half-days.

P. 23   Most outcasts belonged to the Jodo Shinshu (True Pure Land) sect of Buddhism that had been founded by Shinran (1173–1262). A reformist sect, it taught that merely chanting the phrase "Praise be to Amida Buddha" was enough to attain salvation.

P. 24   Hideyoshi Toyotomi (1536–98) was virtual ruler of Japan (1585–98) between the warlords Nobunaga Oda (1534–82) and Ieyasu Tokugawa (1532–1616).

P. 28   The name given to the deities of the indigenous Shinto religion, the word *kami* means literally something that is superior; it does not really correspond to the idea of a 'god' in the Western sense. It includes not only the deities of mythology such as Izanagi and Izanami, who created the islands of Japan, and Amaterasu Omikami, the Sun Goddess and progenetrix of the Imperial family, but also the spirits that act as protectors of the local community and the family, and even natural phenomena inspiring awe, like a great tree, or rock, or mountain; the emperors, too, and many other legendary and semi-historical figures are all *kami*.

P. 39 The *doma* (literally, earth room) is an earth-floored area extending from the front entrance to the back; it served not only as a passageway, but also as the place where the cooking was done. Outdoor shoes were left here before stepping up into the raised "living area."

P. 54 The *mura* is the smallest unit of administration in rural areas, comprising several *aza,* or villages.

P. 65 The Edict of Emanicipation, which abolished the title of *eta* and granted the outcasts full legal equality, was passed in 1871.

P. 65 The *eta* were often called *yotsu,* meaning either "Four-Fingers" or "Four-Legged"; the term was used to imply that someone was less than human, or animal-like. People would often simply hold up four fingers to mean the same thing.

P. 66 A *tan* is equivalent to about a quarter of an acre, and was the usual size of a rice paddy; therefore, the meaning here is all the straw from one rice paddy.

P. 67 In 1873, the Gregorian calendar was officially adopted in Japan, but in rural areas people continued to use the old lunar calendar, according to which New Year's Day fell in early February. This was more convenient for the farmers, who were often still busy husking and packing the rice from the harvest and unable to observe the Western New Year's holidays in January.

P. 73 The novel *Hakai* [The Broken Commandment] was written by Toson Shimazaki (1872–1943) and first published in 1906. It has been translated into English by Kenneth Strong (University of Tokyo Press, 1974).

P. 77 The Three Great Festivals were: the New Year's ceremony at the court (January 1), the anniversary of Emperor Jinmu's accession to the throne (February 11), and the Emperor Meiji's official Birthday (November 3).

P. 126 One *sho* is equal to about 1.9 quarts.

P. 126 The name Shichimero is a pun on the *hachi* of Hachimero, which also means eight, and *shichi,* which means seven.

P. 149 The period known as *doyo* lasts for about eighteen days at the end of July and the beginning of August and is usually the hottest part of the summer.

P. 154 Hidari ("Left-Handed") Jingoro (1594–1634) was a famous sculptor; he is thought to have carved the well-known "Sleeping Cat" in the Toshogu Shrine at Nikko.

P. 169 The *koto* is a stringed musical instrument much like a long horizontal zither.

P. 172 There was another outcast group known as the *hinin* (literally, non-persons). Unlike the *eta*, however, they were not considered hereditarily impure and included commoners who had fallen into disgrace and might occasionally be able to regain their former status.

P. 194 Sazanami Iwaya (1870–1933) was an author of children's books.

P. 198 The 210th day from *risshun*, the first day of spring, according to the old calendar, falls on about September 1, a time of year when there are many typhoons, which is why it is considered an unlucky day by the farmers.

P. 202 The Niiname-sai is a ceremony that takes place on November 23, during which the emperor offers the new crop to the *kami*.

P. 210 The *daimyo* were feudal lords with an estate worth more that fifty-thousand bushels of rice.

P. 222 A *gohei* is a sacred staff with paper streamers on one end that is placed at a shrine as an offering to the *kami;* it is often used by Shinto priests in purification rituals.

P. 223 A *kuyo* is a Buddhist rite of offering to the Three Treasures (the Buddha, the Doctrine, and the Buddhist priesthood) or to the dead. There are all sorts of *kuyo,* from ceremonies for the dedication of new temple buildings or images to the recitation of sutras or the offering of incense, food, or money. *Ho-on* is the repaying of the indebtedness that one automatically incurs from life to life to one's ancestors, parents, teachers, etc.

P. 244 This refers to Kyoto's Nishi Honganji is the head temple of the Honganji branch of the Jodo Shinshu sect.

P. 259 One *to* is equal to about 4.8 U.S. gallons.

P. 261 Buddhism had little connection with the emperor system, whereas the belief in the divine descent of the imperial house from the Sun Goddess was central to the state cult of Shinto. It would have been very strange, therefore, to pray for the emperor at a Buddhist temple instead of at a Shinto shrine.

P. 265 Taiyaki are little fish-shaped griddle cakes filled with sweetened adzuki-bean paste.

P. 281 Seppuku, often known by the vulgar term hara-kiri in the West, is ritual suicide by disembowelment. General Maresuke Nogi and his wife sacrificed their lives in order to "serve their emperor as well in death as in life."

P. 301 One *shaku* is equal to 0.995 ft (0.303 m). Thus, although Mount Fuji is actually 12,389 ft (3,776 m) in height, the figure of 12,365 *shaku* was a mnemonic device to help children memorize the approximate height.

P. 302 A *haramaki* is a cloth band wrapped around one's middle to keep the stomach and lower back warm.

P. 325 The bodhisattva Jizo (Skt., Ksitigarbha) is the Buddhist guardian deity of travelers and children.

P. 328 Offerings are made on the forty-ninth day after a death to mark the end of the transitional state of the soul between one incarnation and the next. It would be unlucky for an unmarried girl to have one of these dumplings because of the connection with death, which Shintoism sees as defiling.

P. 347 Kané was eating a jelly-like substance made from the edible root of the devil's-tongue plant.

P. 347 One *kan* is equal to about eight pounds.

P. 348 The Three Duties of a Japanese citizen were: 1) to receive an education; 2) to do military service; and 3) to pay taxes.

P. 354 Ise suggests the emperor because the Great Shrine at Ise is dedicated to the Sun Goddess, the progenetrix of the imperial house.

❧❧❧❧TUTTLE CLASSICS❧❧❧❧

LITERATURE

ABE, Kobo　安部公房
The Box Man　箱男　4-8053-0395-6
The Face of Another　他人の顔　4-8053-0120-1
Inter Ice Age 4　第四間氷期　4-8053-0268-2
Secret Rendezvous　密会　4-8053-0472-3
The Woman in the Dunes　砂の女　4-8053-0207-0

AKUTAGAWA, Ryunosuke　芥川龍之介
Japanese Short Stories　芥川龍之介短編集　4-8053-0464-2
Kappa　河童　0-8048-3251-X
Rashomon and Other Stories　羅生門　0-8048-1457-0

ATODA, Takashi　阿刀田高
The Square Persimmon and Other Stories　四角い柿　0-8048-1644-1

DAZAI, Osamu　太宰治
Crackling Mountain and Other Stories　太宰治短編集　0-8048-3342-7
No Longer Human　人間失格　4-8053-0756-0
The Setting Sun　斜陽　4-8053-0672-6

EDOGAWA, Rampo　江戸川乱歩
Japanese Tales of Mystery & Imagination　乱歩短編集　0-8048-0319-6

ENDO, Shusaku　遠藤周作
Deep River　深い河　0-8048-2013-9
The Final Martyrs　最後の殉教者　4-8053-0625-4
Foreign Studies　留学　0-8048-1626-3
The Golden Country　黄金の国　0-8048-3337-0
A Life of Jesus　イエスの生涯　4-8053-0668-8
Scandal　スキャンダル　0-8048-1558-5
Stained Glass Elegies　短編集　4-8053-0624-6
The Sea and Poison　海と毒薬　4-8053-0330-1
Volcano　火山　4-8053-0664-5
When I Whistle　口笛を吹くとき　4-8053-0627-0
Wonderful Fool　おバカさん　4-8053-0376-X